Smoke Screen

D1711633

Smoke Screen

Charles Girsky

Copyright © 2009 by Charles Girsky.

Library of Congress Control Number: 2008909433
ISBN: Hardcover   978-1-4363-7965-6
                 Softcover   978-1-4363-7964-9

All rights reserved. No part of this book may be reproduced or transmitted in any form or by any means, electronic or mechanical, including photocopying, recording, or by any information storage and retrieval system, without permission in writing from the copyright owner.

This is a work of fiction. Names, characters, places and incidents either are the product of the author's imagination or are used fictitiously, and any resemblance to any actual persons, living or dead, events, or locales is entirely coincidental.

This book was printed in the United States of America.

To order additional copies of this book, contact:
Xlibris Corporation
1-888-795-4274
www.Xlibris.com
Orders@Xlibris.com
51807

Chapter One

His body shuddered as the ringing of the phone interrupted his dream. Sinking that putt for a birdie on the eighteenth green at Pebble Beach would win him a night with . . . "Shit!" Eyes opened, he couldn't remember the woman with whom he dreamt he was going to spend the night with.

Stuart lifted his head and glanced at the clock. Who would be calling on this line at six in the morning? He waited for the answering machine to kick in.

"Stuart, I know you're there. Pick up the phone, it's your mother."

Reaching over, he lifted the receiver. "Mom, it's six AM."

"Happy birthday to you, happy birthday to you, happy birthday dear Stuart, happy birthday to you."

Stuart shook his head, rubbed his eyes, and exhaled. "Mom, if you bought me a present, return it and get yourself some singing lessons."

"Don't worry, I didn't get you a present. Sixty-four-year-olds have to watch their pennies. Will I see you this weekend for dinner?"

"It's only Tuesday. Maybe I'll get lucky and have a date?"

"You've been saying that ever since Linda divorced you fifteen years ago. Which reminds me, did the kids call?"

"They're not kids, and no they haven't, but it's a little early yet."

"The only time they call is on your birthday."

"So how about hanging up and giving them a chance."

"I still wonder if that job was worth losing your wife and children. I never understood what it was you did."

"It wasn't a big deal, just a lot of traveling that wasn't conducive to family life. At least, that's what Linda said."

"I still think you should've quit sooner."

"Mom, not today, it's my birthday."

"You're right, Stuart. Enjoy yourself and call me about dinner."

Before he could reply, she was gone.

He sat on the side of the bed with his feet on the floor and looked at the digital clock that displayed time and date. It was May 11, 2001.

Forty-four fuckin' years old, he thought to himself. *My life is half over, and what do I have to show for it?*

He picked up the phone and dialed. His call was answered on the second ring.

"Whoever you are, this call better be important." The voice was hoarse and cranky.

"Peter, it's me. I want to put my affairs in order."

"At six fifteen in the morning?"

Peter Weber was Stuart Taylor's closest friend. They had worked together under the auspices of the Alcohol, Tobacco, and Firearms Department. That is, until the accomplice of a reported drug dealer they were trying to arrest shot Peter in the back. Stuart killed the woman, but the dealer was reported to have escaped and was never heard of again. Peter retired from the Service and went back to practicing law. Six years later, Stuart was still working for the government.

"I'm not getting any younger," Stuart replied sheepishly as he pictured Peter turning to his wife Joan and shrugging his shoulders.

"We just got back from vacation. How about coming over tomorrow night for dinner?"

"I don't want to put Joan out." Stuart heard Peter relay his concerns to his wife.

"She says bring a bottle of good wine and we'll celebrate your birthday. She also says to bring a date. If you want, she'll call one of her friends."

"I'll bring the wine and tell her: no friends. Where was your vacation?"

Peter hesitated a second. "San Francisco. We traveled the wine country."

"And you need a good bottle from me?"

"Okay, bring pretzels." Peter laughed and hung up the phone.

Stuart stretched, scratching the back of his head. He winced when a muscle in his back tightened. *I'll have to spend more time in the gym; everything starts to go at this age.*

Yesterday's suit laid across a chair on top of the one he had worn the day before. *Thank god I have five suits,* he thought as he shoved them into the bag that the dry cleaners picked up off the front steps every other day.

After an hour on the treadmill and another thirty minutes of weight training, Stuart was tired and irritable. The TV mounted on the wall had nothing but bad news, including the stock market being down twenty some odd points at the opening bell. To make matters worse, the newspaper wasn't in front of his house. A breakfast of champions and a cold shower improved nothing. *This day is starting off great.*

Chapter Two

The bus stop was a two-block walk; on most days he used the time to think about what was going on at the office. Today, however, all he could think about was being forty-four. Turning the corner, he saw his daughter walking in his direction on the other side of the tree-lined street. She was with a girl he didn't know, but that wasn't unusual, he didn't know any of her friends. He wasn't sure if he should cross the street or wait to see if she was coming to wish him a happy birthday.

"What the hell," he mumbled and started to cross. Waiting for a four-door Lexus with a dented front right fender to pass, he saw it pull up at the curb a few feet from the girls. He started across and saw three boys of perhaps eighteen or twenty step out of the car. Stuart smelled trouble before the first words were spoken. Two of the boys were black, their eyes showing that vacant look which comes with too much drugs and alcohol. Their pants with holes at the knees hung low on their hips, their tee shirts were three sizes too big. The third kid was white and carried himself like he was on a mission and nothing was going to stand in his way. His eyes were clear, his lips set in a sneer that was pure evil. The two other kids leaned against the car and flicked cigarette ashes onto the sidewalk.

"Hey, girls, where are you headed?" he said loudly.

Marilyn and her friend hesitated and then started walking in a wide arc around the boys.

"They think they're too good for us," the boy told his companions.

"I think they need to be taught a lesson," one of his pals said with a nasty laugh.

Stuart approached the group, hands in his pockets. "Sorry, boys," he said calmly. "I think the girls have to be somewhere else now."

The three boys stared as he held a finger to his lips, signaling his daughter not to say anything.

"Hey, Grandpa," taunted the leader, "just mind your own business and keep on walking."

Grandpa. I wish he hadn't said that. "Look, son, you really don't want to get into trouble, so let the girls go on their way . . ."

"Shut the hell up old man, didn't you hear Augie say to keep walking?"

Another country heard from. "I heard your friend give some bad advice," Stuart said to the kid. "If I were you I'd get back in the car and leave."

The sound of a switchblade is unmistakable. You can't hear the button being pushed, but that blade springing open and coming to a quick stop is a sound that once heard is never forgotten.

Stuart turned and stared at the leader. He wasn't looking at an eighteen-year-old street punk, but a man twenty-eight or thirty with lines etched at the corner of his eyes that only came with time.

"You're not very smart, Augie. I now know your name, the type of car you drive, and the license plate number."

Confusion swept the leader's face. "You don't know shit," he yelled, flipping the knife from one hand to the other.

Out of the corner of his eye, Stuart saw that Marilyn and her friend had backed off and were edging closer to the curb.

"Girls, I suggest you cross the street and keep on walking."

"Don't move!" demanded Augie.

Stuart realized Augie had lost control and didn't know how to get it back. Stepping closer, Stuart said in a hoarse whisper, "It's over. Get back in your car and leave."

The switchblade continued to shift from hand to hand. "I'm the one with the knife," said Augie. "And I'm the one that's gonna teach you a lesson. After that, it's the girls' turn."

Stuart had closed to within three feet of the braggart. In one fluid motion, he kicked the knife into the air, stepped forward, and planted a fist so deeply into the young man's stomach that it felt like it reached his spine. Augie's eyes opened wide as air discharged from his lungs. Stuart turned quickly and stomped down on the closest foot. The third kid proved to be the smartest. He took off running and never looked back.

"You broke my foot, you broke my foot," howled the boy whose foot was stepped on.

As Augie struggled to sit up, Stuart leaned over and removed his wallet. "Take a deep breath, you'll feel better." He flipped the wallet open to the driver's license. "Well, August Meridian," he said in a voice so low that only the boy on the ground could hear him. "I now have a name and address to go along with your ugly face, which if I ever see again . . . well I think you can guess the outcome." Stuart smiled pleasantly. "Not so bad for an old man."

Stuart looked inside the wallet and counted ten brand-new hundred-dollar bills. Throwing the wallet on the ground, he walked over and took the wallet from the kid who was sitting on the sidewalk holding his foot.

"Well, Samuel Baker, let's see how much money you have."

"That's my money!"

"I know it's yours, I just want to see how much you have." Rifling through the bills he counted six fifties. Biting his lip, he looked at both men and told himself, *Now was not the time.* He shook his head and walked toward his daughter and her friend.

"Are you girls okay?"

"Dad, you almost killed them. What are you doing here?"

"I live two blocks away. Weren't you coming to visit me?"

"Visit you?" She appeared baffled.

Stuart looked at his daughter. If she had forgotten it was his birthday, so be it. He didn't like being forty-four anyway.

"Maybe I missed something here. These three clowns were harassing you . . ."

"But you almost killed them."

Marilyn's friend, obviously shaken, grabbed her arm. "Marilyn, why don't we just thank your father for his help and go on to school?"

"He's always been like this." Her voice was tinged with anger, her hands balled in fists. "My mother used to tell us stories, he's lucky he's not in jail."

Stuart looked at his daughter and then extended his hand to her friend. "Hi, my name is Stuart Taylor, or maybe just Grandpa." He glanced back at the two boys.

"I'm Sarah Winston," said the girl, "and I would like to thank you for your help." Her hand was cool and her demeanor strangely poised for an eighteen-year-old. Any signs of the frightening encounter were already gone.

"What's going on over there?"

Stuart and the girls turned and saw a uniformed policeman, one arm raised to stop traffic as he crossed the street.

"Oh great, now you're in trouble," said Marilyn as the cop approached.

"Let me do the talking," mumbled Stuart as he gave his daughter a warning look.

"What happened to these two?" asked the policeman.

"Officer, these two and one other stopped these girls on their way to school. This one"—pointing to Augie—"pulled a knife and I had to step in to help them. The girls were just leaving after thanking me, and if it's all right with you, I'd like to be on my way. You can do what you want with the boys, but I think they learned their lesson." Stuart spoke fast, trying to stop the cop from asking too many questions.

"That son of a bitch broke my foot!" yelled the boy on the ground.

"What's wrong with the other one?" asked the officer, pointing at Augie, who still sat hunched over at the curb.

"He'll be fine in a couple of minutes, just had the wind knocked out of him. Let me show you some identification." He reached for his wallet and stepped two paces away from the girls, blocking their view with his back.

"I don't want them to see this," he said under his breath. "I work for the FBI, and my boss would have a fit if he knew I got involved in a street brawl." Stuart flashed an FBI card and stepped back quickly. "Thanks for understanding, I'll be on my way."

The officer nodded. "I'll walk the girls to the corner. Thanks for your help. It's great to see senior citizens get involved."

He could feel his ears turning hot. *Senior citizen my ass.* "Thanks for understanding." Turning toward his daughter, he said, "Say hello to your brother for me."

Marilyn stared at her father, a teenage scowl distorting her mouth. "You could call and say hello yourself."

Before Stuart could answer, Sarah took Marilyn's arm and called out, "Thanks again for your help, and it was nice meeting you."

"Same here," he replied, crossing the street before the cop asked for a closer look at the card.

Chapter Three

Stuart hadn't been in the office thirty minutes when he received an invitation to enter his boss's inner sanctum.

"Stuart, how many times have I told you to stay the hell out of what goes on in the civilian world?"

Stuart was almost standing at attention as Michael Burnett tore him a new asshole.

"What the hell were you thinking, telling the cop you worked for the FBI? The FBI? You couldn't tell him the CIA or something?"

"It was my daughter," Stuart countered. "What would you expect me to do?"

His boss hesitated just for a second. "You should've taken care of those idiots and then left the area. There was no reason to have to explain to the men in blue."

"I thought she was on her way to my house to . . ." He stopped, not about to go into the birthday thing again.

"To what?" The man's voice was demanding. "You know we can only operate under the strictest code of silence. When you signed on, you were made aware of the rules, right?"

"That was twenty years ago," replied Stuart. "Things have changed." At least he could show a little backbone.

"Nothing has changed," said Burnett. There are only thirty people in this department and sixteen others who know of its existence that includes the four people who have left and the President of the United States." He stopped shouting long enough to take a deep breath. "And that's twenty too many." The phone on his desk started ringing. He punched the hands-free button and yelled, "I thought I told you not to disturb me."

Stuart smiled inwardly. It was good to have Michael yell at someone else other than himself, even if only for a minute.

"The President is on the phone," said the voice on the other side of the speaker.

"What President?"

"The President of the United States, sir," came the weakened reply.

Motioning for Stuart to be seated, Burnett cleared his throat and picked up his receiver.

"Good morning, Mr. President. Michael Burnett here. How may I serve you?"

His face turned red as his lips compressed into a straight line. "Yes, sir." He responded to something the President said, "I understand, sir, but . . . yes, sir, he's here now."

Stuart sat up straighter.

"I'll take care of it, Mr. President. Thank you, sir." He hung up the phone and glared at his subordinate.

Stuart smiled. "I guess he didn't call to wish me a happy birthday?"

Shaking his head, Michael sighed. "Today's your birthday?"

Stuart shrugged.

"Why the fuck didn't you stay in bed?"

"What's he so upset about?" Stuart asked. "Someone piss on his roses?"

"What'd you say that girl's name was? The one with your daughter?"

"Sarah Winston, why?"

"It seems her mother is a congresswoman from California. The girl told her mom what happened, and she promptly called the FBI to thank them. When you didn't show up on their roster, she sent one of her staff to find you. The search somehow came to the attention of the Speaker of the House. You know he doesn't like us, and of course he called the President."

"What does the President want?"

"He wants you to stay out of the limelight. If we come under the scrutiny of the House Oversight Committee, we could be in deep shit. The only reason the Speaker doesn't jump all over us is because he and the President are in the same party."

"Meanwhile, you know this congresswoman is going to be able to find me. All she has to do is ask my daughter where I live."

Michael started to gnaw on his fingernail. Every time he did that, Stuart ended up with a headache.

"If she calls to thank you, be gracious and tell her the Bureau must have made a mistake. I'll call the attorney general and have him take care of it."

"Be gracious? What does that mean?"

"I don't know, just make sure I don't get another call from the President. What are you working on?"

"There've been fourteen bank robberies in the last sixteen weeks, and they have all the earmarks of being done by the same people."

"What's the Bureau think?"

"That six of them are related."

"The difference between you and the Bureau is . . . ?"

"Those six have a blonde with a shotgun along with a man in dark glasses."

"And you disagree?"

"Each of the fourteen robberies has two people, one with a shotgun. I think they're six, and the other eight are all committed by the same group but they keep changing drivers."

When Burnett seemed confused, Stuart explained, "The six they're counting have taken place every fourth week. When you include the ones I think are part of it, you have a robbery almost every other week."

"What do they say?"

"That I'm wrong, the robberies are too scattered."

"They're entitled to their thoughts, keep on it, and keep me up to date."

Standing up, Stuart headed toward the door as his boss added, "And don't forget, be gracious."

Stuart turned quickly, a smart-ass comment on the tip of his tongue. When he saw that his boss was smiling, he nodded and walked out.

Chapter Four

Stuart sat at his desk and read reports of bank robberies until his eyes hurt. The clock on the wall had both hands pointing straight up, and he still hadn't heard from his kids.

Christine Bakey stuck her head inside his office and asked, "Got any plans for lunch?" She was the office secretary, file keeper, and all-round den mother to the entire group. Her husband had spent thirty years in the navy and now occupied himself making high-end furniture. It had become more than a hobby; he hired four people to keep up with the orders he was getting.

"No plans," said Stuart. "What do you have in mind?"

"A couple of us are going to the deli, thought you might want to come along."

"Sounds great," he told her, thinking of their corned beef sandwiches.

As he stood and stretched, the phone rang. He held up his hand to Christine as he picked up the receiver.

"This is Agent Weaver of the FBI. My boss Deputy Director Bradley wants to see you."

"I'm on my way to lunch. Call back after one thirty and you can make an appointment," Stuart replied flippantly.

"What I don't need is some wannabe wiseass who tells people he works for the Bureau telling me what to do. Mr. Bradley wants to see you now."

"Let's compromise," said Stuart. "Tell your boss I left for lunch and I'll come by around two."

"Maybe you didn't hear me. My boss is the deputy director."

"The point being?" Stuart replied. He knew he was taking this too far, but it wasn't one of his better days.

"When the deputy director says he wants to see you now, you come now."

"Then tell the deputy director to call me himself. What I'm hearing is some ill-mannered flunky passing on hearsay information." Stuart slammed the receiver into its cradle and started walking out of his office.

"What deputy director?" Christine asked.

"Of the FBI," he said with a smile.

"Ray Bradley?" Her voice was incredulous.

"You know him?"

Christine sat back down. "I don't know him, and I don't want to know him. The story is he's going to be the next director, and it's supposed to happen soon."

Stuart stopped and looked down at her. "I thought the director was on pretty good terms with the President."

"He is, but the word is there've been too many errors that can't be overlooked. The director's taking the blame, and the President can't protect him any longer."

"What kind of errors?"

"I just heard the rumors, not specifics. If I were you, I'd be careful who I antagonize." Christine picked up her bag and started walking toward the door.

Before they reached the door, the roar of "Stuart!" emanated from Michael Burnett's office, followed by, "Get your ass in here."

"Want me to bring you back something?" Christine whispered.

Shaking his head, Stuart walked into his boss's office. "I was just going to lunch," he explained.

"I just arranged a lunch date for you," Michael stated quietly.

"Why don't I think I'm going to be happy about this?" Stuart sat down and waited.

"Don't get comfortable, the director of the FBI is expecting you in twenty minutes."

"The director?"

"Something wrong with your hearing?"

"I just got off the phone with the deputy director's flunky, and he didn't say anything about the director."

Burnett stared silently, the silence lasted so long that Stuart felt compelled to speak. "Did I pass wind or something?"

Burnett closed his eyes and ran his hand through his thinning hair. "Stuart, this is not the time. Just tell me about your phone call."

"Some guy named Agent Weaver who said he worked for the Deputy Director Bradley who wanted to see me in twenty minutes."

"And what did you say?"

"I told him I was on my way to lunch and he could call back later."

"You what?"

"I told him I was on my way—"

"I heard you. Are you out of your mind?"

Stuart stood up and started walking toward the door. "We've been friends for a long time, Michael, so I'll make this simple: Fuck you, I quit. I'm getting too old to take this shit."

"Sit your butt down and pay attention."

Stuart sat down and stared at his boss with a look of defiance.

"Ray Bradley is up and coming. Not a lot of people know this, but there's talk of him replacing Jake Levitt as director."

"That's bullshit," said Stuart. "Christine told me that story two minutes ago, and if she knows, so does half of Washington."

"Didn't I tell you to pay attention? What they don't know is that Jake has cancer. It's in remission, but he wants out." Running his hands through his hair, he stopped for a second. "He also wants Bradley to take his place, but there's a problem. There are rumors that the committee overseeing the selection will blackball Bradley."

"How many people on that committee?"

"Nine."

"How many of them would vote no and why?"

"Every count we get says he'd get at least seven of the nine."

"Then what's the problem?"

"If the President sent the recommendation to the committee, and it somehow gets turned down, he'll have a mess on his hands. With all the FBI's problems, he can't take that chance."

"So what do you want me to do?"

Looking at his watch, Michael said, "You have ten minutes to get over there. I'll call the deputy director and tell him you're on your way. I'll tell him there was a miscommunication. On second thought, maybe I'll just tell him that you're a pain in the ass. Either way, be nice and listen to what they have to say."

Stuart turned to leave. "This is some great day. My mother wakes me, my kids haven't called, I have a run-in with street punks, I'm told to be gracious, then to be nice, and on top of all that, you're going to tell the director of the FBI that I'm a pain in the ass."

Michael laughed, "You forgot to mention that the President called."

Stuart nodded and smiled, but his smiled faded when Michael handed him a piece of paper.

Be careful, something smells to high heaven over at the bureau.

Stuart returned the note. "All right," he said as if nothing had passed between them. "I'll be nice, I'll even be gracious, but I don't have to like it." Standing, Stuart looked around the room wondering if his boss was concerned with some kind of listening devices. "Just tell me where I'm supposed to meet him."

"You'll like this. There's a hot dog stand a half block from the front of the Lincoln Memorial. Jake says they have the best hot dogs in town. He's buying, so if I were you I'd put my ass in gear and get down there in a hurry."

Stuart looked at his watch. "I have ten minutes. Okay if I take a taxi?"

"As long as you pay for it," Michael said still smiling.

Chapter Five

Stuart started to get into the first cab in line and thought better of it. He walked down to the third cab and opened the door.

"Top of the line," said the cabbie, not bothering to look up from his paper. "I don't have time to argue. I have to get to the Vietnam Wall Memorial, and there's a twenty in it if you get me there in less than ten minutes."

"You have to take the first cab," he repeated, glancing at the twenty.

Stuart added another five. "I'm sure the next cab will take me."

"Get in," the driver said, "I hate to argue with a passenger."

The Vietnam Wall was less than a few blocks from the Lincoln Memorial. That slip of paper had made Stuart wary, and he watched out the back window to see if he was being followed.

The taxi made every light, and the trip took less than six minutes. The meter read $3.60. Stuart gave the driver the two tens and a five.

"Hey, I thought the twenty-five was on top of the meter."

Stuart glared at the driver. "You thought wrong, so move on before I turn you over to the cops."

"Cheap bastard!" the driver yelled as he took off, tires squealing.

Laughing, Stuart walked briskly toward the Lincoln Memorial. He spotted Jake Levitt standing in front of a catering truck that sold hot dogs, sandwiches, soda, and ice cream. He noted at least three men nearby, all of them agents. Putting on his sunglasses and sticking a wad of gum in his cheek, he walked to the large opened window on the side of the truck and nodded to the director but said nothing. A quick glance toward the man selling the hot dogs told him there was yet another agent.

"Two dogs with mustard and kraut please, and a Diet Coke."

The director kept glancing at his watch. He didn't know what Stuart looked like, and his body language was saying he was getting pissed at being stood up.

"Eight fifty," said the man in the roach coach.

"Charge it to the man next to me," said Stuart. "That is unless he answers the next question correctly, in which case I'll pay for mine and his."

The director looked at Stuart and nodded to the man behind the counter.

"What's the question?" asked the man behind the counter.

Stuart turned to the director. "Besides you, how many men do you have in the area?"

The director looked at the vendor. "Two aside from him."

"Wrong answer," said Stuart. "Take the eight fifty out of my ten and please don't talk to me. Too many people know who I am already. I'll call you later for another appointment."

"What are you talking about?" asked the director, looking around.

"I counted at least three," said Stuart. "Since they're not yours, the extra ones belong to someone else. After you leave, I'll hang around and let you know later who they are."

Stuart took his change and strolled toward a bench about fifty feet away. He placed the hot dogs on the bench and took a sip of his drink. Opening the newspaper, he pretended he was scanning the second page. Folding the paper on his lap, he picked up one of the hot dogs, removed the paper, and took a bite, his eyes never leaving the director or the three men he thought were with him. The director kept looking at his watch and after five minutes, stomped off. One of the men had started off seconds before the director, which told Stuart the director had a microphone in his jacket and was in constant contact with his men. The second man started at almost the same time, leaving a third, who was standing against a tree and looking around. He was obviously not with them and took a cell phone from his pocket to make a call.

Stuart watched this one, nodded, and started walking quickly in the opposite direction. Stuart rose and took a route that bisected him about fifteen yards away. Tourists crowded the street as Stuart stumbled in front of the man spilling his Coke down the front of the man's suit.

"You clumsy idiot!" the man shouted as the crowd separated.

Stuart sat on the ground and looked up, a confused look on his face.

"You ran into me," he declared, turning to one of the bystanders. "You saw it, tell him it was his fault."

"Look what you did to my suit!" yelled the third man.

Stuart stood and used his newspaper to clumsily wipe down the man's suit.

"What the hell are you doing?" The man pushed Stuart away.

"You should stop yelling, I'm only trying to help." Stuart pointed somewhere behind the man's back. "Here comes a policeman, he'll straighten this out."

The man turned, ignoring Stuart as he patted down the front of the suit. "I don't see a cop, and stop rubbing your dirty paper into my clothes." He pushed Stuart aside and walked away.

"He must be a New Yorker," Stuart said to the dispersing crowd.

Stuart walked several blocks in the other direction before stepping into a doorway and hitting the recall button on the cell phone he took from the man's pocket. "You might yell a lot," mumbled Stuart writing the number," but you're a patsy for a good pickpocket." It was an out-of-town number. With the amount of new exchanges he wasn't sure exactly where, but he knew 571 was not a Washington or surrounding-area number. Pocketing the phone, he dialed his office on his and asked for Michael.

"Burnett here," came the abrupt reply.

"Hi there, Mr. Burnett, that was some great lunch you set up for me."

After a second's delay, Michael replied, "Meet me in front in ten minutes, and don't be late."

Stuart made it in five and stood in a doorway across the street from his office where he could observe people coming and going. Everyone was in a hurry to get somewhere, yet smiling as if they didn't have a care in the world. *Maybe my mother was right, I should've given up this job fifteen years ago.*

Stuart watched his boss exit the front door and turn left without glancing in his direction. Less than fifteen seconds behind came Joe Gates, Michael's personal bodyguard. Joe looked at Stuart and motioned for him to follow Michael. Walking on the opposite side of the street, he watched as Michael walked into the restaurant on the corner. This was the same deli that Christine had asked him to go to an hour and a half ago.

"They're probably throwing me a surprise party," he said aloud as he hurried into the deli. He waved at the cashier, who said with a smile, "They're waiting in the back room."

"Knew it!" he replied, rushing to the back and flinging open the door.

Chapter Six

"Have a seat," Michael said as Stuart came into the room.

Stuart looked around. There was only his boss Michael and two other men. He recognized Jake Levitt, the director of the FBI. The other one, dressed in a blue sport jacket and gray slacks, he didn't know. The man stood and held out his hand.

"Ray Bradley," he said. "Deputy director of the bureau. I understand you had a misunderstanding with one of my men earlier this morning."

Stuart glanced at his boss and saw he was grinning, but the message being sent was *be gracious and be nice.* "Sorry for the misunderstanding," said Stuart, shaking his hand.

"I don't know if you've met the director," said Bradley, "let me introduce you."

Jake Levitt stood. He was two or three inches taller than Bradley but a good fifteen pounds lighter.

"Mr. Levitt, my pleasure," Stuart said, holding out his hand.

"The pleasure's mine," responded the director. "I've heard some very good things about you, and please call me Jake."

"If they're good things, I hope they're from women," Stuart said with a smile.

"Let's get right down to business." Everyone sat and he continued. "I checked, and we had two men plus the man selling hot dogs. What made you think there were three?"

Stuart looked at his boss before answering.

"Let me set the record straight," said Michael Burnett. "These two men are counted among the very few that I call friends. Whatever you would say to me, you can say to them. I trust them implicitly and so should you."

Stuart nodded and waited a moment before speaking. "I got there two or three minutes early and looked over the crowd. Two of them were standing an equal distance from you. One on each side, I expected that. The third stood like he was hiding from the other two, which is why I asked the question."

"My man selling hot dogs told us that you started out after someone but tripped and spilled your drink all over some guy."

Stuart took the cell phone from his pocket. "The man I tripped and spilled the drink on was the third man. He made one call to area code 571." He handed the phone to Bradley, hitting the recall button. "The phone company can probably give you a comprehensive list of all the calls made on this phone. You might want to have your people take a look at any numbers he has stored in memory."

"Anything else?" asked Bradley.

"That's it, unless you want a description. He's five foot five, dark hair, blue eyes, and has a little scar above his right eye. He chews his nails and wears Aramis cologne."

Levitt smiled. Looking at a little notepad, he replied, "Not bad. According to my man, you missed the height by three of four inches, but we missed the scar, the nail biting, and the Aramis."

"Your man also missed the three-inch heels he was wearing."

Stuart glanced at his boss who was chewing on his nails, and then turned back to the director. "Might I ask why someone would be following you?"

"When Ray checks out the cell phone, we'll have some answers."

There was a pause in the conversation as everyone seemed to be lost in thought.

"Before you do that," Stuart said, directing his comment at the deputy director, "I'd like to know why you wanted to meet with me."

The deputy director looked at his boss who nodded.

"There are very few secrets in this town, and I guess one of the worst kept is Jake's wanting to retire." Pausing, he looked at his boss who was staring at the floor. "The second worst kept secret is that I'd like his job. The President is prepared to put my name up as soon as Jake announces his retirement, but there are veiled threats that my name will be turned down in committee. I could live with that, but the President can't. We've had some problems that we're trying to solve. If Jake retires and I can't get confirmed, there will be no one there to clean up the mess."

"Who's in line behind you?" Stuart asked.

"That's one of the problems there is no one. The man some people think is in line behind me." Swallowing some Coke, he started again, "I think is causing the problems."

Stuart noticed that the words came out in a rush, as if he were trying to spit them out.

Stuart started to think through why he was invited to this meeting. "Why not fire him?"

"Two reasons," the director interceded. "The first is that we're not absolutely sure he's responsible, and the second, if he is, there is someone very powerful behind him. We want that person."

"And the reason for wanting to meet with me?" Stuart took his elbows off the table and sat back.

The director nodded at Michael Burnett who started speaking, "Stuart, that little run-in you had this morning with those punks has started a chain reaction that may work to our advantage."

"Our advantage?" Stuart asked sarcastically. One look from his boss and he fell immediately silent.

"Congresswoman Winston received a phone call ten minutes after she heard from her daughter. The caller told her that her daughter had a little problem on the way to school, and if she didn't play ball the next time would be worse. She was also told not to say anything to anyone about the call."

"That makes the actions of those kids you met premeditated, and the caller obviously hadn't heard back from the kids yet," the director interrupted.

"What did she say?" Stuart asked.

"She told him never to call her again."

"Him?"

"She said it was a him," answered the director.

Stuart sat there and thought it through. "What kind of ball is she supposed to play?"

"We don't know," replied the deputy director. "What we do know is that she might be on the committee that decides whether or not to send my name forward."

"She must be on other committees as well."

"We've thought of that, but this is the hottest potato on the plate. Four other members of that committee have started wavering over the past five weeks and, . . . well let's just call it a hunch."

"What is it exactly that you want from me?"

The room went silent. Stuart thought everyone had stopped breathing. The director stood and held out his hand. "I want nothing from you. Ray and I just thought it would be nice for us to meet, now we have to go." Turning to Stuart's boss, he said, "Michael it's been a pleasure seeing you again. Keep in touch."

His assistant rose and shook Stuart's hand. "I'm sure we'll see each other again."

The two men left by the back door.

"Did I miss something?" Stuart asked his boss.

"Accountability. If they don't know, then they're not responsible." He moved closer to Stuart. "They both know of our department, but they can say under oath they didn't know what we were doing."

"What are we doing?" Stuart asked.

"The operative word isn't *we*, it's you. I want you to find out what's going on, and at the same time make sure nothing happens to the congresswoman."

"I'm working on this bank robbery thing."

"I didn't say to stop working on it, I said find out what's going on. I can reassign it but thought that because one of your kids was involved you'd want the assignment."

Stuart drew little circles on the tabletop. As the circles got larger, he asked, "And the rules of engagement are?"

"You know the rules. Same as always."

"This congresswoman, does she know about me?"

"I'd like to tell you no, but I'm not sure. She has some friends in high places. Let's assume she knows, or at least knows part of the story. Use your own judgment and keep me up to date."

"I'm reporting to you, not the Bureau?" Stuart made the statement sound like a question.

"As always, I'm the only one you answer to. You in?"

The circles became smaller. "I'm in," Stuart said as he ran the palm of his hand over the drawing. "I do have one question. What's the name of the person who some people think is the next in line?"

"Eric Weaver."

"Not that asshole I spoke to on the phone?"

"One and the same." He looked at his watch. "I've set up a meeting for two and a half hours from now."

"Who with?"

"The congresswoman, Jessica Winston."

"I hate being that predictable." Stuart stood and looked at his boss. "Where's the meeting?"

"Neutral ground," said Michael smiling, "Library of Congress, second floor, cartoon exhibit. I don't know if you've been there, but there are two staircases. When you enter, go up on the right one."

"Who knows about this meeting?"

"Just the three of us. She was asked not to tell her people where she was going."

"I've got some homework," said Stuart. "I'll stay in touch." He waved as he walked out of the restaurant.

Chapter Seven

Stuart spent almost the entire two hours educating himself on who Jessica Winston was. His attention was so focused that he didn't notice Christine enter his office.

"Rumor has it you're working on a new case," she said, sitting down across from him.

"I wonder where those rumors start." He placed the pad facedown on his desk.

"Mr. Burnett said to give you all the help you needed, but not to say a word about the case to anyone else."

"How much did he tell you?"

"Nothing," she replied. Except that it has to do with some congresswoman."

"Jessica Winston," he stated quietly.

"The one from California?" Christine asked eyebrows rose. "She's the darling of Washington."

"Suppose you tell me what you know about her. It might be more than I was able to get from the computer."

Sitting up straight and putting her elbows on the edge of his desk, she started, "Jessica Winston is in her second term. She lives in Maryland with her only child a daughter. Her husband died six years ago in an auto accident. The driver of the other car was drunk, and she got involved with MADD, Mothers Against Drunk Drivers." Christine stopped and looked at Stuart who motioned for her to keep talking. "She made such an impact that she was selected to run for Congress. Since she's been here, she's made everyone sit up and notice. Unlike most first-term congressmen, she didn't sit back and wait her turn to speak. Instead, she got right into the thick of things. She was interviewed on television and said she might not be reelected, which is why she had to say what she believed, and said it quickly. She was reelected by a larger plurality than the President, and the word is that she'll run for the Senate in the next election."

Stuart wrote something on a piece of paper and then asked, "Do you know what committees she's on?"

"Definitely Transportation," she said, picking up a pencil from Stuart's desk and tapping the eraser against her teeth. "And maybe Judiciary. I think I saw her name mentioned when they had the budget hearings a few months ago, so maybe that one also."

Stuart nodded, "See if you can get a full list of the committees she's on. She must belong to a gym find out the name. One more thing, does she have a boyfriend or several?"

"She goes to state dinners by herself, and she's seldom seen in public with someone attached to her arm. There was a piece in the Sunday edition a few months back, where she said she wouldn't take dinner from a lobbyist and hadn't found anyone in Washington who was single and interesting enough to spend time with."

"How about in California?"

"Don't know, but I doubt it. She's very involved with her daughter and she mentioned a mother, but I don't remember where the woman lives."

Stuart rose and walked to the door, leaving Christine at his desk.

"If it rings, take a message. And get that info for me, I'll check in later." *I don't watch enough TV,* he thought to himself as he walked to the elevator.

Stuart arrived at the Library of Congress twenty minutes early, entered and went up the left staircase. Walking to the back, he was able to observe the entrance without being seen.

Twenty-five minutes later, Congresswoman Winston entered through the front door. Stuart had never seen her in person, but there was no mistaking her. She wore a gray business jacket with matching skirt; a single strand of pearls decorated the opening of a pale blue blouse. The medium high heels gave her legs the look of a model as she climbed the stairs. She wasn't beautiful, but Jessica Winston was striking, and more than a few heads turned as she sped past them up the stairs.

When she reached the top step, she looked around as if expecting someone to approach her. Stuart saw that she looked at her watch, as if to verify that she was only five minutes fashionably late. Stuart began to walk toward her when he noticed a man entering the library. It was the same man on whom he spilled soda.

The stranger scanned the crowd, looked up, and saw the congresswoman and then quickly exited.

Stuart remained out of the line of sight of the front door as he made his way toward Jessica Winston. When only a few steps away, he murmured, "Mrs. Winston?"

She turned with a questioning look on her face. "Are you Mr. Taylor? Marilyn's father?"

"Yes, and please walk back toward me, I have to show you something."

She looked behind her. "What's wrong?"

"Nothing yet. Please come back here."

She held back a moment before taking a deep breath and walking behind the bookcase. Holding out her hand, she said, "Mr. Taylor, I'm pleased to meet you. I don't know why your office picked this spot. I could have come to where you work. I just wanted to say thank you for this morning."

"My office is a pigsty, and there's really nothing to thank me for. It was just a couple of street kids feeling their oats and trying to hit on two good-looking girls."

"That's not exactly the way my daughter explained it, but I'm sure you're right. Is there somewhere around here that we could get a cup of coffee? I missed lunch, and I would love to spend a few minutes talking."

"There's a Starbucks or someplace like it about a half block away, if you don't mind walking?"

She smiled and motioned for him to lead the way.

Stuart held out his hand, and she hesitated before reaching out. Her face reddened as he grasped her elbow and guided her down the stairs.

They walked slowly talking about the weather and about how beautiful Washington was in April.

"I understand you're from California?" prompted Stuart, when the conversation stalled. "How does this compare?"

"I find it hard to compare anything against California. I've been in Montana, Hawaii, Oregon, you name it, and found them to be beautiful. But day after day, Southern California has got to be my favorite. Where are you from?"

"I've been to all of those places. I do a lot of traveling. Right now I'm calling here home."

"Here as in Washington, or here as in Maryland?"

"Both of them. I spend a lot of time in Washington and a lot of time in Maryland."

"You're a tough man to pin down, Mr. Taylor. Your daughter said you were never home, which is why your wife left you. She also said she thought you would end up in jail. I wonder what would make her say that."

Before he could answer two of the boys from the incident in the morning, Samuel Baker and his friend who ran away, came running from behind them. Stuart took Jessica's hand and pulled her so that he was between her and the boys.

"Samuel my friend," he said aloud, exaggerating each word. "I see you found your buddy. I thought he was the smart one, but I guess I was wrong."

"What does that mean?"

"That he ran away and didn't get hurt like you did. I'm sure you can trust him to hang around this time."

"Joey isn't running away this time, and I owe you for my foot, mudderfucker!" Samuel yelled.

"You have a dirty mouth, Samuel. You're lucky I don't have any soap." Stuart shifted his weight.

"What do you need soap for?"

"Samuel, I'm leaving, it's been nice, but I have to go." Stuart held out his hand as if to shake Samuel's, and as a reflex action, Samuel raised his arm. Stuart grabbed the boy's hand and pulled him forward stepping on the same instep. There was no mistaking the sounds of bones breaking. Samuel dropped, and Stuart took two step, grabbing Joey.

"You're running around with some nasty boys," said Stuart. "If I see you again you won't be this lucky." He turned Joey around and kicked him in the butt, sending him running up the street.

He turned and looked at Samuel who was clutching his foot, his face etched in pain. "Samuel," said Stuart. "What am I going to do with you?" Before the boy could respond, he asked, "Who told you where I was?"

"Call me a doctor," demanded Samuel. "You broke my damn foot."

Stuart released an impatient sigh. "Samuel, you're not listening. Who told you where to find me?"

The congresswomen approached Stuart. "Should we get him some help? Before he could answer, she added, "Why did you hit him? He wasn't doing anything."

"Let me introduce you to Samuel Baker, one of the boys that hassled our daughters. At some point, Congresswoman, we're going to have to find out what they're after, and it might as well be now."

"I'd rather not be part of this." She was becoming agitated. "I still want to talk to you about this morning, but"—she shook her head—"maybe we should call the police?"

Stuart stood there, looking at the boy on the ground. He took a deep breath and asked, "Samuel, do you still live at the same address?"

"What you care where I live, mudderfucker, you broke my foot."

"And the next time I see you, I'll break your teeth. And," Stuart continued, "if I ever see you again, you better hope that your foot is better 'cause you can't run fast enough if it isn't." With that, he turned to the congresswoman and said, "Let's get some coffee." The two walked away, leaving Samuel on the ground rubbing his foot.

"You're an interesting man, Mr. Taylor." Looking at her watch, she said, "I have to get back by eight, they're calling a vote that I don't want to miss."

"Can we share a cab?" Stuart whistled for a cab that was cruising by, opened the door, and waited for her to climb in.

"Where to?" the driver asked.

"Give us a minute," Stuart answered. Turning to the woman, he said, "We didn't get to discuss what went on today with the girls.

She smiled, "I have time for something quick. I know a little Italian restaurant not far from here, do you like Italian?"

"I enjoy pasta, pizza, and the sauce they come in," he replied, smiling. She got better looking every minute he was with her.

Jessica Winston gave the driver the directions and sat back.

"As I said before, you're an interesting man, Mr. Taylor. My daughter was very impressed with you, but after watching that display, I can understand your daughter Marilyn's comment about you."

"She's always been a little dramatic, she gets it from her mother."

"How long have you been divorced?"

The question showed she had done some of her own homework.

"Fifteen years give or take a month."

"And you're still involved with your children?"

"I don't know if *involved* is the right word. I talk to them infrequently, but I send them money on birthdays and holidays."

The cab pulled up in front of a small restaurant. When they walked inside, the owner put on a big show of welcoming the congresswoman. He led them to a table in the back. "Caesar is a friend of mine," she told Stuart, "and I can guarantee that anything you order you'll like."

"How about you ordering for me. That way I'm sure not to be disappointed."

Stuart lifted the glass of wine that Caesar brought to the table. He looked over the rim as he watched the first woman he had gone out to dinner with in over nine months order in fluent Italian. This woman was becoming more impressive every minute.

"So tell me," she inquired, handing the menu back to Caesar. "Where is it you work? And please don't tell me the FBI."

"You can always call them and check up on me," he replied with a smile.

She took a cell phone from her purse and dialed six digits. "Should I continue?"

"Why not?"

She hit the seventh digit and held the phone away from her ear.

"Bradley!" came the voice out of the phone.

"Congresswoman Winston here . . . . Listen, I had one of my people check earlier on the status of a Stuart Taylor. I've been told he works for the bureau." She smiled at Stuart. "Of course I'll hold." She took a sip of wine and said, "You know Mr. Bradley, of course."

"I've met Ray." He matched her smile with his.

"Yes, I'm here," she said into the phone, and then added, "beige shirt, tan slacks, blue sport jacket." Her face turned red. "Forty, forty-five, dark hair, six foot two or three, one eighty. No, he didn't make a pass or insult me." She listened for another minute and then asked, "How come my aide didn't find this information earlier?" She snapped the phone closed and stared at Stuart. "I'm sorry for the mix-up, Mr. Bradley didn't know how it happened."

"No harm done, except I can't believe that Ray would ask if I made a pass."

"Do you normally?"

"Do I normally what?"

"Make passes."

"No, I don't. That's just Ray trying to be funny."

Their food arrived, and Stuart was grateful she had stopped asking questions. They ate in silence, as if neither was willing to take the lead. When they finished, it was the congresswoman who asked for the bill.

Stuart held out his hand. "Let me get it. I haven't been on a date in over a year. When I think back to tonight, I can lie to myself and say that I've had one."

She shook her head. "My daughter said you took on those three kids like a kung fu master." She studied him for a moment. "You handled the situation earlier with a minimum of violence, yet you admit to not being on a date for almost a year. It's not something I'd think a he-man would admit to."

"I may not tell the truth, but I don't lie."

"Someday you'll have to explain the difference."

"How about tomorrow night?" he asked quickly. "My only friend and his wife have invited me to dinner, and I hate going alone. It would give us a chance to talk about our kids."

She stared at him. "I haven't had a date for over five years. Are you asking me out on a date? I mean I've been to dinners, but no date. What will I tell my daughter?"

"Anything, just don't tell her it's with me. She'll call my daughter, and all our family secrets will be out of the bag."

"What time?" she asked in a rush, getting the words out before she changed her mind.

"I'll pick you up at six fifteen. He lives in Chevy Chase and dinner is usually at seven."

"You know where I live?" she asked in a surprised tone.

"It goes with the job."

She looked at her watch and began gathering her things. "One part of me is dying to find out more about you, the other has me petrified of what I'll find."

They said their good-byes, and she disappeared into a cab.

"I'm not that bad," he said quietly as the cab pulled away.

Chapter Eight

Stuart signaled for the next taxi in line and jumped in. "Follow that cab."

"You shitting me?" The driver looked into his rearview mirror.

"Move it," he said, flipping open his wallet to expose a badge.

"There won't be any shooting, right?"

"I'm checking up on my wife, so don't get too close, I just want to make sure she's going to work."

"Where does she work?"

"Follow her and hold the commentary."

The cab arrived at the Capitol without incident, and Stuart then directed his cabbie to take him to an address on the outskirts of Washington.

"I ain't waiting," the driver said as Stuart exited the cab. "This isn't the nicest part of town."

"Always nice to meet a concerned citizen," responded Stuart, slamming the door.

Stuart walked two blocks and found the address he had taken from the wallet of Augie Meridian earlier that day. The neighborhood wasn't all that bad. There were no garbage cans lining the street, and for most part, the buildings weren't in disrepair. He stood before a two-story brownstone. Three mailboxes were attached to the wrought iron fence that protected the downstairs apartment. Meridian's unit was downstairs, which didn't surprise Stuart at all.

He looked up and down the street. Seeing no one, he descended the three steps to the basement apartment and knocked. When no one answered, he took another look around, picked the lock, and let himself in.

Using the little flashlight attached to his key ring, Stuart ran the beam run around the room until he had a feeling for what was where. The Murphy bed was opened, and he figured it probably stayed that way. There were two chairs, one with an ottoman facing a thirty-six-inch TV. A small Formica table with two chairs was in front of the sink between the refrigerator and stove. There were two doors. He figured one led to a bathroom, and the other because there was no dresser or chest of drawers, to a closet. Someone in the building flushed a toilet. Stuart heard water running loudly through the pipes. Slowly he opened the door on the left. Inside the closet he found a chest of drawers, a stack of dirty clothes piled in the corner, and Samuel's friend Joey.

The body was warm. Stuart figured it hadn't been here for more than a few hours. Joey's pockets were empty, turned inside out meaning whoever did this was looking for the money or making sure there was no identification. Stuart leaned closer and saw there was no blood, but there were needle tracks on Joey's arm. *Maybe an overdose,* he told himself, *but I don't see the needle.* Backing out of the closet, he decided to call the police and then realized there was no phone in the apartment. How did Augie keep in touch with the rest of the world?

Stuart walked over to the refrigerator and opened the door. Two Diet Cokes on the top shelf a six-pack of iced tea on the bottom. This place was for meetings only. Stuart headed for the door reminding himself to have Christine try and find out who rented the place. He was half way to the door when he thought to take a quick look in the bathroom. Augie wasn't there; but Samuel was, sprawled out in the bathtub, a bullet hole just above his nose, right between his eyes. His bare right foot hung over the side of the tub. Stuart looked over the scene with his lips compressed. The DC police didn't have a chance in hell of solving these murders if they even bothered to try. Stuart guessed that Augie was either responsible for this mess or lying dead in someone else's closet.

From a phone booth three blocks away, he dialed 911 and explained to the operator that he heard screaming an hour earlier and decided to call it in. He had walked another two blocks away before hearing the sirens.

The bells at Saint Malachy's were halfway through their 10:00 PM hourly ringing, as he entered his house. The blinking red light on his phone advised him of new messages. The first was from Christine. "Stuart, if you're home before nine call me. Otherwise I'll give you the information tomorrow."

He pushed the button for the second call. "Father, this is your son Kenneth. I wanted to wish you a happy birthday." There was a slight pause. "I think I'd like to see you, maybe meet for lunch or something. I know you have my number." Each sentence came out in staccato. Stuart stood holding the phone as the dial tone rang in his ear and then he saved the message.

The third one was far different. "Listen carefully, old man," whispered a voice. "Stay away from things that don't concern you. We know where your daughter lives."

Stuart's hand tightened around the receiver. The caller forgot to mention he also knew where Stuart lived, and that list was had by a very few people.

He put in a call to the duty officer. Regulations demanded that anytime someone unauthorized knew his number, his people had to be advised. The number he called was an 800 number, with a cutout that allowed him to reach a live person twenty-four seven.

"This is the Cigar Store. Please repeat the following number for a voice check 44-21-35."

Stuart replied, "Two hundred." The code was simple, add the three numbers and in Stuart's case double them.

"Name is?"

"Stuart Taylor."

The phone went silent. After a moment, the duty officer asked, "What's the problem?"

"I'm going to play a message left on my machine."

Stuart hit the button.

"We'll have someone watching her in about twenty minutes," said the voice. "You also have a son. What should we do about him?"

"He's away at boarding school and only returns home on weekends. I'll let you know about him tomorrow."

"Do you want a safe house for tonight?"

"Thanks, but I should be fine here. The caller threatened my daughter, not me. If I get lucky, he'll change his mind and come calling. I'll be in the office early tomorrow. You can pass this upward; the DC police got a 911 call tonight around nine thirty. When they arrived at the house, they found two dead bodies. I think we're interested in what else they find."

Stuart hung up, knowing that there would be someone outside his house within a half hour. Nothing he could say would ever change procedure.

Chapter Nine

Stuart arrived at his office before seven in the morning and found his boss and Christine waiting for him.

"I thought you told the duty officer you'd be in early!" Michael shouted.

"This is early!" Stuart yelled back, tossing his jacket over the back of his chair as he headed to the coffee bar. Christine stood and followed him.

"I'll take mine black and get in here." Michael snapped.

"He always wants the last word," Stuart whispered as Christine filled her cup.

"Close the door!" Michael Burnett barked as Stuart and Christine started to sit down.

Stuart picked up a pencil and wrote "CLEAN?" in block letters on the notepad in front of him.

"I had it swept last night and again this morning," said Michael

"Find anything?" Stuart asked.

"No," he answered curtly. "Let's get started." When Michael saw Christine take out her pad, he told her to put it away. "I don't think I want to be reminded about what we talked about." Nodding at Stuart, he said, "Why don't you fill us in on what transpired yesterday?"

"I met the congresswoman and ended up taking her to dinner." Stuart couldn't help notice the look between Christine and Michael but said nothing. "On the way there, we met up with Samuel Baker and his friend Joey. I made sure she reached her office at Rayburn, and then went to say hello to Augie Meridian, their leader. He wasn't home, but I found the bodies of Samuel and Joey. Their pockets were clean as was the apartment."

"Explain clean," said Burnett.

"No phone, no food, no lived-in appearance. Two Diet Cokes and a six-pack of iced tea in the fridge, like it was rented for meetings."

Michael pushed back his chair and put one foot on the desk. "Okay, now tell me your thoughts about the phone message."

"I've had time to think about it," replied Stuart, "and I don't think they know who I am or who I work for. For one thing,—he held up a finger—"they called me old man, which was the same term used yesterday." He raised a second finger. "My daughter called me Dad. Once they knew that, it was easy to look me up. My phone's not listed, but anyone with some smarts could probably get the number." Raising a third finger, he concluded, "they didn't mention my son, which tells me they don't know about him, and this was a warning to keep my mouth shut."

"Any idea what they're after?" Christine asked.

"Not yet. Did you find out what committees Winston's on?"

Opening her pad, Christine read, "There are nineteen standing committees, two select committees four joint committees. Every congressperson serves on at least two, some on three or four. Winston serves on three, Transportation and Infrastructure, Appropriations, Ways and Means."

"Which would take up the question of the's new director?" Michael asked.

"Not sure," Christine replied. "The President sends the name to the Senate House Judiciary committee, where they discuss it and then send it to the Senate for confirmation. All confirmations go through the Senate.

"But she's not on Judiciary," said Stuart.

"Not as of two days ago," said Christine. "And she's not a senator either."

The room became silent; Stuart and Christine looked at their boss.

"I guess there are still some secrets in Washington," said Michael, returning their gaze. "Senator Chilicote from Colorado who is the majority whip, is announcing his retirement two weeks from Friday. The Speaker is going to ask Mrs. Winston to fill that vacancy. She won't be on the Judiciary committee, but she'll have an awful lot to say about what goes on."

"Why is he retiring?" Stuart asked.

"That's the sixty-four-dollar question. He says it's for personal reasons, but we're not sure."

"Two weeks from Friday," repeated Stuart. "And her appointment is being announced?"

"The following Monday."

Christine shifted in the chair, stretching against the hard surface. "Will she have to give up her seat on any committees?" Christine asked.

"I'm not sure," said Michael. "I'm not even sure she'll say yes."

"Maybe we have to figure out which seats are the most important?" offered Stuart, "And why wouldn't she?"

Michael shrugged. "Who knows what she wants." He looked at the list of committees that Christine had put in front of him. "Anything with money attached to it has to be important. But then so is every other committee, depending upon the day of the week or the mood of the country. We fall under Appropriations, which makes that important."

Standing, Stuart said, "I get the picture. We don't know what's going on, we don't know who's responsible; you want me to keep an eye on her and find out who's causing the problem, and why people are getting killed."

"Sit back down, Stuart, there's more. The DC police found the bodies, but when they checked, they also found out when Samuel Baker rented the place. They're treating this as a drug deal gone wrong. They'll try and spend some time trying to find out who made the call, but it's a low priority." He finished off the coffee and turned toward Christine. "Why don't you tell Stuart what you found out."

"When Baker rented the apartment, he paid twelve months in advance and in cash." She paused and ran fingers through her hair. "According to the source, this Baker was Caucasian."

Stuart stared at Christine. "The police don't think that's strange?"

"They don't know," she replied. "When the landlord told me the story, I asked him if he thought it was strange for some black kid to lay out that kind of cash in advance. That's when I found out the police never asked the question."

The room fell silent. There were still questions Stuart wanted to ask but preferred not to in front of Christine. As if reading his thoughts, Michael said, "Christine, why don't you leave us alone? I want to talk to Stuart about his daughter."

Christine stood, nodded at Stuart, and left the room.

"You have something you want to say?" Michael asked as the door closed.

"Yesterday, you were concerned about someone listening in on our conversation. Who do you suspect?"

"There's something wrong over at the bureau. Both Jake and Ray are friends of mine, and I'd do anything to help, but it could be this guy Weaver."

"How would he know to bug this place?"

"He wouldn't, but there's been some things that are making me a little paranoid."

"Any idea who was following Jake Levitt yesterday?"

"We still don't know. They traced the number that was on that cell phone, and it was for a phone booth in Pennsylvania, which happened to be in the middle of nowhere."

"Nowhere?"

"Literally. It was at some crossroad twenty miles outside of Allentown. One of those illuminated phones for drivers who're in need of assistance."

Stuart mulled over this for a moment. "Were there any other numbers programmed into that phone?"

"No numbers, and the instrument wasn't even registered."

Stuart rose to leave and then sat back down. "This agent Weaver, how bad do you think he is?"

"I don't know," responded Michael. "He was a political appointee from the last administration. He always seemed to be in the right place at the right time and was promoted accordingly. He's been with the for four short years, and his rise has been way too rapid."

Stuart sat back, deep in thought, appreciative that his boss was giving him time to put his thoughts in order. When Michael finally asked what his plans were, Stuart was ready to respond.

"I'm going to have my phone ring through the Cigar Store so they can trace every call. Next, I'll get closer to the congresswoman and will hopefully head off any problems there. Last, I need to learn more about Agent Weaver. I'll have a background check done and have someone look into those cases where he's been in the right places."

Stuart stood. "And, oh yes, I'll find the people that are robbing the banks." Smiling, he started toward the door.

"I forgot to tell you one more thing," said Michael, clearing his throat. "The President has requested that you attend a black tie dinner at the White House on Saturday night."

Stuart walked back and sat down. "I'm becoming very visible very quickly. I thought one of the rules was never to be seen or heard."

"Yeah, well there's a new set of rules, and the paperwork is being processed as we speak. By days end, you'll be part of the hierarchy of the on temporary duty with the ATF and now returning to the fold."

"I report to Weaver?"

"No, you report directly to Bradley."

"Which makes me the number three man in the Bureau?"

"Yes, it does, but don't let it go to your head, you still work for me. I'm just making it easier for you to track down the bank robbers."

Chapter Ten

Christine walked into Stuart's office and placed a cup of coffee on his desk before he realized he wanted one.

"Thanks."

"Don't thank me," she said. "Just tell me what you want me to do."

"You sound pissed." He put the cup to his lips.

"What went on that I couldn't hear? All of a sudden you don't trust me?" Her eyes registered more hurt than anger.

Stuart put the cup down and sighed. "It's not you. Michael was concerned about someone eavesdropping, and I wanted to know if the office had been swept."

"That's bullshit, Stuart, and you know it. I sweep the office every morning, so it has to be more than that."

"I'm being transferred," he said quietly.

Christine's eyebrows rose. "People don't get transferred out of here."

"It looks like some things are changing, and this is the first of them."

She sat down. "I don't believe it."

"Before I go, there are some things you have to do for me."

"Where are you being transferred to?"

"The FBI."

Christine stared at Stuart for a long and uncomfortable beat. With lips compressed, the words came out forced. "After all the years we've worked together, I'd rather you said nothing than lie to me. I might have believed the CIA or some other part of Treasury, but not the FBI." She shook her head. "What do you want me to do?"

Stuart was drawing circles with his finger on the desk. He glanced up at her and knew that after all these years, she understood that when he erased those invisible circles he'd start talking.

"You're one of the few people in this world I wouldn't lie to," he said, his hand sweeping away the imaginary circles. "I'm being moved to the number three position in the bureau. The paperwork will say that I've been on temporary duty with the ATF."

"Number three person? What about Eric Weaver?"

"One of the things about the is if you want to find out the hierarchy, you find out who they report to. Weaver reports to Bradley and so will I. The only difference is that Bradley will favor me in all decisions."

"You're serious about this." When Stuart nodded, she added, "I've heard that Weaver is not someone you want as an enemy."

Stuart gave her his best smile. "I don't want anyone as an enemy, so make sure you get me good information."

Christine took out her pad. "What do you want me to do?"

"First off, I need to rent a tuxedo for Saturday night."

"A tuxedo?"

"The President has invited me to dinner, black tie of course." The look of astonishment on Christine's face caused Stuart to grin.

"The President invited you? How do I get a transfer? Your new job looks like more fun than we have here."

Stuart motioned toward her notepad. "The second thing you need to do is tell the Cigar Store to put a trace on all calls made to my number, and then, get me a new cell phone. I'll give that number to a few select people."

"Will I be one of them?" she interrupted.

He nodded. "Most important, I need a background check on Eric Weaver."

Christine stopped writing. "Eric Weaver?"

"Him. I want to know where he went to school, with whom, and who's his priest in the government. Someone got him into the bureau. I want to know who. This guy's been in the right place, at the right time more than once, it can't be a coincidence. I also want to know the cases he's been on, how he solved them, and who he leapfrogged to get there. While you're at it, find out if he's married, fools around, et cetera."

He waited until she finished writing before adding, "I want the answers yesterday, and I want only our people used to get the information."

Christine finished writing and sat back. "You're really moving over to the?"

"On paper anyway," Stuart replied.

"If Levitt resigns and Bradley takes his place, that would make you second in command, and it wouldn't be on paper any longer."

"If that happens, I'll arrange for your transfer, I promise."

"I'll hold you to that," Christine said as she rose. "I'll get that cell phone for you right now, the remainder of your wish list will take a little longer."

The rest of the day went faster than normal. When Stuart got his new cell phone, he called his mother who was not home. "Mom," he said into her answering machine, "I got a new phone number. For the next two days you can call my old one, and it'll transfer to me. I'm busy Saturday night. I have a black tie dinner to attend. I'll call you later." Each sentence was a statement all its own, which he knew would drive his mother crazy. He stopped at Tuxedo Junction across from Fords Theater and was fitted for a tuxedo. After that, he headed for Jessica Winston's. Before he had traveled two blocks, his phone rang.

"Stuart, I'm glad I found you," said Christine, the words tumbling out. "Congresswoman Winston called your house and left a message."

"What did she say?"

"You're to pick her up in front of the Jefferson Memorial at six."

"What's she doing there?"

"I haven't got the slightest. The message was relayed from the Cigar Store ten minutes ago."

Stuart looked at the street sign. "I'll take Hoover to Fourteenth, hopefully it won't be too bad."

"One more thing. I set up a file I'm calling Dresser. You can access it on the Internet using Stuartdresser."

"Dresser?"

"Like file, only dresser."

"Why the ruse?"

"I have a funny feeling, like someone's looking over my shoulder."

"Christine, tell Michael about this."

"It's nothing, I'll get over it."

"Tell Michael," he repeated, his voice stronger. "I've learned to trust your instincts a long time ago."

"As soon as he returns, I will."

Stuart was about to hang up when he remembered. "One thing, ask the Cigar Store where the congresswoman's call was made from."

"Anything special you're looking for?"

"I don't remember giving her my home phone number."

Christine was silent. "Don't meet her until I call you back, please."

"You worry too much. I'm trying to find out where the Congress people get their information."

"You're a terrible liar, Stuart. Please," she whispered, "be careful." And then the phone went dead.

Stuart realized he had about twenty minutes before the Cigar Store dispatched men to the Jefferson Memorial. At this time of night, he had perhaps forty-five minutes at most. Ten minutes later, he pulled into the administrative parking zone across the street from the memorial. There were flashbulbs going off from tourists' cameras, their lights casting golden flares against the deepening dusk.

Nothing seemed out of order except for two kids who were leaning against a car with its motor running. Stuart couldn't make out the third person behind the wheel, but had the feeling it was his friend Augie. He removed his pistol from his shoulder holster and walked briskly up to the driver's side. As he approached, he made out the face of the driver. It was Augie. Using the butt of his pistol, he smashed it against the window, showering glass throughout the car. The two men he previously thought were kids jumped in alarm. Before they could react, Stuart reached in the window and grabbed Augie by the hair. At the same time he yelled, "Either of you move and you're dead!"

One man said to the other, "He's full of shit!" and drew his weapon.

Stuart shot both of them and then turned the gun on Augie. "Your turn?"

"Don't shoot, don't shoot!" Augie begged.

Stuart opened the car door and pulled him out, ordering him onto the ground.

The security guards alerted by the shots came running down the memorial's steps.

"Call the police!" Stuart hollered. "I'm with the FBI, and these men are possible terrorists." Holding up his badge in the dim light brought the guards to a stop.

"Check those two on the ground," he ordered. But be careful, they've got guns."

One of the guards leaned over and pressed a finger against each of their necks. "They're both dead," he proclaimed. "Jesus, you killed them both."

The guards shifted quickly into action, taking control of the scene. They all turned at the sound of an approaching siren, except for Stuart, who stared at Congresswoman Jessica Winston now standing at the base of the steps and looking at the scene before her.

It took the better part of an hour, even with the men from the Cigar Store in attendance, to straighten out what happened with the local police. Stuart's story was simple. He was watching over the congresswoman when he received a call that she would meet him here instead of at the Capitol; he knew something was wrong. She confirmed that she made no such call but had received one that announced the change of meeting place. The police told them they would take Augie in tow, and that Stuart and the congresswoman could be on their way.

Stuart called his friend and host Peter and explained they'd be late and ushered Jessica into his car. When she turned toward him, her expression was not friendly.

"Mr. Taylor," she demanded, "before you move this car a single inch, you're going to explain to me what it is you do, and who were those men!"

Chapter Eleven

Stuart locked eyes with Jessica and then looked away. "What I'm about to tell you comes under the heading of Official Secrets Act. If you repeat this, you can go to jail." He put the car into drive and waited for the policeman to stop traffic and let him pull out.

"At least you didn't say 'If you repeat this, I'll have to kill you.'" The smile on her face was forced. When Stuart didn't respond, her expression shifted to confusion.

"Up until three hours ago," he explained, "I was assigned to the ATF, Alcohol, Tobacco—"

"I know what it stand for," she interrupted

"And Firearms." Stuart didn't like being interrupted and suspected that she did this to slow down a conversation. "In reality I worked for Michael Burnett and . . ."

"I don't think I know the name."

She did it again, he thought. "Michael works very hard at keeping a low profile. He's known to a very select few, and that includes the majority and minority leaders of both parties, the heads of the CIA and FBI, the attorney general, and the President." Stuart glanced over to see how she was taking the news. "When I say he's known, that doesn't mean they know what his group is doing, only that they know him . . . or know of him."

"And you are part of that group?"

Looking over, he saw that she was sitting with her eyes closed as if absorbing everything he said. "Yes, I am, but let me try to explain what I do.

In the silence of the car, Stuart explained how, five years earlier, he and Peter Weber were tracking a serial killer. Unlike the FBI that followed all the rules of engagement and therefore were always a day late, Stuart and Peter had no such restrictions. They caught up with the serial killer and his girlfriend in San Diego."

"My neck of the woods," said Jessica, again interrupting the flow of conversation.

This time Stuart let it slide. "The girlfriend almost killed Peter, and I ended up killing her."

"I remember the story," nodded Jessica. "The killer escaped, and the FBI couldn't find him. I don't remember reading your name."

"May I call you Jessica?" asked Stuart, stopping for a red light.

She hesitated. "Why?"

"I'm having a problem getting the word *congresswoman* out of my mouth."

"Sure," she said. "You can call me Jessica."

"Good. Jessica, can you please stop interrupting me?"

Stuart watched her eyes take on an angry glow. She didn't say a word, but her body language told him he was treading on dangerous ground.

He put the car into motion. "I started with this story because it has a moral, the FBI couldn't find him and neither will anyone else. If they had taken him alive, he would've blamed the girlfriend for the deaths and would've stood trial as an accomplice. Part of my job, aside from catching them is to make sure the criminals receive the full penalty for their actions."

"You're an assassin?"

"I like to think of myself as another James Bond, with a license to kill. The difference is I normally don't leave the country. We've got lots of laws protecting the innocent, and in some cases they protect the guilty."

"You're a paid assassin!" she repeated, this time as a declaration rather than a question.

"Jessica, you're talking when you should be listening."

"I'm talking when I should be . . . sorry, please continue."

"Most of what I do has nothing to do with people getting killed. Now, for example, I'm working on a series of bank robberies. The FBI is trying to find the criminals, and I think they're going about it wrong. My job is to find the bad guys, stop the robberies, and turn the culprits over to the bureau. The department I work for doesn't concern itself with state lines or local authorities, nor do we concern ourselves with the niceties of law enforcement. What we do is make sure the crimes stop. We don't look for credit, in fact we always try to shift the credit to local people or agencies."

This time Jessica didn't say a word. Instead she sat and appeared pensive. After a long silence, she asked, "Would you kill someone for robbing a bank?"

"I'm not judge and jury. My function is to stop them. Would I kill them for robbing the bank? Probably not, but if the next question is, would I kill them to stop them from killing someone else? The answer is yes."

The congresswoman said nothing. She sat with her eyes squeezed shut. After a moment, she asked, "The incident with the kids and what happened tonight, what do you think is going on?"

"Some people think that it is related to the next director of the bureau."

"Ray Bradley?"

"You would vote for Ray?" he asked.

"I don't get a vote, but yes."

"The story going around is that Chilicote will announce his retirement this Friday, and the Speaker would like to name you as his replacement. If my information is correct, that committee has the ability to look into his background before rendering its opinion. Rumor has it this committee will come out with a no vote of confidence before his name is brought to the Senate for a vote."

"That would be disastrous for the President," she replied in a surprised tone.

Stuart decided to play his hole card. "I also hear that you're going to run for the Senate, and you'll probably announce within the next two months." He looked at her for some reaction but got none. She was probably a great poker player.

"So you asked me to your friends' house to keep an eye on me," she said. "Your intended death tonight, with me watching, and my daughter's intended mugging, all this was meant to get me in line with whomever is orchestrating this scenario."

"I asked you to my friends' house because . . ." Stuart stared straight ahead. "I don't know why, but it wasn't because I'm supposed to watch you. I thought we could be friends, maybe. As far as the second part, I don't know why they were after me, since no one knows what I do for a living. Having you there to see what was going on, that doesn't make sense either."

"Why not?"

"Because you now know that I can handle myself and you have no reason to be afraid."

"Those men who arrived to help you, were they ATF?" She turned in the seat to face him, her skirt riding up her leg.

Stuart averted his eyes, her legs distracting him. "They were from the Cigar Store." When she said nothing, he explained, "It's a name someone made up. Remember the surgeon general's message that was on cigarette packs? Smoking being harmful to your health?"

"It's not there anymore?"

"They changed it to say the same thing but differently. Anyway those men are backup, which is why we say they're from the Cigar Store."

"Suppose you tell me about your friend we're visiting tonight. I don't want to look like a complete idiot."

"Peter Weber may be the only real friend I have in the world. He belonged to the ATF. When he got shot, he had to retire. He's thirty-eight, six years younger than I." He tried to determine how she took the news of his age. "Married, his wife's name is Joan and he's an accountant, a business advisor type."

"Do they have children?"

"They had a daughter who was killed by a drunk driver nine years ago. I guess you know how that feels?"

"Losing a child is tougher than losing a husband. The hurt, the anger, the rage, and responsibility are all there, but the loss of someone who was a part of you can't be replaced."

Stuart watched discreetly as she wiped her eye. When she moved, a shadow fell across the front of her dress. Between the skirt rising and that shadow, Stuart was almost afraid to speak. They rode in silence until he said, "Peter's house is a few blocks away. Are you all right?"

She gave him a little smile. "I hate being a baby, but sometimes it gets to me."

They pulled into a circular driveway that was lit like a runway at Dulles. The car stopped, the front door opened, and Peter and Joan walked out.

After Joan gave Stuart a kiss on the cheek, she turned to Jessica.

"Congresswoman Winston, welcome to our home. I'm Joan, and this is my husband Peter."

Jessica held out her hand. "Please, call me Jessica. I feel as if I know you both, after listening to Stuart all the way here."

Stuart watched Jessica, who was noting the glance between the husband and wife. It was one of those looks that said "this is different."

"I didn't talk that much," protested Stuart, a little embarrassed. With a smile he added, "I need a drink."

Joan took Jessica's arm. "Let me show you around, and you can tell me how you met Stuart. Perhaps you can also explain what would ever induce you to be seen in public with him."

Jessica laughed. "I'm still having a problem with that second part, but I would love to see your home."

As the two women started their tour, Peter put his hand on Stuart's arm.

"Stop worrying," he said. "Joan won't say anything she shouldn't. Now tell me about what happened earlier."

"I'm not worried about what Joan will say, and it probably won't matter. I can't see anything romantic happening between us." As if having to explain, he added, "We're from different worlds, and it shows every time we get into a conversation. I'm going to keep it all business."

Peter looked at his friend. "That's a good idea," he said without conviction. "Now tell me about tonight."

Stuart was finishing the story as the women returned.

"I hear you saw my friend in action," Peter said to Jessica.

Stuart stepped into the conversation. "I told you it was no big deal."

"What do you think they're going to do with the kid they arrested?" Peter again directed his question to Jessica.

"Forget that kid," said Stuart, raising his voice, "I need a drink."

Peter smiled and turned to Jessica. "How about a drink?"

"A glass of wine would be fine. You have a beautiful home."

"The decorating is all Joan, she keeps telling me to work harder."

"Stuart says you're very good at what you do."

Peter laughed, "How would he know? Fifteen years ago he started investing in small companies, and six years ago he turned his account over to me."

When Jessica seemed skeptical, he added, "He had already bought IBM, and four thousand shares of a little company calling itself Microsoft. He had some GE, Ford, General Motors, and a few other names from *Who's Who* in the stock market. The secret was, Stuart never sold anything, just kept adding to his portfolio. Believe me, it's been a no-brainer."

"You're talking about hundreds of thousands of dollars!" declared Jessica.

"I'm talking about a lot more than that."

"Come on," said Stuart, "we're not here to talk about me." At the same time he threw Peter a warning look.

Jessica turned to face Stuart. "Why are you still working for the government?"

His face turned red as he replied, "I guess it's because I meet the nicest people. Now how about something to eat, I'm starving."

The evening went by much too quickly for Stuart. Jessica and Joan did most of the talking, with the two men starting conversations that the women finished. As Stuart and Jessica walked out the front door, Joan leaned over and kissed his cheek.

"Don't you dare lose her," she insisted, "she's great."

Peter held the car door open for Jessica, and as she slid in, he asked, bending over, "Has Stuart asked you to join him at the President's dinner Saturday night?"

Jessica turned her head to look at Stuart, just as Peter closed the door. She didn't say a word until the gates at the end of the driveway were closed behind them.

"You've been invited to have dinner with the President?"

Chapter Twelve

Stuart turned on to the Beltway, the silence in the car was obvious.

"Is something wrong?" Jessica asked.

"I've never been to a dinner with the President." Stuart stared straight ahead.

"I'm sure you'll do fine."

After another long silence, Stuart said, "I wish Peter hadn't mentioned it." He felt Jessica's eyes on him and spoke before thinking. "I wasn't sure we'd get along, you and me, and wanted to wait before asking you."

"You were intending to invite me?"

"If we got along tonight, I was thinking about it." He glanced toward Jessica and saw at once she was offended.

"Well, you can stop thinking because I don't jump into bed with every—"

"Going to bed with you wasn't part of my plan," he said, interrupting her, and then regretted haven spoken.

The congresswoman turned away from Stuart. "Thank you," she said. "It's always nice to know that I'm not considered pretty enough or sexy enough to want to take to bed."

"That's not what I meant!" Stuart replied now utterly confused.

With a forced smile, Jessica asked, "Why don't you tell me what you meant and keep in mind that you still haven't asked me."

Stuart glanced over, but she was staring out the side window. "I wasn't sure you'd be willing to go out with me again after meeting my friends or finding out what I do for a living. That's what I meant."

When she didn't reply, he pressed his lips together and continued to drive in silence. He kept the speed at a constant sixty-five until he suddenly pushed the pedal to the floor and the car speedometer jumped up to eighty-five. He felt Jessica turn, but before she said anything, she looked at his eyes. They were riveted on the rearview mirror.

"Stuart, what's wrong?"

"Who knows where you are tonight?"

"No one. Even I didn't know where I'd be." She twisted her body and looked out the back window.

"We're being followed," Stuart said through compressed lips.

"Are you sure? I mean there are so many cars on the Beltway, how do you know?"

"Hold on," he warned, turning at the last second onto an off ramp exit, the tires squealing and the car tilting precariously. At the bottom of the ramp, he shut the headlights and turned right. After about thirty yards he spun the wheel, throwing the car into a one-hundred-and-eighty-degree spin and pulled to a stop. "Get down!" he commanded.

Jessica bent forward, her face turned toward Stuart. He removed a gun from under the dashboard. It was nearly pitch-black outside, but she saw his expression harden before her eyes. He unbuckled his seat belt, and the clicking made her jump.

"Here they come," he murmured. "Stay down."

She peeked out the front window. A car had come to the bottom of the off ramp and stopped. "What are we going to do?" she whispered.

When Stuart didn't answer, she repeated herself, speaking a little louder.

Stuart held up a finger. The car started moving slowly and then turned onto the ramp leading back to the highway. He sat back and took a deep breath. "Let's wait a minute and make sure they don't double back."

Jessica had never seen a man so calm in such an intense situation. So many of the powerful men in Congress developed beads of sweat just by talking about a bill being passed. She watched Stuart start the car and hit a button on the phone. The phone rang once before it was answered.

"This is the Cigar Store. Please repeat the following numbers for a voice check. twenty six, seventy five, eighty three."

"Three sixty-eight," Stuart responded.

"Your name is?"

"Stuart Taylor."

"Is there a problem?"

"I'm being followed by a light gray Oldsmobile, three men inside. They picked me up after I left Peter Weber's. I've lost them at exit 21 on the Beltway. I'll drive Congresswoman Winston home and head toward my place. Where can I expect help if I need it?"

The phone seemed to go dead and then came to life. "Get off one exit early and look for two Janus Florist delivery vans. One of them will stay at the congresswoman's, the other will follow you home."

Jessica watched Stuart program her address into the GPS system. "Are they staying in front of my house all night?"

"I doubt if you'll even see them. They'll make sure you get inside, hang around for a while, and then leave as quietly as they arrived."

"Why don't you?" She stopped.

"Why don't I what?"

"Never mind, I'll be fine."

Stuart smiled. "Were you going to ask why don't I stay over at your place?"

"Absolutely not. I wouldn't even think about it." She turned and faced away.

"First off, it might start some gossip that neither of us need."

"And secondly?" she asked when he didn't continue.

"Secondly, I wasn't invited." He saw her smile reflected in the window and was glad that she didn't come out with some smart-ass comment.

"Should I have someone watching my daughter?" she asked, turning toward him.

"Call the Secret Service in the morning. That's their job."

They rode in silence for another ten miles before he asked, "So what about Saturday night?"

"Peter said it was black tie?" she evaded his question with one of her own.

"That's what the invitation said. Are you in?"

"Do you know what the function is?" she asked again, dodging his question.

"Function?"

"The President usually has these dinners for a special reason." Jessica looked up through the moon roof of the car. "Tongues will start wagging if I showed up with you."

"I'm not sure anyone knows who I am."

"They'll know by the end of the night."

"Will you go?" he asked again, only this time his voice was quieter.

Smiling, she replied, "Would this be considered a date?"

He liked the way she smiled. Her teeth were a little crooked, barely enough to notice, but it added to her attractiveness. "I'd like it to be." When she said nothing, he began to feel like he felt when he asked Susan Dale to his high school prom twenty-seven years ago.

"I don't like what you do for a living," she told him. "I'm torn between my concern as a mother and my job as a member of Congress. There's a part of me that wants to have one of the committees I'm on to start an investigation, and it's running head on into my daughter's welfare. I believe you could probably take care of the problem, whatever it is, and I have a feeling your methods would scare the hell out of me."

"Let me help you. Any committee that started an investigation would find itself with nowhere to go and no one to talk to. The Official Secrets Act would make most of the people that know anything keep as quiet as church mice. The committee chairman would be told of impending cutbacks in funding that would affect his pet projects. If that didn't work, pictures of men in compromising positions would suddenly appear. Before you ask, stories or pictures about the women would be circulated."

"That's outrageous!"

"Maybe, but you've been here long enough, you know how the game is played. Now take a look at the other side." He stopped and blinked his lights at a florist delivery truck parked on the side of the road. "I'll find out who's been trying to get you in line, and make sure both our kids are safe. If nothing else, you can bet the farm on that."

Jessica watched the truck pull out in front of them and lead them back onto the Beltway toward her house. "I thought there was going to be two of them?"

"Take a look behind us."

She turned. "All I can see are the lights."

"You can take my word, they're there."

"I guess I can." She looked again out the back window. "The answer is yes, but not as a date, only a companion."

He smiled. "I can live with that."

Chapter Thirteen

Stuart arrived home a little before midnight. He took a beer from the refrigerator and walked into his study. Three of the walls supported built-in bookshelves, the fourth held a forty-eight-inch TV and a fish tank that ran for nearly nine feet. It's three way aeration system creates air bubbles that set the plants into a state of continuous movement. This acted as a distraction from one basic reality—there were no fish in the tank. Stuart had decided that, with his frequent trips, fish would be a liability.

The books on the shelves were arranged in an order more precise than the Dewey Decimal System. They were all about the States. Alabama on the far left, working around to Wyoming on the right. Each section had a set of law books pertaining to that state and a set of maps. A modern double-pedestal desk faced the television. It was bare, other than a twenty-one-inch flat panel monitor. An eight-button telephone were the only things on top of it. When sitting at this desk, Stuart could push a button and view the person with whom he was having a conversation. The computer software allowed him to bring up any map he wanted to see although even this large monitor was inadequate for viewing all the details.

There were two chairs matching the one he had behind the desk. The difference was they had never been sat in. Stuart didn't have much company, and those that did come weren't invited into his study. If they had been, they would have noticed right away there were no windows.

Stuart sat at his desk and turned on the television and the computer. He checked his e-mail and found three messages from Christine. The first one had to do with a phone call from Peter, informing her that he had received a call from Eric Weaver asking about Stuart. The second one was from the Cigar Store advising him that his son had called from Vermont. The last message told him that they were not able to trace the call that sent him to the Jefferson Memorial, but it had originated from the Maryland area.

Taking out a piece of paper, Stuart began to write some thoughts that needed to be checked out.

1. What can Jessica do to influence FBI vote?
2. Is she working on something else?
3. Who is Weaver connected to?
4. Why threaten her kid? Would only make her resolve stronger.
5. Who doesn't want Ray to head up the Bureau?
6. Why did the President ask me to dinner?

"You have a message," announced the computer. He looked at the questions and added (7) Why didn't Peter tell me about Weaver's call? He saved the program he was in, hit the print button and switched back to his e-mail. It was from the bureau.

"There was another bank robbery that fit the pattern you laid out. It was in Norfolk, Virginia. The two last week were in California."

Stuart shook his head as he read the message, his brow furrowed in confusion. He went back to his "Bank Robberies" file where the robberies were listed alphabetically.

Arvin, California	10/04	Thursday	(13)
Bismarck, North Dakota	09/13	Thursday	(9)
Durango, Colorado	10/01	Monday	(12)
Hannibal, Missouri	08/21	Tuesday	(5)
Harrisburg, Pennsylvania	9/24	Monday	(11)
Memphis, Tennessee	08/15	Wednesday	(4)
Milpitas, California	10/08	Monday	(14)
Milwaukee, Wisconsin	09/19	Wednesday	(10)
Norfolk, Virginia	10/10	Wednesday	(15)
Reno, Nevada	08/28	Tuesday	(6)
Richmond, Virginia	08/07	Tuesday	(3)
Roanoke, Virginia	09/03	Monday	(7)
Scottsboro, Alabama	09/07	Friday	(8)
Spanish Fork, Utah	07/12	Thursday	(2)
Tucumcari, New Mexico	07/03	Tuesday	(1)

Stuart understood why the didn't think they were the same people. There was no rhyme or reason for the days, the frequency, or the locations. He brought up a map of the United States and added a dot next to Norfolk. Maybe the crooks were spelling a word or making a design. "I could drive to half of these," he said aloud. It also could mean he was wrong and the Bureau was right, but he refused to even consider that possibility. His reverie was broken by the television, and he increased the volume.

"A man being held as a terrorist was found in his cell hanging by his belt. The suspected terrorist's name was Meridian, and he was arrested earlier this evening by guards at the Jefferson Memorial where two suspected terrorists were shot and killed. We will keep you advised as more facts come into this station."

Stuart dialed the Cigar Store.

"Please repeat the following numbers for voice check. Three, nine, thirteen."

"Fifty," said Stuart.

"Your name."

"Stuart Taylor."

What do you need?"

"A man was killed in jail about an hour ago, a prime witness. Have someone check out all the circumstances leading to his death."

"Anything else?"

"No, that's it."

He sat at the desk staring at the screen. He began to type, thinking there could be two groups working together. As soon as he looked at the words, he deleted them. It was the same group, he was positive.

Turning out the light, Stuart walked into the bedroom. Unlike the study, designed strictly for work, the bedroom looked like a pleasure palace out of some long-forgotten Chinese movie. The bed was a California king mattress resting on a four-poster frame. There were oversized night tables on each side and a matching twelve-foot dresser along the left side of the room. The television was even larger: At sixty inches, Stuart could watch and feel he was in the set. There were recessed ceiling lights that worked on dimmer switches, by the bed, the entrance, and next to a third door that led to the bathroom. Someone entering the room for the first time might not notice there weren't any windows.

The outside of Stuart's home was equally as planned. State-of-the-art cameras were installed around the perimeter and were activated by even the smallest movement. Anyone or anything coming to within six feet of the house would unknowingly trigger the surveillance cameras while automatically turning on all seven televisions located in different parts of the house. In the six years since they'd been installed, they had been activated only once, and that was an eight-year-old boy chasing his kite.

Stuart's mother, when she visited couldn't believe he lived without windows in those two rooms. What she didn't know was the windows in the rest of the house were constructed of shatter-resistant plastic.

Stuart lay down on the bed and wondered what Jessica would say if she ever came into his bedroom. She would probably think he was paranoid, and maybe he was. Both hands of the clock pointing to twelve, he closed his eyes.

When the phone rang, he thought it was ten minutes later. Stirring, he glanced at the clock and saw that it was after two. "Yeah," he answered groggily.

"Stuart, it's Jessica. Jessica Winston."

He sat up. How many Jessica's' did she think he knew?

"It's ten after two, what's wrong?"

"I just got a phone call from someone who said to give you a message or else."

"Or else what?"

"I don't know; he didn't say." When Stuart said nothing, she asked, "Are you still there?"

"I'm here. What's the message?"

"He said to stay out of things that didn't concern you, and then he gave me this phone number to call. He said if I didn't make the call immediately, he would know. Stuart, I'm starting to get more than a little worried."

"I wonder why he didn't call me directly."

"Maybe he only had your answering Service number?"

"My answering Service number?"

"He gave me an 800 hundred number to call, and I was transferred to you."

Stuart whistled the first six bars of Dixie, which were immediately answered by the next two bars, "Hurrah, hurrah."

"What's that?" Jessica demanded.

"It's something I do when I'm thinking. Go back to sleep, there's nothing to worry about." The moment she disconnected, a voice came on the line. "We'll have to change this number. Whatever it is you're involved in, get it done in a hurry; you're taxing our assets."

Stuart tried to go back to sleep. After sleeping in fits and starts, he went downstairs and began working out in his gym. He got himself up to a five-minute mile when the television image suddenly switched to Michael approaching his front door. For his boss to come here, he knew something bad was happening. He watched Michael search for the bell and, not finding one, resorted to banging on the door.

"Hold on," said Stuart into the intercom. "I'll be up in a second."

Opening the door, he said, "I haven't made any coffee yet, would you like some instant?"

Michael's eyes were bloodshot, and he was unshaven. "We don't have time for coffee. I came to tell you this in person before you heard it on the radio." He started chewing on his thumbnail. "Got scotch?"

Stuart blinked. "Plain or with water?"

"Straight up!"

Stuart began pouring just as Michael blurted out, "Christine's been shot." Stuart raised the glass to his lips and swallowed.

"Stuart, they don't think she's going to make it," Michael continued.

"Who did it?" Stuart asked as he poured scotch in a second glass for his boss. His eyes had turned gray and his lips compressed until white.

"We don't know. She was doing research until around two. When she got home, someone shot her. Her purse was missing; they're calling it a robbery gone bad."

"No one heard the shot?" Stuart asked.

"Her husband heard the garage door open. When she didn't come up to bed, he went looking for her. The police got the call at two thirty-five; I was called at three fifteen."

"I'll throw on some clothes," Stuart said. When he reached the stairs, Michael's phone started ringing.

"Burnett!" barked Michael into the phone.

Stuart watched his boss, saw that he was visibly shaken as he sat on the nearest chair and closed the phone. There were tears in his eyes.

"Michael?" Stuart whispered.

"She didn't make it."

Late Thursday afternoon, Michael called Stuart into his office. "Just got an unofficial courtesy call from the chief of police. The case won't be officially closed, but it's not getting any special treatment either. He says there are no leads, no suspects, and nowhere to go. If something comes up, he'll give us a call."

"Meaning?" demanded Stuart, his body set for an argument.

"Meaning catch me the bank robbers, find out who's screwing with the congresswoman, solve Jake's problem, and get your ass back to your desk. And while you're at it, hire Christine's replacement." He rose from his desk and walked out, leaving Stuart sitting there to stew.

Chapter Fourteen

Stuart called the take out number, ordered a large pepperoni pizza and a six-pack of Coke. He gave the address of his new office at the and told himself that without Christine, a lot of the detail work would fall on his shoulders.

The first items on his to-do list were to discover who had access to the Cigar Store's 800 number and why Senator Chilicote was retiring.

He started drafting a memo to Jake and Ray that asked for a meeting and listed items to which he needed answers. He wanted Ray to think back and see if he could remember anything derogatory in Weaver's background. Stuart also wanted access to the file on Weaver, his original hire sheet, and the name of the person who assigned him to the cases he was on. He was trying to decide if he should ask why the President invited him to a dinner, when the door to his office opened and a stranger entered.

"So you're Stuart Taylor," said the man. He was wearing a three-piece suit, minus the jacket. He was clean-shaven, which was odd for that time of day, and he didn't have a hair on his head out of place.

Stuart stood, mentally measuring the stranger's height and weight. Six foot one, one ninety-five. A closer look revealed a five-thousand-dollar remodeling of teeth. "Yep, that's me," he said. "And who might you be?"

"My name is Eric Weaver. We spoke briefly on the phone the other day."

Stuart sat back down. "Did we? It must have been about something unimportant because I don't remember the conversation."

Weaver's face turned red, the smile never leaving his face. "When I called, I had to go through the ATF switchboard. Is that where you were working?"

"I worked out of their offices." Stuart smiled back at him as he spoke.

Weaver slid into the seat in front of Stuart's desk. "What jobs were you on?"

"Are you the welcoming committee?"

"No, shit head, I'm your boss, so you'll answer my questions without the smart mouth."

"Don't let the door hit you in the ass on your way out," Stuart said through compressed lips.

Weaver jumped to his feet. "What did you say? I get respect around here!"

Stuart leaned forward, arms on his desk. "You want a conversation with me, you don't ride in on some high horse and demand respect. As far as I'm concerned, you're like a lady of the night who I don't have to respect in the morning."

Weaver was speechless. Twice he started to say something, but Stuart's smile stopped him cold. His eyes turn a steely gray, and red blotches appeared on his cheeks. He finally spoke. "No one talks like that to me and gets away with it," he announced. "I'll have you up on charges and out of here so quick you won't know what happened."

"And when that doesn't work?" taunted Stuart.

Weaver turned and walked into the closed door.

"I said don't let it hit you in the ass," laughed Stuart, watching the man yank open the door and stalk out.

It took less than five minutes for Ray Bradley to call. "I just had an irate Eric Weaver storm into my office," he said. "He's screaming that you insulted him and made him look foolish. Is that true?"

"I didn't insult him," said Stuart, his voice calm. "As far as his looking foolish, he did that all by himself."

"So I don't have to congratulate you for anything you did?"

Stuart smiled. "No congratulations in order, but if you get a phone call from anyone on the Hill, let me know."

"You did it on purpose?"

"I didn't know he was coming, but it looked like the right thing to do." Stuart heard the smile on Ray's face.

"I'm going to enjoy working with you," said Ray. "Meanwhile, I better bring Jake up to date."

Ray disconnected from his call with Stuart and laughed aloud. This was the most fun he'd had in a month. Jake Levitt always had an open-door policy, so Ray walked right into the man's office. The director waved him in, holding a finger to his lips. Ray recognized the voice on the speakerphone immediately as belonging to Senator Daniel Conrad of Arizona. Conrad was the ranking member of Ways and Means, had spent more than twenty years in the Senate, and had always been a party man ready to carry out the wishes of the President, and the party on every crucial vote. Both Jake and Ray considered him a friend. It was from Daniel Conrad that they were getting their information on what would happen when the vote was held.

"Where did this guy come from?" resonated Conrad's voice over the speaker.

"He's been on special assignment over at ATF, and the job is finished. We're bringing him back inside."

Bradley knew immediately to whom the senator and Jake were referring.

"Who does he report to?" the senator asked.

"He reports directly to Ray. Why the sudden interest?" Jake asked.

The senator's voice became wary. "I thought Eric Weaver was next in line."

"Daniel, you know there's no next in line behind Ray; it doesn't work that way. Eric's one of the top people around here, but there's no org chart that puts him higher than anyone else."

"I've seen one," the senator responded.

"What you've seen is the org chart of different departments. If I remember correctly, there are five departments. Karen Ortega, heads up one, Eric another, then there's Jerry Pettit—"

"That's the one," he interrupted. "But I was under the impression that Eric has the inside track if you retire."

"I haven't announced my retirement yet."

"Jake, this is me you're talking to. Tell me you support Eric to take Ray's place if you retire and I'm off the phone."

"Senator, you know nothing I say holds water after I leave."

Ray knew that shifting back to this formal address moved the conversation to a different level.

The senator must have realized it as well because the phone went quiet, followed by "Jake, I have to go. Don't disappoint me."

Jake looked up at Ray, who said, "That was quick."

"What does that mean?" the director asked.

"I came straight from Stuart's office," said Jake. "He had a run-in with Eric. It's got Eric screaming like a stuck pig. Stuart wants to know the first person who complains, so I guess that's the senator."

"What was the run-in about?"

"According to Stuart, Weaver came in and started pushing, so he pushed back. I get the feeling Stuart's pretty good at that. He's asked for a meeting tomorrow, and he's sending us a list of questions he'd like answered."

"Do you know the questions?"

"I can guess."

The intercom went on, and the voice of the director's secretary filled the room.

"Mr. Levitt, I've got the Speaker of the House on line 1."

The director picked up the phone and started talking. "Gary, to what do I owe the honor of this call?" After listening a few seconds, he replied, "I think he was out of line. Ray's deputy director; after that we only have department heads. Eric's one of them." He listened and then responded, "Stuart Taylor is back from temporary duty with ATF. He is not and never has been considered heir apparent to Ray, so Daniel Conrad is wrong." Listening and nodding for another few seconds did nothing to assuage his discomfort. "I understand, Mr. Speaker." He hung up and took a deep breath.

"That did not sound like a nice conversation," said the deputy director.

"It wasn't, and it's the second call about Eric not being in line for your job. Why don't you tell Stuart to get the list of questions to us before midnight and schedule the meeting for eight tomorrow morning?"

Chapter Fifteen

"Mom, I can't believe you went on a date!" Sarah Winston was seated at the kitchen table and was eating a piece of Kentucky Fried Chicken straight out of the container.

"Why don't you use a plate?" said her mother in mock frustration.

"You didn't tell me his name. Is he another congressman or senator?"

"No, he works for the government, but not in the legislature."

"Well, who is he? Do I know him?"

Jessica put a plate down in front of her daughter. "I'll get you a napkin."

"Mom! Who is he?"

She took a deep breath. "He's your friend Marilyn's father, Stuart Taylor."

Sarah stopped eating. "Marilyn's father! Where did you meet him?"

Jessica nearly laughed at her daughter's expression. "It's a long story, and it wasn't really a date. I called to thank him after you told me what happened, and we met for coffee. And then we ran into two of those kids who'd been hassling you, and they started doing the same thing to me. After Stuart straightened them out, he asked me to join him at a dinner party, and I guess I felt obligated."

"Wow, did he try to kiss you? Where was the dinner party? Who else was there?"

The questions were spilling out faster than Jessica could digest them and reply. "Slow down," she laughed. "He took me to a friend's who lives in Chevy Chase, and no, he did not try to kiss me good night."

"I think he's kind of sexy," said the girl, still gnawing on a piece of chicken.

"Stop that! He's a very strange man. Sometimes he's nice and then, quick as you can snap your fingers, he's entirely different."

"I hope he asked you out again."

"As a matter of fact," said Jessica, licking sauce off her finger, "he's invited me to a dinner at the White House this Saturday night."

"With the President? You never had dinner with the President!" After a moment, the girl shrieked, "Mom, what are you going to wear? I bet it's formal."

"I thought I'd wear that black dress."

"You can't wear that old thing! You have all day tomorrow. I'll help you pick it out."

Jessica stood there looking at her daughter. Just watching the girl's enthusiasm, started getting her excited.

Sarah made a squealing sound and jumped up from the table. "I have to call Marilyn. She'll never believe you're going out with her dad!"

Jessica turned serious. "Maybe you should hold off. I'm not sure where her father works or for whom, but I get the impression it's a job one doesn't talk about."

The girl sat down on the chair. "Can we still go shopping tomorrow?"

"Beep me when you're done at school, and I'll see what I'm doing."

Sarah pushed the chair back. "I've got homework, gotta go." She rushed out of the kitchen and into her bedroom. Pushing aside her mother's admonition, she phoned her friend.

"Marilyn, I just wanted you to know that I might leave school early tomorrow."

"Where are you going?"

"My mom's invited to a dinner at the White House, and she needs a new dress. I told her I would help pick one out. It's a date!"

"With some representative?"

"I'm supposed to keep it a secret."

"A secret?" laughed Marilyn. "In this town, that's not likely."

"You're probably right, but you have to promise not to tell."

"I promise."

"It's your dad."

"Who?"

"Your dad. She called to thank him for his help the other morning, and they had coffee and he ended up asking her. Isn't that exciting?" Sarah heard nothing. "Are you there?"

"I'm here, I was just surprised by what you said. Are you sure it's my dad?"

"Of course I'm sure. Now remember, you can't tell anyone."

There was no answer, but this time Sarah heard the dial tone. Marilyn had hung up.

The e-mail was sent to both Jake Levitt and Ray Bradley. Stuart decided that he would direct each question toward one of them and ask for comments. The message said, Gentlemen, please answer the following for tomorrow's meeting.

For Jake Levitt:

1. Since Jessica Winston isn't in the Senate, what can she do to derail Ray's appointment?
2. Was Eric Weaver sponsored by anyone?
3. Who would like to see you gone and Ray not appointed in your place?
4. Have you had a background check done on Weaver in the past four years?

For Ray Bradley:

1. Who doesn't like you? Think back to the time prior to Weaver joining the bureau.
2. After Weaver joined the bureau, who handed him his assignments, and who worked with him?
3. May I see a copy of his reviews?

For both of you:

Why do you think the President invited me to a dinner at the White House?

He sent a blind copy to Michael Burnett with some additional questions:

1. Who has access to the Cigar Store number?
2. Any results on my request for information on Eric Weaver?
3. Did Christine speak to you about her premonitions?
4. Any results on Augie Meridian's death?

Stuart hit the Send button on his computer just as the phone started ringing.

"Stuart here!"

"Father? This is your son, Kenneth. You didn't return my call, so I decided to try again."

"I just listened to your phone call, but you didn't leave a number."

"I thought you had it," the young man replied.

"I just moved into a new office, and my stuff hasn't caught up with me yet. What's up?"

"I know you work for the government, so can I speak over the phone?"

"I don't have that sensitive of a job, Ken. You can say anything you want."

"Marilyn told me you're taking a congresswoman to dinner Saturday night."

"Your sister must be trying to get a job at the Inquirer." When there was a silence, he explained, "I asked the woman last night and your sister already knows."

"She told me. I'm not supposed to say anything, but she heard it from the woman's daughter."

"Is that why you called?"

There was a hesitation before he started, "There were two men from the Department of Justice here last week asking about you."

"You mean the FBI?"

"No, I mean the DOJ, and they were asking funny-type questions, like you were in some kind of trouble. They told me not to say anything, but I figured what the hell, you're my father."

"Do you remember the questions?"

"They asked them pretty fast, almost like they didn't care what the answer was. The one that sticks in my mind was where you'd get your hands on six to eight million dollars."

Stuart sat holding the phone and didn't respond.

"Father, are you there?"

"I'm here."

"Do you have six to eight million dollars?"

"No, but some people might think so. Have you told this story to anyone?"

"I was afraid to. I had the feeling these men weren't friends of yours. I thought you stopped working for the government years ago."

"Kenneth, you're old enough for us to have a father-son conversation, but not over the phone. When's your next break?"

"School closes a week from Monday; I can come down next Friday night."

Stuart heard questioning and anticipation in his son's voice. "Next Friday night it is. What time can you be here?"

"I can arrive in Washington by seven thirty."

"I have a better idea. Fly to JFK and look for a limo driver holding a card with your name on it. There's a flight that'll get you in around five thirty. We'll have dinner, spend Saturday together, and I'll get tickets for the Knicks. They're playing LA, it should be a great game."

"That sounds great, but I have one question."

"What's that?" Stuart asked warily.

"What do I call you? I can't keep saying father."

Stuart smiled. "What do you call your mother?"

"Mom."

"Then how about dad? Or if that's a little too hard, you could try Stuart."

This time Kenneth was quiet. "I have a week to decide, so I'll surprise you. One more thing, I'm not going to tell Marilyn or mom what I'm doing."

"Your choice." When the line was quiet, Stuart reminded him to look for the man with the sign, and then he hung up.

"I've put a lot of time and effort into you. I hope I haven't wasted my time," said the voice on the phone.

Eric Weaver's upper lip was sweating. "Don't worry about a thing. This guy is an idiot. He's got his ass way out on a limb with some bank robberies, so no one will ever listen to him."

"You better be right," stated the voice, and then ended the conversation without giving Weaver a chance to respond. Weaver pushed the button on his phone that summoned his secretary. "Bring me the entire file on open bank robberies, anywhere in the United States, and do it now."

Chapter Sixteen

Stuart was reading his e-mail replies from Ray and Jake when his phone rang. "Taylor here!"

"When did Christine have this feeling of being watched?" Michael Burnett barked into the phone.

"When she called me to relay the phony message from the congresswoman."

"She never said a word. Did she say anything else to you?"

"No, she didn't," replied Stuart. "In fact, she sent me a couple of e-mails later that night and didn't mention anything."

"Was she in the office when you spoke to her?"

"I assumed she was. Why?" Stuart started to feel uncomfortable. *Maybe he missed something.*

"Christine had an uncanny sense about her. If she felt something, I'd bet it was here. I'm going to have background checks done on everyone . . . again."

"Hey, boss, let me ask you a question." Trying to act nonchalant, Stuart tapped his hand repeatedly on the desk as he waited for a response. Receiving none, he asked, "Why would two DOJ men be questioning my son about me?"

"What kind of questions?"

This wasn't the response he expected, and Stuart became immediately wary. "Background-type stuff, as close as I can determine. When my son mentioned it, I downplayed the whole thing."

"I'll see if I can find out," offered Burnett. "Talk to you later."

Stuart put his feet up on the desk. Michael's response should have been yes or no, not what kind of questions. Stuart stared at the wall thinking. Things were changing and maybe not for the better. Perhaps it was time to retire. He lowered his feet back down and said, "As soon as I clean up the work on my desk."

At the other end of the building, Eric Weaver pounded his desk in frustration.

"Miriam!" he yelled at the top of his lungs. As his secretary Miriam entered his office, he continued shouting, "This list has over fifteen hundred names on it!"

"I only listed those that were under open investigation. Did you want them all?"

"Did I want them all? How many are there?"

"If you want me to include the last three years, there are over four thousand unsolved bank robberies."

Weaver sat behind his desk as if he were in a trance. *There was no way this Taylor could pick out fourteen and solve them. He was an idiot.*

"Thanks, Miriam. You've been a big help."

Miriam started toward the door and stopped. "Mr. Weaver, you know of course that they catch about ten to fifteen a month."

"Ten to fifteen what?" Weaver replied.

"People that hold up banks," his secretary answered as she walked out of his office.

Weaver stood and walked over to the window. He pulled the string raising the blinds halfway up the window. Looking down at the street, he could see taxis lined up waiting for passengers. At the end of the block, there was a coffee truck with four people waiting to get coffee. The truck was parked in a no-parking zone right in front of a bank. How great it would be to catch someone robbing that bank. I'll have to suggest it.

"Mr. Weaver."

He let go of the string at the sound of his secretary's voice and jumped backward.

"Miriam! How many times have I told you not to sneak up on me?"

"I buzzed, but you didn't answer. The director is on the phone."

"The director? Why didn't you say something?" He waved Miriam out of the room as he pushed down the hands-free button on the phone. "Jake, to what do I owe the honor of this call?"

"Do you have some time for me this morning? I'd like to go over these bank robberies that Stuart has been investigating. I think he may have something and can use your help."

"It's funny you should mention that," he replied almost breathlessly. "I had my secretary pull a list of all open bank robberies, and I find that we have a little more than fifteen hundred. I was going to ask him how he decided to follow up on only fourteen."

"Good, I like it when my top men are on their toes. See you at my office at eleven this morning."

"Miriam!" he yelled as he punched the disconnect button.

"You could try using the phone once in a while," she answered as she entered his office.

"Get in touch with the agent in charge of bank robberies and see if you can find out which fourteen the new guy Stuart Taylor is working on." With a smug look on his face, he sat down behind his desk. "And I need the information before my meeting with the director at eleven."

"How long is the meeting going to last?"

"I don't know," he replied like a spoiled child.

"You know I made reservations at the Hyatt for lunch and for a room this afternoon."

"I know, but this is more important."

"That's always nice to know," she replied as she walked out the door. "I'll get you the information you need. You can never tell, maybe the meeting will be over by noon."

He nodded his head as he watched her walk out. She has one great set of legs.

At eleven on the button, Weaver presented himself at the director Jake Levitt's door. Mrs. Nagy told him to go right in. He couldn't understand why Jake Levitt would want a secretary that had to be fifty if she was a day, with gray hair, and was probably thirty pounds overweight. Upon entering he found Ray Bradley sitting at the conference table reading some reports and the director on the phone.

"Yes, Mr. President, I read the Attorney General's report. I will take it up with my staff this afternoon. Good-bye, sir." The director looked up. "Have a seat, Eric, as soon as Stuart gets here we can start the meeting."

"He's not here yet?" Weaver asked. "Didn't he know you called the meeting for eleven sharp? I guess they weren't so time oriented at ATF."

Jake Levitt looked at Ray and nodded toward the door. Ray stood and started walking toward it when the intercom went on and the director's secretary announced, "Mr. Taylor is on his way in, sir."

Stuart entered the room, looked around, and acknowledged both Ray Bradley and Eric Weaver with a nod of his head. "Good morning, sir," he said to the director. "Sorry I'm late. I've never been on this floor before, and while it's probably a good thing not to put names outside of the offices, it certainly plays havoc trying to find someone."

Jake Levitt smiled, "Have a seat, I want to discuss the bank robberies you've been following. Do you want something to drink?"

Stuart looked around the room. "Sir, can I ask why Weaver is here?"

"You can ask, but I'm not so sure you're going to like the answer. I want Eric brought up to date on what your thoughts are so that he can compare them against what our specialists think."

Stuart's eyes went dark. His clenched teeth brought tightness to his face that made Weaver sitting across the table uneasy.

This guys a psycho. For a second Weaver thought he had voiced the words aloud.

"I don't usually share my work, sir."

"Let's just say I don't think this is usually, and in this department, we learn to share."

The room was silent as a three-in-the-morning movie on television with the mute button in effect. Stuart hoped he was playing his part correctly. His meeting earlier with Jake had set the guidelines, but they were playing it by ear.

With an exaggerated show of teeth, Stuart finally broke the silence. "I'd be happy to share my thoughts with Agent Weaver. How would you like us to proceed?"

The director smiled. "Ray, give Eric and Stuart a copy of what our department head thinks. Stuart, you start with what got you started and why you think you're right."

Stuart sighed as if in resignation before he started talking, "I have what I think are fifteen definite and maybe another eleven possible. Two people in the bank and another in a car outside committed the fifteen robberies. One of the three, is a woman. I believe they rotated each robbery to throw us off. The other eleven were committed by a man and a woman using the same type of shotguns, but they were last year and there was no driver of the car outside."

Weaver shrugged, unimpressed. "Of the fifteen hundred bank robberies under investigation, two hundred were done by three people."

Stuart stared at him. "We have surveillance photos, and after checking each of them more than once, I found that the shoes worn by the three people were the same in all the pictures."

"The shoes?" Weaver again interrupted.

"Yes, the shoes. I believe one of the men is wearing Cole Haan, very upscale, not cheap. The other man is wearing black basketball sneakers with gray supports on the inner sides. They are manufactured by Brooks and can only be bought in specialty shops."

"Have you learned anything about the woman?" Jake asked.

"She wears a fake scar on the side of her cheek. It's one of those tricks that spies learn. People tend to look at the scar and forget the rest of the face."

"How do you know it's a fake?" Weaver asked.

"It's off by almost a half inch in one of the tapes. That fact by itself tells me that she's probably not a blonde, since blonde hair on a woman has the same effect."

"Anything else you can tell us about either the robbers or the robberies?"

"I don't think the woman or the man with the mustache are ready to kill anyone, but the third man could be a problem."

"How the hell would you know that unless you know the people?" Eric again jumped into the conversation.

Stuart stared at him and replied, "You have a big mouth and a small brain. Look at the pictures. Neither one of them has the shotgun cocked, but the other guy does."

The three other people seated at the table looked at the photographs in the packages in front of them.

"If you look closely at photo number 37," Stuart continued, "I think you'll notice that he's not wearing a ring, but there is a ring mark on his finger from the sun. I get the feeling that he takes off his jewelry before the robberies, but maybe he was on vacation when this one was taken."

All three men turned over photo 37 at the same time.

"Reno, Nevada," the director said aloud.

"Do you think that's where he lives?" asked Weaver.

A look of disgust showed on Stuart's face. "No, I think that's where he robbed the bank."

"I don't understand," Weaver said.

Before Stuart could answer, Jake Levitt, the director, intervened, "Eric, that's why I wanted you at this meeting. You understand our procedures better than Stuart, who's been on loan to another department. I want you to take over this investigation. I think Stuart's been too close."

"Wait a second." Stuart stood and leaned on both palms. "This is my investigation. I don't want to give it up."

"Sit down, Taylor. You do what I say. I've had just about enough of your outbursts."

Stuart stared at Jake Levitt for a full ten seconds before sitting.

Jake looked at his watch. "It's time for lunch. Stuart, you get something to eat and cool down. You're off that assignment and that's final. Eric, you're in charge. See me tomorrow morning, and let me know how you're going to proceed. Ray, come with me upstairs for lunch, I want to talk to you. Gentlemen, thank you all for stopping by."

"You're back. Do I have to cancel the reservations, or are you available?"

Eric smiled as he openly stared at Miriam's breast. "Cancel the lunch and order something sent up from room Service. Have them leave it in the room, we'll be there in half an hour. I have to make one phone call."

Jake Levitt looked at the caller ID on his cell phone. "Stuart! You put on a great performance."

"Do you think he bought it?"

"I did and I was in on it. Let's see what happens now. See you in a couple of hours."

Chapter Seventeen

"I see you ordered finger food," Eric said to his secretary as they entered the room on the fourteenth floor of the hotel. He picked up a shrimp and dipped it in the cocktail sauce on his way to the window where he looked out at the Potomac River in the distance. He popped the shrimp in his mouth and wiped his fingers on the drapes. He started tugging at his tie as he raised his voice over the sound of CNN that she had turned on when they entered. "We'll have to hurry, I have a meeting this afternoon."

"Can we talk for a minute? I have a few things I would like to get straightened out." Her voice was a little strong, which made him stop unbuttoning his shirt.

"Can't we talk later? You know being in a bedroom with you drives me crazy."

"Being anywhere with me drives you crazy." She stood and shimmied out of her skirt. "I want to know where this relationship is going?" Her slip rustled to the floor, leaving her in a sweater, high heels, and panties.

Eric continued unbuttoning his shirt, his tongue running over his parted lips. "As soon as I get the promotion I'll tell my wife I'm leaving her, and then you and I can be seen together in public."

"Do I have your word on that?" Her words were muffled as she pulled her cashmere sweater over her head.

Eric almost tripped getting out of his pants. "Of course you do."

"This is the Cigar Store. Please repeat the following for a voice check. One, two, fifteen."

"Thirty-six," Stuart responded.

"Your name is?"

"Stuart Taylor."

"Your friend is playing patty cake with his secretary. They're on the fourteenth floor of the Hyatt. We did a check on his credit card for past stays, and he's checked in there at least nine times in the last three months."

"Put a researcher on the secretary and send me the usual background check."

When there was silence on the other end, Stuart asked, "Something wrong?"

"This is the first time in our history that an agent has been able to call the shots without getting prior approval from up top. You're sorely taxing our resources. Do you have any idea how much longer this will go on?"

"Sorry, I don't. When I see daylight, I'll let you know."

"They put me in charge of him," Eric Weaver whispered into his cell phone. "From what I can see he's got his head up his butt. He thinks he can solve fifteen bank robberies out of a couple of thousand. I'm still trying to find out what he did over at ATF that made them think he was a hotshot of some kind."

"I think it would be a mistake to underestimate him," the steely voice warned. "Remember what I said about mistakes." The phone went dead.

"Miriam! Get me someone at ATF. I want to find out what's holding up the information I requested."

"Mr. Burnett, Eric Weaver from the FBI is on the phone again. He's demanding information on Stuart. What would you like me to tell him?"

"Tell him it's sensitive information, and if he would like to come in person, we would be willing to talk to him."

"Where should I tell him to meet you?"

"Tell him to go to the Enforcement Operation Center here in Washington and ask for a Mr. Richardson. Remind him that we need a three-hour prior notice of his arrival."

Smiling, Michael's secretary, Sally Kim, couldn't wait to give this obnoxious Weaver person the answer. She had worked inside of the department long enough to know Michael Burnett had the clout to get away with almost anything.

"Mr. Weaver? Are you still there? I've been told that if you call the Enforcement Center and give Mr. Richardson a three-hour notice, he'll be happy to talk to you."

"Listen, honey, what's the person's name who this Richardson reports to?"

"I'm sorry, my name is Sally Kim. I guess you misunderstood me earlier. Mr. Richardson's boss is classified. Would you like to make an appointment?"

"That's a good idea. I'm tied up until about six, tell him I'll be there around six thirty."

"I'll tell him, but he leaves at five. How about Monday?"

Bitch. Eric thought to himself. Aloud he replied, "That'll work fine. What time does he get to work?"

"Since he needs three hours prior notice, I'll put you down for seven thirty Monday morning."

"He starts work at four thirty?" Eric asked with amazement in his voice.

"Actually he starts at four, but I know people over at the Bureau don't start that early."

Eric sat at his desk, wondering if she was playing with him or if she was serious. Shaking his head, he said, "Put me down for seven," he said, shaking his head and hung up.

The phone rang twice before Sarah picked it up. Her mother taught her well. The Washington axiom was that you were always too busy to pick up the phone on the first ring, but you shouldn't keep anyone waiting past the second ring.

"Hello?" she said quietly into the phone.

"Hi, this is Stuart Taylor. Is your mother home?"

"Hi, Mr. Taylor," she said his name aloud to alert her mother as to the caller. Her mother nodded yes, which gave Sarah some license to continue a conversation. "She's in the kitchen, I'll get her for you. Mom, it's Mr. Taylor." She shouted over her shoulder. Her mother smiled and motioned that she'd pick up the extension in the den. "She told me about your dinner plans for tomorrow night, I'm very excited. Imagine, dinner with the President."

"I don't think it's dinner with, maybe dinner at his home would be more like it. It's really no big deal."

"I think." Before anything more came out of her mouth, her mother interrupted.

"I think you should finish your homework."

Sarah didn't reply for a second and then said, "Good night, Mr. Taylor. Wait till you see my mom in her new dress." The last part of the sentence rushing out before she pressed down and disconnected her extension.

"She's going to drive me crazy," Jessica said over Stuart's laughter.

"I just wanted to tell you that I'll pick you up at seven tomorrow night and warn you that I rented a limo to drive us there and back."

"I'll be ready, how come you hired a car?"

"To tell you the truth, I had two reasons. The first is I'm trying to impress you." He waited to see if she would reply; when she didn't, he cleared his throat and said, "The second is, I've never been to the White House before, and I'm not sure how to get in. This way, it's the driver's problem."

Jessica smiled, "Make sure your name is on the guest list. We shouldn't have a problem."

"You've been there before?" Stuart wasn't very good at small talk, but he knew he had to give it a try.

"Yes. I've had dinner at four or five state gatherings and breakfast twice."

"What did they serve?"

Jessica realized he was a little nervous. They were questions designed to keep a conversation going when a person had nothing to say. On the spur of the moment, she decided to make it easier for him.

"It's only seven thirty. Why don't you come on over for a cup of coffee and I can go over some of the protocols."

"I'd like that. Do you want me to pick up some donuts or something?"

"No. I'm sure I have something. How long will it take you to get here?

"About ten minutes," he replied before he realized she would know he was close by. "That is unless you think I should take a half hour?"

"Ten minutes is fine. I live in a gated community. I'll call the guard and leave your name."

"Sarah, Mr. Taylor is coming over. Call the guard and give him Mr. Taylor's name."

"As soon as I get off the phone," Sarah yelled back. "Marilyn, your dad's coming over tonight to visit. This is so exciting. I have to change. I'll tell you tomorrow what happens."

Promptly ten minutes later, Stuart arrived at the open gates of Jessica's development. The light in the guard shack was out, which surprised him. Driving through, he stopped his car on the inside, left the motor running, and got out of his car and walked slowly toward the shack. The green and red lights on the control panel gave off just enough illumination for him to see that the phone was off the hook. He ran back to his car and dialed Jessica. She answered on the first ring.

"Hello," her voice sounded strained.

"Jessica, this is Stuart. I won't be able to make it tonight. I have to get back to headquarters. I hope this won't inconvenience you?"

As he spoke, his car was moving with the lights out toward Jessica's home. There was no moon, and he was glad he had visited earlier to get the lay of the land.

"No. It won't be an inconvenience. We can discuss the boys we met earlier, tomorrow."

She was trying to send him a signal. He hoped she wouldn't do anything dumb.

"I'll see you tomorrow," he said before she could say anything else and hung up.

The car rolled to a stop two houses away from hers. He could see a dark Lincoln Continental with its motor running in the driveway. Someone was sitting behind the wheel. He approached the car from the passenger side, which gave him the most protection. He took a Swiss Army knife from his pocket and after opening it wedged it against the tire. The lights on the first floor of Jessica's house went out, making it even darker in the driveway. He heard the front door open and saw Jessica and Sarah being pushed by two men toward the car. He dropped to the floor and rolled under the car. He heard the car window being opened, and the man inside of the car yelled out to the other two.

"Anyone else in the house?"

He's speaking Spanish Stuart said to himself.

"No" came the reply.

"Burn the house down" Came the reply from the car.

"Set it on fire?"

These guys are crazy, Stuart thought to himself as he translated their words. He rolled out from under the car on the driver's side and yelled at the top of his lungs, "Hey, amigo." The man holding Jessica and Sarah pushed them away from himself and turned, facing Stuart with his gun drawn. Stuart fired twice, both shots finding their mark in the center of his chest. The man who had started toward the house turned and fired one shot at Stuart. It was the last thing he ever did. Stuart's next shot was a half inch away from the man's nose.

Stuart heard the man behind the wheel say, "Damn," as he shifted the car into drive and hit the gas. The wheels started skidding as they ran over the open knife propelling the car into a tree in the middle of Jessica's lawn. The car burst into flames and exploded less than ten seconds later. It was at that point that Stuart realized Sarah was screaming.

"Is she alright?" he asked Jessica.

In the light from the flames, Stuart could see Jessica's ashen face. She didn't say a word but put her arms around Sarah and held her.

Alerted by neighbors, the police started arriving within five minutes. Stuart had used the time to go through the pockets of the two dead men and then call the Cigar Store.

"This is the Cigar Store. Please repeat the following numbers for a voice check. One, thirty, fifty."

"One hundred and sixty two."

"Your name is?"

"Stuart Taylor."

"What can I do for you?" the Cigar Store answered in an apprehensive voice.

"I'm at the home of Congresswoman Winston. There are three dead men, two of them with my bullets in them. The police are on their way, I can hear them in the distance."

"Use your FBI credentials. I'll have someone attach themselves to the investigation and report back later."

"For our records, the men spoke Spanish," Stuart added.

"Noted. Anything else?"

"Not right now, the police have arrived."

It was almost midnight when the police finally left. They had found the guard unconscious behind the guard shack. He told them the men asked for directions and when he leaned over to give them, they must have hit him. He didn't remember anything else. Stuart waited for the two women security agents he requested to arrive before he decided to call it a night. Jessica had given Sarah a pill to help her sleep and had come down to say good night.

"It looks like I owe you my life."

Stuart stared at her. Her hair was disheveled, her face drawn, but she was extraordinary a woman as he could remember ever knowing. "I don't think they wanted to harm you. If they had, they would have done so inside of the house. They don't want you to do something, or maybe they do want you to do something, I just don't know what that is. You and I will have to spend some time together going over whatever you're doing on the committees you're on. The key has to be there."

She nodded.

"We're still on for tomorrow night, aren't we?" Stuart asked, cutting off whatever she was going to say.

She smiled as she nodded again. "I certainly . . . yes, of course we are. The security agents will still be here, won't they?"

"They'll be around for a while. I've got to go."

Jessica stepped forward and held out her hand. Misunderstanding, Stuart took it, pulled her forward, and kissed her. Jessica started to pull away and then stopped. It was a long time since she had kissed someone that sent a shiver through her spine.

Chapter Eighteen

Saturday was a day without enough hours. The pockets of the dead men were devoid of any type of identification except for a boarding pass on an American Airline flight from Chicago to Washington on Thursday. The airline's records showed that a Hector Cruz had been assigned that seat. Further checking had found that a Hector Cruz had taken a flight from San Diego to Chicago earlier that day. The tickets were purchased using cash, and there was no way to trace the person that purchased them. Stuart had the manifest double-checked and found another person who used cash for the same two flights. Jose Flores was the name of the other person, and a background check showed him to have a record for assault and battery. Since his fingerprints didn't match either of the dead bodies, Stuart had to assume that the man behind the wheel was Flores. Stuart looked at his desk calendar. Christine's funeral was tomorrow. He dialed Sally Kim, the girl he had chosen to take Christine's place.

"This is Sally."

"Sally, do me a favor. Check the flights that Flores and Cruz were on and find out if anyone else was on the same flights but used a credit card or a travel agency."

"Anyone special you're looking for?"

"The third man, or someone else that may have been with them."

"Should have an answer within a couple of hours. I'm starting to get in some of the reports you requested."

"Such as?"

"Your friend Eric Weaver's girlfriend and secretary. She moved to Washington three years ago from Nebraska. She worked for Congressman Gary Brightwell."

"The Speaker of the House?"

"That's him."

"When did she move to the Bureau?"

"When Weaver got his third promotion. By the way, the report I read on one of his promotions had him catching three counterfeiters single-handed."

"Who assigned him that job?"

"No one. The report says he was following a hunch. What the report doesn't say is that all three of them were released after serving only six months in a minimum security prison."

"How could that be?"

"They were given a Presidential pardon."

Stuart got a sinking feeling in the pit of his stomach, a Presidential pardon, after only six months in jail.

"One more thing," Sally interrupted his thoughts. "They were arrested, tried, and convicted inside of thirty days."

Stuart could feel his face getting red. "Check out the other good things this guy has done and get back to me. One more thing, tomorrow's the funeral. Are we supposed to send flowers, or is the boss taking care of it?"

"I'm sorry, I forgot to give you the message. No one from the office is to attend the funeral."

"What!"

"Michael said we were to take a very low profile and not attend the funeral. If anyone wants to visit her husband afterward, that would be acceptable."

"Sally, there seems to be something wrong with this connection. I didn't get the message. I'll talk to you on Monday."

"Stuart, I have an aunt buried at the same cemetery whom I'm visiting tomorrow. I'd be honored if you'd join my husband and I to pay our respects."

"What's your aunt's name?"

Sally didn't answer for a second and then responded, "Auntie."

Three hours later, dressed in his rented tuxedo, Stuart was on the phone to his friend Peter from the back of the limousine. "They've sent out instructions that we're not supposed to go to the funeral."

"What are you going to do?" Peter asked.

"I'm visiting the cemetery with Christine's replacement. Her aunt is buried there, and her family is paying their respects."

"Who was the idiot that said you couldn't go?"

"It came from Michael, but I don't know where it started."

"Look, Joan and I will be there. How about coming back here around four. I'll throw a steak on the barbeque, and we'll sit and swap stories."

"Sounds like a great idea, see you then."

The limo pulled up in front of Jessica's home. The guard had announced their arrival, and Stuart was surprised to see his daughter Marilyn standing next to Sarah on the lawn.

"Hi, Mr. Taylor," Sarah said aloud. "Marilyn wanted to see what you looked like in a tuxedo. The "baby sitters" are taking us to her house after you two leave."

Stuart did a pirouette. "Hi, Marilyn, Sarah, what do you think?"

"I think you look handsome."

"Thank you, Sarah. What about you?"

"I think, no. I know you look like Kenneth."

Stuart smiled, "Thank you. Is your mom ready, Sarah?"

"She should be."

"I'm ready!" Jessica walked out the front door. She stopped and looked at Stuart. He cleaned up real well. "Make sure the door is locked when you leave."

Marilyn couldn't take her eyes off her father. She was annoyed that he was going out with a congresswoman, especially after all the things her mother had said about him; but he was good-looking, and for some reason she felt very proud of him.

Once they were in the limo, Jessica said, "I'm sorry if the girls made you uncomfortable. I haven't gone out a lot, and Sarah is making a big deal about it."

"Actually, it felt pretty good. Those were the nicest things Marilyn has said to me in years."

"What happened between you two?" Jessica wished she could take back the words as soon as they were out of her mouth.

"It wasn't Marilyn and I, it was her mother. She couldn't take my traveling or the hours. She met another man who was stable, ran a pretty big company, and they fell in love. I always believed she felt guilty and had to blame someone. That someone was me, and it rubbed off on the kids."

"What about your son?"

"He and I are getting together next weekend in New York. I'm getting tickets for the Knicks, and we'll see if we like each other."

"That's funny. Sarah and I are going to the Knick game next weekend. They're playing the Lakers, and one of my constituents sent me a couple of tickets."

"Are you allowed to accept them?"

"They're sort of a peace offering. Mark Harper owns a large farm in my district, and we don't see eye to eye on day laborers. There's the White House."

The limo driver drove to the west gate. Lowering his window, he announced, "Mr. Taylor and guest for dinner with the President."

The guard looked at his pad and replied, "I only have Mr. Taylor on my list. I don't show a guest."

Stuart stepped out of the car. "It must be an oversight, I was invited."

"We have your name, Mr. Stuart, but not your guests."

"My guest is Congresswoman Jessica Winston."

"Please hold on while I call it in."

Stuart got back in the car and was explaining the problem to Jessica when there was a tap on the window.

"I'm sorry, Mr. Stuart. The President has told us to tell you that the invitation was for you only, not for a guest. We'll be only too happy to drive the congresswoman home."

"That won't be necessary. I'll drive her home. Please give the President my apologies. Tell him if I'm in the area again, I'll give him a call."

"Pardon me?"

"I am taking the congresswoman out for dinner. If not here somewhere else. It would have been nice to have the President join us, but since he's busy, we'll have to reschedule."

"Mrs. Winston, please explain to Mr. Taylor that he can't do this."

"I'm sorry, but Mr. Taylor asked me out for dinner. He picks the place." Jessica squeezed Stuart's arm as she whispered, "You know you're crazy, but I have never felt so good about anything before in my life."

Stuart pushed the button, raising the window. "Turn this car around, and let's find somewhere to eat."

There was another knock on the window. Stuart lowered it and said, "Yes?"

"The President has found room for one more person. He's sorry for the confusion and has asked that you proceed to the side door."

Stuart turned to Jessica. "Should we?"

Chapter Nineteen

"Mr. Taylor, Congresswoman Winston, welcome to the White House. The President has asked that I take you to where you can meet the other guests and get you a drink." The Secret Service agent took two steps and then stopped. "Before we enter the White House, I'll have to ask, are you carrying any weapons?"

Jessica turned to Stuart. "I'm not. Are you?"

Stuart shook his head.

"There's an alarm that goes off if anyone has any metal as we enter, but I guess we don't have to worry, do we?" He looked straight at Stuart as he spoke.

Stuart patted himself down. "I have a cell phone. Want to take a look?"

The Secret Service man held out his hand. "Would you mind if we held on to this while you're guests of the President?"

"Yes, I would. I'm on duty twenty four hours a day and not having the phone with me would be an inconvenience."

"Maybe if I held it that would be alright," Jessica interceded.

"No. I'm sure Mr. Taylor understands our concern. I'll just check it out and return it."

"In front of me," Stuart replied.

In the short time Jessica had known Stuart, she had seen his eyes change color twice. Neither time did she want to be on the other side of his gaze.

The Secret Service agent smiled, turned the phone on, and dialed a number. The phone on his belt started ringing. Pushing the button to disconnect, he handed the phone back to Stuart. "Thank you," he said politely.

"Can I see your phone a second?" Stuart asked.

A look of concern crossed the agent's face. "Why?"

"Just curious, I just wanted to see if it's one of the new ones they're handing out."

The agent removed it from his belt and handed it to Stuart, who promptly hit the recall button. The phone in his pocket started to ring. Stuart snapped the antenna, took out the batteries, and smashed the phone on the ground. He then took five one-hundred-dollar bills and handed them to the surprised agent. "This will pay for the phone that I dropped. Sorry for the inconvenience."

"Are you out of your mind?" The agent couldn't believe what had just happened.

"No one, and I mean no one, has access to my phone number. It's one of the rules of the agency. You should have known what was going to happen. Since this is my first visit to the White House, I'm paying for it. You can tell the other agents, in the future, I won't."

"I doubt if you'll ever get invited back." The agent winked and smiled as he put the five hundred dollars in his pocket. "Follow me."

"I wasn't sure I was going to have a good time tonight," Jessica whispered as she held Stuart's arm. "But if the first ten minutes are any indication of the rest of the night, it could go down in history."

"Stuart," Michael Burnett greeted him as they entered a room with thirty-foot ceilings that made their voices seem different. "This must be Congresswoman Winston. Why don't you introduce me?"

Stuart stared at his boss Michael. "Why don't you explain why you didn't tell me you'd be here, and then you can explain why I'm not supposed to go to the funeral tomorrow."

"Congresswoman Winston, my name is Michael Burnett. Mr. Taylor seems to have forgotten that I'm his boss, and I don't have to tell him anything." Michael held out his hand.

Jessica shook his hand briefly without saying a word. Putting her hand down at her side, she started, "Mr. Burnett, you've known Stuart longer than I have, and more than likely know him a lot better. I hope you know what it is you're doing. In the few days that I've known him, I've seen him get a little upset. The people that upset him will not forget what happened to them. He is now more than a little upset."

Michael laughed out loud. "He'll probably be more upset before the night is over, but I've lived with him for a long time. He'll get over it." Looking over her shoulder, his expression changed. "Here comes the President." Looking at Stuart, he said, "Be nice, I think you'll enjoy the night."

"Jessica, how nice to see you again. I'm sorry for the confusion at the gate." The President leaned over and pecked her on the cheek. "You must be Stuart Taylor. It's a pleasure to meet you. I see you don't have a drink yet, what would you like?"

"I'll have whatever you're having, Mr. President, as long as it has some alcoholic content."

The President turned to one of the waiters. "Two scotches straight up, and for you, Jessica?"

"I'll have a glass of wine, red preferably."

"And a glass of red wine, preferably from California." Taking Jessica by the arm, he started walking toward one of the waiters carrying a tray of appetizers. "You'll have to tell me how you two met, but wait until my wife joins us. I'm sure she'd love to hear the story." Helping himself to some of the food on the tray, he looked around and in a conspiratorial voice said, "I really should take another couple of pieces before my wife gets here. She doesn't like me indulging."

"I heard that," said the President's wife, Catherine Sherman, as she entered the room. "Sorry I'm late, Jessica, how nice to see you. You look lovely, I didn't know you were going to be here."

"Stuart only asked me two days ago."

"Ronald, why don't you introduce me to our other guests."

The President stepped forward. "Michael you know, and this is Stuart Taylor, the man I told you about."

Catherine accepted a peck on the cheek from Michael before turning to look at Stuart. "Mr. Taylor, it's a pleasure to meet you. Since we're all here, why don't we go into dinner? Taking Stuart's arm, she started walking toward the dining room.

The President took Jessica's arm and held back as he nodded at Michael to precede him.

"Jessica, this is a little awkward. It was supposed to be men only. He never mentioned bringing you, and as far as anyone knew, he wasn't dating anyone. Please bear with me. I promise we'll talk later. Keep in mind this meeting is off the record, far off the record."

Jessica was surprised. The President had never in the three years she'd been in Congress ever spoken to her as a friend. Another thing bothered her, if the dinner was for men only, why was Stuart instructed to wear a tuxedo. She had heard about some of the dinners the President had that turned into five- and ten-dollar poker games, but they were usually held with high-ranking members of Congress or heavy donors.

Stuart was holding a chair for the first lady when Jessica entered the room.

"Why don't you sit across from my wife on my right?" said the President as he held a chair for Jessica. Michael Burnett stood behind the chair next to the first lady, waiting for the President to be seated.

Stuart noticed there was another place setting at the other end of the table.

"Are we missing someone, sir?" Stuart asked.

"No, he'll be right down. He's a guest of mine . . ." Stopping, he looked at Jessica. "I think you may know him, Mark Harper from San Diego."

"Of course she does. We've known each other for years." Stuart stood as the man who was obviously Mark Harper entered. He was maybe an inch or two taller than Stuart's six feet one; he had dark hair, a very bright smile with very white teeth, and he filled the tuxedo jacket with muscles that Stuart believed he knew how to use.

"Sorry I'm late, Ron, oh, excuse me, Mr. President, some pressing business problems. Catherine, you look radiant, and, Jessica, I see the Washington weather is treating you well."

Stuart stood watching as the man approached him.

"Mr. Taylor, I've heard a lot about you."

His grip was firm and his palm was dry. Stuart took an instant dislike to him. Calling the President by his first name was odious, and Stuart believed he was trying to impress both Jessica and himself. Glancing at Michael, Stuart knew they were both on the same wavelength.

"I hope what you heard was something good."

"It was," he replied, turning toward Michael. "I don't believe we've met?"

"You're right, I haven't had the pleasure. My name is Michael Burnett, I'm with the ATF."

"Ah yes, the Ruby Ridge people."

Michael smiled. "Among other things."

"Bring Mr. Harper a drink." The President motioned to one of the waiters.

The serving of dinner took almost two hours. The talk around the table went from baseball to some charities that Harper was supporting. Stuart had the feeling that this was not what the dinner was supposed to be about. At exactly eight, the President's wife asked Jessica if she would like to see some of the gifts they had received since taking office. Jessica stood and followed her out of the room.

"We have about ten minutes before they return," the President started. "Stuart, let me fill you in on why I wanted to meet you. Mr. Harper has a problem in Southern California that he believes we can help him with. Mark, why don't you explain your problem?"

Harper stood, removed his jacket, and hung it on the back of his chair. "I need day laborers to work my fields as does every farmer out my way. The INS with all their inspections keep slowing me down. The President has suggested that I set up places for them to sleep and eat and register them on a weekly basis. He would be willing to push a bill through Congress accomplishing this. My problem is that it's too costly to house feed them and pay them a so called living wage."

"Where do I fit in?" Stuart asked.

"I have asked the President to set up a department that will transport laborers from entry points in Mexico to places where they will work and then back again to Mexico."

Stuart thought to himself, this must be a joke, but no one was smiling.

"I would assume that all the places they have to be transported to are within a thirty- to forty-five-minute ride from the border. In the summer they would stop work by five so they could get home."

"That's the problem. Since I can't house and feed them, the government could do it somewhere close to the border. They could set up camps, and people from all over the Southland would stay there."

Stuart shook his head. "I think the idea is crazy, but I guess that's what some people do for a living."

"Do what for a living?" the President asked.

"Think about crazy ideas and what would make them work or not work."

"Mr. Taylor, I asked you here to see if you were the person to head up this new department."

Stuart looked around the room. "Mr. President, if I wasn't sitting here but in a bar having a few beers, everyone could laugh and joke about what Mr. Harper is looking for. But I am here, and it's not a laughing matter." From the corner of his eye, he saw the first lady and Jessica standing by the door and for a second was unsure if he should continue. When Jessica smiled, it made up his mind. "Any thought given to Mr. Harper's proposal should be considered wasted. It goes against everything our country stands for. I almost feel insulted that you would consider me for this abortion." Stuart stood and said, "I think it's time for me to leave. I'm sorry this dinner didn't go as you planned, and if you want, my resignation will be on your desk in the morning."

"Will you personally deliver it?" the President asked.

"I can."

"I'll be waiting for you at nine in the morning. Thank you for coming, and, Jessica, we'll have to do this again soon." With that, the President walked out of the room. As he reached the door, he turned, "Michael, please wait around for a few minutes, I have to speak to you."

Michael, who was standing, nodded, poured himself a drink, and sat back down.

Chapter Twenty

"He's everything you said he was." The President swirled the brandy around in his glass. "I think he's the right man for the job."

Michael acknowledged the words with a nod of his head. "You have to remember, Mr. President, Stuart sees almost everything in black-and-white. With him, there is very little gray. The kids were bad, he kicked their ass; the men were threatening bodily harm, he kills them. When you talk to him, make sure you spell out what you're after and why; otherwise he's liable to turn you down. There's only one job he wasn't able to complete. It was fifteen years ago, and it's changed his life."

"Catherine, I hate to tell you this, but that Taylor is a strange guy. He's here to be offered a promotion, and he mouths off big time in front of the President."

"I'm sure Ronald will put him in his place tomorrow."

"I hope you're right, it's not nice what he did." Mark Harper yawned and stretched. "I have to make some phone calls and get to bed. I have a whole bunch of people to meet with tomorrow."

"That's the guy that gave you the Knick tickets?" Stuart asked Jessica as they were driven through the gates.

"That's him. My daughter thinks he's good-looking, what do you think?"

"I don't know about good-looking, but he does fill out a tuxedo nicely." Stuart answered begrudgingly.

"This was the first time the President called me by my first name, it felt odd." Jessica sat back and closed her eyes. "So the conversation that I walked in on, is that how you really feel, or were you saying those things for my benefit?"

Taking a deep breath, Stuart started, "I guess it showed, but I didn't like your friend. I'm also having a problem with my boss being there and not saying anything beforehand, and I asked. I was surprised about the job offer because the job is a piece of"—Stuart hesitated—"crap. I had some questions I wanted to ask about Presidential pardons, and I never got the chance. Michael never explained. If I left, who was going to find the bank robbers, certainly not that idiot Burnett, or who was going to track down the killers of the three kids. This whole night made absolutely no sense."

Jessica sitting there listening was more attuned to the way Washington worked. She knew Stuart was right, which meant tomorrow's meeting would be even more important. "Do you want someone to go to the funeral with you?" she asked.

Stuart looked at his watch. "If you would, I have a great idea." Dialing a number on his cell phone, he whispered, "I'm supposed to go to Peter's tomorrow after the funeral for a barbecue. I'll ask him if it's all right to bring you and the girls."

Peter answered the phone on the third ring. "Hello."

"Peter, it's me."

"Jesus, don't you ever sleep?"

"About tomorrow, is it okay if I bring Jessica, her daughter, and my daughter?"

"Marilyn?"

"She's the only one I have."

"Miracles never end. Of course it's okay. Come straight from the funeral. Do the girls eat steaks, or are they vegetarians?"

"Haven't a clue, see you tomorrow."

"How was your date with the congresswoman?"

"See you tomorrow." Stuart laughed as he hung up. "He said it's fine. Do you think it's too late to call the girls?"

Jessica thought to herself, *He's like a kid in a candy store.* "They're probably still watching television. Give me the phone, I'll call."

Marilyn answered on the first ring. "Marilyn it's Mrs. Winston, how are you girls doing? That's fine, I have a question for the two of you, can Sarah pick up the phone on another extension?" After a few seconds with both girls on the phone, she asked the question. "Marilyn's father would like the two of you to join us at a barbecue at his friend Peter's. He has to attend a funeral at which I'm joining him and then we're going to Mr. Weber's home in Chevy Chase." There was no answer from either girl, and Jessica could picture the two of them trying to look at each other.

Sarah finally broke the silence. "I'd love to go."

"I'll have to ask my mother." Marilyn came back a second later.

"Mom, did you have a good time? What did they serve for dinner? How many people were there?"

Sarah was again running on.

"Yes, I did, steak, six, including the President and his wife. Now go to bed, I'll see you tomorrow."

"I thought you told me this guy could be counted on," Harper whispered into the phone.

"I told you he wouldn't be a problem. There was no way he would accept that job."

"Well, you were right about that part. I think the President will fire him in the morning."

The voice on the other end was silent.

"Did you hear me?" Harper again whispered.

"I hear you, I just don't believe you. In fact, I think we should terminate our agreement. Something isn't right. Lose my number and forget you ever heard of me." The phone went dead. Harper made another call.

"He said to forget I ever heard of him. I don't even know his name. You gave me a number to call and this guy on the other end told me that for fifty thousand he would make sure Taylor wasn't a problem. He now says he told me Taylor wouldn't take the job the President would offer. You tell me, what's going on?"

"My sources tell me that he's not in good standing at the bureau, and that if he turned down this job, he's out of the government. I don't know more than that. Did you send the fifty thousand?"

"No, I never got around to it."

"Send it to me, and make sure I have it by Monday at noon."

When Harper hesitated, the voice asked, "Do you have a problem?"

"Yeah, I do. What about the day workers from Mexico?"

"Give me a couple of days after I receive the money through the usual channels."

"Would you like to come in for a cup of coffee?" Jessica asked.

"I'd love to, but this is my transportation. I'll just check out the house to make sure no one is inside."

"Send the driver home, I'll lend you my car. I'd like to talk to you about tonight and your meeting tomorrow."

Stuart rubbed some nonexistent lint off his jacket. "So this would or wouldn't be part of the companionship thing?"

Jessica's lips turned upward and her eyes glistened. "Let's say it's a first step in finding out if we like the same things."

"What kind of coffee do you have?"

"Does it matter?" she replied as she opened the car door.

"Not really, I wasn't planning on sleeping tonight anyway."

"We have to call off Tuesday's job. In fact, we're going to have to call off visiting all the banks we had planned for over the next four weeks." The man speaking on the cell phone looked at the clock on the night table alongside his bed.

"Bullshit. I'm not calling off anything." The voice had a slight Spanish lilt to it.

"Something's wrong. If we continue, we're going to get caught. I'll call you when I'm sure it's safe."

"When you're sure! You call me in the middle of the night, how come I can't contact you? How come I don't know you or your girlfriend's name?" The Spanish accent became more pronounced as he got louder.

"If you knew our names, I'd have to kill you." The words said without a hint of remorse stopped the conversation. "I'll call you when it's safe. Go on vacation and spend the three hundred thousand dollars you made. Don't be an idiot."

Closing his phone, he rolled over and looked at the other side of the bed.

"What did he say?" asked the woman with short dark hair.

"Nothing important, I just hope he goes on vacation."

"Stuart, come on in here," Jessica called as she put the pot of coffee and a box of Girl Scout cookies on the kitchen table. She heard the sound of the TV go off and seconds later followed by Stuart entering the kitchen. "Anything happening in the world I should be aware of?" she asked.

"It's raining in the Pacific Northwest, and there's a heat wave in Texas," Stuart answered. "And I love Girl Scout cookies." Walking to the table, he asked, "Were you a Girl Scout?"

"I was a Brownie and a Girl Scout," she replied, setting down a container of milk.

"I also loved Girl Scouts." Stuart took her arm and pulled her toward him. There was a slight resistance until they embraced. As he moved his hand down her back, she pushed him away.

"It looks like that's something we both like. Let's talk before this goes any further."

Chapter Twenty-One

"One of the things I've learned during my time in Washington is that things are never quite what they seem." Jessica looked at Stuart, who was sitting on the other side of the table eating a Girl Scout shortbread cookie. "This meeting tomorrow has to be the real reason the President wanted to see you."

"He's the President, for God's sake," responded Stuart, brushing shortbread crumbs from his sleeve. "He could've called me anytime and just told me what he wanted. And your friend, Harper." Stuart shook his head in disgust. "How do you put up with guys like that?"

Jessica's first thought was that Stuart was jealous. It made her feel warm, and she felt herself blushing. Rising quickly, she put her cup in the sink. "He's a constituent; he's also a sizeable donor to my campaign and the party. Remember what they say: politics makes strange bedfellows."

"What does that mean?" Stuart snapped

She was taken aback by the tone of his voice. "It means that sometimes, in order to get things done, we have to appear to be friends with people we're not fond of, especially if we think they're important."

Stuart stood and moved toward her. "Sorry, I didn't mean to raise my voice. This whole night has me a little upset, maybe more at Michael than anything else. I have no right to tell you who to like . . . or not." He stopped short of reaching out for her and put his hands in his pockets. "I envisioned the night being a lot different."

"What did you think would happen?" Jessica approached him and thought, *This is crazy*, but didn't stop until she was inches away. They both jumped when his cell phone jangled.

"Damn!" Stuart snapped open the cover. "Taylor here. You, son of a—" He caught himself and started over. "Hi, Michael, I'm glad you called. I wanted to thank you for setting up an enjoyable evening." He listened for a few seconds. "You are definitely crazy. I am not meeting you in twenty minutes, anywhere." He turned at the sound of Jessica's kitchen phone.

She picked it up, listened, and then turned to Stuart. "Your limo is back. The guard wants to know if I should let the driver in."

"Make it thirty minutes," he told Michael. Snapping the phone closed, he shrugged apologetically. "Have him wait for ten minutes and then admit him," she instructed the caller.

"This is Washington," she said. "Things happen." She moved closer. "Now listen carefully, we don't have a lot of time. The President is going to ask you to do something. It's going to be either a favor or something that looks like a great opportunity. Either way, try to get it in writing. You'll be playing ball with one of the all-time great statesmen. He's smooth like glass, and people have a problem telling him no."

"And if he accepts my resignation?"

"Take up golf and learn to live on that five or six million you have. But trust me, he wants something."

"My appointment's at nine. I'll call as soon as it's over, and you can tell me where to pick up you and the girls." Stuart looked down at his shoes. "Does tomorrow qualify as a date?"

Jessica stepped closer, put her hands on his face, and gently kissed him on the lips. "I think having two chaperones watching our every move definitely qualifies it as a date." She kissed him again, this time a little harder. "Now go keep your appointment, I'll see you tomorrow." She turned him around and gave him a little nudge toward the door.

Twenty minutes later, the limo pulled up to a bar with a block-lettered sign: Curious George's. "I was told to drop you here," said the driver, "but the place looks closed. You want me to wait?"

Stuart opened the car door. "No, go ahead, my friend won't be long."

He waited for the taillights to disappear before walking into the darkened doorway. When he was sure there was no one on the street, he pulled a quarter from his pocket and tapped twice on the glass. Sally Kim opened the door and smiled. "Follow me, Michael's in the back." "When did we get this place?" Stuart questioned, looking around the darkened bar.

"Yesterday. I understand something's wrong with our offices."

"Like what?" There was concern in his voice.

"Michael said something about rodents."

"What about the Cigar Store?"

"As far as I know, they're okay."

"If you two are finished talking, I have to get some sleep."

Stuart turned at the sound of Michael's voice.

"I didn't see you sitting there," said Stuart, peering into the corner of the room. When Michael didn't respond, he asked, "What kind of rodents did you find?"

Michael forced a smile. "Sally, why don't you get Stuart a drink and then leave us alone for about thirty minutes? I think he's drinking scotch."

Sally looked at Stuart, who shook his head to the negative. She reached for a bottle and poured him a glassful. Handing him the drink, he said, "If you want more, it's on the counter." Having fulfilled her boss's wishes, she left the room. Stuart took a sip and nodded when the ginger ale hit his palate. The moment they were alone, Michael began talking, "Tomorrow, listen carefully to what the President says. I don't want to preempt him, but this could be one of the most important decisions of your life."

"Jessica said almost the same thing."

"What's with you and the congresswoman?"

Stuart felt the muscles in his jaw tightening. "Meaning?"

"Are you two getting close or something?"

"Not yet, but I'm working on it." Hesitating, he took another sip. "Now I'd like some answers."

"Such as?"

"How come you didn't tell me you were going to be there? Did you know about the Presidential pardons that were given to the men Weaver arrested? Why was I instructed to wear a tuxedo and not expected to bring a guest? And lastly, was he serious about even considering Mark Harper's idea of housing and transporting Mexicans so they could work the fields for cheap labor?"

"Harper is a big party donor, Stuart. That means access to the President and other ranking members of Congress. But that doesn't mean that the President will consider his request. As for the date part, it was a mistake. The tuxedos were meant to make the meeting seem important to Harper. There were only going to be the four of us for dinner, and then the President was going to call Jake and a few others for a card game. Jessica's arrival changed all that. As far as the pardons, that's part of the problem. The list is submitted to the President almost as a rubber stamp. He usually asks one of his staffers to go over it, submit it to the FBI, and then they okay it."

"The FBI said the list was okay?"

"Someone at the FBI did."

"Weaver?"

Michael nodded. "I was given instructions not to tell you who was going to be there tonight nor what's going to be said tomorrow. The funeral is a little dicey. I'm trying not to connect you to our operation. In case someone's watching, your being there would be a tip-off."

Stuart downed his drink and asked, "What do you want me to do?"

"Listen to the President. Find out who killed Christine and who's trying to hurt your girlfriend."

"She not my girlfriend," Stuart interrupted a little too quickly.

"Whatever," Michael responded with a flip of his hand. "While you're doing this, find out who killed the three kids. Oh, and in your spare time, catch the bank robbers."

"That's it?" Stuart asked sarcastically.

"No, one more thing: when I invite you to have a drink, I didn't mean ginger ale."

Stuart smiled; nothing got past Michael. "Do we know who had access to the Cigar Store phone number?"

"Too many people to pin it down. There are four operatives, plus yourself, the six men who man the phones 'round the clock. There's Sally, me, Longstreet from ATF, three ex-operatives, and maybe the spouses of any or all of the above."

Stuart thought for a second. "What about the rodents?"

"The place was swept yesterday morning. This afternoon, we found three listening devices—your office, mine, and the main switchboard."

"You should be able to pin down who was in there since yesterday."

"Two operatives, plus Sally, me, and six cleaning men. I checked the cleaners, and they swear they only sent four men and a supervisor. I'm having those five questioned to see if they remember the other person."

Both men turned at the sound of the door. "You told me to return in thirty minutes," said Sally.

Michael stood. "Keep in touch, okay? And try and stay out of trouble."

Stuart headed for the door, feeling Michael's eyes on him. "I'll do my best," he said. "But I'm still going to the funeral."

"Big surprise," mumbled Michael as Stuart walked out.

Chapter Twenty-Two

"I thought we were going out for dinner?" Stuart's mother scolded him over the phone.

"Mom, in case you forgot, I'm forty-four years old. You can't call me at six thirty in the morning and start talking to me like I'm a child."

"Why can't I? You obviously didn't have a date last night or you wouldn't have been home when I called."

"As a matter of fact, I did have a date, and I took her to the White House for dinner with the President."

His mother was silent as she digested this information. "Are you telling the truth?"

"I am, and I have even more news: I'm taking her to Peter's today for a barbecue and Marilyn is joining us."

"Who is this woman?"

When Stuart didn't answer, she continued, "Come next weekend for dinner, you can bring me up to date."

"Sorry, I'm meeting Kenneth in New York for our weekend of bonding. How about Thursday night? I'll take you to that Italian restaurant you like."

"Pick me up at six, and you better be ready to tell me what's going on in your life."

Shaking his head, Stuart hung up and adjusted the light gray tie that the salesman swore went well with the dark gray suit. He filled a tote with slacks, a golf shirt, loafers, and a sweater. At the last moment, he slipped his forty-five between the folds of the shirt. When he arrived at the White House gate, it was eight thirty. He was asked to step out of his car as they ran mirrors under the frame and looked in the trunk and backseat.

"Do you have any weapons to declare?" asked the guard with the starched white shirt.

"Only my forty-five, which is inside the tote in the trunk that your partner just closed."

The two guards looked at each other.

Stuart took out his FBI credentials and showed them to the closer guard.

"Any weapons on your person?" asked the second guard. "No."

We're going to pull your car into the parking area. You can pick up the keys when you return. Now, we're going to have to pat you down."

Stuart lifted both arms and held them straight out. The guard doing the patting came across the cell phone. "May I see that, please?"

Stuart turned it on and dialed a number. He held the phone so the guard could hear the reply: "The time is eight forty-one."

"I still have to check," replied the guard, reaching for the phone.

Stuart slid it back into his pocket.

The two guards looked at each other and then asked. "Were you here last night?" asked the taller one.

Stuart nodded and looked at his watch. "It's eight forty-five, so how about one of you calling the President and letting him know that I'm going to be late."

The shorter guard scowled, "Gary said you were a smart-ass."

"Gary was right about that," responded Stuart, watching a well-dressed man in his late fifties approach. Both guards stood a little straighter as the stranger entered their sphere.

"Good morning, Mr. Gastner," they said in unison.

"Good morning." He looked straight at Stuart. "Is there a problem?"

Stuart recognized the name of the White House chief of staff.

"Thanks, but my job requires that I carry my cell phone. It wasn't a problem last night, and I don't expect it to be one today."

"You must be Stuart Taylor." David Gastner pulled a watch fob from his pocket. "Follow me," he said. "And we have to hurry or we'll be late."

Stuart followed the man into the White House.

They entered the Oval Office at two minutes before the hour and one minute before the President's arrival. When he entered, both Gastner and Stuart leapt to their feet.

"Stuart, thank you for coming. I understand that Michael spoke to you last night."

"Yes, sir, he did."

"What did he say?"

"He told me to listen."

"And what did the congresswoman have to say?"

"She said you were one of the all-time great statesmen and I should hear you out."

"Neither said anything about you resigning?" Gastner asked.

"The congresswoman did."

"What did she say?"

Stuart faced Gastner. "She said that if I didn't like what I heard, I should be prepared to learn to play golf."

Both men laughed. Finally, the President said, "Let's get down to business" and David Gastner handed Stuart a set of papers. "I'm going to ask Congress for permission to set up a new department, Stuart. It'll be called Home Guard or something like that, but what it'll be is an anti-terrorist organization. I want you to head it up."

Stuart sat back. When he realized that his mouth had popped open, he closed it.

"Any questions?" asked the President. "Several, but could you please give me a second to arrange my thoughts?"

No one said a word until Stuart gave the sign.

"I'm very honored," he said. "But the first question has to be why me, and not someone like Michael?"

"Michael's going to take Jake's place at the FBI. Before you ask," he added, holding up a hand, "Bradley will be moved over to head up ATF. We're closing down the Cigar Store operation. Too many people are starting to take notice, and it could become embarrassing." The President poured himself a glass of water and nodded at his chief of staff.

"The way we envision it working," explained Gastner, "is to move Bradley over to ATF as second in command to Longstreet. Before his replacement is named, Michael's will be submitted to Congress to replace Jake Levitt. During the hearings, Michael will announce that he wants Karen Ortega as his second in command. Those in Congress who look like they're going to object will be shown data on Weaver's affair with his secretary. Over the past three months, the CIA has been hearing rumors about some of the lunatic fringe groups getting ready to start car bombings, germ warfare, and something to do with hijacking planes inside our borders. On the second day of Michael's hearings, we're going to announce the new department and the reason for it. Your name will be placed in nomination and a fast confirmation hearing requested. We'll put pressure on Senator Conrad to bring both confirmations to a speedy and happy end."

"What do you propose this new department do?"

Gastner studied Stuart's face for a moment. "Our country has thousands of people walking around who don't belong here. They've entered the country as visitors and then disappear, or they enter illegally and join a network of terrorists. This new department will find them and stop them before they do damage."

The silence in the room caused Stuart to fidget, but experience had taught him this was the moment to say nothing.

"Can you imagine what would happen if someone threw poison into our reservoirs?" asked Gastner, and then brushed the question away. "Listen, the CIA will continue to operate overseas, hopefully find out who these people are and stop them before they get here. As for the FBI, once Michael has it straightened out, it'll continue its domestic work. Your department will figure out how to stop these lunatics before they get started. And if they do get started, you'll find them and make sure they don't do it again, whatever it is."

"When do you expect this new department to be operational?" Stuart asked.

"Four weeks from tomorrow," the President replied.

Questions and concerns buzzed around Stuart's head. "Mr. President, I'm honored and flattered that you would consider me, but I do have a few more questions. I'm not a politician and have no experience interfacing with Congress or the press."

"If you accept this offer, Chilicote will announce his retirement from the Senate and come on temporarily as your chief of staff. He's a lawyer and a gifted politician. Over the next four weeks, you'll have to pick some key people, and he could be a great asset. I don't expect you to hire every person working for the department, but I do expect you to be responsible for all of them. Chilicote will help train his replacement."

"Is there a budget to fund this?"

The President smiled. "I like a practical man. There's no money now, but there will be in four weeks. Congresswoman Winston was right, you know. I am a great statesman." He smiled shamelessly.

Stuart remembered to smile, but his mind was still racing. "Mr. President, two more questions before I leave. The first is about the congresswoman. Does my friendship with her present a problem for you?"

The President took another sip of water. "I don't think so, although I must tell you that it does present some interesting possibilities." He sat back and said nothing more.

Stuart was tempted to ask what those possibilities could be but held back. "The other question is, will I have access to you?"

"You'll get your formal thirty-minute meetings every Monday afternoon at three forty-five and some not-so-formal ones at either of our whims."

"Mr. President," said Stuart, his voice taking on a more formal timbre, "there are probably a dozen more questions I should be asking but lack the intelligence to think of what they might be. If you will accept my answer now, it's yes, and I thank you for the opportunity."

The President stood and placed both hands on his desk. "Don't get too far ahead of me, Stuart, you know the timetable. I'm having lunch with the Senate Majority and Minority leaders today and will start the ball rolling. If I know

Washington, by this time tomorrow there will be leaks to the press. Will you be seeing Jessica soon?"

"I'm meeting her today."

"Send my best wishes, and tell her to act surprised when she hears the story through channels." With that, the President shook Stuart's hand. "I think you're going to enjoy the position."

David Gastner motioned for Stuart to follow him, just as the phone on the President's desk rang.

Chapter Twenty-Three

The chief of staff informed Stuart that his first meeting with the President would be in seven days, and then instructed an agent to take Stuart to the basement where he was photographed for an all-access pass to the White House. It was the same Secret Service agent whose phone he had smashed on Saturday night.

"Here's your five hundred back," the agent said as they were walking toward the exit. "They give us the phones."

Stuart pocketed the money. "You could have kept it. You can't earn a lot in this job."

"I don't do badly. With the hazardous duty pay and my wife's job, we do all right."

"Would you like to move to another department?"

"Which one?"

"They haven't named it yet, but I'm going to be looking for some good people."

The agent didn't answer, but when they got to the door, he asked, "Why me?"

"I like honest people."

"I'd like to think about it; can I have a couple of days?"

"I'll be back a week from tomorrow, you can let me know then. By the way, what's your name?"

"Gary. Gary Williams."

Stuart held out his hand. "See you next Monday, Agent Williams."

Forty minutes later, Stuart arrived at Jessica's home. Before he could walk up to the door, she stepped onto the porch, dressed in a business suit, and carrying a black leather overnight bag.

"Something to change into," she said, hoisting the bag.

"Where are the girls?" he asked, looking behind her.

"I thought it better if we picked them up after the funeral. It'll give us a chance to talk, and I didn't see any reason to start off with them at a cemetery."

Stuart put her bag in the trunk next to his and felt awkward, the two bags lying side by side, as if hinting at an intimacy they had not yet reached. After last night, he wasn't sure if he should kiss her or shake her hand.

Jessica solved his problem by kissing him on the cheek and saying, "This is a date!"

They traveled a short distance before Jessica asked, "So what did he say?"

"Who?"

She playfully punched his arm. "Who do you think?"

"The President said you should act surprised when you hear the story through channels."

"He knew you would tell me?"

"He surmised as much, especially when I asked if our being friends was a problem."

"Is it?"

"He didn't seem to think so."

"What did he offer?"

"The head of a new agency."

Her head jerked in his direction. "I haven't heard of any new agency."

Stuart explained how they were going to close down his department, make Michael the head of the FBI, and keep Ray Bradley as deputy director." He glanced at Jessica, but she remained silent.

"They're also going to form a new department. I'm not sure what it will be called, maybe Home Guard. In any case, it'll be an antiterrorist organization. They've gotten signals from the CIA that some crazies are planning to hijack planes, start fires, release toxic chemicals into the air, et cetera, but they haven't been able to put a finger on them. It looks like they're coming out of Iraq, Iran, and Afghanistan, maybe even Palestine. The CIA will continue to hunt them overseas, but we're going to have to start acting on it here. The President has asked me to head up that organization."

"What does he expect you, or that organization, to do?"

Stuart didn't like the sound of her voice. "What do you mean by that?"

"I know you're into . . ." She stopped, thought for a second, and then restarted. "Your background is solving problems. Is that what this department is going to do? Solve problems outside of due process?"

Stuart felt his ears turning red. "If you don't like what you hear, vote against it."

Jessica took a deep breath. "Is it funded yet?"

"He's starting on that today, meeting with both the majority and minority leaders for lunch."

"I'm on the budget committee. If they go for it, they'll be talking to me tomorrow. I wonder how much they're going to ask for."

"I don't know, but I don't think he's prepared to go second-class."

Jessica put her hand on his arm. "I'm sorry, I shouldn't have said what I did."

They drove in silence for a while, each in their own thoughts, until Stuart said, "My birthday was last week. I turned forty-four. I'm probably more than halfway through life, with nothing to show for those years but a broken marriage, two kids that I'm estranged from, and a job that I can't discuss with anyone."

"Am I supposed to feel sorry for you?" said Jessica, stepping in on his words. "I'm almost as old as you are, and I work for the government. You have twice as many children as I do, and I see you trying to get back together with them. As far as not having anything to show for those years, how many criminals have you taken off the streets? What about the money you've amassed? What about this new job the President has offered you?"

"Some job. I tell you about it, and the first thing I get is some comment about working outside of the law."

"I said I was sorry."

"Did I ever tell you I was a lawyer?" He glanced over to see if there was a reaction. "I know the law, and I understand why some of the laws were passed. I also understand that some of them are being used to circumvent their original purpose. So what do we do? We keep passing more laws to correct the old ones." When she remained silent, Stuart took this as encouragement to continue. "Someone has to protect the people. This job will be about stopping terrorists from killing Americans, and I intend to do everything in my power to make sure that happens. Hopefully, it'll all be within whatever laws are in effect at the moment."

Jessica shifted around until she was nearly facing Stuart. "I'm only going to say this once more," she told him. "I'm sorry for what I said. And to prove it, I'll vote for and throw my support behind this new department. But with one caveat."

"Which is?"

"If you're not chosen to head it up, I'll fight like hell for its defeat."

They again rode in silence for several minutes before Stuart asked, "Almost as old?"

Jessica smiled. "Yes, and I refuse to answer any more questions on that subject."

They shared a laugh as the car approached the gates of the cemetery.

Chapter Twenty-Four

There were less than thirty people at the gravesite. Two women flanked Christine's husband. One looked like Christine, maybe a few years older. Stuart learned later that the other woman was the husband's sister. Michael was there, but he stood out of the way. Sally Kim and her husband were dressed in black, neither acknowledging Stuart's presence. Two men, obviously police, stood opposite Christine's husband and looked over the crowd. Like the policemen, Stuart's eyes never stopped moving. He recognized two men who worked for the department and another man with a camera hidden under his coat. Jessica walked over to where Peter and Joan were standing; Stuart stepped back behind a tree and dialed a number.

"This is the Cigar Store. Please repeat the following numbers for a voice check. Seven, twenty-one, twenty-two."

"One hundred," Stuart replied.

"Your name is?"

"Stuart Taylor."

"How can I help?"

"I'm at the cemetery, and I see a couple of our men. I also see someone with a camera under his coat. Can you make sure no pictures are taken, and if they are, that they're not developed?"

"You're there with the congresswoman?"

"I am."

"Do you see the boss standing against the tree?"

Stuart glanced around. There was obviously surveillance nearby.

"He's behind the tree, but I see him."

"I'll take care of it. Anything else?"

"Yeah, I'd like to know who the guy with the camera is working for?"

"Consider it done."

Stuart rejoined Jessica, who looked at him questioningly. He kissed Joan on the cheek and shook Peter's hand.

After the services, Stuart and Jessica paid their respects to Christine's husband. After the obligatory words of condolence, Stuart whispered to Peter that they would see them within the hour. Joining Michael, they stood in silence and watched their agents push the man with the camera into a waiting car.

"What's that all about?" asked Jessica, gesturing toward the action. Turning to Stuart, she demanded, "Why don't you do something!"

"I'll explain later," he said softly, noting the tension in Jessica's face.

Michael turned toward Stuart. "How was the meeting with the President?"

"I accepted his offer."

Michael nodded toward Jessica. "I suppose you know." She forced a smile. "He told me just enough to get me started asking questions."

Michael smiled. "I have no right to ask this, but given what you know, would you support this in the House?"

Stuart saw her body tighten while her face showed no reaction.

"Mr. Burnett," she said, "I'd like to keep my options open. I've heard Stuart's version, and I'm sure I'll soon be hearing someone else's. After all the information is in, I'll make my decision."

"Spoken like a true politician." Michael's voice was more than a little hard.

"That's what I am," replied Jessica, her voice every bit as hard.

Stuart stepped in with "Hey, you two, this is a funeral, okay?" To Michael, he added, "And just so you understand, I expect Jessica to vote her conscience, and I know her well enough to know that she'll vote for what she thinks is right."

Michael looked at both of them. "You're right, I apologize, I shouldn't have asked."

"Doesn't the President think he has enough votes even without mine?" she asked, sugar dripping from every word.

"I'm not privy to what the President thinks," Michael replied, almost as sweetly.

Jessica held out her hand. "Spoken like a true politician."

Michael shook her hand and smiled. "Good, then let's call it a draw."

Chapter Twenty-Five

"Would you mind telling me what that was about?" Jessica asked before the car cleared the grounds of the cemetery.

"I'm not sure," said Stuart. "I guess Michael's concerned about his new job."

"I'm talking about the man who was shoved into the car."

"Oh, him." Stuart glanced into the side-view mirror as he entered the Beltway.

"Well?" she prompted.

"He had a camera under his coat, and it wasn't exactly your high-visibility, star-studded funeral. I wanted to know who he was shooting and why. If he's some innocent reporter, he'll be turned loose." Stuart looked at the dashboard clock. "He's probably on his way home."

"And if he's not?" she fired back.

"Then I want to know all about him and whoever hired him. Don't, for even one second, forget that our daughters were threatened, that three men broke into your home at gunpoint, and that the one I captured died in jail. Oh yes, and someone's called both of us at home, trying to scare us."

"But you treated him like a criminal before you knew anything about him."

"In my job, I can't afford to wait until someone gets hurt. Think about it. What was he doing with a hidden camera?"

"I don't know, but we have laws."

"That were made to protect the innocent, and someone has to enforce them."

"You make everything seem black-and-white, but there are shades of gray."

Stuart watched Jessica out of the corner of his eye. Her anger only made her more beautiful. "Maybe for you, there's gray, but not for me. Listen," he added quickly, before she could speak, "I'm having a real problem here. The angrier you get, the more desirable you become. I'm starting to think I'm getting you angry on purpose."

Jessica's face turned blank, all signs of anger suddenly gone. "You get me angry on purpose?"

"I hope not, but I've got to tell you before we pick up the kids: I find you very attractive."

Jessica turned away from Stuart and faced forward, brushing imaginary lint from her jacket. "This isn't going to work, Stuart. Every time I get upset with something you say or do, you change. You're like a chameleon."

"Are those the little pets that everyone loves to cuddle?"

"No, they're the . . ." She stopped when she saw his smiling face.

The car came to a stop in front of the home belonging to Stuart's former wife. Marilyn and Sarah were standing on the lawn. In the driveway sat three Mercedes. A Chevrolet was parked at the curb. Stuart recognized the two men inside. He waved at the girls and walked over to the Chevy.

"I'll take it from here," he told the men. "Thanks for watching over my daughter."

One of them leaned closer to Stuart. "Keep an eye open for a green Olds. It came by an hour ago, but the plates were so dirty I couldn't make them out."

"Never came back?"

The man sitting behind the wheel shook his head. "It just seemed out of place for this neighborhood."

"Thanks for the heads-up." Stuart stepped away from the car as it pulled away and saw his ex-wife talking to Jessica. *This should be fun,* he thought.

"They were fine," she was assuring Jessica but stopped speaking as Stuart approached.

"Hi, Linda," he said. "You know Sarah's mom, Jessica?"

"We've just met," she responded. When she spoke again, her voice was less friendly. "You know I don't like your type hanging around where I live."

"It couldn't be helped."

Linda turned back to Jessica. "Some of the people he associates with are lowlifes. It's one of the reasons we split up."

"Mom," Marilyn interrupted, appearing at her mother's side. "You promised you wouldn't."

Linda studied her daughter's face for a moment. "You're right, I promised." Turning back to Jessica, she said, "If you ever have a few hours to spare, give me a call and I'll tell you all the other reasons we couldn't make a go of it."

"I'll have her home before seven," Stuart said, quickly hustling everyone toward the car.

"See that you do," she called out just as he closed his door.

"My mother's been a little uptight about those men," explained Marilyn, attempting to diffuse what she considered an ugly situation.

"It's the only way the Secret Service will allow Sarah to stay with you," Jessica said over her shoulder.

Sarah leaned forward and asked, "So how was dinner with the President?"

Stuart looked into the rearview mirror and saw the anticipation on Sarah's face. Clearly, both girls wanted all the details, and he shared their curiosity. How *was* their evening at the White House?

"Oh my God!" exclaimed Marilyn. "Dad, you really said that to the Secret Service man?"

After forty minutes of Jessica's recounting, this was the first question asked by either girl.

"Don't go making a big deal out of it," insisted Stuart. "I was starving, and then all of a sudden I thought they'd asked me there to work. It seemed the right thing to say." He felt a reprieve when they arrived at Peter's house. "I hope Joan's doing the cooking," he announced, "because Peter's a terrible chef."

Stuart reclined on a chaise lounge and admired the backyard. A six-foot chain link fence that circled the property was almost completely hidden behind a ten-foot privet. The lawn was well manicured, and the water in the pool was aquamarine. Smoke from the barbecue was drifting his way: with the aroma of filet mignon, and his mouth was watering. "You look like you're having a good time," Peter said, handing Stuart a can of Diet Coke. "You sure you don't want anything stronger?"

"This is fine, thanks, and you're right. I don't remember the last time I felt this good." He gestured toward the yard. "Is this your work?"

"We have a guy who comes in twice a week."

"You'll have to give me his name, he does a great job."

"Turned out to be a nice day," mused Peter, settling into the other lounge chair.

"It's always a great day when Marilyn treats me like a human being. It's also nice to see Jessica and Joan talking like friends."

"She's a nice lady. Are you two getting along?"

"It gets a little dicey at times, but for the most part we're putting up with each other."

"How'd your dinner with the President go?"

"If you can believe it, he only invited me."

"No one else was there?"

"No, I mean the invitation didn't include a guest."

Peter let go with a low whistle. "No shit. What did you do?"

"It's a long story, but the evening ended up okay."

"So why did he invite you?"

"To offer me a job."

"You turned him down, didn't you?"

Stuart thought for a second. "I did."

"How'd he react to that?"

"He handled it pretty well. In fact, he offered me another one today."

"Doing what?"

"Heading up a new agency."

The statement caused Peter's expression to change. "A new agency . . . what?"

"The CIA and the FBI are getting information that some crazies plan on setting off bombs here. The President wants an agency in place that'll stop them."

Peter took a long sip of beer. "I'd love to be back in the action, doing something important like that."

"You are," said Stuart. "You're watching over my money. Speaking of which, how am I doing?"

"The market was up nearly ten percent this week, meaning you gained a little over eight hundred thousand. I think it's time you switched half of that over to triple-A government bonds. That'd still leave you with close to five mill in stocks and . . ."

Stuart held up his hand. "Do whatever you think best." That financial decision made, he shifted his attention to his daughter. "Look at her," he said. "She's getting to be a woman."

Peter looked over at Marilyn. The girls were standing together, towel drying their hair after coming out of the pool. "Sarah's is going to be a beauty, like her mother. Try not to lose this one."

"I don't know, Peter, we're from different sides of the spectrum."

"At least give it a chance, okay? And don't blow her off the first time you don't see eye to eye."

They sat there, behind their sunglasses, watching the women and the two girls. They didn't budge until Joan called out that the steaks were ready.

All of them sat around the patio table, laughing and joking about Stuart's dinner with the President, and Jessica's Senate committees.

There was a lull in the conversation into which Sarah turned to her hostess and asked, "Have you ever been to California?"

"We were in San Francisco last fall," Joan replied. "We did the whole tourist bit. Is that where you're from?"

"No, we're from around San Diego. San Francisco is up north."

"Anywhere near Arvin?" asked Joan.

"Arvin's near Bakersfield," said the girl. "We live in Carlsbad. How do you know Arvin?"

Joan looked at Peter, who answered for her, "I have a client outside of Arvin, but I think I flew into LA."

"You probably did, it's north of LA."

"Anyone want ice cream?" asked Joan, heading into the kitchen.

"I'll help," said Jessica, swinging her legs out from under the table. Standing, she gave Stuart a look. His face turned red with the realization that she had caught him staring at her legs.

The women stood in the kitchen while Joan stacked bowls onto the tray.

"Do you travel often with Peter?" Jessica asked. "More than I used to," she replied. "Peter is getting bored, he misses the excitement."

"I understand it almost got him killed," said Jessica, folding the paper napkins. How were you able to cope with his job?"

"It wasn't easy. That's why Linda left Stuart for another man." She crossed the room to the dishwasher and removed the basket of clean utensils. "I couldn't do that, so I volunteered at a shelter for battered women. I also made sure to learn all I could about baseball and football so we could talk about that when he was home. I learned to shoot a pistol, a rifle and took golf lessons. I became pretty good too with a seventeen handicap. The trick was to find things we could do together. When he was shot, I don't remember whether I was upset or relieved." Joan opened the freezer and stared at the vapor forming as the cold air hit the warmth of the day. "That's not true. I was relieved when he was shot because it meant that I wouldn't have to worry anymore. If he died, I was finished; if he lived, I was finished. The only problem was that he wasn't happy."

"How did you handle it?"

"Like I said, I made sure we did things together. I go on business trips with him, we take a lot of vacations."

"Hey in there!" The women turned and saw Peter at the door. "Where's the ice cream?"

Looking embarrassed, Joan yelled back that it was on its way.

The sun was starting to get lost behind the hills of Chevy Chase when Stuart gave Joan a kiss on the cheek and whispered, "That birthday cake was a nice touch. I think it impressed Jessica. Thank you."

"Peter thought that a picture of Jack Benny and a big thirty-nine would be fun. Now get out of here," she said, giving him a nudge. "They're waiting for you."

Stuart drove toward Jessica's home and felt wonderful. The girls were asleep in the back, and Jessica was dozing, her head leaning against the window. In fact, he couldn't remember when he had enjoyed himself like this. Maybe Peter was right, he had enough money and Jessica seemed to like him. His mind began flights of fancy. He and Jessica could take vacations like Peter and Joan, perhaps even go with them. He stared into the distance, his brow creased. "What was the name of that place they visited?" he thought aloud.

Jessica turned her head in his direction. "Did you say something?"

"I was just thinking about what a great time I had today."

"Me too," she said. She shifted closer, leaned her head against his shoulder, and was instantly asleep.

Chapter Twenty-Six

Stuart was at his desk by six thirty Monday morning. There was a message from the Cigar Store: The man with the camera was a freelance photographer who spent Sundays at the cemetery, hoping to get interesting pictures to sell. They did as thorough an investigation as possible in eight hours and he looked clean, but they would continue to check.

Stuart leaned into the chair, his feet on the desk, and he thought back to the funeral. He was going to miss her. "Dumb," he snarled, sitting upright and turning on the computer. Christine had told him she left a message in a file she started called dresser. After typing in his password to retrieve the file, he began tapping his feet in a staccato rhythm.

"What's wrong?" Sally asked, passing his office.

"I must have the slowest computer in the office," he declared. He no sooner got the words out when the screen lit up with Stuartdresser.

"Can I help?" Sally asked.

"No thanks, I think I can handle it."

"Just a feeling," was how it started. Christine's last words had a chilling effect upon him. If only he had called her when he heard her message on his machine. Leaning forward, he read the entire message:

> Just a feeling, but I think someone is looking over my shoulder. I get the impression that every phone call I make, someone is listening in. I know I might be paranoid since we clean the lines every week but . . .
>
> The people I know tell me Chilicote will not resign. He's looking for another job somewhere else in government. I've done some checking on Weaver, and here's where it gets scary. One of the people he's indebted to is Senator Daniel Conrad. The odd part is, he doesn't

come from Conrad's district. He originally comes from San Diego, where he was an assistant DA. His biggest contributor and supporter is someone named Mark Harper. I've got some questions out, but no answers yet. Harper is some kind of big shot back in California. Maybe he knows Congresswoman Winston. When I get more information, I'll call you.

Stuart sat back and stared at the screen. *Michael was right,* he thought. Christine had good instincts.

"I have some more information about the three guys you killed," announced Sally, entering his office. "Jose Flores, the one arrested for assault and battery, was convicted but given a suspended sentence . . . at the urging of an assistant district attorney in San Diego."

"Eric Weaver?"

"You must be psychic. How did you know that?"

"That's why I get paid the big bucks. What else have you found out?"

"There was one other person on both flights. I don't think he's connected with them, he's a high-powered attorney."

"What's his name?"

"Kenneth Hall."

Stuart sat for several seconds with his eyes closed before speaking. "Find out the name of his firm and see if you can get a list of his clients."

Sally stood there for a moment and then asked, "I have a couple of things I'd like to know."

"Such as?"

"What went on with that guy at the funeral?"

"And?"

"There's a story going around that they're closing up the Cigar Store."

"The guy was a freelance photographer, nothing more. As for closing up, it's because we're sudden getting high visibility. They're going to transfer everyone to either ATF or the Bureau."

"Which one are you going to?"

"Wherever I go, you'll be going with me."

Sally smiled. "That's good enough for me. Now, let's see if I can get you that information." Walking to the door, she turned. "You and the congresswoman looked very nice together yesterday." Before Stuart could respond, she closed the door behind her.

Stuart felt restless. Drawing circles on his pad, tapping his feet, glancing at the clock on his desk didn't make the feeling go away. At exactly seven fifteen, he decided that Jessica and Sarah should both be awake. As he reached for the phone, it surprised him by ringing.

"Hello," he said, a hint of annoyance in his voice as he pushed the Speaker button.

"Aren't we the grumpy one this morning." Jessica's voice came through loud and clear.

"Jessica, how nice of you to call," he was stammering, caught off guard. "I was just going to call you."

"Why?"

"Why? Well, uh, to say good morning." He stopped and composed himself. "And to thank you for yesterday."

She didn't reply for a second. When she spoke, her voice was softer. "That's why I called, to tell you that Sarah had a very nice time. It's not often that we get to go out and have fun like that."

"And what about you, did you have a very nice time as well?"

"Yes, as a matter of record, I did."

The comment widened his smile. "Where are you staying in New York this weekend?"

"We're booked into the Midtown Marriott."

"You're kidding, that's where my son and I are staying." He slid the notepad closer and quickly wrote the name of the hotel.

"Maybe we'll run into each other," said Jessica. I'm sure Sarah would love to meet Marilyn's brother."

Stuart checked his calendar. "Kenneth arrives at two thirty, and he should be in the city by seven. How about joining us for dinner? I'll make reservations at an Italian place I know."

"That would be an imposition," said Jessica. "Besides, isn't this supposed to be a bonding weekend between father and son?"

"Having you and Sarah joining us might help break the ice. You'd be doing me a favor."

"Okay, Friday night, seven thirty, in the lobby. And Stuart," she added, "thanks again for yesterday."

The moment the line went dead, Stuart hollered "Sally!" through the open door.

"What?" Appearing as if by magic, she replied.

"Were you listening in on my phone conversation?"

Sally crossed her arms and smiled impishly. "If you don't want anyone to hear what you're saying, pick up the receiver and hold it next to your ear."

"You aren't supposed to eavesdrop."

"So I guess you don't want me to make reservations at the Midtown Marriott."

Stuart shook his head and laughed. "Arriving Friday, checking out Sunday, and tell them I want two nice rooms next to each other."

In less than ten minutes, Sally stuck her head through the door and announced, "You have a two-bedroom suite at the special rate of eight ninety-five a night, which I guaranteed against your credit card. I also made reservations at an Italian restaurant called San Jaco. My husband and I ate there four months ago. You can tell her that the one you liked closed down."

"Thanks," he said, pushing back from the desk and standing. "If anyone needs me, I'll be in the audiovisual room. It's time to take another look at those bank pictures."

Chapter Twenty-Seven

Sally Kim was sorting through files in the cabinet when Eric Weaver walked through the door.

"I work right under Ray Bradley," he told her, "and I make it a point to meet all the new people. I understand you transferred over with my friend, Stuart." Having said this, he extended his hand.

Sally placed the papers face down on the desk and shook his hand. "Sally Kim," she responded. "And yes, I did."

"Kim," he repeated. "Name sounds familiar. How long have you worked with Stu?"

"Not long."

After an uncomfortably lengthy pause, Weaver asked, "Where is he?"

"Mr. Taylor had some things that needed doing. He can be reached on his cell phone. Would you like me to page him?"

"No need, thanks. I'm in charge of the task force investigating some bank robberies. Stu has some papers I need for background information. I wonder if you could let me see the files."

Sally had a perplexed expression on her face. "Mr. Taylor said that investigation was going nowhere and had me send all the files to Mr. Levitt. I'll call his secretary and have her forward them to you."

"No, that's not necessary," said Weaver. "I'll stop by Jake's office and pick them up."

"Jake?"

"I'm sorry, I forgot you're new here. Jake is Mr. Levitt's first name." Weaver took at step toward the door and turned back. "Okay if I call you Sally?"

"I'd rather you didn't. It's my experience that using first names change the business atmosphere."

Weaver stared at her, as if not quite knowing what to say. "You're right, but over here we tend to think of ourselves as family."

"I've heard that," said Sally. "Your secretary's Miriam, am I correct?"

Weaver's eyes got smaller. "What have you heard?"

"Only that she's very pretty, and she's like a member of the family. I think someone mentioned that she's a friend of your wife."

"She does a lot of things for me and my wife, so I can see why they say that." This time, Weaver moved decidedly toward the door. "In any case, welcome to the bureau. I'm sure we'll get along just fine."

Sally smiled as he left the room.

Chapter Twenty-Eight

Stuart spent two days going over the videos from the bank robberies. On late Tuesday afternoon, Ray Bradley walked into Stuart's office and found him studying charts and graphs. "My spies tell me you've been at it without a break. Find anything new?"

"I think so," said Stuart. "I've limited my search to robberies committed by two people with shotguns over the past twelve months. So far, I've found thirty-seven. After that, I narrowed it down to twenty-eight robberies where someone was waiting in a van."

"What about the shoes? Or was that just for Weaver's benefit?"

"No, that part was true. Unfortunately, not all the videos show everything. What I have been able to determine is that one of the men is about six feet tall; the second, the one with the gun cocked, is about five ten, and the woman around five six. What I haven't figured out is why they chose banks that are geographically scattered."

Bradley looked at the map and sighed. "I came down to talk to you about the change in jobs. No one has said anything to Karen Ortega, and I'm not sure who's supposed to. I haven't seen a thing in the press about Michael taking over the Bureau about this new cabinet post. Have you heard anything?"

Stuart shook his head. "But it's only been three days, right? And don't forget, I'm an outsider without a clue as to how the system works." He watched the man and sensed there was more to it than he was revealing. "Spit it out," said Stuart, turning off the video machine.

"You have a friend in Congress. Maybe you could ask her what's going on."

"You not serious."

"Something's not right, Stuart. This should be a big thing with the Congress, not to mention the media, but so far nothing. It's like the President has a different agenda, and we're not privy to it."

"Have you spoken to Jake?"

"He's in Switzerland on private business. So how about it, will you speak to Michael or the congresswoman?"

"I expect to see her Friday night, I'll ask her then. If she doesn't have the answers, I'll ask the President on Monday."

A look of relief passed across Bradley's face. "I'll leave you to your dilemma, thanks." Before Stuart could respond, he added, "You know, it could be that we're dealing with three retired people who only rob banks while they're on vacation." Bradley laughed, waved, and disappeared through the door.

Stuart stared at the space where the man had been standing. "While they're on vacation," he murmured. "Damn, why didn't I think of that?" Picking up the phone, he punched in Sally's extension.

"Sally Kim."

"It's me," he said.

"Ah, well, your closest friend in the whole world was here looking for some files on the bank robberies."

"What'd you tell him?"

"That you sent them to the director's office, and that if he wanted them, I'd be happy to get them forwarded to him."

"And he said?"

"He said he'd like to call me by my first name."

"Nice. I need you to do something."

"Will it aggravate your friend?"

"Probably."

"In that case, tell me what you want."

Stuart smiled, imagining the expression of disdain on her face. "In my desk is a list of the robberies I'm checking. On that list is also the city where each bank is located and the date of the robbery. Find the nearest big airport to each of those cities and check with car rental agencies. I'm looking for one to two days earlier than the robberies, where someone has either rented or returned a white or gray van. If you find any duplicates, any at all, have them fax you a copy of the driver's licenses or credit cards, anything you can get."

Sally was quiet and then said, "So that's why they pay you the big bucks. It may take a couple of days, but it's a stroke of genius. If I do find a name, what next?"

"Hold it for me. You probably won't get an answer until next week, and I've got some other ideas." Stuart paused for a moment, able to hear his assistant's fingers fly across the keyboard. "Anything else?" he finally asked.

"I've set up a meeting with Senator Chilicote for tomorrow morning, nine o'clock. He seemed a little hesitant until I dropped the President's name."

Stuart smiled and then asked if he had received any calls.

"No, she didn't call," said Sally. "If she does, I'll beep you."

"I wasn't talking about her specifically."

"Yeah, I know that. Like I said, if she calls, I'll beep you."

Chapter Twenty-Nine

"Why do you want to see me?" Chilicote asked, looking at his watch. "I don't have much time."

Stuart looked around the senator's office. On the walls were pictures of the man shaking hands with four past Presidents. The desk held a carafe and two glasses, but Stuart was not offered a drink. He studied the man's attire; blue shirt, red and yellow, and blue-striped tie; wide suspenders, their clips covered by new silver dollars—the consummate politician.

"Senator, I understand you're considering retiring?"

"Whoever told you that cock and bull story?" snapped Chilicote.

"I heard it during a meeting with the President."

"Well, you heard wrong. If you've got nothing else to say, I'm a busy man."

Despite the dismissal, Stuart held his ground. "You know why I'm here. Just tell me what's bothering you, and let's see if we can fix it."

Chilicote removed his glasses and rubbed his eyes. "You can't be this dumb. I agreed to see you because I thought the President was sending me a message. What do you think this is, fun and games? If you have a message to deliver, let's have it. Otherwise, get the hell out of my office."

Stuart leaned against the doorjamb, making it clear that he no intention of leaving. "What did you think the message was going to be?"

Chilicote leaned forward, his eyes narrowing. "Mr. Taylor, I know all about you: you're a professional killer working for the government. To be honest, I expected something like 'fall in line or else' with you being the *or else*."

"That's not why I'm here."

"Then maybe something to the effect that you're sleeping with a certain congresswoman, and if I don't fall in line, she's going to take my job next year."

Stuart looked around the room, thought back to the Nixon days and wondered if everyone taped all these conversations. "Senator," he finally said, "you're a sick old man. If you had half the scruples of the congresswoman, that thought wouldn't even cross your mind. Just to keep the record straight, I'm not sleeping with her. In fact, I'm a bodyguard, not a delivery boy. As for this message from the President, you'll just have to keep waiting. Trust me, you don't want me delivering anything to you." Taking one more look around the room, Stuart walked out, leaving the door open behind him.

"He just left. Never told me what he wanted, but now I know he's nothing more than a high-priced bodyguard." Smiling, the senator listened to the voice on the phone. As the conversation came to an end, a scowl crossed his face. "Of course I'm paying attention. In the next two weeks, your proposal will come up for a vote. Right now, I've got almost enough pledges to see it through. You get the President behind it, it's a shoo-in."

"Just remember," came the reply, a western twang giving it a homey quality. "I've got a lot of time and money invested in this project, and I don't want it to fail."

Before the senator could speak, the line went dead. "Someone's got to teach that boy manners," he muttered, glancing at a framed photograph of himself standing in front of the White House. "If I were fifteen years younger."

Sally was lost in airline and car rental data when the phone rang. Hearing Stuart's voice and his request for yet another favor, she grimaced. "Now I understand why the people downstairs think you're a pain in the butt. What do you need now?"

"Senator Chilicote. I need to know how much money he has in cash, how much in stocks, and which stocks. It would also be nice if I could find out how much insurance he has, whether or not he owns any property, and where it is."

"And you need this by . . ."

"Next Monday would be nice."

"Would it be too much to ask why?"

"You can ask, but I'm not so sure I know. There's something going on, but I still don't know what."

"Has this got something to do with your new job?"

"Afraid so."

"Just remember that when I move over to work in the new department, I'm getting a raise."

"I'll see what I can do. Meanwhile, get me that information."

"Mr. Gastner's office."

"Put Gastner on the phone."

"And who shall I say is calling?" asked the woman while jotting down the number shown on caller ID.

"Tell him it's Mark Harper."

The woman punched in a number. "Mr. Gastner, there's an obnoxious person on the phone demanding to talk to you."

"Did he give you his name?"

"Mark Harper."

"Tell him I'm busy."

She hit the Hold button. "Mr. Harper, Mr. Gastner is busy. Could you please? . . ."

"Tell him I'm busier and to pick up the damn phone."

"I'm sorry, sir, but he is chief of staff to the President. Please call back." Taking a deep breath, she hung up.

"You tell that flunky of the President that when I call, he responds."

"Mark, be reasonable, he's one of the busiest people in Washington."

"Then you find out what the hell is going on because it's been almost a week and nothing's happened. Has that guy Taylor been fired? Are they going to take a vote on what to do with the people I have to hire? I put a lot of money into your pockets," he went on. "What am I getting out of it?"

"Mark, I'll call you after I speak to the President." Senator Chilicote hung up the phone and glanced around his office. Taking a small phone book out of his drawer, he looked up a name and then poured himself some scotch from the carafe on his desk. After swallowing it in one gulp, he dialed Weaver's secretary. "It's me, we have to meet."

Chapter Thirty

"Ray, Stuart here. I hate leaving messages on a machine, but your secretary says you'll be out of town for the next few days. Let me make this simple. *You are right. This is Denmark.*"

"Miriam, I need your expertise. You've got to get close to Taylor and find out what's happening. The President offered him the job taking care of illegal immigrants, and he turned it down. Then the President offered to put him in charge of a new task force, one that I'm holding up by the skin of my teeth. In exchange for my support, I'm trying to get a promise to move Eric into the number two position at the bureau. There's lots of resistance. I think that either this guy or his boss, Michael Burnett, has something on the President or the chief of staff. If they offer Eric the job of feeding and transporting the people out of Mexico, I can switch my position, but I need to know the lay of the land before I do that."

"Would that be a promotion for Eric?"

"What difference does that make?"

"He's promised to leave his wife and marry me once he gets a promotion."

Senator Chilicote stared at her. "Miriam, we've been through this before. When you worked in Brightwell's office, you thought his aide was going to marry you, and now Weaver? I don't think so. I pay you two hundred thousand a year to keep me informed about what goes on in different places. Don't go get religion on me."

"I'm thirty-five years old. How much longer am I going to be able to keep getting you information? I've got to think about my future."

The senator walked over to where Miriam was sitting. With a smile, he touched her breast. "Keep these firm and your waist narrow in five years, you can retire with whomever you want."

A shudder went through her, and she moved her shoulders, knocking his hand away. "What do you need?"

"I have to know what, if anything, he has on the President. What's he working on? And is anything going on between him and Congresswoman Winston."

Miriam stood, running her hands down the sides of her skirt. "I still think Eric will marry me. But just in case, I'll see what I can do."

The senator's hand reached out to touch her again, and she took two steps away. "You know I have a soft spot in my heart for you, so how about I add an extra thousand this month and you hang around to show a little kindness to an old man?"

Miriam's eyes shimmered with unshed tears. She set her jaw to stop the shaking and walked out the door.

"I have more information about Weaver's secretary."

"Hold on, Sally, let me pull over." Stuart shifted to the soft shoulder and took out a pad. "Shoot."

"Remember when you said I'd move with you to your new job?"

"I remember, but what's that got to do with Weaver's secretary?"

"Nothing, except that she's got a little over six hundred thousand squirreled away in the Caymans."

"What?"

"I said, she has—"

"I heard what you said, but where the hell would she get that kind of money?"

"I can't wait to go with you. They must get great pay on that side of the Capitol."

Stuart put the pad on the passenger seat and pulled back onto the road. "Very funny. Now go see if you can tap into those accounts and find out where her money comes from."

"You know how they are down there, they don't give out spit."

"Just see what you can do. Oh, and call Michael and tell him I'm coming by this afternoon."

"Michael's in Europe."

"Doing what?"

"Haven't got the slightest, he doesn't report to me."

"You have ways of finding out."

"Probably."

"So find out."

"Give me an hour."

"Okay, anything else going on?"

"No, she hasn't called. I told you I'd let you know if she does."

"I wasn't asking about her."

"Oh, so sorry, my mistake."

"This'd better be a good restaurant you're sending me to tomorrow night."

"Or?"

"Or I'll tell Weaver that you have a thing for him and he should try harder." The little shriek on the other end of the line made him smile.

"I've got to go," said Sally. "This to-do list gets longer every time you call." She chuckled as she hung up.

Less than thirty seconds later, her phone rang again. "Mr. Taylor's office, Sally speaking."

"Sally, this is Miriam, Eric Weaver's secretary. I have to speak to Mr. Taylor."

"He's not in right now. Is there something I can do for you?"

"Yes, please contact him and tell him I need to speak to him immediately. It's very important."

"Where can he reach you?"

"I'll be in my office for the next hour. If you can't reach him by then, it might not matter. And, Sally, can't we be friends? I've always gotten along with Chinese people."

"The next time I see one, I'll tell them to give you a call. My parents were born in Korea."

"Stuart, Weaver's secretary just called and says it's urgent. Her exact words were, 'I'll be in my office for the next hour. If you can't reach him by then, it might not matter.'"

"Where does she want me to contact her? It's almost four o'clock."

"She's in her office, extension four-four-zero-seven."

"Miriam? Stuart Taylor returning your call."

"Thank you for calling back so promptly. I must talk to you about some things that are going on around here."

"Such as?"

"Not over the phone. Can you meet me in about two hours?"

"Why don't you go to Eric?"

"Eric's too nice a person. I don't think he's up to doing what I think needs to be done."

"Give me a second." Stuart studied the landscape out of his car window. "Okay, meet me at the front gate of the zoo at six fifteen."

"At the zoo? Why not a restaurant or one of the hotels?"

"I'm in the middle of an investigation, and the only place I can get to and be secure is the zoo."

"I thought you were relieved of the bank robberies?"

"I have other cases." In the ensuing silence, Stuart was positive that she was waiting to hear about the other cases.

"All right," she said. "In front of the main entrance of the zoo, six fifteen." Miriam looked up and saw Eric Weaver standing at her desk. "He's going to meet me," she told him, "but he insists on the zoo."

"Find out what other cases he's working on. My records don't show him doing anything else."

"Where can I get in touch with you later?" she asked as he started to leave.

"It'll have to wait until tomorrow. I have to take my wife to the Kennedy Center tonight."

Miriam watched him leave without a backward glance. Biting her lower lip, she picked up the phone and dialed a number. When the answering machine started, she said, "He's meeting me in front of the zoo at six fifteen tonight."

Chapter Thirty-One

"This is the Cigar Store. Please repeat the following numbers for a voice check. One, three, nine."

"One, three, nine." came the response.

"Your name is?"

"Stuart Taylor."

"What can we do for you?"

"I'm on my way to a six-fifteen meeting in front of the zoo. I want you to arrange backup if it's needed."

"How will we know?"

"The woman I'm meeting works at the Bureau. If anyone besides her shows up, come running."

"Will do. You sound a little strange, Stuart, is everything alright?"

"I'm just a little nervous. I've been working on this case a long time."

"Cigar Store out."

"Listen, everyone, we've been compromised. Close down now. Contact the four agents in the field and give them backup numbers to call. I want this place to look like a morgue in fifteen minutes."

The agent in charge placed a call to Michael Burnett. After a series of cutouts, he was routed to Burnett's cell phone in Switzerland.

"Burnett, here."

"Mr. Burnett, I'm closing down the Cigar Store, we've been compromised."

"Which agent?"

"Taylor."

"It figures. You're moving to location B?"

"No, location N. It'll take a while longer, but it'll be safer."

"Do what you have to, I'm still three days from getting home."

"I know how to reach you. I'm going to try and find Taylor."

"Do your best to keep him safe," said Michael, and then closed his cell phone.

"Sally, this is the Cigar Store. Can you do a voice check for me?"

"Go ahead."

"Seven, eight, nine."

"Ninety-six," Sally replied after multiplying the number by four.

"Your name is?"

"Sally Kim."

"Find Stuart. We keep getting a busy signal on his cell phone. Someone called in using his name but didn't know about the voice check. Whoever it was requested backup at the zoo at six fifteen."

"That's when he's supposed to meet someone there."

"The caller said a woman and not to move in unless other people showed up."

"What other people?"

"Don't know. When and if you find him, tell him we've moved and to use the N phone number."

"Will you have help standing by?"

"Yes, but not at the zoo. We don't respond to strange calls."

Sally listened to the busy signal on Stuart's phone. Frustrated, she dialed his car phone and left a message. She paced back and forth, glancing out the window for perhaps the tenth time in the last five minutes. Finally, she put the palms of her hands against the pane and looked down. After a few seconds, she said, "Why not?"

Sally took the elevator from the sixth floor, where her office was, down to the fourth floor. Walking down the long hallway, she came to room 4407. The door was open, and she entered without knocking.

"Miriam, I decided you were right, we should become friends."

Weaver's secretary stood and looked at Sally. She was taller than Sally remembered and was wearing very expensive clothes. "I'm surprised to see you," said Miriam, glancing at her watch. "I thought you went home at four thirty."

"Sometimes I do," said Sally. "But tonight's special. My husband's giving a lecture over at Johns Hopkins, Stuart has a meeting, and something came up that I felt you and I had to talk about."

"What was that?" Miriam asked.

"Not here. Let's go downstairs where it's a little more private."

Miriam frowned. "I have an appointment in about an hour."

"This'll only take five or ten minutes."

Miriam shrugged and followed Sally to the elevator. When they reached the bottom floor, Sally led the way to a bench a good distance from the front door.

"I know you're supposed to meet Stuart at the zoo at six fifteen. What I don't know is who else knows about the meeting."

"What does that mean?" Miriam asked.

"That means someone else knows and is arranging for something bad to happen. I don't know if the something bad is to you or to Stuart."

"I don't believe you."

"Keep your voice down," Sally admonished. "Right now, this is between you and me. If anything goes wrong, it'll be between you and the attorney general, when he puts you away."

"Eric would never let that happen." Her words were devoid of conviction. "Is Weaver the one who knows?"

"I don't have to tell you anything," replied Miriam. "Eric is going to be the next assistant director of the FBI, and he'll take care of me."

"If something happens to Stuart, I will personally make sure that the attorney general puts you away for life."

An expression crossed Miriam's face that resembled a smirk. "Nothing's going to happen. And if you don't believe me, come with me and you'll see."

"Were you planning on driving?"

"I'm taking a taxi and having Stuart drive me home."

"What makes you think he'd do that?"

Miriam put her hand on her hip and looked at Sally as if she were from another planet. "I'm pretty good at getting men to do what I ask."

Sally stared at Miriam and then shrugged. "We'll take my car. That way, if you're as good as you think you are, I'll have a way home."

"And if I'm not?" Miriam asked, the smirk returning.

"I'll drop you at a bus stop."

"Senator, you've had me on the phone for over an hour."

"Mr. Taylor, I'm a busy man. My phone at the end of the day never seems to stop ringing. I'm willing to meet with you again tomorrow afternoon, around four thirty."

"Sorry, Senator, but by then I'll be on my way to meet my son."

"Oh? And where's your son?"

"He's in New Hampshire. If you've done your homework, you know that I've been divorced for fifteen years. This is our first real chance to, I think the word is *bond*."

"New Hampshire? Tell you what; let's schedule the meeting for Monday night at Papillion's, around six thirty. You know where it is?"

"I've been there, and I'm looking forward to meeting you."

Turning up the volume on his car radio, Stuart reflected on the conversation. Aside from constantly being put on hold, the tone was cordial, almost to the point that he sensed something else was going on at the same time. The senator had just maneuvered him into having dinner after his meeting with the President. Stuart had to admit that Chilicote was good, maybe even a good man to have on the team. The ringing phone startled him. "Stuart."

"Who have you been you talking to?"

"Why?" Stuart replied to Sally's question.

"You've been compromised. The Cigar Store closed shop, and they're moving to N location."

"What do you mean, I've been compromised?"

"Someone called in and asked for backup at the zoo. The store was told not to do anything but watch unless you called. I'll be with Miriam when she meets you there, and I think she's told Weaver."

"Why didn't you call earlier?"

"I tried, but your line's been busy, and they've shut down your cell phone."

"Shit, I just spent the hour chatting with Chilicote. I wouldn't put it past him to try to keep me tied up."

"Here comes Miriam, I have to go."

"Sally, don't get out of the car. Sally, answer me."

Chapter Thirty-Two

Stuart put the car into drive and pressed the pedal to the floor. The tires squealed as he pulled away from the curb and headed toward the zoo. Reaching onto the floor behind him, his hand found the emergency flasher. "Today, I am a policeman," he said as he applied it to the roof of the car. Other cars immediately moved out of his way. Racing ahead, his car phone rang again.

"Sally, did you hear what I said?" he shouted.

"Who's Sally," asked Jessica. "And why are you yelling?"

"Jessica, I'm sorry. I thought it was my secretary."

"What did she do, forget to put sugar in your coffee?"

"No, we got cut off in the middle of a conversation. How are you?"

"I'm fine, thanks for asking."

Was that sarcasm he detected in her voice?

"The reason I called is that I'm flying to New York around two thirty and wondered what time you were heading up."

"I don't know. I haven't made reservations yet."

There was a strange silence, and Stuart wondered what he said wrong.

Jessica finally said, "I'll see you in the lobby at seven thirty" and then hung up.

Stuart hit the brakes, barely missing a car, and turned onto the drive leading to the zoo. The phone rang again.

"This is Stuart."

"I'm glad you answered the phone, I was beginning to worry."

"Mom, what are you worrying about?"

"You forgot that you were supposed to take me to dinner tonight?"

"Today's Thursday?"

"Today's Thursday. Does this mean we're not going to dinner?"

"Mom, I'll call you later. I'm in the middle of something."

"When you call me, aside from the story about this woman you're dating, I'd really like to go into what you do for a living."

"Later, Mom, I have to go."

Stuart pulled into the zoo's parking lot and walked to the entrance. There were very few cars still parked there, and as far as he could tell, they were empty. He took up a position against the fence, in the shadows, and waited. At six ten, he saw Sally's car pulled into the parking lot and parked five rows from the entrance. As the door opened on the driver's side, he stepped out from the shadow and commanded, "Don't get out of the car."

The passenger door opened, and he sprinted toward the car. "Stay inside!" he shouted just as the front window erupted, sending glass everywhere. Stuart turned just as one of the cars parked in the next aisle sped out of the parking lot. He watched a van move to block the speeding car's exit. Three men jumped out of the back of the van and started shooting at the moving car, which then turned and headed back toward Stuart. He pulled his pistol. Before he could get off a shot, the front tire of the car was hit, sending it into a skid. It didn't come to a stop until it slammed into a parked car. Both doors flew open as two gunmen, one from each side, came out of the vehicle firing. They both fell in the hail of bullets coming from the van. The three men started walking to where the men laid on the ground.

Stuart was amazed that, with all the shooting, no one from inside the zoo, not even the animals, were making a sound.

"Help me," Sally called, breaking the reverie.

Stuart ran over to her car. "Are you hurt?"

"I have a piece of glass in my arm, nothing serious, but Miriam's a mess."

Stuart looked into the car and saw that Weaver's secretary was bleeding from a dozen small lacerations on her face and neck. "Can you see?" he asked.

"Of course I can see, it's my face that's bleeding."

"Get out of the car, we'll take you to a doctor."

One of the men from the van was standing behind Stuart. "Why don't you take her, we'll watch Sally and clean up this mess."

Stuart nodded and held his hand out for Miriam. She climbed shakily from the car, took one step, and stumbled into his arms. As he supported her, she looked over his shoulder at Sally and winked.

Chapter Thirty-Three

"Where are you taking me?" Miriam asked, using a paper tissue and spit to clean her face.

"There's a twenty-four-hour emergency center three exits down the beltway."

"Do you think I'll have scars?"

"You're lucky you're not dead. Who did you tell about the meeting?"

"I didn't tell anyone. You must have told somebody."

"Miriam, whoever you told tried to kill you. Let me try and help you."

"Maybe they wanted to kill you?"

"Then they would have shot at me. Think about it: they wanted you dead and me blamed for it, or somehow involved." Stuart pulled into the lane leading to the entrance of the emergency room.

Miriam stared straight ahead jaw set, as she considered Stuart's analysis. "Maybe you're right, I don't know." She looked at the building. "This doesn't look like a very good hospital."

"Shows you how looks can be deceiving." He stopped at the curb adjacent to the front door, in the no parking zone.

At the front desk they were greeted by the on-duty physician. "Your secretary called and said to expect you," he said. "You're to give her a call when you're free."

Stuart nodded his thanks. "Where are you taking her?" he asked, gesturing toward Miriam.

"Room 3. You can wait in my office."

"No, I want Stuart with me," Miriam said, her eyes becoming larger. "I don't like operating rooms."

"This isn't an operating room, it's just, . . ."

"I don't care, I want him with me."

Stuart exchanged glances with the doctor and reminded himself to be pleasant. "I'll be there in a second, okay? I want to check on Sally."

Miriam ran her tongue over her lips. "Don't be long."

The doctor helped her into a wheelchair and proceeded to push her down the hall.

Stuart found a corner, pulled out his cell phone, and called Sally. "What's going on?"

"The dead men have no identification, and it's a rented car. The police are here asking questions. What's the party line?"

"We're FBI on the trail of terrorists. One of our agents was shot and transported to a hospital, not this one, and died on the way. Tell them we'll provide the agent's name after we notify next of kin."

"And if they won't buy it?"

"Throw out Jake's name. He's in Europe and can't be questioned. How's your arm?"

"A little sore, but Dennis took the piece of glass out and bandaged it. How's Miriam?"

"She'll be fine. She's getting looked at now." Stuart watched an ambulance pull up, and noted how the pace quickened around him. "On second thought, see if you can get the locals to push for the name of the dead agent, and then give them Miriam's name. Call Weaver and give him the news. Tell him the story we made up, I'm sure he'll understand."

"You're as bad as that guy in ancient history, Machiavelli, or something."

"I'll take that as a compliment. By the way, take tomorrow off. And, Sally, thanks." He closed the cell phone and reflected on how his relationship with Sally was in so many ways like the one he had with Christine, only different.

Stuart entered the treatment room and stopped short. Miriam was perched on the bed, her blouse and brassiere lying beside her, the blue hospital gown draped over her shoulders. The doctor was standing knee to knee with her, peering at her face through a large magnifying glass illuminated by a halo light.

"This shouldn't hurt," he said, holding a pair of tweezers.

Stuart started to back out, but Miriam saw him and called his name.

"Don't leave, please," she said. "Come hold my hand, I'm a little nervous."

When Stuart didn't move, she asked, "Have you called Eric yet?"

"Sit still," ordered the doctor, glancing at Stuart.

"That's not part of my job," said Stuart. "Sally is calling him."

She smiled. "I like that in a man, someone who has his subordinates do the work. Come hold my hand."

Stuart approached her but did not take her outstretched hand. "We still have some important things to discuss."

"I know," she said, and then asked the doctor how much longer he would be.

"Much longer," he replied, "unless you sit still and keep quiet."

"Ouch!" she complained, reaching for Stuart.

"One more to go," murmured the doctor, dabbing at her forehead with cotton. Miriam pulled Stuart's hand until it rested on her lap. Closing her eyes, she said, "Don't hurt me."

The doctor looked at her, smiled at Stuart, and replied, "Don't worry, we won't let anything happen to you."

Twenty minutes later, as they entered Stuart's car, Miriam asked, "Where are you taking me now?"

"Home."

"Yours or mine?"

"Yours."

"That's okay, I have some very good scotch there."

"Miriam, maybe you don't understand the predicament you're in. You call me and set up an appointment so you can tell me some cock and bull story about something going on inside the department. You then tell your boss, and two guys show up to kill you. It sounds like you know something you shouldn't."

"Did it ever occur to you that they were after you, not me?"

Stuart noted how her comment came much too quickly. "I'll tell you what has occurred to me, and that is it was a setup. You were supposed to be killed, and I was going to be implicated. It didn't matter if I was convicted or not, implication was all that was needed; the Washington rumor mill would take care of the rest. I can see the headlines: FBI Agent with License to Kill Involved with Secretary's Murder. My usefulness would be finished, your friend Eric would become the new assistant director, but you would be dead."

"Eric would never let that happen."

"Don't tell me you believe that he loves you?"

She moved farther away and did not answer his barb.

"Miriam, do you think for one second that no one knows about your lunchtime meetings on the fourteenth floor of the Hyatt, or your bank account in the Caymans? Do you think no one's followed your career moves from Nebraska to working for Weaver? There's a file on you so thick that someone could write a book." The woman's face took on three or four different expressions, shifting from anger to surprise, and then concern. Through all of them, there was accompanying confusion.

Stuart knew he had her on the ropes. "Eric's been under investigation for over three months, and the only reason he's still walking around free is that we're trying to find his contact. I think you know who that person is, which is why they wanted to kill two birds with one killing: yours. That way, they'd be rid of you and the investigation would stop." He stopped the car in front of her apartment. "You can get out and go about your business, or you can be smart and let us put you in hiding. You have my word that you'll never have to testify against anyone. We've already told the TV, radio, and newspapers that you're dead. If you decide not to help us, that story will only be twenty-four hours premature."

Miriam sat looking out the window, fingers gripping the door handle. She inhaled, threw her shoulders back, and turned toward Stuart. There was a smile on her face. "You would be watching over me, right?"

"No, not right, we have special people to do that, but I'll make sure you got the protection and end up wherever in the world you want. But you won't see me again, and it's for your own protection."

"What about tonight? I don't want to be alone."

"If you agree to help us, I'll have two people here inside thirty minutes. They'll help you pack, and you'll be gone in an hour."

She reached out and touched his arm. "That means we have thirty minutes, let's get upstairs."

Stuart smiled. "I have to make one call."

Chapter Thirty-Four

"This is the Marlboro man, how may I help you?"

Station M meant that all calls were answered with the letter M, and all agents replied in kind.

"This is Captain Midnight," Stuart answered. "Did you find out where the phone call came from that used my name?"

"A phone booth on Interstate 5, in San Juan Capistrano."

"What about those guys at the zoo?"

"Both clean, but the car was a rental. We're checking it out now."

"How's Sally?"

"They gave her a tetanus shot and sent her home." The voice on the other end chuckled. "She asked us to keep an eye on you; she thinks you're in a fish tank with a barracuda."

Stuart smiled. "She's probably right. Meanwhile, the barracuda has agreed to talk to us. All we have to do is make sure she gets to somewhere of her choosing and with no strings attached."

"We'll have to get authorization for that."

"Get it. Meanwhile, send a team to her apartment. You have the address?"

"What if the boss says no deal?"

"After I have the name, I don't give a shit."

"I'll find the boss and let him know what's going on."

"Where is he?"

"Need-to-know basis, and no one needs to know."

"Will he be back by Monday?"

"Yeah he'll . . . , who said he was away?"

"You did, but that's okay, I won't tell, as long as you get those people to her apartment posthaste."

"I'll do my best."

Stuart took the stairs to the porch two at a time. He pressed the button and pushed the front door open when he heard the buzzer. Miriam lived on the first floor of a three-story brownstone walk-up. Her door was ajar, but he knocked anyway, just in case.

"It's open," she yelled from somewhere in the back.

Stuart pushed open the door and looked around. The room was a cross between a living room and a den. There was no permanent wall separating the spaces; this was accomplished with an étagère that was over six feet high and four feet long. The living room area had a sofa, two chairs, floor-to-ceiling drapes, and an off-white Berber carpet. The den area had light hardwood floors, a large television, and leather sofa and chairs. Nothing fancy, but certainly livable. "I'm in here," called out Miriam.

"Where's that drink?" he called back.

Miriam appeared wearing a camisole that draped down to her thighs and high-heeled shoes. She picked up what looked like a television remote control, pushed a button, and a bar slid out from the wall separating the den and the kitchen. "Help yourself and pour me whatever you're having."

Stuart was pouring two drinks when she beckoned him from down the hall to bring the drinks.

"Why don't you come out here and we can talk," he responded.

She appeared again, this time without shoes. "We only have twenty minutes," she announced, a smile on her face. "And I don't like being hurried."

"Telling me the name I need will only take twenty seconds," replied Stuart, handing her the drink.

She sat down on the sofa, curling both feet under her and making it obvious that she was wearing nothing under that camisole.

Stuart watched her but kept his distance.

"Sit next to me," she whispered, taking a sip of the drink.

"The name first," he replied, wetting his lips with the scotch.

"I'm still not sure I should do this. Eric's been pretty good to me over the years."

"Miriam, the name!"

She ran her fingers up the side of her leg, leaving white marks on her bronze skin. She glanced up at Stuart and said quickly, "Chilicote, Senator Chilicote." Once the name was out of her mouth, the story came quickly. "He was a guest lecturer at the junior college I was attending in Nebraska. I was chosen to take him back to his hotel after his talk. It was snowing and he asked me if I would join him for something to eat. He said he hadn't eaten before the meeting, and I thought it would be exciting having dinner with a senator. It was. After a couple of drinks we went up to his suite. It was one of the largest hotel rooms I had ever seen. He told me to pour myself a drink while he called the President." She stopped and looked at Stuart.

"Did he?" Stuart asked the question because he knew he was supposed to.

"He spoke to someone he said was the President. I was never so impressed with anyone in my whole life. After his call, I remember saying that the snow was getting thick on the ground, and the next thing I knew, we were in bed. The next day, he asked me to come back to Washington. He knew a congressman from Nebraska who was looking for an intern and believed I'd fill the bill. He offered me a job that paid twenty-five thousand a year, off the books, reporting back to him on things the congressman was doing. The congressman had an aide that I became sort of close to." She glanced up to see Stuart's reaction. "Actually, more than a little close. I thought we were going to get married, but he changed his mind. I told my problem to Senator Chilicote, and he got me a job working for the bureau. Two years later, I became Eric's secretary." She took a sip of the scotch, the first since she had started talking. "We've become close. In fact, when he gets promoted, he's going to leave his wife for me." She stopped talking, and a tear appeared on her cheek. "I don't care what the senator thinks, he'll marry me." Her voice had become stronger.

"Did the senator give you cash or checks?"

"Always cash. He suggested that I open an account in the Cayman Islands, and he said that no one would ever be able to find it." Again, she stopped and looked at the ceiling. "Somehow, you did."

There was a knock on the door, and Stuart asked who was there. When the response was "Mickey and Minnie," he opened the door, and the two agents walked in.

"Get her somewhere safe," he told them. "And keep her off the phone." Turning back to Miriam, he said, "I have to go somewhere tomorrow. These two agents will look after you until I return on Monday or Tuesday. Don't give them a hard time, and remember that you're supposed to be dead."

Chapter Thirty-Five

It was ten minutes after midnight when Stuart walked into his den and saw the light blinking on the telephone. He pushed the button, heard the voice, and smiled.

"Hi, it's Jessica. Wanted to apologize for my rudeness on the phone earlier. Heard the news about the agent being killed, and I realize now why you seemed so distracted. Sarah and I will be on the two thirty to JFK, and I've arranged for a limo to drive us into the city. If you're arriving any time near us," she hesitated, and then added, "call me and we can drive into the city together."

Stuart smiled again, strange how the sound of her voice conjured up visions of good times. There was another message, this one from his son.

"Hi, Dad. How does that sound? I've been practicing, and I think it sounds better than Father. Marilyn called me, said I'm going to meet her friend, Sarah. She wants me to behave. Sarah is supposed to be hot. I think the real reason for her call was to tell me to call her and let her know how the weekend goes. She didn't sound as upset with our meeting as she was when she first heard about it. Have you seen her lately? I'll see you tomorrow. My plane is supposed to arrive at two forty-four. I'll take a taxi into the city. Meet you in the hotel, bye."

Stuart heard in his son's voice the same hesitation he felt when leaving messages on a phone. Logging on to the Internet, he found both flights. According to the screen, they would be landing only three gates apart. There were no open seats on Jessica's plane, but there were some first-class tickets on the flight that left an hour earlier. Stuart reserved one of those seats and left his return flight open. He placed a call to the Cigar Store, regulations being that he had to advise them of any planned trip.

"This is the Marlboro man."

"Captain Midnight calling in."

"Don't you ever sleep?"

"Give me five minutes. I just wanted you to know that my plane leaves at one thirty tomorrow. I haven't made return arrangements yet."

"I already booked you on the seven fifteen; you would've gotten your wake-up call at five thirty. You have an eight thirty meeting in the Admirals Club at JFK. You have your card?"

"I have it. Who's the meeting with?"

"The boss is landing at eight ten, and he'll meet you at the club. We've reserved a conference room from eight to noon."

"Just the two of us?"

"Don't know. I was told to reserve the room and tell you to be there."

Stuart looked at his watch. "It's twelve twenty. How about making me a reservation at the Holiday Inn at JFK and tell the company jet to stand by. I'll be at National in fifty minutes, which gives me an hour of sleep on the plane and another five at the hotel. It's been a long day."

"Consider it done. Have a good time, and oh yes, be careful. The last part is from Sally. She's more than a little worried about you."

It took Stuart less than ten minutes to pack, and since he was taking the company jet, there was no need to break down his weapon and hide it in his luggage. He put the red light back on top of the car and broke every speed limit while driving to the airport. There was a company parking lot with valet parking where he gave the attendant his estimated time of return and his ID number. After his trip, the car would be filled with gas and freshly washed. It was one of the perks of the job.

The engines had already started as Stuart ran across the tarmac to the waiting plane. He was the only passenger on the Boeing 727 with two stewards. He no sooner sat down when the plane started down the runway.

"You better put on your seat belt. Seth isn't happy, and he's not waiting around for introductions," shouted the taller of the stewards above the roar of the plane as it headed down the runway.

"What's he pissed about?" Stuart yelled back as the plane left the ground.

The two stewards looked at each other and smiled. The smaller one answered, "Usually there's a steward and a stewardess on each flight. Tonight, Seth talked Marie into dinner and a movie at his place. Your request came through just as the movie was over, which means he's now piloting the plane, and she's sleeping in his bed, alone."

"Tell Seth to book a table at any restaurant he likes in New York, and I'll pick up the bill for him and the sweet Marie. Wake me when we're on the ground." Stuart was asleep before the plane banked to the left and headed to New York and remained in a deep sleep until someone shook him awake.

"We're on the ground," said the man. "I hear that airport security sent one of their cars to take you wherever you need to go."

"Who are you?" Stuart asked.

"My name's Seth Roberts, I'm the pilot. I hope the flight was smooth enough."

"It was, and I understand I may have ruined your night."

"Actually, it was the weekend, but maybe she'll give me another chance."

"Flying with you leaves me with an unused ticket. Why don't you give her a call and get her on the first plane in the morning? I'll pay for the ticket, the hotel room, and dinner."

"That's okay," said Seth, waving his hand. "On second thought, maybe it's a good idea, I'll give it a try."

Stuart stood and stretched. "Seth, how'd you like to work for another department?"

"Which one?"

"It's just forming, but I like you, and your being on board would be a plus."

"I'd love to talk to you about it when you're ready," the pilot said, stepping back to let Stuart pass.

The June night air was cold, and Stuart closed his jacket before walking down the steps of the plane. The airport police vehicle was waiting at the bottom with two uniformed police standing by the doors. As he reached the tarmac, one of them opened the rear door and said, "If you're Mr. Midnight, we're told to bring you to the International Hotel."

"By who?" Stuart asked.

"He said his name was Marlboro."

"Then the International it is."

The International Hotel, being located at the entrance to JFK, took less than five minutes to reach. As he checked in, Stuart was given a message to call a Mr. Marlboro from the front desk.

"This is Mr. Midnight, you have a message for me?"

"In thirty seconds, I will start transmitting four pages that you must read prior to your meeting tomorrow. Please stand at the fax machine to receive the transmission."

"Where's your fax machine?" Stuart asked as he hung up the phone.

"It's in the back room, but there were no faxes for you."

"The machine will go on in less than fifteen seconds, and I must be standing there when it does."

"I'm sorry, sir, but no one is allowed back there."

Stuart took out his FBI card. "I am."

The clerk's forehead wrinkled with concern. He had never seen an FBI card and wasn't sure what to do. "I'll call the night manager," he replied.

"No time for that," said Stuart as he put both palms on the counter and jumped over. Walking past the surprised clerk, he continued into the adjoining room and arrived just as the machine began spitting out paper. Taking the four sheets, he walked back out and asked, "Where is my room key?"

Locking the door behind him and leaving a wake-up call for seven, Stuart scanned the four pages. They were from Michael and supplied the background information he'd need at the meeting. There were no marks to help him ascertain where Michael was or who would be at the meeting. Glancing at the clock on the bedside table, he realized that he was now down to four hours' sleep . . . he hoped.

The phone rang at seven, interrupting a night's sleep from hell. Stuart had dreamt of his mother, his son, his daughter, and his ex-wife; and those were the good parts. After acknowledging the wake-up call, he sat with his feet dangling off the side of the bed, rubbed his eyes and yawned. He grabbed the TV remote off the nightstand and turned on the news. Four Israelis had died when a terrorist blew himself to bits at a bus stop. Israel was screaming for retaliation. As yet, no one had stepped forward to claim responsibility.

There were two other stories, one from Mexico and the other from Canada, followed by a picture of Jake Levitt, photographed while boarding a plane in Switzerland. The announcer said he had visited one of the country's famous clinics for cancer treatment, and that the plane was due to land in Washington at eight fifteen, and further news would be forthcoming. Stuart did some calculating and realized that Jake was scheduled to arrive an hour and fifteen minutes later than that flight normally took. *I wonder where he's really getting off that plane,* Stuart mused, stretching before his exercises.

Chapter Thirty-Six

After twenty minutes of sit-ups and push-ups, Stuart stood under a steaming shower, his thoughts focused on the information in the four-page memo. The Israelis were positive there was a Saudi-based terrorist group of Pakistanis located either in Pakistan or across the border in Afghanistan. It was also believed this group was planning acts of terrorism that defied logic. The problem faced by the Israelis was getting infiltrating and finding out. They had approached the United States and Great Britain, hoping to find assets in place that they could use. Michael had accompanied Jake to Europe to attend the meeting, along with Brett Daniels, the head of the British Terrorist Response Team. Stuart had met Brett three years earlier when a drug dealer he was tracking turned out to have connections to a wing of the IRA. He remembered Daniels as a no-nonsense guy when it came to terrorist activities. He stood a shade under six feet, had jet-black hair, was a little heavy across the chest, and a very sloppy dresser, which Stuart remembered because it seemed out of character for a Brit.

Stuart looked out the window on the eleventh floor, the June morning showing all the makings of a beautiful day in the Big Apple. The eight o'clock news was just starting, which galvanized him into action. He had twenty minutes to reach the Admirals Club if he wanted to arrive at least ten minutes before the meeting started.

Just as he left his room, he heard the elevator stop on his floor and saw a man enter. Hollering for him to hold the door, he sprinted the last ten yards and stepped into the mirrored space.

"Thanks," he said, the door closing behind him. The man nodded, and for an instant, Stuart thought he looked familiar. He positioned himself with his back against the wall and realized that something about this stranger bothered him. He had unruly blonde hair and thick-rimmed glasses. He was well dressed, wearing a three-piece gray suit with a pale blue button-down shirt.

The elevator stopped on the sixth floor, and two women entered. The man with the glasses looked at their legs and smiled. At that instant, Stuart knew that he was looking at Brett Daniels in disguise. By the time the elevator made two more stops and arrived at the first floor, Stuart was no longer sure if the Brett Daniels he had known in the past was the disguise, or this one. The two women exited first with Stuart holding back until the top antiterrorist expert in England exited the car.

After a few seconds, the man said, "They did have nice legs. So are we going to stand here all day, or are we going to the meeting?"

"I have a car waiting," Stuart replied, following Daniels out. "When did you arrive?"

"About twenty minutes after you."

"So you beat Jake by almost five hours."

"I took the Concorde; I didn't want to be seen with Jake." They walked to the front door. At the curb sat a waiting taxi, the sign in its window saying, Mr. Stuart Taylor. No words were exchanged during the ten-minute ride to the American Airlines domestic terminal. Entering the building, Stuart led the way to the escalator. When they reached the second floor, Daniels walked into a bookstore and bought a newspaper.

Stuart walked half the length of the corridor to the Admirals Club with Daniels hanging back to be sure that no one was following. Convinced, he proceeded through the same door.

There were four hostesses seated behind the waist-high counter. The one on the far left asked, "May I help you?"

Daniels took a ticket from his pocket and handed it to her.

"The one o'clock flight to Los Angeles will start boarding at twelve thirty, sir. I suggest you start down a little early, it's a full flight."

Daniels nodded, took his ticket, and walked into the main waiting area. When Stuart entered a room at the far end of the club, the Brit sat down in a lounge chair and got comfortable. Less than five minutes later, the two women from the elevator entered the club, took a cup of coffee, and sat down near Daniels. He made brief eye contact with each of them and then rose, crossed the room, and joined Stuart in the conference room.

Stuart was seated at the long, burl wood table. Stirring his coffee, he looked up at Daniels and asked, "Your two playmates get here okay?"

"You still don't miss much, do you?"

"Aside from nice legs, one of them has a nice butt; and if you look closely, which I did, you'll see the outline of a small caliber gun."

"I'll bring it to her attention," he replied, walking over to Stuart and extending his hand. "Long time no see, I understand you just had a birthday."

"It's been about five years," responded Stuart, "and I'm not discussing birthdays, thank you. What brings you to our side of the pond?"

"Let's wait for the others to arrive before we get into world events." Daniels waved his hand in a circle, which Stuart understood immediately. "I hear you're dating a congresswoman. Anything serious?"

Stuart grimaced. "Word sure gets around," he groused. "Not serious, I think, but we only met two weeks ago, and most of our contact has been business related. I'm seeing her this weekend, but our kids will be with us."

The door opened, and Michael entered with Jake Levitt close behind. Jake held up a hand, looked around the room, and then stepped aside for two men carrying scanning devices. No one said a word as they covered the room, waving wands in all directions. "Clean," one of them announced, and they both walked out.

"Have a nice trip?" Stuart asked, looking at Jake and Michael. "Had to change planes during an unscheduled stop in Newfoundland," replied Michael. "Aside from that, it wasn't bad. You two bring each other up to date?"

"Not really," Daniels answered. "We only arrived a short time ago and decided to hold conversation until you a got here and the room was swept."

Stuart looked at the others. "Is this everyone?"

Jake shook his head. "We're waiting for Marc Frankel, Jose Vargas, and Bill Cook."

The names were familiar to Stuart. Marc Frankel was with Israeli intelligence, Bill Cook was with the Royal Canadian Mounties, and Jose Vargas ran security for Mexico. Stuart had met Vargas fifteen years earlier on another case.

The door opened, and the three men entered. Marc smiled at the group and gestured toward the waiting area. "It's starting to look like a spooks convention out there."

Before anyone could answer, Michael's cell phone rang. He turned his back on everyone, said a few words, and hung up. "We're all set," he told them. "Brett, you have two agents, both women. Marc, you've got a family traveling together: father, mother, twenty-one-year-old son, his wife, and their two-year-old child." Turning to Jose, he continued, "You've got two men who look like they're in a rodeo. Bill, the two men in military uniform are yours. If I've covered it all, we can get started." He scanned the faces as if making sure that everyone understood whose meeting it was, and then walked over and poured himself some coffee. "Anybody want something before we start?"

Stuart looked at his watch and saw that it was exactly eight thirty. It took another two or three minutes for everyone to get comfortable before Jake began to speak.

"Just so we're all singing off the same song sheet," he said, "let me reiterate why we're all here. Marc's people are positive that there's a group of terrorists close to unleashing some of the worst acts of violence we've ever seen. They think they're located either in Pakistan or Afghanistan with ties to Saudi Arabia or Iraq." Jake turned and nodded to the Israeli. "Marc, why don't you tell the group the whys and wherefores?"

Marc Frankel stood, his tan sports jacket and dark brown slacks a perfect complement to his olive-toned skin. It struck Stuart that this man could pass for someone from any country in the Middle East. The fact that he was fluent in three or four Arab dialects, along with Italian and Greek, added to his ability to blend in.

"Three weeks ago," Marc began, "in a sweep outside of Hebron, our people came upon an Irishman who, unfortunately, decided he didn't want to be taken alive."

Brett Daniels interrupted, "They contacted us, picture included. His name is or was Robert Tylor, and he's been on our Most Wanted list for over five years. We had no idea he was in the Middle East."

"Anyway," Marc continued, "thanks to papers we found and some people who were with him, we were able to piece together the following: Tylor's been acting as a conduit for funds that are being transferred from holding companies around the world to groups of individuals in different countries. The passport he was carrying indicated one trip to the U.S., two into Canada, and three to Mexico. Being Caucasian, it's only a hop and a skip to cross the border back and forth. When we found him, he had instructions to search out vulnerable targets of opportunity here and in Great Britain."

The seven men looked at each other, as if no one knew quite how to respond. Stuart broke the silence.

"Since he didn't make it, we still don't know who was paying him and who his contacts were. What do you suggest we do?"

Marc nodded and said, "Through means I'd rather not discuss, we found out that some of his past contacts were told to get jobs in train stations, airports, national monuments, and federal buildings. One of the people we were holding mentioned that Tylor was taking credit for a plane that crashed off Long Island."

"I would have liked my people to question that detainee," Jake murmured. "Our investigation didn't turn up anything that looked like a bomb in the cargo area."

"Unfortunately, she didn't make it either," Marc said, his voice almost nonchalant.

Bill Cook, the Canadian, said what Stuart was only thinking. "That seems to happen to a lot of people in your part of the world."

"If I am correct, and I am sure that I am, your time is coming," Marc answered testily.

Jake Levitt held up both hands. "Gentlemen, let's not argue. The implications are clear, and the President is preparing to send Congress a bill that will set up a new department. We're going to call it Home Security, and Stuart has been asked to head it up." The others glanced toward Stuart, who kept his eyes on Jake.

"This department will have full authority to deal with terrorists inside of the U.S.," Jake explained. "The CIA will continue to deal with events happening outside of the States, which is why they're not here today. The FBI's task is to keep the peace with everything other than terrorists. Our job today is to pool our resources of information and see if we can stop whatever is going to happen before it starts. Michael," he said, turning to his friend, "I'd like to hear from you first. Any thoughts on how to proceed?"

Taking his cue, Michael stood, crossed to the blackboard, and picked up a piece of chalk. "My first thought is to list possible targets in England and all of North America. Unfortunately, the list is so long that it might take the United Nations to guard them." Turning his back on the others, he said, "These are most pressing," and wrote, "Niagara Falls, Empire State Building, Statue of Liberty, Golden Gate Bridge, Madison Square Garden." When he finished writing the last, he glanced toward Stuart, as if to acknowledge his friend's weekend plans.

"For that matter," interjected Jose Vargas, "any soccer game or sports arena holding more than fifty thousand would be a target."

"The list goes on forever," agreed the Israeli, "which is why we have to cut off the heads of the terrorists, wherever they are."

Stuart paid close attention and suddenly realized that Marc Frankel knew the answers before this meeting started.

Chapter Thirty-Seven

For three hours, the men went over all terrorist activities worldwide. Jake ran the meeting, but it was evident after the first thirty minutes no one veered far from their own party lines. Marc Frankel wanted a hard line taken with any country that allowed terrorists to operate inside Israeli borders, and that included breaking diplomatic relations and, if necessary, using force. Brett Daniels kept pressing for a UN resolution condemning the killing of civilians by any group, and only after this resolution would Special Forces go after not the countries, but the individuals. Jose Vargas kept coming back to the need to cut off drug traffickers, arguing that Mexico believed drugs were supporting terrorist actions. Bill Cook wanted a clearer description of who was to be considered a terrorist. "After all," he argued more than once, "even anti-Castro forces could be placed in that category."

Stuart sat there listening. Israel was prepared to fight; England would, but wanted to be able to negotiate first. Mexico wasn't ready to fight but was willing to work to stop drugs from passing through their country, and Canada, always an ally was for some reason holding back.

During a break, Stuart pulled Michael aside. "What's with Bill?" he asked.

"His government is concerned about how we categorize the separatists in Quebec. If an opposition party is put in the same category as terrorists blowing up buses in Israel, Canada has a major problem."

The meeting resumed and went on for several more hours. Just as it was drawing to a close, Jake looked at Stuart and said, "You've been very quiet this morning. As the man who's been picked to head up the U.S. side, do you have any thoughts before we break up?"

Stuart stood and made eye contact with every man in the room. "Obviously, anything I say is my opinion, not my government's. I don't have the job yet, and I'm not sure of the party line. However, after listening to you, gentlemen, all morning, I think someone needs to identify who we're going to call a terrorist.

While we're deciding that question, each country should step up security at its borders. I get the feeling that unless we decide to go to war against someone, this will never be a multinational force. Nevertheless, we're going to have to be more open with our information. If there is going to be terrorist activity in the States, I'd rather the people being questioned are kept alive, at least until we get a shot at them. I would think the same applies to each of you." Again, he looked around the table. "I also think someone needs to contact the Russians and the Chinese. To be truly effective, we must have them sitting beside us."

"Is that how you feel," Marc asked, "or was it a slip of the tongue?" When Stuart appeared confused, he continued, "You said that you'd rather they be kept alive until you get a shot at them. That implies after you're finished talking, it wouldn't matter if they were kept alive."

"It's not fair to put Stuart under the gun like that," Michael interrupted.

All eyes turned back to Stuart. No one said a word, but it was evident that they were expecting something.

"I don't mind answering." Stuart looked at Michael. "Unless my orders change, I'm against filling our jails with people who have caused willful and premeditated death to civilians." He watched glances being exchanged between the men. "This is the first time some of us have met, but we're all cut from the same cloth. I don't know this to be a fact, but I have the feeling that we've all killed in the line of duty. When the time comes, I'm sure we'll do what is required of us." Looking at his watch, he sat down.

"Gentlemen, I've been taking notes," Jake started. "I have what I think are some action items and a few other things that need taking care of. I'll contact each of you tomorrow and go over what needs to be done."

"Subject, of course, to our own country's needs," Marc added.

"I'm talking of our collective fight against terrorism," Jake retorted, his voice suggesting that his patience was wearing thin.

"Our collective fight?" repeated Marc. "Where are you Americans when those animals are killing our people, with no regard for their own lives, let alone the lives of innocent Israelis?"

Stuart felt his ears get hot but said nothing.

"You know," stated Brett Daniels, "Marc has a point. The IRA was setting bombs off in stores, buses, and schools while their political wing was traveling around the States collecting money for bombs and guns. The first time it looks like you Colonials have a problem, it becomes our collective fight."

Jake glanced at Stuart; his eyes begging for help. Stuart drew circles on the table, took a deep breath, stood, and stared pointedly at the Brit.

"Us Colonials kicked your ass twice, saved it twice more, and we've been there every time you needed help." Turning to the Israeli, he continued, "And as far as Israel is concerned, we stood on the front line when it was time to vote for statehood. We supplied guns, planes, military expertise, money, and a friend every time you needed it, which was often. Unless you heard something I didn't, we're not asking you to defend us, just to help us get information . . . and then stay the hell out of our way while we're taking care of the problem." Stuart glanced around the table. "You're either with us or against us. If you're against us, you'll have to deal with me now or in the near future, so take your pick." He did one more sweep around the table and sat down.

The room was silent. After a lengthy pause, Jose Vargas stood. "Stuart, you're at least four inches taller and twenty pounds heavier than I, and I certainly don't need anyone else pissed off at me. Count me in personally, which means that more than likely, Mexico is in too."

Bill Cook, sitting next to Jose, said, "I couldn't live with myself if I let Jose have all the fun. My boss said Canada would stand alongside the U.S. and Mexico."

"You Colonials always were cheeky bastards," smiled the Brit. "We're with you as well."

All eyes turned to the Israeli. Marc looked at each of them, his expression making it clear that he knew he could count on them whenever the need arose. "Unlike Jose," he said to Stuart, "I'm as tall as you and may even have a few pounds on you, and having one more person upset with me doesn't bother me at all. In this business, however, you have to trust your gut. I'll trust you until you do something that tells me I made a mistake. Count me in."

Stuart nodded and turned to Jake.

Jake looked relieved. "So that's decided. I'll contact each of you tomorrow. We may be a month or two away from putting this to bed here in the States. Until then, it'll fall under the auspices of the FBI. As of this moment, Stuart is assigned to the bureau, and I'll make sure he's given the time to respond to every situation that develops. Now," he concluded, "I suggest we don't all walk out together. Anyone in a hurry?"

Everyone looked at his watch, and Michael spoke up first, "Jake, why don't you go first. You're going to have to explain why you weren't on the plane that landed in Washington this morning."

"I'm sure they'll have lots of questions when I show up in Minnesota," he replied.

No one said a word, each man conjuring up the same explanation for why Jake would be visiting that state. All of them knew that Minnesota was the home of the world's most renowned cancer clinic.

"Don't worry," Jake told them with a smile. "I'm not visiting the Mayo. There's a police convention in St. Paul that I'm addressing this evening."

As the door closed behind Jake, Bill Cook turned to the group and asked, "And how far is that from Rochester?" Stuart pushed away the thought that he was losing a dear friend.

Chapter Thirty-Eight

Stuart spent the next two hours reading reports given to him by the other men. It was one thing to read about terrorist activities in the morning papers or watch their results on CNN, but reading reports not cleaned up for public consumption made him glad he hadn't eaten breakfast. One thing was evident: there were no nice guys when it came to some of the atrocities.

He continued reading and learned the fate of some of the captured men. Soldiers and police with families torn apart by bombs were put in charge of the prisoners. Those who survived the interrogation were put in prisons with inmates who had lost families and were more than willing to get even.

While many of the people were religious fanatics, Stuart understood that it took money to train them, arm them, and transfer them from place to place. He also realized that if they were going to put a stop to the exporting of terrorism, they would have to dry up the supply of money.

The clock on the wall said two o'clock. He checked the arrival board and saw that his son was arriving ten minutes early and Jessica's flight was five minutes late.

It took Stuart almost five minutes to locate the limo driver who was waiting for Jessica, and then advise him of the change in plans. He paid the driver in cash and took possession of the sign with *Winston* written across it.

Kenneth's plane landed first, and Stuart watched the boy walk into the terminal and look up at the exit sign. He had grown since their last meeting, and Stuart could see why Marilyn thought they looked alike. Kenneth was over six feet tall, thin, and muscular, more from sports more than working out in a gym. He was wearing Dockers and a white golf shirt that showed off his tanned face.

"Kenneth!" Stuart called. "Over here!"

Kenneth turned and smiled that infectious smile. Stuart found himself grinning back. The boy started toward his father, hesitancy in his steps. He glanced up and down, as if reaffirming that the man in front of him was his father.

"Hi, Dad," he said, holding out a hand. "I'm surprised to see you."

"I took an earlier plane and decided to wait for you and the congresswoman. She's due in at the gate across the way," he added, motioning toward the doorway that had just opened. "How was your trip?"

"It was fine. Do you follow basketball?"

Stuart smiled at his son's attempt to find some common ground. "I follow the NBA enough to know who Shaq and Kobe are, but not enough to tell you which college teams made the Final Four. How are your grades?"

"Not bad," said Kenneth.

"What's 'not bad'?"

"I'm almost 4:0," he said, glancing toward the deplaning passengers. "Has she come out yet?"

"You'll recognize her when she does."

"I've never met her," said the boy, scanning each face.

"I'm sure your sister has described Sarah. Like mother, like daughter."

Kenneth started to blush. "She did say she was tall and skinny."

"You can decide for yourself, here they come."

Stuart watched his son's mouth open as he caught sight of the girl. Jessica saw Stuart and waved.

"This must be your son, Kenneth," Jessica said, her lips brushing Stuart's cheek.

Kenneth had to force himself to take his eyes off Sarah. "Mrs. Winston, it's a pleasure. Marilyn has mentioned you and Sarah many times."

"Marilyn was right," said Sarah, entering the conversation. "She said you looked like your father."

Jessica and Stuart smiled as they watched their two children size up each other.

"Have you seen my driver?" Jessica finally asked.

"I paid him and sent him home. I have my own car and driver. It didn't make sense for us to take two cars to the same hotel. He's waiting in front."

Stuart heard Kenneth ask if he could help Sarah with her bag. He glanced at Jessica, who was smiling.

"Nice start to the weekend," Jessica whispered. "I haven't seen her look this happy in months."

It took nearly eighty minutes to get into Manhattan. During the ride, Kenneth and Sarah monopolized the conversation. On occasion, they included one or both parents with a question like, Do you remember? but they never waited for an answer.

When Jessica began to register at the front desk, she was told that Mark Harper had reserved and paid for a suite, and that all other expenses had been taken care as well, including meals and use of the spa.

Stuart saw her concerned look and asked, "What's wrong, did they give away your room?"

Jessica turned away from the desk clerk and, in a low voice, said, "Mark booked a suite that runs nine hundred dollars a night. He's already paid for it, plus some very expensive incidentals." "Nice of him," Stuart replied, a touch of hardness in his voice.

"Too nice of him," corrected Jessica. "A couple of tickets to a game is one thing, but this is insane. I can't accept such a gift."

Nodding, Stuart leaned over the counter. "There seems to be a mistake. I'm paying for Mrs. Winston and her daughter. I think someone misunderstood Mr. Harper."

"His instructions were specific. He said—"

Stuart leaned closer and interrupted. "Let's not make a big deal out of this, okay? Mrs. Winston's bill will be added to mine." He took out his wallet and flashed his FBI credentials. "Understand?"

It took a very nervous clerk no more than sixty seconds to make the changes.

"I'll write you a check when we get back to DC," she told Stuart. "And thanks."

The two suites were across the hall from each other. Before the women disappeared inside, Stuart told them he made reservations at an Italian restaurant for seven, and he would knock on their door at six fifteen.

"Dad, this place is enormous!" Kenneth exclaimed, coming out of one of the two bedrooms that bordered the enormous living room. Sitting down on one of the leather wing-backed chairs, he put his feet up on the matching ottoman and cleared his throat. "Dad, do you really have six or eight million dollars?"

"The visit by the FBI still bothers you?" Stuart was hoping that he had formulated an answer that Kenneth could live with.

Kenneth put his feet on the floor and leaned toward his father. "It's not their visit that bothered me, even if they didn't go to see Marilyn. It's that I'm not sure what you do for a living. I guess you still have something to do with the government, but Grandma says you don't. Those men weren't sure of how much you have, but they did say that it was an awful lot of money."

Stuart studied his son's face for a moment. "I guess you're old enough to hear part of the story," he said. "But you've got to keep it quiet. That means you can't tell your mother or your sister what I'm about to say." When Kenneth nodded, Stuart continued, "I never left the government. I was working for a division that focused on solving major crimes. Our job was to track down serial killers, bank robbers, and major drug lords . . . build a case so strong that the outcome would never be in doubt. That is, where no lawyer would be able to pull a rabbit out of a hat and get them off. The job took me all over the United

States and sometimes out of the country. Last week, the President asked me to head up a new task force that's being formed to deal with terrorists who may be planning to screw with the U.S. of A. I have three weeks to clear my desk of the cases I'm working on, which includes a series of bank robberies, a group of murders, and maybe a mole inside our government."

Kenneth looked slightly awed by what he had just learned. It was a moment before he could organize his thoughts. "So what part of the government is that? And how much are they paying you? I mean, it sounds like an awesome job."

"The pay's not bad. Don't forget that, when your mother left me, she married a man with lots of money. She didn't need anything from me, nor did she ask. So everything I didn't spend was invested in the stock market. You remember Peter Weber? After he almost died, he changed jobs and took full control of my finances, which is why I can honestly say I don't have those six or eight million dollars. At any given time, I may have that much in stocks, but I'm never sure of the exact amount. Those men came by and asked because of this new appointment. I'm told that I'll need approval from Congress."

"Is that why you're seeing the congresswoman?"

Stuart smiled. "I met her before I met the President. And just so you know, Kenneth, she's the first woman I've gone out with more than twice in the past ten years. If you ask her, she'll tell you we've only gone out once and those other times were business."

"Do you think her daughter likes me?"

"If I'm any judge of first impressions, I'd say that's a definite *yes*."

Before Kenneth could ask anything else, the phone rang. Stuart picked it up and said, "Taylor!" After a moment, he added, "Sure, hold on." He held the phone out to Kenneth. "It's Sarah."

Kenneth jumped up and raced toward the bedroom, calling over his shoulder that he's taking it in the other room. Ten minutes later, he emerged with a grin on his face. "She wanted to know if I'd like to go to a movie after dinner."

Chapter Thirty Nine

The dinner was excellent, and the two teenagers never stopped talking. Stuart and Jessica were bystanders in the formation of this new friendship, and they enjoyed every minute of it. At eight thirty, Kenneth mentioned the movie started at nine fifteen and they needed to leave. Stuart told them to take the limo waiting in front; he and Jessica would take a taxi.

"The limo will be there after the movie," he added. "You can use it to go out for ice cream."

"I can get us around," Kenneth retorted, not wanting to look like a kid in front of Sarah.

"I'm sure you can," said his father. "But Sarah is the daughter of a sitting U.S. congresswoman, so it's either the limo, or I'll have Secret Service men accompany you into the movie."

Kenneth looked at Sarah, who nodded and smiled. He shrugged, and they got up to leave. Sarah bent over and kissed her mother's cheek, while Kenneth shook Stuart's hand and restrained himself from commenting when his father slipped him two-hundred-dollar bills.

After the kids walked out the door and stepped into the waiting limousine, Stuart asked for the check. "This is a new experience for me," he admitted. "Do you wait up for her or go to sleep?"

Jessica smiled rather sheepishly. "If I know the boy or his family, I'll wait up in bed. If I don't, I find work to do and try not to get anxious."

He signed the bill and pulled out Jessica's chair. Walking toward the exit, he asked, "And what about now, here?"

"I always have work with me," she replied. When Stuart didn't respond, she added, "Tonight, however, I know the family well enough."

He smiled and held her hand as he waved down a taxi.

Settled inside, they looked out their windows, lost in their own thoughts. Nothing was said during the ten-minute ride down the Great White Way.

Upon reaching the hotel, Stuart finally asked, "Would you like to join me for a nightcap?"

"Let me go to my room for a minute," she responded. "I'll knock on your door in a few minutes."

Stuart waited for her door to close before entering his room. The moment he was inside, he picked up the phone and asked for room service. "I'd like a bottle of merlot sent up to my room," he instructed. "There's an extra ten if you're here in five minutes."

"Mr. Taylor," said the voice on the other end. "If you take a look in your cabinet, you'll find five choices of wine, two champagnes, and individual bottles of liqueurs. Fresh ice was just delivered, and there's a small refrigerator with soft drinks and bottled water. If you desire something to eat, there's a menu by the phone. Is there anything else I can do for you?"

Stuart hesitated. "Tell me your name and you'll find an envelope with the ten in it when you come to work tomorrow."

The man on the other end laughed. "Sir, at the price you're paying for that suite, it's the least we can do. Thanks anyway, and have a good night."

Before Stuart could answer, there was a knock on the door. He rushed over and found an ashen-faced Jessica.

"What's the matter?" he asked, looking up and down the hall. Before she could answer, he pulled her into the room and locked the door.

"There were two messages on my phone. The first was from Mark, asking if anything was wrong because the hotel had told him he wasn't paying for the room. The second call was from someone who warned me that if I didn't fall in line, Sarah might end up getting hurt. How did they know I was here?"

Stuart took out his cell phone and pushed three numbers. The phone was answered on the first ring. "Are the kids okay?" he asked.

"We've got two people behind them in the movie, another outside, and I'm in the car. What's the problem?"

"The congresswoman got a phone call telling her that Sarah might get hurt."

There was silence on the other end, followed by "It won't happen on my watch." The words arrived with such finality that there was no room left for conversation.

Stuart looked at Jessica, who was pressed against him and listening to the conversation.

"I'll have two more people here by morning," said the voice, "and you'll have four new tickets for tomorrow night's game delivered to your room by noon. Have the congresswoman leave her tickets at the front desk for Mrs. Marvel. We'll have two women sitting in those seats tomorrow night. Who knows? We may get lucky. Anything else?"

Stuart looked at Jessica, who shook her head. "I think you've got it covered," he responded. "If I think of anything, I'll call."

Stuart closed the phone, and Jessica put her arms around him. "Thank you," she whispered as her mouth found his.

"I didn't do anything yet," he responded.

"But I know you will." She headed toward the bedroom and then asked, "Is this one yours?"

He nodded, but only because his mouth was too dry to speak.

Chapter Forty

"I guess you never forget how," teased Jessica, leaning on her elbow, her face close to Stuart's. "It's been a very long time since I've been with a man; I was more than a little concerned."

Stuart moved closer and knew that she was looking for a reply. He ran his forefinger down the bridge of her nose, stopping at her lips. "I'm not so active in the sex arena that I could be called a connoisseur, but I have to tell you I don't remember ever making love to anyone as beautiful and as sexy as you."

Jessica leaned forward and kissed him lightly on the lips. "Thank you. I remember you telling me, you felt you were halfway through life. From what I've just experienced, I very much doubt it."

Before Stuart could reply, he heard the door open in the living room. The children weren't due home for at least another hour. Jessica felt his body stiffen as he looked at the clock on the nightstand. He slid out of bed and moved to where his clothes lay on the floor.

Jessica didn't move, nearly incredulous to find that she was admiring his muscled body in this situation. She watched him take a pistol from the pile of clothing and slowly pull on his slacks. They had left the door to the living room ajar and could now hear someone moving away from their bedroom to the one with the closed door.

Stuart stopped and put the gun at his side. He tiptoed back to the bed and whispered, "It's the kids. They must have come home early, and they think we're in your room."

"What are we going to do?" she mouthed, panic in her eyes.

"Get dressed," he told her. Pointing to the door leading out to hallway, he said, "That door leads to your room. I'll take care of the kids."

As Jessica gathered up her clothes, she heard the television and her shoulders relaxed. It was evident the children didn't know their parents were in the other room. Slipping her dress over her head, she blushed as Stuart stood there and stared. When she was ready, he held open the outside door and kissed her on the cheek.

"I feel terrible," she murmured.

"There will be other times," he replied, closing the door behind her. He waited until she was safely in her suite and then walked over to the door with the gun in his hand. Kicking open the door, he yelled, "Don't anyone move."

Kenneth jumped up and yelled back, "Don't shoot! It's us."

Stuart could see that they had been sitting on the king-sized sofa, perhaps three feet apart, and drinking Cokes.

"What are you doing here?" he asked sternly.

"We didn't like the movie and decided to come back," Sarah replied, her voice shaky. "Where's my mom?"

"Isn't she in her room?"

Kenneth and Sarah looked at each other. "We didn't look," said Kenneth. "We thought that the two of you were," he told his father. And then gestured toward the bedroom and added, "in there."

Stuart walked over to the phone. "Let's make sure she's there."

"Please, don't call my mom."

Stuart hesitated.

"She hasn't gone on a date in years, and I was afraid of screwing it up."

Stuart hung up the phone. "Your mom is one of the nicest people I've ever met. She's intelligent and good-looking. We had a nice time and decided to turn in early. You didn't mess up anything, and I wouldn't worry about her. If you kids want to sit here and watch television, it's okay by me, just keep it down. I need my beauty sleep."

"No, I'd better go back to my own room," said Sarah. Turning to Kenneth, she told him, "I had a great time. What are we doing tomorrow before the game?"

"Let's talk about it tomorrow. I'll walk you to your room."

Stuart called Jessica as soon as the door closed. "Don't worry, they never even tried your room. Sarah didn't want to *screw up your date*." He listened for a second and then replied, "Me too. See you tomorrow."

Stuart was asleep before Kenneth returned.

Chapter Forty-One

Stuart was halfway through his daily exercises when Kenneth knocked on his door.

"Dad, are you up?"

"Come in."

Kenneth stood in the doorway and watched his father lying on his back, with his feet stuck under a chair as he did sit-ups. "How many of those do you do?"

"On a good day, a hundred sit-ups and fifty push-ups. Today, I'll probably do half of that." Stuart stopped and sat upright. "In fact, since this is a special day, I'll call it quits now."

"How many are you up to?"

"I already did fifty push-ups and twenty-five sit-ups."

Stuart stood and draped a towel over his head. Kenneth sat on the chair that had been used for ballast.

"How dangerous is your job?" Kenneth asked, staring at the floor. "Sarah told me about the run-in you had with those three kids, and then later on with some men at her house. She thinks you're very brave, but that you could've been killed."

"Sarah's a little dramatic," said Stuart. "Those three punks were amateurs; there was never any real danger."

"What about the men who were going to burn down their house? You ended up killing them!"

"They were a different story. As far as we could tell, they were semi-professionals. Unfortunately for them, I happened upon the scene and didn't realize they were only there to scare Sarah and her mom, not harm them."

"Unfortunately for them? Dad, you killed them! I would say that's unfortunate."

"Kenneth, I told you yesterday I worked for a special branch of the government. If you read the newspapers, I'm sure you've heard of the Alcohol, Tobacco, and Firearms group."

"The Ruby Ridge people?"

Stuart nodded. "I worked under their auspices, but I didn't report to them. My group is a little more like . . . James Bond." He used the towel to wipe sweat from his face. "We're not spies or anything; we just do a job that not a lot of people are suited for. Part of that job sometimes entails people getting killed. Hopefully, other people."

"Does Mom know what you do?"

"No, and neither does Marilyn, but she saw me handle those three and has probably heard the same story you got about the men. But no, she doesn't."

Kenneth thought for a moment before asking, "Will this new job make you famous?"

"It's a job with a lot more visibility. But make me famous? I don't think so."

The ringing phone cut off Kenneth's next question. Stuart motioned for him to answer.

"This is Kenneth." The boy's face broke into a grin. "Good morning, Mrs. Winston, is Sarah up yet?" He turned to his father. "Dad, Mrs. Winston wants to talk to you." Handing over the phone, he whispered, "Don't hang up, I want to say hello to Sarah."

"Good morning, Jessica, how'd you sleep?"

"Like a baby," she said.

"Me too. It must be the air or something. What did you have in mind for today?"

They discussed the plans, and he finished the conversation with, "In twenty minutes, we can be ready. Oh, and hold on. Kenneth wants to say something to Sarah." He passed the phone to his son and mouthed the words, "Breakfast downstairs in twenty minutes."

Summer was only a week and a half along and already the Big Apple was showing why it was one of the greatest places to visit. The mayor had done a great job of getting the streets cleaned up, and they were now filled with tourists. Over breakfast, Sarah and Kenny, as she was now calling him, did most of the planning. It was decided that they would visit the Statue of Liberty, the Empire State Building, and take the Rockefeller Center tour. The Knicks game didn't start until eight, which left them plenty of time to take in the sights. Sarah mentioned a club she had heard about, and Kenneth looked at his father.

"No problem," said Stuart. "Give me fifteen minutes to arrange everything and we're on our way."

The day went like no other that Stuart could remember. He and Jessica stood at the rail of the ferry as it traveled from the tip of Manhattan to the Statue of

Liberty. The fresh air brought color to their cheeks, the wind lifted Jessica's shoulder-length hair and tossed it across her face, creating a look that not even the most gifted hairdresser could hope to imitate.

With their children nearby, Stuart didn't have a chance to discuss last night. He had decided that his best course of action would be to act nonchalant. He didn't want to seem smitten, but at the same time didn't want to appear aloof. His plan blew up in his face when they boarded the elevator for the ride to the top of the Empire State Building. The car went nonstop to the eighty-sixth floor, and Stuart was sure there were at least four people too many inside. He was pressed up against Jessica, who stood slightly behind him and managed to maintain a straight face. Before reaching the top, she moved her hand lightly against his thigh until she found his fingers and held on. He turned to smile, but she didn't acknowledge his glance. Instead, she just squeezed a little harder. By the time they reached the eighty-sixth floor, he had an overwhelming desire to push everyone aside and put his arms around her.

The four of them circled the viewing platform. While their children were peering through telescopes facing Central Park, Stuart took Jessica's hand and led her to the other side of the building.

"We have to talk," he said as they looked out over Manhattan and the Statue of Liberty.

"About what?"

"Last night."

"What about last night?" Her lips were pursed, giving her a questioning look.

"We didn't get much of a chance when the kids came in."

"Okay," she said, "let's talk. I enjoyed the dinner, I enjoyed the ride home in the taxi, and I enjoyed what happened next. I didn't enjoy having to sneak out of the room, but in retrospect, and after knowing you for almost three weeks, I probably should have expected it."

"What does that mean?"

"It means that if I'm going to spend any time with you, I've got to learn to expect the unexpected. Now you." Having passed the gauntlet, she waited for him to speak.

"This isn't what I meant when I said we had to talk. But," he added, and then looked in the direction of their children, "last night, after the dinner and after the taxi ride home, was as good as it gets. I'm concerned about being able to do my job when you're around. You have an effect upon me that I haven't felt in years and . . ."

"There you are," declared Sarah, causing Stuart and Jessica to jump. "We thought we lost you."

Kenneth came up to her father's side. "This is some view, Dad. You can see the Bronx from that side, New Jersey from over there, and Staten Island

down there. You know, all the times that we've come, I've never been up here."
Kenneth looked strangely at his father and then at Sarah's mom. "Did we
interrupt something?"

Sarah did a quick study of the adults' faces. "Something wrong?"

Jessica touched her daughter's face, pushed a loose curl behind her ear.
"Kenneth's father was just telling me about his new job. He thinks it might be
too much for him." As she spoke, her eyes never left Stuart.

"Jeez, Dad, after what I've heard, you can probably handle anything."

"That's what I was about to tell him," agreed Jessica. Sarah never said a
word. Instead, she studied her mother's face and smiled.

They collectively decided to skip Rockefeller Center and walk from the
Empire State Building, on Thirty-fourth Street, to their hotel, which was about
ten blocks away. Sarah and Jessica wanted to do some window-shopping, and
Kenneth wanted to do anything Sarah did. They arrived at the hotel at four,
tired but happy. Jessica and Sarah decided to have their nails done, leaving
Kenneth and Stuart to fend for themselves.

"What do you say to taking a nap?" Stuart suggested hopefully.

"Sounds good to me," Kenneth replied. "I'll probably fall asleep in front
of the TV, watching a movie."

As they walked toward the elevator, Stuart noticed one of the men from the
Cigar Store standing in front of the mirrored columns. Their eyes locked, and
the agent motioned him toward a bank of phone booths.

"Go ahead up," he said. "I'll be there in a minute."

"That's okay, Dad, I'll wait."

"No, really, go on up."

Kenneth looked around the lobby. "Is everything okay?"

"Of course it is. I just have to check on tonight's tickets."

The moment Kenneth entered the elevator, Stuart walked over to the
phones.

The operative held up a newspaper. "Michael suggested that we deliver
this to you tonight. He has a friend at the paper, and this was scheduled for
Sunday's Potomac Happenings column."

Stuart scanned the headline and then read the article.

Which Congresswomen Is Accepting Expensive Weekends in New York

This paper has learned that one of California's representatives has accepted
a weekend in New York, paid for by one of her constituents. Aside from the
luxury suite, meals and entertainment have also been included. When this
paper called the congresswoman's office to verify, everyone was gone for the
weekend.

No name, no hotel, nothing, but it could start a feeding frenzy with the
press corps.

"Any idea where the info came from?"

"Michael's working on it. If he can find out, he'll let you know."

Taking the envelope, Stuart walked to the elevator and thought, *Harper is starting to piss me off*. He found Kenneth lying on the sofa, a pillow from the bedroom propped under his head. The television was on, but the boy was fast asleep. Stuart thought, *like father, like son,* and ten minutes later, he was asleep on the bed.

Stuart had always believed that he had a built-in alarm clock. When he awoke at six on the button, he felt a slight panic. Rushing into the living room, he found Kenneth fast asleep.

"Time to get up, sleepyhead," he urged, giving the boy a gentle shake. "We don't want to keep the ladies waiting."

Kenneth did a slow turn on the couch and pulled himself up to a sitting position. After several moments, he asked, "Dad, how come you and Mom split up?"

The timing of the question surprised Stuart. "What did your mother say?"

"She said you were never home, your friends weren't nice, and you didn't love her."

Stuart sat down on one of the chairs. "She was partially right. I traveled a lot for my job." He leaned back and rubbed his face. "The only friends I had were from the department, and these were men I staked my life on. When your mother decided she wouldn't have anything to do with them, it created a chasm we couldn't span. I loved her when we got married and had you, but the time came when we did nothing but argue. When she found Louis, I was hurt, and I guess relieved. I offered to give them child support, but he had more than enough money to take care of the two of you."

"If you and Mrs. Winston decide to get together, will the same thing happen? Will she not like your friends?"

"We're not anywhere close to that yet."

"But if you do?"

They both turned as the phone rang.

"Saved by the bell," laughed Stuart. "I'll get it, you start getting dressed." He grabbed the phone and announced, "Taylor!"

"Hi, this is Marilyn. Are you two having a good time?"

"I am, and I hope Kenneth is. Maybe you and I should do this sometime."

"That might be fun. Is he there? I'd like to talk to him."

"I'll get him for you." Turning toward the second bedroom, he called out "Kenneth, it's your sister. You can pick it up in your room." Stuart held the phone to his ear, waiting for his son to pick up. He heard the boy greet his sister. When she asked if he was having a good time, the boy answered, "I'm having a great time!"

That's when Stuart hung up the receiver.

Chapter Forty-Two

"These seats are great!" declared Kenneth. "You must know someone to be able to get four of them together on such short notice."

"I wonder where our other seats were." Sarah asked her mother while scanning the far reaches of Madison Square Garden.

"Who cares?" Jessica replied. Stuart had shown her the article scheduled for the Sunday paper, and she was in a bad mood ever since.

Stuart knew exactly where the original seats were, and he had been keeping an eye on them since the game started. Two women, nicely dressed, similar in size and shape to Jessica and Sarah, were seated there and enjoying the game with every Laker basket. Everyone around them was sure they were from Los Angeles and big Lakers fans.

As for Kenneth and Sarah, they were in their own little world. Kenneth jumped up and down, every time Sprewell or Camby scored for the Knicks. Sarah screamed "Shaq attack!" at the top of her lungs every time her hero passed the ball off to Kobe or moved inside for a dunk. It got so that the fans in the surrounding seats got into the fun, yelling "Beat LA" every time the Knicks scored.

Halfway through the second period, a photographer walked down the aisle where the substitute Jessica and Sarah were sitting, passed them, and then quickly turned and snapped off three or four shots. The women put on a show of being upset, one of them throwing a cupful of soda at the photographer. Stuart thought it was very convincing and couldn't wait to see the results.

With seven minutes to go in the game, the Lakers were winning by fifteen points. Stuart and Jessica conferred and decided that it was a good time to leave. There was no argument from Sarah and Kenneth, who had been laughing all night and couldn't wait to get away from their parents.

"Are you sure you don't want the limo?" Kenneth asked for the third time. "We can take a taxi."

"We're sure, just try to get back to the hotel before . . ." Stuart looked at Jessica, who finished the sentence. "One o'clock."

"Mom, were in New York! How about two?"

Jessica nodded. "Two it is, but don't be late."

After the lights of the limo were lost in the blend of a hundred cars and taxis, Jessica turned to Stuart. "Do you mind walking for a while?"

He held out his hand, but she shook her head and started walking. "I'm upset," she started. "If you weren't with me, that newspaper article would've been right. I would have accepted a constituent's gift worth several thousand dollars and been branded a taker."

"But you tried to correct the misunderstanding," said Stuart.

"Stuart, I would have accepted the situation and then sent a check to Mark next week. It never occurred to me that it might cause an immediate problem. You said earlier that you didn't know if you could do your job when I was around. Well, I'm having the same problem. I'm not used to not being in charge, and I should've seen this coming. You have a way of clouding my vision. By Monday, the papers will have the whole story, and what do I tell them? That I went away with my daughter, and that the man I had sex with paid for my weekend?"

"I'm not a constituent, if that's any consolation."

"No, you're someone who needs my vote, which makes it even worse."

Stuart stopped walking and turned to face her. "Jessica, let me tell you how it looks to me, not that we could tell this to the papers, but it is the truth. Someone is trying to scare you off from something. They've threatened you and your daughter; they've broken into your house, and now they're trying to intimidate you through this trumped-up story. Just so you know the rest of it, I had two women placed in the seats you and Sarah were supposed to have. A photographer came by and snapped their picture. He got a cup of soda dumped all over him. With any kind of luck, the paper will run the stories with a picture of the women and name them as you and Sarah. Anyone looking at the picture will know it's not you and will get a laugh out of it. The papers following up on the rooms will find that I, a government agent, who was guarding you and your daughter on a trip to New York, paid for them. The money will be repaid to me in the form of a check, and that will be that. I know you don't want to hear this, but I'm certain that Mark is behind this. The idiot honestly believes he can get support for his plan to have the taxpayers' house and feed migrants crossing the border from Mexico to work in his plant."

"Mark would never do that," she insisted. "It has to be someone else."

"I've had people go over the committees that you serve on and the bills pending. There is nothing we can see, aside from Mark's problem, that's worth the aggravation."

Her eyes narrowed and a muscle twitched in her jaw. "What do you mean 'go over the committees'?"

"Remember what you said about being prepared to expect the unexpected when dealing with me? This should not have been unexpected. When you first called to thank me for helping the girls, you also called the Speaker of the House. That call set off alarms, and I had to find out who and what you were all about. My secretary was killed when she started asking questions."

"I thought she was killed by an intruder."

"That's the party line. I will find out who killed her and why, even if it takes time."

"In other words, I'm a case you're working on."

They arrived at the hotel, and Stuart remained on the sidewalk. "I'm going to check on the kids." Taking out his phone, he hit three buttons. "Everything all right?"

"They just went into a disco on the East Side. I've got four people in there watching them. The two watching you are tired. Are you calling it a night?"

Stuart glanced around and didn't see anyone out of the ordinary. "Tell them to go home."

"Have a good night's sleep," said the voice and then the line went dead.

"What did they say?" Jessica asked.

"The kids are in a disco on the East Side, and the two people watching us are going home."

In the elevator, Stuart asked, "So you think you're just some case I'm working on?" When she didn't respond, he pulled her closer and kissed her.

"No, I don't," she finally responded. "But I do think you're becoming a problem that I'm going to have to solve."

He kissed her again as the door opened on their floor. The minute they stepped out, Stuart saw four people standing in the hall. The two men had cameras, the two women were carrying note pads.

"Are you Congresswoman Winston?" one of the women called out.

Before Jessica could answer, Stuart stepped forward and replied, "Do I look like a congresswoman? Let me pass or I'll call the police."

They stepped back as Stuart led Jessica into his suite. The first thing he did was call the front desk. "There are people all over the hallway. Get someone up here in a hurry and get them out before I sue this hotel for everything it's got. I don't know if you're aware of the law, but Section 11 of the innkeepers code states that you are responsible for any and all violations of a guest's civil rights, and this is a gross violation. If I find out that anyone tells the reporters where the congresswoman is, we will own this hotel." He slammed down the phone and smiled at Jessica. "Now, where were we?"

She did not return the smile. "Stuart, I've got to get back to Washington, this is getting out of hand."

Taking a deep breath, Stuart sat down at the desk. He made two calls, the first to the airport where he had left the company plane. "You have a pilot, Seth Robert, somewhere around there. Can you put me through to his cell phone?"

He watched Jessica sit on the couch and click on the television. The picture came on, and she muted the sound. Leaning back, she closed her eyes, running her tongue over her lips.

"Seth, this is your passenger from Thursday night. Did the sweet Marie come up to join you?"

"She did, thanks."

That's nice. Now, I need another favor. In about three hours, two kids will be delivered to the plane. Thirty minutes later, I'll arrive with another guest. That means at two thirty we'll be ready for takeoff back to Washington. For the record, the others on that plane will be only Marie and I. She can keep her mouth shut, can't she?"

Seth excused himself, and Stuart could hear him explaining the situation to Marie. He came back on the line and said, "She can, except she wants another weekend, preferably where you can't find us."

"Tell her she's got a deal," said Stuart. Hanging up, he turned toward Jessica. "Take a look through the outside door leading into Kenneth's room and tell me if the hall is empty." While she looked, he made a second call to the men watching Sarah and Kenneth. "I've got the press all over my ass. At two, when the kids are finished, take them directly to the airport. I'll meet you there with the congresswoman at two fifteen. The plane will have us back in Washington by three thirty and you can go to sleep."

"There's no one there," Jessica said, coming back into the room.

"Go in and pack all of your things. I'll be in and help you carry the suitcases back here. Meanwhile, I'll pack our stuff."

Ten minutes later, Stuart entered Jessica's room and saw the light blinking on the phone. "You have a message."

"I know. I was afraid to answer it."

"I have a little tape recorder. Is it okay to tape the messages?" When she nodded, he hit the Speaker button.

"You have four messages. To listen to your messages, please push 3."

The first message said, "Mrs. Winston, this is Carol Gund from the *Washington Post*. I'm trying to check on a story we were given about your trip to New York. Please call my office at 1-800-888-1000 so that we can verify what is being said. Thank you."

Next came Mark Harper. "Sarah, what is going on in New York? The first thing I heard is that you decided to pay for your own room at the hotel. Now there's a story about you being drunk and throwing beer all over a photographer at the Knicks game, and I'm getting phone calls about giving you thousands of dollars worth of gifts. I don't need this kind of publicity. On Monday, I'm holding a press conference, and I suggest you call me before then and either get on board or . . . well, you can guess or what."

"Nice guy your friend," Stuart said, pushing the button for the next call.

"Congresswoman Winston, this is Eric Weaver from the Federal of Investigation. There have been some questions raised over the deaths of a people who were purportedly threatening your daughter. The story being circulated is that you knew the person who killed them, maybe even hired him. I know it's absurd, but I'm required to investigate. Please call the on Monday and ask for Eric Weaver."

"This is getting insane," complained Jessica. "Do you know what he's talking about?"

"I have a small idea, but don't let it worry you." Stuart pushed the button for the last message.

"Sarah, this is Neil Chilicote. You are in a heap of trouble. Avoid the press until you can talk to me. We've got to figure a way out of this for you. You know how to reach me."

"Are you two close?" Stuart asked.

"No, he's a pig. He tried to get friendly when I first came to Washington, and I've avoided him whenever possible."

"That's a good idea. He's going down."

Jessica's eyes widened. "Just what does that mean?"

"We're working on some things that have his name attached. It won't take long before he's out. Come on," he added, "let's get out of here." He grabbed her bags and led Jessica back across the hall to his suite. "We have about three hours to kill, you should take a nap. Tomorrow is going to be a long day."

Jessica sat on the sofa, closed her eyes, and listened to the music Stuart had put on a CD of show tunes, and their melodies soon filled the room. "Someone once said that listening to songs without the words is one of the most relaxing things we can do. Our minds block out everything else while following the music." He looked over at Jessica and saw that she wasn't listening. "What is it?" he asked, concern evident in his voice.

"This weekend ended up a disaster; I so wanted everything to be perfect."

He crossed to her. "Jessica, it was. The kids are having the time of their lives, I'm bonding with my son, and I have no regrets about how you and I seem to be getting along."

Jessica smiled and patted the cushion next to her. "We should talk before we get back to Washington."

"There's not a lot to talk about," he said, joining her. "I've added Harper and Chilicote to my list of things that have to get done."

"It's Washington, Stuart, and nothing is ever black-and-white. In fact, everything is open to negotiation. I'm sure that when we get back, I'll be told what they want from me. As long as I have some room to wiggle, everything will come out fine. It's you and me we should talk about."

Stuart leaned closer and ran his fingers through her hair. "What could we say?" He put a little pressure on the back of her head and drew her closer.

"We could say that"—a shiver ran up her spine—"we should be careful about when and where we meet."

Stuart's lips brushed hers. "We could say that." His right hand caressed her throat as his fingers drew little circles on her chest.

"We could say that we shouldn't meet anymore." Her voice was less than a whisper and then she kissed him hard on the mouth.

"We could say that, but it would be a lie." Stuart stood, helped Jessica off the couch, and led her to the bedroom. "What we could say is that,"

Before he could finish, she pressed a finger to his lips. "We could say that we talk too much." She kissed him again.

Chapter Forty-Three

After he handed the first taxi in line a twenty-dollar bill, Stuart and Jessica got into the second cab and directed the driver to take the Queens Midtown Tunnel and the Long Island Expressway. As they approached Lefferts Boulevard, Stuart told the driver to exit and park at the bottom of the ramp. He counted ten cars coming off behind them and told the confused cabbie to drive back onto the expressway and go directly to the American Airlines terminal at LaGuardia. When they arrived, he gave the driver a hundred dollars. When the cab was out of sight, he hailed another taxi for the thirty-minute ride to Kennedy.

Stuart was glad to find their children waiting for them.

"What's going on, Dad?" Kenneth asked as they boarded the plane.

"There's a mob of reporters searching for Mrs. Winston. We're taking her home before they find her."

"Why are they looking for you?" Sarah asked her mother.

"Someone notified the newspapers that your mother was taking illegal gifts from a constituent," explained Stuart. "Now they're trying to get a story." He hustled everyone toward the plane. "Let's get on board, so we can get home before it gets light."

"Mr. Loring isn't going to like this," said Kenneth, climbing the stairs.

"Who's Mr. Loring?" Sarah asked. "Is he the headmaster?"

"No, he's my mother's husband, and he gets very upset when someone or something doesn't go the way he thinks they should. He's paranoid about the family getting their name in the papers."

"Don't worry," Stuart told him. "First off, you won't get your name in the paper; second, you're with me and that should count for something."

They settled into their seats and were quickly met by Seth's girlfriend.

"Hi, I'm Marie," she said, flashing her dazzling smile. "If you'd like a soft drink or a snack, I'm the person to see." And then she added in a singsong voice, "Buckle yourselves in, Seth is in a hurry."

Stuart smiled and said, "I'm Stuart and I understand that I owe you a weekend. How about Bermuda?"

Marie laughed and responded, "That's very nice, thank you, but I'm fine. As far as I'm concerned, the weekend was a huge success. I hope yours was as nice." She looked from Stuart to Jessica, and then raised an eyebrow when Stuart started to blush.

Forty minutes later, the jet landed in Washington and taxied to the private terminal. Seth Roberts came out of the cockpit to say good-bye.

"Good job," said Stuart, shaking his hand.

"I was thinking about that job you offered me," said Seth. "If you have an opening, keep me in mind. I like your style."

Stuart thanked the crew and herded everyone to his car. "Jessica, I'll drop you and Sarah off at your house. Kenneth, you have a choice. You can come home with me, or I'll drop you at your mom's."

"I'll stay at your place," said the boy. "Mr. Loring would be very upset if I arrived at four in the morning."

A strange look passed over Stuart's face. It wasn't until Stuart drove through the security gate near her home that Jessica realized he had been reacting to Kenneth's use of the formal *Mr. Loring*.

As they pulled up in front of the house, Stuart turned to Jessica. "You're a big girl and with a lot more experience than I have when it comes to Washington politics. Nevertheless, for the record, give me a check for two thousand four hundred dollars and date it today. As far as anyone's concerned, you will have paid for your room. This morning's paper will have a picture of two other women sitting in those seats at the Garden. All you did was take your daughter to New York for the weekend and go to dinner with a friend and the kids. If they want the friend's name, give it to them. And just remember, I'm not as polite as you."

"I understand," she said, making no move to get out of the car. "And I want you to know, Stuart, that I had a wonderful time."

"Mom!" called out Sarah. "Kiss him good night, or do whatever people your age do, and let's get to sleep."

Jessica held out her hand. "We're back in Washington, I'm a congresswoman, and I need to go back to acting the part."

Stuart looked at her outstretched hand, pulled her close, and kissed her full on the lips. "People our age don't have time to waste; I'll call you tomorrow."

Stuart drove into his garage at four thirty in the morning. Kenneth had fallen asleep five minutes into the ride home, and Stuart had to shake him awake.

Groggy, the boy looked at his father and said, "Dad, I can't believe you kissed Sarah's mom. Are you two going to become an item?" Stuart smiled and popped open the trunk. "Stranger things have happened."

"Marilyn's going to have a cow," said Kenneth, taking his suitcase from his father.

"Maybe you shouldn't say anything to her."

The boy shrugged. "I'm sure Sarah's going to tell her."

"Well, let her be first. Maybe she'll surprise us."

Kenneth shrugged again and headed for the front door. He hadn't taken five steps when his father called him back.

"I'd want to ask you something that's been bothering me."

The boy appeared suddenly alert. "Sure, go ahead."

"Twice you referred to Louis as Mr. Loring. Is that what you and Marilyn call him?"

Kenneth scowled, and the expression wasn't lost on his father. "Marilyn's allowed to call him Louis, not me. Five or six years ago, we were having an argument, and I told him I didn't have to listen to him because he wasn't my father. He got all upset. Plus, he tried to adopt us, and you wouldn't let him. Anyway, he said that was true, he wasn't my father, and from that day forward I could call him Mr. Loring."

Stuart picked up his bag and closed the trunk. "If it's any consolation, there was no way I would allow him to adopt you two. I guess I knew that someday, it would be fun having kids. Now let's get some sleep."

The two entered the house, and Kenneth smiled all the way up the stairs to bed.

Chapter Forty-Four

The first thing Stuart did Sunday morning was to open the paper to the Potomac Happenings column. The story read,

California Congresswoman Accused of Taking Kickbacks.

This paper has learned that California Congresswoman Jessica Winston has been accused of accepting over two thousand dollars in hotel and entertainment gifts from a constituent who may need her help in pending legislation. As of press time, this paper could not contact either Congresswoman Winston or her constituent to confirm, but we were able to get a photo of her and her daughter at a Knicks game at Madison Square Garden. Witnesses confirmed that the congresswoman threw a glass of beer at our photographer and created a scene.

The picture that was attached to the story was a little fuzzy, but it was clear enough so that anyone who knew Jessica would recognize the error. Stuart turned on the television and saw that CNN was running the story at the top of the news. They were reporting that the newspaper was apologizing, it being obvious that the woman in the photograph was not the congresswoman. CNN also reported a conversation with the congresswoman, now at her home in the Washington area. Congresswoman Winston acknowledged she was at the Knicks game with her daughter, as well as a friend and his son. Her friend got the tickets, but she paid for her own hotel room. She doesn't understand what the furor is about, but she is going to take it up with the ethics committee on Monday.

"Morning," said Kenneth, walking into the den. "This room looks like a library." Inspecting the shelves, he observed that there was a law book from every state in the union. He circled the room, finally stopping at the fish tank. "What kind of fish do you have, Dad? I don't see them."

"There are none. I travel so much that I found it difficult to keep them fed, so I had the sand and bubbles put in." Stuart watched his son wander around the room.

"I know what's missing," announced Kenneth. "There are no windows."

"A lot of people never seem to notice that. You're observant."

The boy smiled at the compliment. "I heard them mention Congresswoman Winston and her daughter. Something wrong?"

"No, everything's right. A newspaper ran the story about her accepting gifts, and it even ran a photo of women they thought were Jessica and Sarah that was taken at the game. Now they're falling all over themselves trying to apologize." Turning off the TV, Stuart asked Kenneth if he was hungry. "I'm going to call your grandmother and ask her out to breakfast. I'm sure she'd love to see you."

"I'm always hungry. Can I call Mom to say hello?"

"Sure, and why don't you ask Marilyn if she wants to join us?"

Kenneth picked up the phone on the desk, the one that automatically taped all conversations. Stuart nearly stopped him, but he didn't want to go through the story of why he taped everything. "It's eight fifteen," he said. "Tell her that if she wants to join us, we can either pick her up or she can meet us at the Potomac Country Club at nine thirty. That should give her plenty of time."

"Are you going to invite Mrs. Winston?"

"No. I think she's got her hands full this morning. We'll make it a family affair. I'll call your grandmother on the other phone."

"Hey, Mom," Stuart said to his mom, "do you feel like joining Kenneth and me for breakfast at the country club?"

"I'd love that, and you can tell me all about your weekend in New York, especially the parts that CNBC left out."

"What are you talking about?"

"CNBC just reported that you were the person with Jessica Winston in New York."

"They have anything else to say?"

"Only that you were with the FBI and you've only known her for three weeks. I thought you quit working for the government?"

"It's a long story."

"I hope it's a good one. The networks are falling over themselves trying to scoop the newspapers and one another."

"Mom, my other phone is beeping, I'll see you at the club." He answered the phone with his typical "Taylor!"

"Stuart, it's Jessica. I'm sorry about all of this. Somehow they found out you were with us and the questions are starting."

"Jessica, let me ask you a question. Is there anything wrong with the two of us being in New York with our kids?"

"No. In fact, in retrospect, I think it was pretty good."

"Only pretty good?" he replied, his smile so big he was certain she could see it over the phone.

"Okay, very good. But listen, the questions really are coming fast and furious. I want to run them by you. They want to know who paid for the rooms, how we got home, and were we ever alone without the kids."

"My first answer would be that it's none of their business. I know you're a public figure and subject to scrutiny, so you might as well tell the truth. I charged the rooms against my credit card to avoid a sticky situation, and you gave me a check after we left the hotel. We got home on a jet that I arranged. They can call me for answers to that one, if you're more comfortable. And yes, we were alone. After dinner, the kids went to a movie, for which they only stayed for a part. After the game, they went to a disco. I'll tell them that a threat was received against your daughter and we had four agents with them, plus the two who stayed with us whenever we weren't with the kids."

"I'd love to tell you that this will all be over by tomorrow, but it usually lasts until they find something more interesting. I have to go," she added, and then stopped talking but didn't hang up.

Stuart felt his body tense. "Jessica, you there?"

"I'm here," she said after a long pause. "I was wondering if I'm going to see you this week."

"I hope so, I miss you already."

"Good, call me." And then she hung up.

Kenneth entered the room, his face downcast. "Marilyn can't come."

"That's too bad. How come?"

"Mr. Loring is having a fit. Sarah called early this morning and told them about the weekend, and he wants me to return to school immediately."

"What are you going to do?"

"What would you like me to do?"

"I'd like you to come to breakfast with your grandmother, but I'll understand if you don't."

Kenneth smiled. "I bet there's a plane that leaves an hour after we finish eating."

"I'd bet you're right. Finish getting dressed and we'll leave."

Kenneth went running up the stairs, and Stuart returned to the library and closed the door. He pushed the Rewind button and listened to the recording of Kenneth's phone call.

"Mr. Loring, good morning. This is Kenneth, is Marilyn up yet?"

"You listen to me, you ungrateful piece of shit. You know how I feel about getting my name in the paper. I heard about your escapades from Marilyn, who got a call from her friend, Sarah. I hear your father's shacking up with Sarah's mother."

"That's not true."

"Don't lie to me. Like father like son."

"I didn't do anything." Stuart could hear panic in Kenneth's voice.

"I heard he hired a private jet to get everyone back to Washington."

"He works for the FBI, it was one of their planes."

"He never worked for the FBI until last week. What's he been doing the past ten years?"

"I don't know."

"You're lying. I know he told you all about his new job."

After a brief silence, Kenneth said, "You can always call and ask him, he has no reason to lie."

"You listen to me. I want you on the next plane back to school, and I don't want an argument."

Stuart winced as the phone was slammed down on Kenneth's ear. Erasing the tape, he muttered, "That's one more thing I have to do before taking this job."

Chapter Forty-Five

"You know, you look a lot like your father."

"That's what Marilyn said, Grandmother."

"Grandmother! You're going to have to call me something else, that makes me feel old."

Kenneth nodded, his mouth full of food.

"Are you getting good marks?"

"Almost straight As."

"Do you have a girlfriend?"

Kenneth blushed and shook his head.

"Okay, enough of the small talk. Tell me about the weekend in New York."

"What would you like to know, Grams?"

"I like that. Tell me what's she like, this congresswoman, is she pretty?"

"I think so. She's a little old, but her daughter is very pretty."

"The television is saying that she spent the weekend in New York with your father. Did they really spend the weekend together?"

"Mom!"

"Be quiet. Let me get the story from someone who was there."

"Well, I guess they were together, but Sarah and I were with them. The first night Sarah and I went to a movie and got back to the hotel early. She thought they might be together in her mom's room, so we went back to Dad's suite. We sat down to watch television, and Dad came out of the bedroom with a gun in his hand. We had awakened him, and Sarah's mom wasn't even there."

"What were you doing with a gun?" she asked Stuart.

"I told you, Mom, it's a long story. I'll tell you when we have more time, okay? Right now I have to get Kenneth to the airport."

"When will I see you again?" she asked, looking at her grandson.

"Summer vacation starts June twenty-ninth, so let's make plans to get together that weekend."

"Saturday, the thirtieth of June it is. I'll make dinner."

Kenneth kissed his grandmother and started out the door.

The woman turned to Stuart. "He's a nice boy, I like him."

Stuart nodded and smiled. "Me too." Standing, he followed his son outside.

In the parking lot, Stuart hailed a cab and put his hand on Kenneth's shoulder. "I hate to do this, but business calls. The taxi will take you to the airport where the plane we came in on last night is preparing for a test flight up to New Hampshire. They have room for one more person, and that's you. Have a nice flight, and I'll see you in a couple of weeks."

Kenneth held out his hand. "Dad, I had a great time. I'm sorry for all the years we've missed."

Stuart pulled him close and hugged him. "Me too, son."

"I guess I won't need insurance on this flight," Kenneth said as he entered the taxi.

"What do you mean?"

"Mr. Loring's personal attorney, Kenneth Hall, says that I should always buy insurance before I get on a commercial plane."

"Who?"

"Kenneth Hall, his personal attorney."

"And who does he say should be the beneficiary?" Stuart felt his heart thumping.

"Mom."

Stuart remembered Sally's words about the man being a high-powered lawyer.

"See you in a few weeks," he promised, and the taxi took off almost before the door was closed.

"What are you doing for the rest of the day?"

Stuart turned at the sound of his mother's voice.

"I'd love to hear the story of where you work and why."

"Not today, Mom. My life's becoming complicated again."

"Just tell me you're not doing anything dangerous."

Stuart looked at his mother. This was the first time he could remember her ever saying anything that resembled concern. "I'm not doing anything different today than I've been doing for the past twenty years. Why are you worrying now?"

"I didn't know what you were doing during those twenty years."

"You still don't." He smiled and gave her a hug. "I can tell you this: things are definitely looking up."

Chapter Forty-Six

Stuart spent the better part of Sunday sitting at his computer, using the Internet to bring up as much information as he could find on Mark Harper and Louis Loring. Tomorrow, he would have Sally find out even more about them; but for today, he wanted a feel of their businesses, their finances, outside activities, and their families. He knew from past experience that by tomorrow afternoon, Sally would be able to tell him how many times a day they went to the bathroom. He kept the television muted, except when he saw Jessica's picture, which seemed to be every thirty or forty minutes. The story stayed basically the same. With nothing new to report, they were showing photos of the people in Southern California and asking them what they thought of their congresswoman. Aside from one woman who said "Where's there's smoke, there's fire," the people were 100 percent supportive.

It was five thirty when he got up and stretched. He walked over to the printer and put everything he had downloaded and printed into two piles, one for Mark Harper and the other for Louis Loring. He decided to go through Harper's first. There was something about Loring that bothered him; he wanted to make sure it wasn't personal.

Mark Harper was born in September of 1970 in a place called Ramona, California, not far from San Diego. Both parents died in October 1991 when a fire swept through their house and burned it to the ground in a matter of minutes. The local fire department termed the fire suspicious since it started in the middle of the night in an unattached garage where they stored paint used on their barn. The two Mexican families lived on the property didn't have a phone and were unable to call for help. Mark Harper, after returning from college, married his childhood sweetheart, Denise Loring. They have three daughters.

"Denise Loring?" murmured Stuart. "Now that's a coincidence." He jotted notes to himself on a pad.

> *Over the past ten years, Harper has turned a twenty-acre farm into two thousand acres. He has added a four-thousand-acre cattle ranch and a two thousand-acre orchard. His estimated net worth is approximately twenty-five million dollars. He's a patron of the arts and a big supporter of 4H clubs of America.*

Stuart heard the bell that told him when someone was approaching the front door. Changing the channel, he watched his boss, Michael, walk up the steps and ring the bell.

"Hold on. I'll be right there," he said into the intercom.

When Michael stepped inside, the first words out of his mouth were, "I could use a drink."

"Help yourself, you know where the makings are."

Michael fixed his drink then sat down on the sofa. "Can you tell me what the hell is going on? I've been on the phone with the President for over an hour. This thing with the congresswoman is blowing up in everyone's face."

"What thing?" Stuart asked, making the words sound very hard.

Michael held up both hands. "Hey, don't get pissed at me. Everyone's asking questions, and now your name is in the middle. People want to know where you work, where did you work, and what it is that you're doing. They smell blood, Stuart, and they don't care whose it is."

"And?"

"And the President can't tell them what you've been doing or what he has planned, this thing's got him boxed in."

"And?"

"Stop saying and, and sit down so we can talk."

Stuart sat across from Michael at his desk. "Okay, talk."

"Bring me up to date on where you're at and what the plan is."

"What makes you think I have a plan?"

"Because I know you, we've worked together for too many years."

Stuart put his elbows on the desk. "This is between us, I don't want any politicians jumping the gun."

When Michael nodded, Stuart began. He explained how the whole thing started when someone sent three young thugs to hassle Jessica's daughter. "I got involved because my daughter happened to be with her," he said. "The congresswoman started getting calls at her office, and I was getting them on my private line, which told me that someone inside our community was involved."

"Any ideas about who that person is?"

"At the moment, my first guess is Eric Weaver."

"Aside from his being an asshole, any other reasons?"

"His girlfriend, Miriam, who was also his secretary, was placed there by Senator Chilicote who, if you remember, is the person the President wants to run this new organization on the inside. He's made some arrests of people who the President has pardoned after serving six months of ten-year sentences. Weaver was also an assistant DA in San Diego, and one of the guys he let walk was someone I killed at the congresswoman's home. How's that for a reason?"

"Not bad. What else you got?"

"This one's a little dicey. Yesterday, my son mentioned the name of his stepfather's lawyer, Kenneth Hall. That's the same name that came up in a report that Sally ran for me. It had to do with people taking the same plane as the two men I shot. The only other name that came up was Kenneth Hall, a high-powered attorney from DC."

"You mean your ex's husband may be involved?"

"I haven't checked yet to see if it's the same person; I just found out today."

"How does it all tie together?"

"Oh, one more thing. Mark Harper's wife, her maiden name was Loring."

That piece of information silenced Michael. Stuart was waiting for a response when Jessica's face reappeared on the television. Superimposed with the words LIVE. Stuart raised the sound.

"When I became a congresswoman," Jessica said, "I understood that I was giving up some of my rights to privacy. But this weekend borders on something far beyond that." She was reading from a statement and her voice left no doubt as to her anger. "I have a friend who also happens to be a constituent. Two months ago, he offered me two tickets to a Knicks game. He suggested that I stay at the Marriott in midtown Manhattan because of its convenience and offered to make the reservations for me. Two weeks ago, Stuart Taylor, who happens to work for the Federal of Investigation, mentioned that he was taking his son to the same game. We decided to meet for dinner and go sightseeing with our children. When I checked into the hotel, there was some confusion as to who was paying for my room. Since it was guaranteed by my friend, the hotel wanted to use his card. In order to avoid what I perceived to be a conflict of interest, Mr. Taylor offered his credit card to the clerk." At this point, Jessica smiled. "My daughter and I had a great time in the city. We visited the Statue of Liberty and the Empire State Building. In fact, we even walked from the Empire State Building to our hotel, doing some of the most wonderful window-shopping imaginable." Her face turned suddenly somber. "While we were there, someone called the hotel and threatened my daughter with bodily harm. I told Agent Taylor, and he arranged for protection for both my daughter and me. I never saw the people who were protecting me, but I understand that two women from the sat in the seats I had been given. Partly because of the commotion at the game, and to avoid any further confrontation, Agent Taylor decided that we should fly home on a company plane in the middle of the night."

Jessica looked straight into the camera. "I would like to thank all the people from the for their protection, especially the two women whose picture was in the paper. What's more, I want to tell whoever is threatening my daughter that it won't work. I'm a sitting member of Congress and, as such, will not and cannot knuckle under to demands that are made against the best interests of my country. My daughter fully understands and supports my position. I will take a few questions."

"Congresswoman Winston, are you and Stuart Taylor an item?"

Smiling, Jessica answered, "Stuart is someone I've known for a short period of time. He's charming and fun to be with and . . ." She paused, as if reconsidering, and then said, "That's all I'm going to say."

"Congresswoman Winston, do you have any idea why someone would threaten you or your daughter?

"I have no idea at all."

"Congresswoman Winston, it's obvious that someone has tried to damage your reputation. Do you have any idea who it is, and why they are doing it?"

Jessica smiled at the female reporter. "Since I've come to Washington, I've tried to do my very best for the people of my district, my state, and the citizens of this country. In certain cases, this is in direct conflict with what some people would like. Very soon, members of Congress will be resigning or will move back to the private sector. It is my intention that when seats on certain committees become available that require more responsibility, I will ask the people to support me. If someone wants to stop me from one of these positions, this was a good place for them to start. What's more effective than manufacturing an embarrassing scenario to get me out of their way? I'm sure that as I go forward, they will try again."

"Congresswoman Winston, do I understand you say that you are throwing your hat in the ring for Vice President?"

"No, not Vice President, but I believe there are some other positions that will open up soon."

"Congresswoman Winston, which ones?"

"That's not what we're here for. I have asked for a meeting tomorrow with the ethics committee. When they give me a clean bill, we can discuss my future. Thank you all for coming on such short notice."

With that, she turned and walked away.

"She's some woman," Michael mused. "Now they don't know who or what to chase. The vast majority will perceive her as a heroic figure that won't cave in to pressure. Did you notice how she moved your name in and out, from Mr.

Taylor to Stuart Taylor of the FBI and to just Stuart, a very close friend. She's good."

Stuart turned off the television and turned his full attention to Michael. "If I'm right about Harper, he could be working with my ex's husband and Chilicote. They could be a dangerous combination."

Michael mulled this over for a moment before asking, "What's your plan?"

"First, I have to ask you a question. It's been a week since I spoke to the President. I haven't seen a thing in the newspaper, and as far as I know, nothing has come up in Congress. I spoke to Ray, and nothing has been said to anyone at the bureau. If Jake is getting ready to resign, you should be preparing to take his place." He paused, then jumped in with, "So is the President serious about this new job?"

Michael took another sip of his drink. "I would like to tell you that he definitely is, but suddenly I'm not so sure. What I can say is that he's getting a lot of pressure from sources unknown."

The two men sat there, few words passing between them. Michael finished his drink and got up to pour another. He raised the bottle to Stuart, who shook his head.

Stuart walked over to the fish tank and stared at the water. "I might as well start releasing the pressure."

"Are you going to tell me how?"

"I don't think so, Michael. What I've learned in the past week is to leave people with the ability to deny."

Chapter Forty-Seven

Stuart walked out of his house at six fourteen, the Eastern sky just starting to brighten. At exactly six fifteen, a black Lincoln Town Car pulled up into the driveway.

"Captain Midnight?" the driver asked.

"That's me."

"There's coffee and Danish in the armrest. I have a copy of the *Wall Street Journal* up front, if you prefer, there's a TV built into the backseat. Reception isn't always so good, but it beats listening to the radio. It'll take thirty to forty minutes to reach where we're going, so enjoy yourself."

Stuart poured some coffee and looked longingly at the Danish, which he decided to forego. The side windows were darkened as was the glass partition between the front and back seats. He would not know where he was when he arrived, but his training told him that they were headed west toward Germantown. The television reception was better than he expected from a moving vehicle, and he watched the local news station. At six thirty, the world news came on, and the top story was the President telling the nation that he would find the truth about who wanted to smear the reputation of Jessica Winston. "Everything I have heard so far points to someone trying to unseat her when she comes up for reelection. I consider her one of the hardest working public servants in Washington."

Sounds like he's trying to jump on her bandwagon, thought Stuart.

The next story showed photos of the damage done by a Palestinian terrorist who blew himself up in an open market, killing three innocent bystanders and hurting fourteen others. Marc Frankel was not going to be a happy camper.

The weather report was just starting when the car left the highway. Stuart looked at his watch and noted that it had taken thirty-five minutes to drive to this point. Five minutes later, the car came to a stop. Stuart exited and looked around. There were two fences surrounding the house, each fence about five feet high and separated by four feet of empty space. Stuart surmised that there was more than enough room for two or three guard dogs to roam in that space at night. As he approached the house, he noticed two cameras covering the entrance, which meant there were probably a half dozen more in other places. Walking through the front door, he set off an alarm.

"We'd like you to leave any weapons up front for safekeeping." A woman with jet-black hair and very prominent white teeth, which flashed when she smiled, delivered the statement. "Please sign the register, first name only."

"How many guests do you have?" Stuart asked, signing the single sheet of paper.

"I'm not quite sure," she lied, the smile never leaving her face. "Here's the key to locker 11. You can hang up your jacket and leave behind anything else you won't need. Be sure to put on the blue jacket." Stuart stowed his belongings and donned the blue jacket. He knew the routine: if everyone is dressed alike, the visitors can't be identified. He walked through another detector and followed the woman.

"You're leaving the desk unattended?" he asked.

"Someone will watch it," she replied, preceding Stuart down a hallway. Her high heels clicked on the tile floor, bringing Stuart's attention to her legs, which he decided were very nice. Reaching the staircase, she pointed up. "Someone will meet you at the top. Have a nice day."

At the top of the stairs, a man wearing tan Dockers, a white shirt, and a blue jacket met him. "You've come to visit Miriam," he stated. "I'm here to remind you that anyone else you see or inadvertently meet, you will forget. She's in the second room on the right."

Stuart knocked once and entered. The room had to be more than six hundred square feet. It dwarfed the sofa, two chairs, a desk, a large television, and the king-sized bed on which Miriam sat. Stuart glanced at the television screen and saw two couples in various degrees of nakedness. Miriam smiled at Stuart's expression. "Not your type of movie?" she asked.

"I'm not a movie fan. When I watch, I like mysteries."

"You're not interested in which guy gets which girl?"

"From past experience, I would say that both guys get both girls or Vice versa."

"You're probably right," she replied, hitting the clicker and turning off the set. "When am I getting out of here?"

Stuart settled into a nearby chair. He knew better than to sit next to her on the bed. "Miriam, you have more than enough money stashed away to live comfortably. At the moment, everyone thinks you're dead. If they find out that you're alive, I wouldn't give you a plug nickel for your ability to spend it."

"So what am I going to do?"

"Help me."

"Come sit on the bed," she cooed, "and then I'll help you."

"Not that kind of help. Tell me about Eric."

Miriam stood and walked over to the window. "What do you want to know?"

"He got his promotions by being in the right place at the right time, but someone had to make sure something was going to happen at those places. I have to know who that someone is."

"It's not complicated," she responded, gazing at the security fences. "Eric would talk to someone, I'm not sure of his name, and tell him what type of arrest he needed, and that person would set it up."

"You have no idea who that person is?"

"No, but Eric was told not to use his gun because the people he was arresting would surrender."

"I need to know how he set it up. Think."

"He never told me, but he's getting ready to do it again."

Stuart's head jerked up. "When?"

"I'm not sure, but I do know that from his window, he can see a bank, and he's always talked about how great it would be if on his way to lunch, he interrupted a bank robbery and caught the crooks."

Stuart sat with this information for a moment. What he needed to know next was of great importance, so he had to word it just right. "We know that all of the crooks he caught got out of jail in less than six months. Any idea how he managed that?"

Miriam turned away from the window and smiled. "Oh, Senator Chilicote helped him with that one. See, every year there's a list of people the President pardons. Congressmen get to submit the names of prisoners from their districts, and then those names are turned over to the FBI. It was so easy! Eric got himself appointed to the job of getting those lists, and then he made sure that the people he wanted released were listed."

"Do you have any idea how many names are submitted to the President?"

Miriam sighed, as if bored with this line of inquiry. "I think Eric told me there were more than four hundred."

Stuart rose and headed toward the door. "You've been a big help, thanks. I'll tell the people in charge to bring you travel folders so you can start planning your retirement." With that, he opened the door to leave.

"Wait! Do you have to go?" Miriam gave him a provocative smile, stretching her arms above her head and causing her blouse to ride, exposing creamy white skin.

Stuart smiled and said, "Sorry, but I'm a monogamous person."

Miriam's arms dropped to her side. "Don't tell me you have a thing for that congresswoman they're talking about on TV."

"Why would you say that?" he asked, curious about how she made that connection.

"I heard your name mentioned with hers."

"On television?"

"No, when Eric was talking. He hired this kid called Augie to scare some girl. Augie was supposed to make it look like a robbery, but then you happened by and beat him up, along with a couple of his friends. This congresswoman's daughter was with the other girl, so all of a sudden they had to make Winston's daughter look like the target. They only wanted to shake her up, so Eric was really pissed off when you killed some of the men. He complained that he should have been the one who saved the congresswoman."

Stuart was gripping the doorknob with such force that his hand began to hurt. There was no way for Miriam to know that "the other girl" was his daughter. "Who are they?"

"Eric never told me their names, but some high-powered lawyer brought the guys from California."

Stuart's stomach was in a knot. It was bad enough that Marilyn was the original target, but even worse, knowing who was responsible.

Chapter Forty-Eight

Stuart dashed out of the safe house and found the car awaiting him, its motor running. The minute he climbed in, the driver said, "The office called, Sally says it's important, and I'm supposed to get you there in a hurry. There's a phone with a scrambler attached in the armrest." With that, the window between the front and back seats rose, cutting off further conversation.

The phone was answered on the first ring. "Sally, what's up?"

"No calls are accepted at the safe house and all hell's broken out down here."

"Fill me in."

"First off, the President's office called to postpone this afternoon's meeting."

"Did they say why?"

"Their exact words were tell Mr. Taylor the four o'clock meeting is postponed. Nothing else."

"Who called?"

"The chief of staff."

Stuart made a few mental notes and then asked, "What else is going on?"

"You received a call from Marc Frankel, but I don't know who or where he is. He'll call back. Brett Daniels called, again, someone else I don't know, but obviously British and he's in San Francisco. You can reach him at the Fairmont."

"Anything else?"

"Two anythings. A call from Eric Weaver who wants to know where Miriam's body is buried and more about the bodies you found last week. The second call, which I guess is almost anticlimactic, is that we got a hit from the car rental."

Stuart ran through his memory and drew a blank. "What car rental?"

"You asked us to run all the car rentals, looking for a van rented forty-eight hours prior to any of the robberies."

"Oh right, I remember. And?"

"And they found six vans rented to a Kevin Kinsella, who used an American Express company credit card. The name on the card is Green Tree Lawn and Garden, located in Virginia."

"See if you can find out anything about the company. You might try, the IRS or the Better Business Bureau, you know the drill. I'll call Brett now. If Marc calls, patch him through to me. I should be in the office in thirty minutes."

"What about your friend Eric Weaver?"

"When I get back, I'll deal with that son of a bitch."

A woman answered the phone when Stuart was put through to Brett's room. "Mr. Daniel's room."

"This is Stuart Taylor returning a call from Mr. Daniels."

"He's expecting your call. May I have the number you're calling from? He'll return your call in less than one minute."

Stuart's cell phone rang almost immediately. "That was quick."

"You heard about the terrorist bombing this morning in Israel?"

"Just what they showed on TV."

"I heard from Marc. One of the people who got hurt was a Saudi. He had explosives wrapped around his body. The first bomb went off prematurely and knocked him cold. The guy never got a chance to pull the string on his dynamite."

"Some people got lucky."

"Maybe us. He was carrying an American passport, posing as a tourist who spent four days in London before continuing on to Israel. They also found a key for a hotel room in Jerusalem. It was occupied by an American couple of Iraqi descent. We detained them, and they screamed like banshees that their rights were being violated. After some persuasion, they decided to tell all. Their group consisted of six men and two women. The Israelis have accounted for three of the men—one of whom blew himself up—and one of the women. The other couple is carrying British passports, and they left yesterday for Canada. The fourth man has disappeared. Marc is hoping that when the suicide bomber wakes up, they'll get more information. He's got the home address of the couple they arrested and wants you to check it out."

"He's keeping their arrest quiet?"

Brett Daniel didn't answer.

"Is he keeping their arrest quiet?" Stuart asked again.

"You'll have to ask him, but I think two Iraqis with American passports died in the bombing."

"Son of a bitch, I said we wanted to talk to anyone they found."

"He may not be to blame. He was visiting relatives in New York and spent the Sabbath with them, so Marc didn't arrive home until three hours before the bombing." Stuart looked at the tinted windows that shut out the light of day.

"Are you still there?" asked Brett.

"I'm here. I was just thinking of what it must be like to live in a country where life is so cheap."

"It's very different, trust me. I'll contact you when I have more information."

The line went dead, and Stuart replaced the receiver. Protecting his eyes from the glare outside, he climbed out of the car. A group of children were being led by their teacher up the stairs and into the front door of the building. "Stay in line," said one of the accompanying adults. "This is a very busy place. And remember what we learned the FBI is here to protect all the citizens of our country and to catch criminals."

Stuart followed them through the front door and watched them line up for the metal detectors. Each child made a big deal of going through pockets and emptying everything onto trays. The alarm went off on a few of them, mainly due to pens in their jackets or oversized zippers.

"Letting these kids in here shouldn't be allowed."

Stuart turned and found himself face-to-face with Eric Weaver.

"Why not?"

"They disrupt the flow."

"How so? They're not allowed upstairs, and the tour only shows them the lighter side of the building." Stuart felt himself getting aggravated. "I have something to talk to you about, whenever you have time."

"What is it?" Weaver asked.

"Not here. Meet me after lunch. It has to do with the bank robberies I was working on." Stuart watched closely and noted how Weaver's eyes took on a gleam and thought to himself, *He's a piece of shit, and he's forgotten all about Miriam.*

"Don't play game with me, Taylor. I want to know now."

Stuart looked at his watch. "I have an important meeting in twenty minutes. I'll come to your office in an hour, and we can discuss it."

Weaver wasn't happy with Stuart calling the plays, but he nodded. When Stuart walked toward the elevators, Weaver called out "See you then!" as if he had been the one to terminate their meeting.

Chapter Forty-Nine

"He's coming to my office in an hour. I think he's got a line on some bank robberies I've been assigned to."

"What's that mean to me?" The words were hard, sending a shiver through Weaver's body.

Weaver tried to sound professional and make the intimidation he was feeling go away. "If I can solve these robberies, I'll definitely get the promotion."

"What if he only wants to pass the time of day?"

"Maybe," Weaver faltered, almost afraid to continue.

"Maybe what!"

"Maybe you can arrange to have someone try and rob the bank across the street, and I can catch them in the act."

"The last time I did that, it cost me over a quarter of a million dollars."

"But this would be the last time. I'd become deputy director and—"

"And nothing. Let me know what he has to say, you know my number."

For Eric Weaver, the silence that followed was more frightening than the man's voice. He called out "Miriam!" before remembering that she was dead. He meant to ask about the funeral but had forgotten. Instead, he wondered where he could *get* a new secretary. Perhaps the senator could suggest someone. He smiled, now that he knew how to proceed.

Stuart felt impatience rising in his chest. "Ray, I'm sure this'll work. Weaver called a number reached only by dialing the number of a phone booth in some godforsaken place, and then that call is transferred to a cell phone. It's just like Miriam said: he wants to stop a robbery in progress so he can get the credit . . . and a promotion."

Ray Bradley shook his head. "Weaver's got to be out of his mind. Why would he think that catching some scum would advance his career?"

"Probably because he's done it in the past."

Ray paused for a moment, digesting this information. "Okay, I'll discuss it with Jake."

Stuart shook his head emphatically. "It's better if he doesn't know."

Ray stared at the man, trying to comprehend an unspoken message. "Any particular reason?"

"How was his speech in Minnesota?" said Stuart.

The change of topics wasn't lost on Ray. "Fine, just between you and me."

Stuart sat in Eric Weaver's office and suppressed the desire to kill him. Instead, he kept his voice calm, almost placating. "Eric, I know we got off on the wrong foot, but maybe this can soothe the bad feelings."

Weaver sat on the power side of the desk, fingers forming a pyramid and eyes staring, unblinking.

"I think those crooks I've been chasing are headed this way. Remember me telling you about the shoes, and the person who remains in the van? Well, my snitch tells me that he saw these guys in New Jersey last week, at one of the casinos. That means they're getting close. If we get a task force to cover the local banks, we just might catch those bastards in the act." Having spoken, he nearly held his breath in anticipation of the reply.

"How many men would we need?"

Stuart felt the heaviness being lifted off his back. If Weaver wanted to play, the game could only get better. "Since only one of them works with a loaded gun, we could probably get by with one man for each bank we pick."

Weaver nodded, touching his mouth to the pyramid. "Have you shared this idea with Levitt?"

Stuart tried to inject petulance into his voice. "I'm officially off the case. Remember? But I want these people caught so bad that I'm willing to break a few rules."

Weaver managed a little smile. "Don't say anything for a couple of days and let me see what I can do."

Minutes later, Weaver was on the phone with his contact. "Taylor just left here. He thinks the bank robbers are headed toward Virginia. He wants me to assign men to cover some of the smaller banks, but I have a better idea."

"Which is?" asked the man Eric was talking to.

"Can you arrange for three men to rob the National Bank across the street from my office? I'll be there in time to stop the robbery, but the men will get away. I'll blame Taylor for not passing the information upward in a timely manner, which will leave him in disgrace."

"When would you want this to happen?"

"How about Wednesday, at two thirty in the afternoon. I'll take a late lunch and be on my way back when it goes down."

"You're sure no one will get hurt. I can't afford to lose any men."

"I'm positive. I'll be by myself and when they come out of the bank. I'll yell for them to stop and fire over their heads."

"Let me think about it."

"Okay, but remember, two men go in and the third stays in a van that's parked in front."

"I'll call you later today," said the voice in a tone that said the conversation was over.

Shortly after Eric Weaver's private conversation, Stuart was on the phone with Ray Bradley.

"Ray, it's Stuart. He's bought it. They're going to hit the bank across the street on Wednesday at two thirty."

"How do you know?"

Stuart hesitated. As much as he trusted Ray, he still wasn't ready to tell the deputy director of the FBI that he was having phones tapped inside the bureau. Before he could respond, his boss hissed, "Don't tell me you're having his phone tapped."

"Okay, I won't tell you," said Stuart. "Let's just say that I know it's Wednesday at two thirty—and leave it at that."

Ray released what sounded to Stuart like a very heavy sigh and then asked, "Fine, Stuart, what's the plan, and how many agents do you need?"

Stuart felt the adrenaline surging. "The plan is simple, really. And I'll be nearby, so I won't need any men."

"I don't think I'm going to like this."

"Trust me, Ray, this is going to work. I'll send you an internal memo this afternoon. It'll tell you that I think the bank robbers are moving into Virginia, that I've contacted agent Weaver, advised him of my thoughts, and he's investigating."

"And?"

"And nothing. Just be sure to watch CNN or CNBC Wednesday afternoon."

Stuart's phone rang later that day. He'd been reading the preliminary reports on Kevin Kinsella and the nursery he worked for.

"Is this a secure line?"

Stuart recognized Marc Frankel's voice. "It is."

"Give me a secure fax number. I'm sending copies of the documents taken off the, uh, victims from the terrorist attack. The documents say they're Americans on vacation, but my sources say they're Saudis connected to Al-Qaeda."

"I understand your informant has died."

"Unfortunately, yes. I arrived back too late to request a change in the way these things are handled. Hopefully, I can do better in the future."

Stuart gave Marc the safe number. "It takes longer," he explained to the Israeli, "but it's very secure."

"They're on the way." Stuart shifted in his chair and put both feet on his desk. "I've gone over those reports, and I have a question. This Bin Laden character, why hasn't he been dealt with?"

"If we could find him, Stuart, he would be. We think he's somewhere in Afghanistan, perhaps Pakistan. Pinning down his location down has proved daunting."

"Is it a question of offering enough money?"

"Money won't do it. His family is wealthier than some small countries. No, you don't get close to him unless he wants you to, and there aren't many people he wants to see. We have names of many of his top aides, but it's a tough road." After a shared silence, Marc added, "We have come across some things we can't figure out." When Stuart said nothing, he said, "For one thing, they're looking for pilots. This does not bode well."

Stuart felt a chill running up his back. "It certainly doesn't," he said.

"We've got to assume they're going to try to hijack planes."

"Any guesses where they'll do this?"

"Certainly not Israel or Russia. Maybe from France or one of the 'Stans."

"I know that your security is tight, but why not Russia?"

"It's not a security question, Stuart, it's that both countries have a hard policy of not giving in to demands."

"We don't give in," responded Stuart, more out of hurt pride than anything else.

"I know" was all that Marc said. "In any case, let me know if you find out anything from these documents. Meanwhile, I'll keep in touch."

The tone of the disconnect told Stuart that the conversation was over. He dialed the private number of David Gastner, the President's chief of staff, and the call was answered on the first ring. "This is Stuart Taylor. Please tell the President I must see him today."

"Didn't you get his message?"

"I got the message you left. It's now two, I'll be there at three."

It was nearly twenty seconds before a reply arrived. "Make it four thirty."

Chapter Fifty

"Good afternoon, Gary." Stuart smiled at the Secret Service agent he had met during his last visit to the White House.

"Good afternoon. I was told you were coming. How's life treating you?"

"Not bad," Stuart replied as he held his arms up for the perfunctory pat down.

"I heard a name like yours on television yesterday, but no picture."

Stuart smiled broadly. "I take bad pictures."

Gary looked around and, in sotto voce, said, "In that case, I suggest you avoid the front of the building. Someone's called a press conference for four thirty, and it's got your name all over it."

Stuart looked at his watch and nodded. "I owe you one."

"Just remember my name when you start that new organization."

"Mr. Taylor, I'm glad to see that you're early." David Gastner approached Stuart with his hand outstretched. "We've arranged a little press conference so the President can thank you publicly for the way you handled that threat on Congresswoman Winston."

Stuart squared his shoulders and looked the man directly in the eye.

"Mr. Gastner, let me be perfectly honest with you. The only reason I'm here is to talk to the President about terrorist activities that must come to his attention. One week ago, I was told that I would have access to the President, as needed. If he's changed his mind about me, that's fine, but I will not be part of some dog and pony show."

"I've arranged for you to meet with the President for fifteen minutes after the press conference, will that do?"

"Change that to fifteen minutes before and it'll do just fine."

Gastner's eyes narrowed, and his cheeks went red. "I don't think you understand. You don't tell the President what to do, he tells you."

"And I don't think you understand," Stuart shot back. "I'm not telling the President, I'm telling you. If I go to that press gathering first, you can be sure I'll mention the terrorist rumors and how this country is ignoring them."

"You do know you're committing political suicide."

"What I know is, there's a problem and someone has to pay attention. If, after listening to me, the President decides that I need to resign, I'll do it."

Gastner took a cell phone from his pocket and pushed a button. "Tell the press corps that the meeting has been pushed back thirty minutes." He listened to the person on the other end and then erupted, "I don't give a shit what reason you give them. If they don't like it, tell the assholes to go home!" He turned to Stuart. "Follow me."

The two men proceeded along the corridor and came to several guards stationed in front of the double doors leading to the working area. Stuart realized that word was spreading quickly because no one would look at either of them as they sped through the building.

Gastner knocked twice and then entered the President's office. "Mr. President, we have a little problem."

The President looked up, a frown on his face. "What do you consider a little problem?"

"Mr. Taylor refuses to attend the press conference until he speaks to you."

"Did you tell him what the conference was called for?"

"Yes, I did, Mr. President, but he refuses to listen."

"Did you explain to him that I thought he should attend?"

Stuart cleared his throat. "Mr. President, you may not have noticed, but I am standing here."

The President turned his glance to Stuart. "As far as I'm concerned, you aren't here. You are waiting for me to join you on the front steps."

"In that case, Mr. President, I suggest you head out to the front steps and tell the people whatever story you want. Just understand that I will not be there."

A vein suddenly appeared on the President's temple. "I am the President of the United States," he intoned. "You work for this country, which means you work for me. If you won't go to the press briefing, you won't be working for the government." Turning his attention to his chief of staff, he added, "David, walk Mr. Taylor to the front of the building. If he doesn't go with you, see that he's released from government Service . . . today."

Gastner began to walk out, but Stuart did not follow. "Mr. President," he said, "you two men are living on a different planet. In the week since we last met, I've had meetings with representatives from four countries. As a result of those meetings, I've learned that two people involved in yesterday's Israeli bombing were carrying American passports. The Israelis captured one of them and are faxing the address of where they lived in the States. I've also been told that some of the terrorists are taking flying lessons, which points to possible takeover and hostage situations all over the world. I don't know the exact number, but we must have more than ten thousand planes leaving from any given airport in the U.S. alone."

"What are you suggesting, that we close down our airports?"

"Of course not, Mr. President. What I'm suggesting is that you start the ball rolling. Last week, you told me about this new group, which I think you referred to as Home Guard. Don't let your idea die on the vine."

The President looked at his chief of staff. "What do you think, David?"

"I think Taylor's an arrogant bastard."

"Aside from that?"

The chief of staff looked directly at Stuart. "Where is your information coming from?" he demanded.

"A meeting in New York with high-level security men from Israel, Canada, Mexico, and Great Britain. I've had further conversations with two of them since then."

"So the five of you met and—"

"There were more than five of us there," interrupted Stuart. "Michael and Jake were also present."

The chief of staff nodded. "Ah, so that was the screwup with Jake's plane."

"What was decided?" asked the President, his voice now devoid of anger.

"We want to improve communication between our five countries. Consideration would also be given to include other countries in the group."

"Which other countries?" the President asked.

"Russia and China."

The President poured a glass of water. "Mr. Taylor . . . Stuart . . . please give us a couple of minutes alone."

Stuart responded, "I'll be right outside the door," and walked out, wondering if he would still have a job when he returned.

Behind the closed door, the President shook his head and said, "You're right, David, he certainly is an arrogant bastard."

"But he's good," Gastner replied with more than a little admiration.

"Very good, but what do we do with the press outside?"

"How about we tell them everything we were going to say and then add that Taylor will be going on special assignment for the intelligence community?"

"Do you think he'll buy it?"

"He'll have to, at least until we're sure of what's happening and how we want it handled."

"Okay, bring him in and let's get the show on the road."

Gastner left the room and returned moments later with a very curious agent.

"Mr. Taylor," said the chief of staff, "you have the President over the proverbial barrel. He's called the press together to publicly thank you. We understand you may have personal feelings for her, but you acted in the best interest of the country. The President has been having some problems funding this new department, which doesn't mean he isn't committed to proceed; he just needs a little more time. He'd like you to attend the press briefing, where he is prepared to announce that you're being transferred to a high post inside the intelligence community. He can then fall behind the veil of secrecy if questions are asked."

"And if any of those questions are asked of me?" Stuart asked, looking straight at the President.

The President held up a hand, indicating that he wanted to answer this question. "Tell them we're committed to helping achieve peace in the world, and that might mean helping our allies in their time of need."

"Mr. President, does that mean I can continue what I'm doing?"

The President's face hardened, and Stuart understood that the leader of the free world did not want to get pinned down to a course of action he could not control. Before the man had a chance to respond, Stuart spoke again, "Mr. President, I did not ask that question." He saw the President's brow suddenly relax. "What do you think of this: Tell the press corps that I'm being assigned to the intelligence community to investigate and report directly back to you on terrorist activities around the world, and then let it go at that."

The President smiled and stood up. "I like it, let's get to the briefing."

Chapter Fifty-One

Stuart stood to the right and slightly behind the President, listening to Kim Pederson, the President's press secretary.

"Ladies and Gentlemen, if I could please have your attention. You've been clamoring for more information with regard to Congresswoman Winston, and the President will be addressing that issue. He will also discuss the situation in the Middle East. He has a prepared statement and will then take a few questions." She turned and looked at the double doors. "Mr. President."

Stuart watched as the crowd stood, and the President walked to the microphones.

"Good evening. Before we get started, I would like to introduce"—the President turned and nodded to Stuart—"Mr. Taylor, please come join me." Stuart stepped up to where the President was standing, the glare of a hundred flashbulbs forcing him to shield his eyes. "Ladies and Gentlemen, Stuart Taylor." The President put his arm around Stuart's shoulder and smiled as the glare intensified.

"For two days," said the President, "stories have been written, and not all of them are true, about Congresswoman Winston's visit to New York. I've asked the Secret Service to investigate threats made on her and her daughter, and I promise you a complete accounting as soon as I have the answers. I've asked Mr. Taylor to meet with you and answer questions. He acted with courage and forethought to insure their safety, and I'm proud that he is part of our team. I would also like to take this opportunity to tell the world that the United States will not stand still as the forces of evil continue to terrorize our friends. I have, as of this day, assigned Mr. Taylor to the job of coordinating with our allies the war against terrorists. He will report directly to me so that I, along with Congress, can put into effect a program that will hopefully eliminate terrorist activities forever. Yesterday's bombing in Israel took civilian lives. These attacks must be stopped, and we must help stop them. If you have any questions of Stuart or me, we have some time."

Twenty hands shot up simultaneously. The President pointed at Victoria Denson, who always got the first question on even-numbered days, as well as the last question on odd-numbered ones.

"Mr. Taylor, what can you tell us about your relationship with Congresswoman Winston?"

Stuart looked at the President for guidance; the President motioned him closer to the microphone.

"I've known the congresswoman for a few weeks. Our daughters are friends, which is how we met. Any other questions?" The subject was obviously closed.

The President pointed to a man standing in the front row.

"Mr. Stuart, you don't know me, but I write the Potomac Happenings column for my paper." The crowd went quiet. "The story I wrote was correct in every detail, but you somehow were able to change the events so that I looked like a fool. Do you make people look like liars in your everyday duties? And if so, what department do you work in? I have it on very good authority that, until recently, you worked for the ATF doing something that no one will talk about."

"I missed your name," Stuart said lightly, after taking a deep breath.

"My name is Joseph Drake."

"Thank you, Mr. Drake. I noticed that when you wrote that story you didn't put your name on it. I also noticed that you lied." Stuart held up his hand. "Don't bother to deny it. The congresswoman never took those kickbacks you referred to, and no one said she did. A Ms. Gund from your paper called, trying to get some facts after that edition was put to bed. As for where I worked, it was under the auspices of the ATF. Recently, I was transferred to the Federal Bureau of Investigation. As you just heard from the President, I am again being transferred, but there are people inside of the, like my good friend Eric Weaver, who will do me the Service of tracking down the source of your lies. Once that happens, they'll make sure that this person, or persons, ceases to give out false statements to the American public."

The press corps was stunned. No one had ever accused one of their own of outright lying. They had been accused of publishing erroneous information, but never this.

This being an even-numbered day, the President called on Chuck Andres.

"Mr. President, the enormity of what Mr. Taylor just said goes far beyond my ability to ask simple questions. We have never had a journalist accused of lying in front of a nationally televised audience. I hope Mr. Taylor can back up his statement."

Stuart again stepped forward. "Mr. Andres, you're a respected columnist. Rather than take up everyone's valuable time, how about you pick two of your colleagues and then the four of us will meet and go over the proof. The only thing I ask is that the three of you publish the results."

Chuck Andres looked around the room. He'd just been put on the spot on national television, and he was in a bind. If he refused the offer, it would look like he was afraid to follow up on a story. If he accepted, he could be seen as a watchdog on the working press. He removed his glasses and rubbed his eyes. "I'll check with my paper to ensure that they'll publish my findings," he said. "Once I have their permission, I will, of course, contact you. As far as the other two members of this group, I invite anyone interested to please contact me after this meeting."

Kim Pederson stepped to the microphones. "Thank you for attending. Mr. Taylor looks like he's going to keep everyone on his or her toes. Because this meeting started a little late, I had sandwiches delivered, and you're all invited to partake."

Stuart followed the President and his chief of staff back into the White House.

"It's usually not a good idea to call any reporter a liar," said Gastner. "Are you sure you can prove this?" Stuart shrugged and nearly smiled. "If nothing else, I figure I bought another week. We'll see."

"I didn't know that you and Eric Weaver were friends?" interjected the President.

"You know Eric Weaver, sir?" Stuart asked.

"I met him once, when he was the FBI agent in charge of checking out the pardons. He comes highly recommended from some members of Congress."

"So I've heard, Mr. President. Who would you like me to interface with during the week?"

"I've already told you, report directly to me."

"There should be a liaison I can go to in between our meetings."

"Who would you suggest?" the President answered after a few seconds of thought.

"Maybe Michael, if he's going to head up the bureau."

"Michael would be a good choice, but as you know, I haven't announced that move yet."

"Can I ask why you haven't, sir?"

The chief of staff stepped in with "No, you can't."

"Then who would you recommend?" asked Stuart, facing David Gastner.

"That's up to the President," he shot back. Stuart looked at the President, who raised both hands, as if in surrender.

"Okay, it's Michael, but I'll talk to him first. David, ask Michael to stop over tonight around nine." The President stared at Stuart. "I think that you could become one big pain in my butt, but you do have a way of getting things done." Almost as an afterthought, he added, "Michael will contact you tomorrow. Is there anything else you need to know?"

Stuart smiled broadly. "Does this new job come with a raise?"

The President shook his head and waved his hand. "Ask Michael that question."

Stuart knew he was being dismissed but needed to squeeze in one last question. "Mr. President, does Senator Chilicote figure in your long-range plans?"

The President sat down. "Why would you ask that?"

"Because he's dirty, and he's going down."

It took a moment for the President to process that message. "How dirty?"

Stuart looked at the chief of staff. "I'm not sure Mr. Gastner should be in the room when I tell you."

"Why not?"

"Because you may want to deny ever hearing what I have to say, and Mr. Gastner might be forced under oath to refute you."

"That's crazy," protested Gastner loudly.

"Not so crazy," the President replied. "David, why don't you get me a cup of coffee while I say good-bye to Stuart."

As the door closed, the President leaned over and repeated, "How dirty?"

Chapter Fifty-Two

It was approaching six thirty when Stuart entered the restaurant where he was meeting Senator Chilicote. He had never eaten here before and was surprised at the number of people waiting for seats. Standing behind a well-dressed couple, he listened to them arguing with the maître d' about having to wait twenty minutes past their reservation time. The official-looking man tried to placate them by explaining that there was a two-hour wait for anyone without a reservation. As the couple moved off toward the bar, Stuart turned to the man and said, "Six thirty reservations for Stuart Taylor."

The headwaiter looked at his list, smiled, and replied, "Ah yes, here you are. We're running a little behind. Your table will be ready in approximately one hour. If you will wait in the bar, I will find you."

"But you just told those people it would be twenty minutes." Stuart nodded toward the bar.

"Yes, but they did come in before you."

He looked at the tables in the dining area. "I see you have empty tables."

"We expect those people any minute. Now, if you will wait inside, I will call you." He looked past Stuart and smiled. "Mr. Burke, how nice it is to see you again."

The man, well dressed, and with a woman fifteen years his junior, smiled broadly. "Edward, I'm sorry I didn't get a chance to call. Do you have a table against the wall?"

"Of course, Mr. Burke, please follow me."

Stuart watched the three of them walk to the back of the dining area. The frown on his face became a mischievous smile as he leaned over the podium and tore out the page of reservations. Walking into the bar, he laughed out loud and took a seat where he could watch the front door. At six thirty five, the senator entered. *Five minutes late*, thought Stuart. *Exactly the time you keep someone of lesser importance waiting*. He stood and joined the senator at the podium.

"Senator, how nice to see you," he said, watching with interest the reaction of the headwaiter.

"Edward, you look flustered," the senator said, ignoring Stuart. "Is everything all right?"

"Good evening, Senator. I seem to have lost my reservation list. Your reservation was for what time?"

The senator turned to Stuart, his expression quizzical.

"Five minutes ago," offered Stuart. "But that doesn't matter, since your friend, Edward, told me we have nearly an hour's wait."

The senator turned slowly to face the maître d'. "Is that true, Edward?"

The man waved his hand, as if brushing away something unacceptable. "No, of course not, Senator. Your friend must not have understood me. Your table is ready, please follow me."

Stuart reached into his pocket, and when they arrived at their table, he handed Edward a shiny quarter. "Thanks for the Service."

"How much did you give him?" Chilicote asked.

"Twenty-five," Stuart replied.

The man nodded, impressed. "He'll remember you; I only give him a ten spot."

After ordering, the senator started the conversation with "Now what was it you wanted to talk to me about?"

Stuart picked up the large damask napkin and refolded it. Turning his gaze to his dinner partner, he said, "The President has asked me to head up a new department, which is tentatively called Home Guard. Since I've had relatively no experience in the running of a department, only the operations side, he suggested you might be a good choice to work with me."

"So you're asking for my help?"

"Not really, Senator. Last week, I was going to ask for your help; today, I'm going to tell you that the offer has been withdrawn."

The senator sneered as he leaned in. "Did you think for one second that I'd play second fiddle to you?"

Stuart smiled benignly. "At the time that I was prepared to talk to you about the job, it would not have been a second fiddle position. I was prepared to offer you the leadership of the department for two years." He saw the senator's expression change from sarcasm to curiosity. Whatever happened, he knew he was about to have fun.

"Really? And what made you change your mind?"

Stuart leaned closer and said, "I decided I don't like you. On top of that, I have a problem working with people who abuse their position for personal gain."

The senator nearly laughed. "You mean like that bitch you're dating?"

Stuart clenched his jaw for a moment. The last thing he wanted was to be on the defensive with this man. "I'm surprised you'd refer to a sitting member of congress in that tone. Before my friend Eric Weaver's secretary died, I had a conversation with her. She was very much in love with him and told me some stories about you that I'm tempted to share with him."

The senator's face tightened. "What kind of stories?"

"Kickbacks, sexual favors, and the like. I'm not sure what Eric's feelings were for Miriam, but I'm certain that I want no part of you."

"To whom have you told these fairy tales?" asked the man.

Stuart smiled. "No one, mainly because I can't document what she revealed. But Eric might be interested."

The maître d' approached their table and spoke directly to Stuart, "I hate to bother you, but we seem to have lost a page from our reservation book."

"You think I took it?"

The man nearly jumped. "No! Of course not! But well, you were the last person seated, and I'm at a loss about who has reservations and who doesn't."

"Sorry, I can't help you," said Stuart. "In fact, the Service has been so bad that I'm leaving." Stuart stood and faced Chilicote. "Senator, take care of the bill, and remember to leave a big tip." With that, he walked away with a smile on his face.

As Stuart disappeared from sight, the senator took out his cell phone and dialed his longtime benefactor. "We've got to do something about him. He said that before Miriam was killed, she told him some stories about me. All our plans are going to go down the drain."

"The man's a clod," the voice on the other end stated, "and he's been a nonentity for more than fifteen years. There isn't a good report about him anywhere that I can find, and I've followed his career personally. He even thinks Eric is a friend. I'll contact my sources tomorrow and float a trial balloon about your being the next attorney general. Then I'll make arrangements to insure that Eric gets that promotion."

Chapter Fifty-Three

At five thirty the next morning, the ringing of the telephone woke Stuart. "This is Taylor."

"Dad, it's Kenneth, sorry to bother you this early, but I didn't know what to do."

Stuart immediately sat up, body alert. "What's the problem?"

"My step dad's lawyer, Mr. Hall, called last night. He told me my tuitions been revoked, and Friday is my last day at school. If I can't take the finals, the whole year's a waste."

"Did he say why it's been revoked?"

"Something about last weekend and me lying to Mr. Loring."

"I'll call Peter Weber, don't worry. He's my best friend, and this is what he does best. What did your mother say?"

"She wasn't home last night, and it's too early to call her. I don't know what she'll say." After a pause, he added, "You sure this isn't going to be a problem?"

"I'm sure, now go back to sleep. When you wake up, it'll be resolved."

There was a moment of silence and then, "Dad, thanks!"

Stuart glanced at the clock on his nightstand and decided to let Peter sleep another fifteen minutes. He turned on the TV and laid back down on the bed. It was five to seven when he opened his eyes. *Long time since I've done that,* he thought as he dialed Peter's number.

"Don't you ever sleep?" Peter asked, not waiting for Stuart to say hello.

"You won't believe it, but I let you sleep an extra ninety minutes."

"What's the problem that couldn't wait until eight?"

"My ex's husband, Loring, cancelled tuition payments for my son's school. He's only got a couple of weeks until graduation, and I'd like you to take care of it for me."

"I thought you had something hard for me to do. Tell Kenneth not to worry."

"I already told him that. Ask Joan if she's up to going out some night and let me know when."

"How are you doing with Jessica and the bank robberies?" Peter asked. "With all that I'm hearing, I'd be surprised if you had time for anything."

"I think we got a lead on the robberies, but I still have to check it out. As for Jessica, we'll see. I'll fill you in when we get together." He was about to say good-bye when he added, "Before I forget, what's the name of your gardening Service? Jessica thinks your place looks great, and maybe they have time for another customer."

Peter hesitated. "Green Tree Lawns or Green Gardens, something like that. They're located somewhere in Virginia. The number's downstairs."

Stuart hesitated. "Do me a favor and give me a call with their number. I have an eight thirty meeting and need to start getting ready. And thanks for handling this problem with Kenneth's school."

"You sound funny," said Peter. "Is everything okay?"

"It's this new job. When we have dinner, I'll tell you about it."

Replacing the receiver, Stuart mused over the fact that Peter always told him to never trust coincidences. That train of thought was broken when Jessica's picture popped up on the television screen. He raised the sound, his shoulders leaning forward expectantly.

"The rumor today, that of Senator Chilicote's name being thrown into the hopper for the new attorney general, opened another slot in the Senate for Congresswoman Jessica Winston. Washington has been in a frenzy trying to come up with possibilities for the congresswoman, and this would certainly fill the bill. When Senator Chilicote was asked, this was his response."

A talking head shot of the senator filled the screen. "You're all a little premature. What I can tell you, however, is that if I were offered the job of attorney general, I would certainly support the congresswoman to fill my seat in the Senate. She would, of course, have to be elected first."

The camera cut back to the reporter, who announced, "There's an unconfirmed story out of California that Senator Moreland may retire due to bad health. This is, of course, fueling this replacement theory."

The picture changed again, this time to Niagara Falls, and the newscaster spoke of the Canadian border patrol stopping a man with a Saudi passport and then discovering that his car's trunk was filled with explosives. "The man is claiming diplomatic immunity, but the police have informed us that immunity is only in place if he were coming from the United States and was stopped on the Canadian side of the border."

The picture changed again, this time to a map showing the country's weather patterns. Stuart lowered the volume and sighed. It was going to be a busy day.

Halfway through the report that Sally had accumulated on Green Tree, Stuart's phone rang.

"I have to talk to you now," Eric Weaver whispered into the phone.

"Come on over, you know where my office is."

"Two floors below mine," he replied, as if reminding Stuart that the higher the floor, the higher the importance. "I don't want anyone to see us talking," he added.

Stuart shook his head. "Tell you what, there's a men's room halfway down the hall; I'll be there in five minutes. If you happen to stop by, we can talk."

"A men's room?"

"Eric, if you can't talk on the phone, the men's room with tiled walls is the safest place." Stuart smiled; sure that he could hear what Eric was thinking.

"You're right, but come up to my floor. Less people use this bathroom."

Stuart wondered how Eric came to know that useless piece of information but let it pass. "Let's compromise. I'll meet you in the middle in five minutes."

"That's great," Eric, replied, "I really like it when agents can work together."

Five minutes later and after checking out all the closed stalls, Eric began to speak. "Which banks do you think our men should start covering? I think I've only got eight men for two weeks, so I want to make sure we cover the most likely targets."

"I might be able to save you some resources," said Stuart. "The robberies only take place on Fridays or Mondays, which mean we can cover forty banks on those two days."

Eric nodded and then said, "Fine, now which banks?"

"I have some work to do, so I'll get the list to you on Thursday. As close as I can figure it, we have two weeks before they start in this area."

"Stuart, I want to thank you," said Weaver. "A lot of men would've been upset, having to turn this over to someone else."

"No problem, Eric. Like I said, I just want these people caught."

Weaver nodded and then checked his appearance in the wall-length mirror. "I also want to thank you for the kind words you said about me on television. With you being transferred, I'm a shoo-in for this promotion."

Stuart offered his most enthusiastic smile. "Oh, I'm sure you'll get much more than a promotion; you'll be remembered in the annals of the bureau."

Eric smiled at Stuart's reflection in the mirror and then walked out, ignoring his new best friend's outstretched hand.

The address received from Israel was in Clearwater, Florida. Stuart called Ray Bradley for two reasons: to fill him in on the information and to request the man's help.

"Send a team to the address and shake it down thoroughly," suggested Stuart. "The people will be reported killed in the explosion, so it won't be unusual to have the neighborhood canvassed for restaurants, cleaners, or travel agents they might have used. We can say we're looking for relatives."

"Done," said Bradley. "And I'll have our Florida office jump on it immediately. Have you given any more thought to what you're doing tomorrow?"

"I think I'll watch CNN and see what develops."

"Be careful, Stuart."

He smiled at the warning. "You're like my mother, Ray. She's always worrying about me."

"I hate visiting the mothers of agents who weren't careful."

"Message received, I'll watch myself."

Stuart had returned to reading the report when Sally's voice interrupted him. "Congresswoman Winston on line 1. Shall I tell her you're busy?"

"Only if you want to go work for Weaver." He picked up the receiver and said, "Jessica, how's your day going?"

"Wonderfully. I was just wondering what you were going to cook for dinner?"

"Checking up on me?"

"No, just wanting to know what wine to bring."

"I'm glad you called." As soon as he spoke, something changed in the silence between them.

"Is something wrong?"

"No, I'm just glad you called." Her concern cut through his banter. "As for the wine, any kind is fine, as long as you're the one who brings it."

"So how is your day going?" she asked, added warmth in her voice. "Better than most, but I'll tell you about it tonight. See you around six thirty."

"I'll be there." She stopped talking but didn't hang up.

"Jess, are you there?"

"I'm here. I'm . . ." and then she stopped. When she resumed, it was to repeat that she would arrive at six thirty.

Stuart wished the day to pass quickly. "I'll be home by five. If you have the time, come early, okay? I'd love to show you my house."

"I may do just that."

Immediately after their conversation ended, Sally buzzed again. "Bill Cook on line 2," she announced. "And Peter called to say that everything is taken care of. He said you'd understand."

Stuart acknowledged the messages and picked up the receiver. "Bill, I heard you caught some guy at the falls."

"He's screaming," reported the agent. "He's claiming diplomatic immunity and refuses to accept his immunity only counts in the country to which he's assigned to the diplomatic corps. He and his government are saying a diplomat is a diplomat wherever he is."

"Is he one of the people who left Israel yesterday?"

"No, he just turned up in the alert we issued."

"What country is claiming him as a diplomat?"

"Saudi Arabia."

Stuart felt the muscles in his neck tighten. "Are they crazy?"

"I think we're the crazy ones, and I don't think we can hold him."

"Do you at least get to keep the explosives?" asked Stuart, half joking.

"I don't know, these politics are screwing us up." There was frustration in Cook's voice. "We haven't been able to find out how he got into the country, we don't know where he's been staying, and we don't know where he got the explosives."

Stuart knew that Cook needed placating. There were times agents like Cook thought they'd never get a break. "Bill, I have a suggestion."

"I'm listening."

"Give him his car with or without the explosives and send him on his way, but make sure he comes my way. I'll have my people stop him and hold him somewhere where he can't be found."

"Ever?"

"Ever!"

"I'll let you know which way he's headed," said Cook, a new energy in his voice.

Stuart pushed the Intercom button. "Sally, find me Michael now."

Twenty minutes later, he explained to Michael what he wanted done. When Bill Cook phoned back, Stuart was ready.

"Bill, this is what you're going to do. Tomorrow, walk your friend to the Air Canada terminal and make sure he gets on the plane headed for New York. Tell him that he can't transport explosive materials into the States, but you'll have it sent to the Saudi Embassy in New York by truck, if they agree to accept it."

"You're going to pick him up when he lands in New York?"

"Something like that."

"Nice talking to you, Stuart, and good luck."

Moments later, Sally buzzed to announce, "There's a Mr. Loring on the phone. He insists that I put him through. Do you know him?"

"Ask him to hold on while you locate me. Count to thirty and then put him through."

Thirty seconds later, he was saying, "This is Stuart Taylor. How may I help you?"

The voice exploded through the receiver, "You know goddamn well how you can help me," said Loring. "For fifteen years, I've raised those brat kids of yours and without any input from you. Now all of a sudden you want to get involved! You listen to me, Taylor, I'm telling you to stay away from them and me."

"I remember you," said Stuart, his voice quiet and controlled. "You're the guy that dated my wife when I was on assignment. The story going around was that you were impotent and needed a ready-made family. Was that true?"

"I was what!"

"I said," impotent, "that you were—"

"I heard what you said," interrupted Loring. "Now listen to me you, you fucking civil servant. Stay away from the children or else."

"Or else what?" he asked, a hard edge creeping into his voice. "You listen to me, Loring. By some quirk of fate, my kids are back in my life. And another thing: you have no idea how annoying civil servants can be if you get us upset. And I promise you, you are getting close to my being upset. If you'd like to tell me what this call is about, I'll see what I can do."

"You had some obnoxious person call the school and handle the tuition."

"So?"

"I was punishing him."

"And I decided he didn't need to be punished. In the future, you'll check with me before you punish either of them."

"They live under my roof, Taylor, they obey my wishes."

"Don't worry about Kenneth, he won't be coming back. As for Marilyn, if she wants out, I'll let you know."

"Do you have any idea how much it costs to keep those brats in clothes, let alone school?"

"Let's get something straight," responded Stuart. "I don't like you, I never have. I didn't have a really good reason until now. But there's something you need to know. People I don't like seem to have trouble with the IRS, the local police, and sometimes the Better Business Bureau. Consider yourself on that list. You can start looking for me."

"I can start looking for you? You mean *you* can start looking for my people! I don't have to take any of your—"

Stuart hung up. It was time to go home and cook dinner. On his way out, he stopped at Sally's desk. "I'm leaving," he told her. "If Loring calls back, leave him hanging for five minutes before you tell him I'm gone.

Chapter Fifty-Four

"I don't see any fish in the tank," Jessica remarked, tapping the glass with her finger.

"There aren't any," Stuart replied. "With my travel schedule, I was afraid I wouldn't be able to feed them."

Jessica stared at him a moment, looked in the tank, and then took a sip of wine and glanced around the room. "There aren't any windows."

"Not many people notice that."

She had arrived twenty minutes early. A visibly nervous Stuart, after a perfunctory kiss on the cheek, made a show of opening the bottle of wine she handed him. They had started the tour with the kitchen and a brief description of the food he was cooking and were now in the den.

"Where do you sleep?"

He worked to keep a straight face. "Upstairs."

"Does that room have windows?"

"Of course it does," he insisted. "This is the only room that doesn't."

"Are you going to show me the upstairs?" A little smile played on her mouth.

The phone's ring saved an awkward Stuart from answering. He crossed to the table and answered.

"She arrived in a taxi," said the voice. "No one followed her. You'll see that she gets home okay?"

"Will do," Stuart answered and then hung up the phone.

"Something important?" Jessica asked.

"Just the people guarding you, advising me that you arrived in one piece, and it was my job to get you home safely."

"Did they tell you what time I had to be home?"

"Darn, I forgot to ask. Is there a curfew?"

"We'll see," she replied. Taking his arm, she said, "Now show me the rest of the house."

Stuart led her to the staircase. At the landing, he stepped back so that she could go first. Jessica started up the stairs, Stuart right behind her. When she was one step from the top, she stopped abruptly, causing Stuart to walk into her and nearly knock her to the floor. He quickly wrapped both arms around her and stopped her fall. Still holding her, he climbed the last two steps. When she turned, they were nearly eye-to-eye.

"Sorry," she said. "I wasn't thinking."

His mouth went dry. He ran his tongue over his lips, trying to say something, but he couldn't think of any words that made sense. "I was too close," he stammered. "Did I hurt you?"

Jessica stepped back and checked herself. "I don't think so. Do you see any bruises?" She raised her chin for inspection.

"I don't see any bruises," he murmured, moving in closer. Finally, he took her face in his hands and kissed her softly.

Jessica folded her arms around him and pressed her lips against his, slowly opening her mouth. "Where's that room you sleep in?"

"What about dinner?" he stammered.

"I think we should have dessert first."

From the hallway to the foot of the bed, clothes were strewn everywhere. Jessica looked at the clock on the nightstand and noted that it was six thirty. "What time is dinner being served?"

Stuart hoisted himself onto an elbow and faced her. "Jessica, we have to talk."

"About what?" she asked, her face becoming suddenly serious.

"About us. I haven't been in a relationship in years, and this is all new to me. I'm not sure what I'm supposed to do."

She sat up, covering her breasts with the blanket. "And I am? Stuart, you're the first man I've gone to bed with since my husband died. Maybe it's pent-up passion, or maybe it's just you, but I'm enjoying what we're doing. I thought you were enjoying it too."

"Enjoying it? Jessica, I love every second that we're together. I just don't know if I should be buying flowers or an engagement ring."

She let the blanket fall away. "Flowers are always nice. A ring might be a little premature, but keep the thought."

Stuart reached out to touch her, but she took his hand. "Right now," she said, "I could use something to eat."

Stuart slid off the bed laughing. "You're like all the women I've ever known—all you think about is food."

Jessica nearly asked how many women there were, but instead she smiled, her eyes shining with pleasure. This was the first time that she had heard him laugh.

Chapter Fifty-Five

"You're in a happy mood," Sally remarked as Stuart walked by her cubicle. He was humming "Seventy-Six Trombones" from *The Music Man*.

"I love it when a plan comes together," he said over his shoulder.

"I've heard that before. Who said it?"

"George Peppard, from *The A-Team*."

"What position did he play?"

Stuart smiled and shook his head.

"Michael called and said you should leave lunch open. He'll call back when he has the time and place firmed up."

Stuart motioned for Sally to follow him into his office. "Find Michael and tell him I'm busy for lunch, and it's something I can't change. Ask him if he's available around five."

"If I find him, I'll buzz him in and you can work out the time."

"I'm busy until around five, and you won't be able to locate me for anyone, including Michael."

"Boss, you know the rules."

"How'd you like to be working for Weaver tomorrow?"

Sally looked at the floor. "Does that include the congresswoman?"

"I said everyone."

Twenty minutes later, Michael called back. "Put me through, Sally."

"Sorry, Michael, he's been here and gone. He said he's busy for lunch, but he can meet you around five."

"Busy with who?"

"Didn't tell me."

"I'll hold. Call him and tell him we have to talk."

"Mr. Burnett," said Sally, her voice suddenly formal. "I don't know where he is."

"Sally, this is me, and you know better than handing me some song and dance. Where is Stuart?"

"I don't know, honestly. He said to tell you he's free around five."

"Is he with the congresswoman?"

"No, and he said he's not available for her either."

"When he calls in, tell him it's important. And, Sally, remind him of the rules."

"Just sign the card, *keeping the thought*," said Stuart into his phone, eyes never leaving the front of the building across the street.

"Another cup of coffee?" asked the overweight waitress. "I couldn't help but overhear. What kind of flowers did you order?"

"Long-stemmed red roses."

"For your wife or girlfriend?"

"Not married, for my girlfriend."

The waitress poured from the steaming pot. "You look familiar, are you a movie actor?"

"You've got a good eye, you must have seen Forrest Gump."

"I did. Were you in that movie?"

"Do you remember when he was in the hospital and got the Purple Heart?"

The waitress's face went blank. "I'm not sure."

"Well, I'm the guy who played the officer that handed Forrest the medal."

"No kidding, I knew you looked familiar."

Stuart handed the waitress a twenty-dollar bill as he spied Eric Weaver leaving the building. "There's my friend, I have to go."

Weaver was waiting for the light to turn as Stuart was walking toward the corner. They reached the front of the bank at the same time.

"I'm glad I ran into you," said Stuart. "I have to discuss a problem that's developed."

"It'll have to wait," replied Weaver, trying to sidestep Stuart. "I'm in a hurry."

"It can't wait. I just found out you hired some street kids to hassle my daughter, and I'd like to know why."

"What are you talking about?" A look of alarm spread over Eric's face.

"Don't you remember Augie Meridian? He died in jail after I found two of his friends dead in an apartment."

"I remember the story, but I don't remember anything about your daughter."

"Maybe you remember her as Marilyn Loring."

A look of panic broke out on Eric's face. He glanced at his watch and said, "You're crazy," his voice barely above a whisper. Looking around, he added,

"I'm supposed to meet some people, so we'll have to talk later." Those last words were expressed in staccato. Again, he tried to get past Stuart.

"I also have to talk to you about Miriam."

"What about Miriam?" demanded Weaver, his voice taking on an angry edge. "She's still alive."

"What?" he nearly hollered, but the sound of his voice was overwhelmed by the shrill dissonance of the bank alarm. "Oh my god," he added, his voice now a whisper.

At the same moment, Stuart was shouting, "Everyone get down! It's a robbery!"

Two men ran out of the bank, one of them firing a shot into the air.

Eric yelled, "Stop! It isn't supposed to happen this way!" Waving his hands above his head, he started in the direction of the two men.

Stuart, standing behind Eric, crouched and shot the man who had fired his gun. The second man, and then a third who jumped out of a parked car, began firing back. Eric, who was standing between Stuart and the three culprits, took the bullets and slumped to the pavement. Stuart aimed and pulled the trigger three more times, all shots hitting their marks. He ran over to the fallen men, kicked their guns away, and checked each man's neck for a pulse.

When the police arrived, they confirmed what Stuart already knew: one of the robbers and Eric were dead. Another man died on the way to the hospital. Shortly after the incident, Stuart was repeating for television cameras the story he had just told the police.

"I met my good friend and colleague, Eric Weaver, in front of the bank, and we started to discuss FBI business. The alarm went off, and two men came running out. Eric yelled for them to stop, said something like 'This isn't the way it's supposed to happen' and then one of the men shot at him. I returned his fire, and that's when the other two opened up on Eric. He was a brave man and a credit to the department. I know I will miss him, and I'm positive it will be difficult to fill his shoes."

Eight people who had been standing in the street confirmed Stuart's account. One of them even said that he believed Eric had jumped in front of Stuart and saved his life.

It was a quarter to five when Stuart called his office. "Where am I meeting Michael?"

"Curious George's. He said you know where it is."

"Anything else?"

"Yes. I have a question. I've been watching television. How did you know you were going to be busy until around five?"

"Years and years of training," he told her. "See you tomorrow."

"Are you out of your freakin' mind?" Michael nearly yelled as soon as Stuart was seated.

"What did I do? I was standing there talking to one of my good friends, and these guys come out of the bank with their guns blazing."

"Your good friend, my ass. He hires some guys to hassle your daughter and you go on a personal vendetta."

"Are you forgetting something?" asked Stuart. "Eric Weaver was probably responsible for those deaths. Think about it, Michael. With everyone dead, we can't prove anything in a court of law. But I didn't kill him. The truth is, I would've loved to take him alive. He was our best link to Chilicote, not to mention my ex's husband, Loring."

"Stuart, you're in the big time now. You're meeting with the President and giving press interviews. You can't go around making like Rambo."

"I also believe he was responsible for Christine's death."

Michael poured himself a drink and made a gesture with his chin, as if to say, "Go on."

"She was tapping into records, we're sure about that. The night she died, one of the calls I got from her was to tell me that Weaver had called Peter. He had access to our phones, and he was obviously checking up on me. I didn't believe the robbery story and neither did you, but we had to live with it."

"And this was your solution?"

"My solution was to catch the crooks in the act, pin it on Weaver, and have him turn state's evidence."

Both men sat there, silence floating around them. It was Michael who finally spoke, "The President says you're pushing him too fast; he wants you to back off a little."

Stuart shook his head vehemently. "You were there! If he doesn't do something soon, it's going to be too late."

"He knows that, so just give him a little breathing space."

"Maybe I'm not suited for this type of work. I mean, if we know who's rotten, we should do something about it."

"We will," placated Michael. "What do you still have on your plate?"

"The bank robbers, Chilicote, Loring, and Harper."

"The President wants Loring and Harper dealt with."

"And Chilicote?"

"He wants you to get the goods on him, but he'll deal with the senator."

"He's going to let him get away?"

"Let's just say the President needs some votes in Congress, and the senator is the perfect person to get them. Any proof you find is still good next year."

"Did he say when you were taking over the?"

Michael chewed on his lower lip for a moment. "That's another thing he doesn't want to get pushed on. However, I trust him, so you need to trust him too."

"Michael, I trust you, but I'm not sure that extends to anyone else."

"For the time being, he's put me between you and Gastner. He said he promised you that."

"And what about the bank robberies?" Stuart asked nonchalantly.

"Very low priority. It's time to turn them over to the Bureau. Anything I should know about the man the Canadians caught, or about what's happening down in Clearwater?"

Stuart sorted through the facts in his head before speaking, "The plane he'll be taking is a direct flight to New York. However, it'll develop engine trouble upstate and will be forced to make an emergency landing in Boston. The passengers will be told not to leave the gate area, but our diplomat will know more than all of us and he'll take off. He'll rent a car, using his license and credit card, which he says he'll drop off in Manhattan. The car will never be found."

"What about the man?" Michael asked, his voice so casual he could have been discussing the weather.

"If it was his intention to blow himself up, we may accommodate him. If he was just a delivery boy, it may take us a couple of months, but we'll know the names of everyone he ever met. Who knows? We may turn him into a useful human being."

"You think you can get him to work for us?"

"Stranger things have happened."

Michael contemplated what he had just been told and then asked, "And the address in Clearwater?"

"I turned that over to the C.I.A. They have the manpower to investigate."

"So I guess everything's under control?"

"Looks like," Stuart answered as he started to rise.

"You never mentioned the lead you got from the car rental."

Stuart sat back down. "I don't have anything yet. I tried a wild guess and got a name. I'm having it checked out."

"You're not going off on your own with this, are you?"

"No, Michael, it's like you said: low priority. I'll keep checking into it. Who knows? Maybe we'll get something." Stuart rose again and headed toward the door. Over his shoulder he said, "I'll keep in touch."

Michael waved good-bye while thinking, *I wonder what he's not telling me.*

Chapter Fifty-Six

"You knew!" Jessica shouted over the phone. "When you said you were going to be busy tonight, you knew this was going to happen."

"Jess, slow down," placated Stuart. "Nothing happened."

"You killed two men and wounded a third, and you say nothing happened?"

Stuart groped around for something to break the tension. The best he could come up with was, "Tell me about your day."

"My day was going fine, Stuart. That is, until this afternoon when reporters began asking questions like 'How does it feel to have your very close friend almost shot?'" After a moment's pause, she added, "And I can't wait until tomorrow when they've had a day to think it over. The media must be all over you."

"They would be, if they could find me. They don't have my number or my address, and it's unlikely they're looking for more stories about my very good friend, Eric."

"That's another thing," said Jessica. "I didn't think you even liked him."

"Between you and me, I didn't, but he was a part of the Bureau, and we honor our own."

Stuart heard Jessica's breathing and decided to let her take the lead. After a few lengthy delays, she told him, "I got the flowers you sent, and they were beautiful. For the record," she added, "Sarah, thinks you're the coolest person, ever. She wanted to know what you meant by *keeping the thought*."

"What did you tell her?"

"I told her you were always speaking in code, and I'd have to ask."

"In other words, you chickened out."

"In other words, you're right. So am I going to see you this week?"

Stuart nearly grinned. He knew what it must have taken for Jessica to ask that question. "How about Friday night? I could take you and Sarah out for dinner."

"That's a good idea, we accept. And how about asking Marilyn to join us?"

"An even better idea, I'll call her."

"Where are we eating?"

"I'll make it a surprise."

"Stuart, do me one favor."

When he made a questioning sound, Jessica said, "Try not to take any unnecessary risks, okay? Not that you'd listen, but—"

"I promise," he interrupted. "How's that?"

Jessica laughed, "Go take a cold shower" and hung up.

Stuart watched the muted television screen while drawing circles on the desktop. Picking up the phone, he dialed his mother's number. "Mom, we have to talk."

Forty minutes later, his car was sitting in his mother's driveway. She opened the door just as he reached her front door.

"Come on in," she said somberly. He followed her into the kitchen where there was a pot of coffee on the stove, a bottle of scotch on the table, and a Sara Lee coffee cake on the counter.

"No ice cream?" he asked, pouring himself a shot of scotch.

She walked to the freezer and took out a quart container of Häagen Dazs vanilla. "Do you want this on top of the cake or in a bowl?"

He smiled and sat down. "Maybe later. Join me for a drink?'

"Is it that bad?"

"I don't think so, but." He shrugged and downed another mouthful of scotch.

She poured herself some scotch and sat down across from her son. "Let's hear it."

Stuart had gone through this scenario and decided to just lay it out. "Fifteen years ago, when Linda divorced me, I told you I was leaving my job and going into another line of work. I was very vague about my new job, and you let me get away with it. Now, things are happening so fast that I need to set the record straight." He looked at his mother expectantly, but she just sat there. "The first job was under the jurisdiction of the Justice Department; the new job was related to Justice, but I reported through the ATF."

"The Ruby Ridge people?"

Stuart sighed and then nodded. "Under their auspices, yes, but at the same time completely separate. I was part of a group that had license to kill, like James Bond, except we could only act within the United States."

Her eyes widened, and she leaned into the table. "To kill?"

"But only under special circumstances," he qualified, as if that would lessen her shock. "Our job was to track down serial killers, rapists, bank robbers, etc., very bad people who crossed state lines. Our first choice, always, was to prosecute, but the unwritten message was clear: if there were problems about bringing them to justice, we were to come up with our own solutions. If we availed ourselves of that license, there was an automatic investigation before a review board. It was done anonymously, but it was done rigidly too. Anyone who stepped over the line was immediately dismissed."

His mother's eyes narrowed for a moment and then she asked, "Were you ever investigated?"

"Three times," he responded. When her expression didn't change, he decided to give her the response she deserved. "The first was when a serial rapist tried to slash his way out of an alley. The next incident had to do with a neo-Nazi group trying to ambush one of the ambassadors from a South American country. The last time was when Peter was shot."

"Why are you telling me this now?"

"Mom, everyone's heard the story about my saving Jessica's daughter and how she won't cave in to the bastards. But it wasn't Sarah they were after, it was Marilyn."

"Marilyn?" There was such shock, and then disbelief, in her voice that he poured her another drink.

Stuart waited until his mother seemed calm before he hit her with the next piece of information. "I have reason to believe that Loring, Linda's husband, wanted Marilyn threatened just enough to frighten me into doing something. His brother-in-law happens to be from Jessica's district and the two of them are trying to get legislation passed that will help their business. The FBI agent that was killed today was on their payroll and so is a sitting senator. An hour ago, Jessica called and told me to be careful. After I spoke to her, I realized things don't always go the way we'd like." He took a sip of scotch and delivered the last part of his message. "According to Peter, I'm worth more than ten million dollars. My will specifies that after you're taken care of, the rest go to the kids. Which brings me to the most important point." Stuart felt his pulse racing and saw a look of concern on his mother's face. "Mom, if anything goes wrong, I need you to do something for me." He reached across the table and rested his hand on hers. "Whatever happens, you've got to make sure that the kids get away from Loring."

His mother pulled her hand away. "What do you mean, if something goes wrong? Stuart, what are you involved in?"

Stuart rose from the chair and walked to the sink. Outside, the world was going on as if all were peaceful and safe. "Nothing's going to go wrong; this is a just-in-case scenario."

She stood up and walked over to him. "I guess I shouldn't worry. You're good at what you do, aren't you?"

"Mom, I am very good at what I do, very."

"What about Jessica?"

"That's another thing I wanted to tell you." This time, he finally smiled. "Mom, I think she could be the one."

Chapter Fifty-Seven

"Stuart, the congresswoman on line 1."

"Her name is Jessica Winston," he yelled through the open door.

"Whatever her name is," Sally responded through the intercom, "she's holding on line 1."

Stuart picked up the phone and said, "Jessica, good morning."

"I have a problem, Stuart."

He sat straighter in his chair. "What's happened?"

"Nothing serious, relax. It's about our date tomorrow night. I forgot that this is the weekend before the Fourth of July. I'm scheduled to be in California to attend a picnic on Saturday morning and a luncheon on Monday. I tried, but I can't get out of them, and I'm scheduled to leave at noon on Friday."

"Are you staying for the rest of the week?"

"I have in the past; I use that time to meet with constituents. You know, show my face and shake as many hands as possible. It's convenient because Congress shuts down for the week."

Stuart wanted to voice his disappointment, but what could he say? This was her job, and it was an important one. "How about tonight?"

"There's a meeting of the leadership, we need to go over the party's agenda and figure out where we need help. They give us information to use when we're talking to voters back home."

"Can you call when it's over?"

"They usually last until after midnight. Will you be awake?"

"I'll be waiting."

"Stuart, I'm sorry."

"I'm used to expecting the unexpected."

"What does that mean?"

"I'll tell you when you call."

He looked up at Sally, who was bringing in a cup of coffee. She put it on his desk and sat down. "You're going to have to learn to close your door."

Stuart gave her a look. "You were listening?"

"I was," she admitted. "And I have more bad news for you."

He leaned back hard in the chair and gestured for her to speak.

"We got another hit on Kevin Kinsella." She saw the confused look on his face and added, "Kevin Kinsella, Green Tree Lawn and Garden."

The light went on and he asked, "What did you get?"

"He reserved a car for next Monday in Phoenix. I checked airline reservations and couldn't find which airline he's using."

Stuart walked over to the wall and took down a map of Arizona. "Did he give a return date? Wait," he quickly added. "Did you say a car?"

"Return date is Monday, and yes, a car."

His brow furrowed. "Strange, they've always used a van. I wonder why he's renting a car."

"Maybe he's on vacation," suggested Sally. "And maybe he's not the bank robber."

Stuart studied the map. "Maybe you're right, but I have this feeling." He replaced the map and returned to his desk. "I need to give this some thought," he told her, dismissing her with "Close the door on your way out."

Alone in the room, he picked up the phone and called his mother. "Do you have any plans for this weekend?"

"I was planning on renting three movies," she replied. "So whatever you're offering, I accept."

"How about calling Marilyn and asking her to join you in California for four or five days? This is the weekend that Kenneth finishes school, so I'll invite him to join us, sort of a family reunion."

"Are the congresswoman and her daughter going to join us too?"

"Actually, we'll be joining them."

"If Marilyn can do it, when and where?"

"Try for tomorrow, around noon, out of Dulles. Call my office, and Sally will arrange your tickets."

Stuart returned to the map, and then walked back to his desk to make another call. "Joan, this is Stuart. Is Peter home?"

"He's in the backyard, I'll call him. When are we getting together?"

"I was hoping for this weekend, but Jessica has to be in California. You guys going to be home?"

"I was planning on it. Peter told me to leave the weekend open, just in case. Why don't you come over? I'm dying to find out what you're doing, and I know that Peter's very jealous."

"I may have some work to do, and I'm thinking of going to California."

"Let me get him in here, maybe you two can work it out." A minute later, Peter came on the line. "Stuart! Joan tells me you're going to California this weekend."

"Listen, this is between the two of us. The trip is an excuse; we've got a possible line on one of the bank robbers. We've been checking on car rentals in a fifty-mile radius of the robberies, and one name came up a half dozen times. He's got a reservation for next Monday, and I want to be there to get a look at him. If something goes wrong, I've told my mom to make sure she gets the kids away from Loring. Peter, I want you to help."

"What do you think will go wrong?"

"Nothing, but you can never tell."

Peter made a little humming sound and then asked, "Where's he renting the car?"

"Arizona, but I'm going to California first to be with Jessica. I'll call you when I get back."

"Want some company?"

"No thanks, I've got the kids and my mom coming along, and that's more than enough company." The men shared a brief laugh before Stuart added, "And please, don't forget what I said about Loring."

"I won't, go have a good time."

The phone was answered on the third ring. "This is Kevin."

"Where are you?"

"Well, if it isn't the mystery man. Why do you give a shit where I am? If I remember correctly, you said you were taking a vacation. Well, I'm not."

"I told you that if you didn't, I would kill you."

"That's big talk from someone who's afraid to give me his name or phone number."

"Just tell me where you're at."

"I'm in Virginia, why?"

"Stay there, don't go anywhere this weekend."

Kevin became quiet. *How does he know?* "No problem."

"I'm planning a job for next Thursday. I'll contact you on Monday."

"Where?"

"Vermont."

"Wednesday's a holiday."

"So?"

"Nothing, call me."

The organizer stared out the window. He trusted Kevin, but the early stages always made him edgy. When the third member of the team asked, "Honey, is everything all right?" he nearly jumped. "That idiot's going to get himself killed," he told her.

She walked over to where he was sitting and put a hand on his shoulder. "Maybe it's time to get out of this business?"

"And do what?" The response came out louder than he intended. He knew she was right—this life wasn't for him.

"Live like normal people."

He sighed. *If only I'd been paying attention.* "I guess it's time."

Chapter Fifty-Eight

"Kenneth, I have a surprise for you. I've decided to go to California for the holidays and would love to have you and your sister join me. Your grandmother is coming along, sort of a chaperone, since I'll be near San Diego with Jessica."

Kenneth didn't answer right away, and Stuart worried he had pushed the family thing too aggressively. "Dad, does Mrs. Winston know you're coming?"

"I'm telling her later tonight. Why, do you have a problem?"

"Well, it's just that I, I mean, Sarah and I were going to San Francisco."

"You were going to San Francisco for . . . what?"

"For one thing, we wanted to watch the fireworks from the Golden Gate Bridge."

"Have you asked her mother?"

"Dad, if Sarah wants her mother to know, she'll tell her."

"Kenneth, I know it's a bit late to start acting like a father but—"

"But what?" interrupted Kenneth, his voicing rising in frustration. "I think Sarah's great, and I think she likes me, so what's wrong with going to San Francisco together?"

Stuart thought about it for a moment and then said, "I guess nothing. Have a good time. Oh," he added, "and be careful."

"Congresswoman Winston on line 2," announced Sally, her voice carried through the intercom.

Stuart finished his call with Kenneth and punched the other line. "Jess?"

"I have another problem."

"What's that?"

"Sarah."

"I just heard."

"You just heard what?"

"That she's going to San Francisco this weekend."

"Where'd you hear that?"

Stuart heard a bell going off in his head. *Dummy, she didn't know!* "It was just wishful thinking," he said, hoping for a good cover-up. "I'm trying to plan a trip to California this weekend, since I have to be in Arizona on Monday."

Jessica laughed. "Don't panic," she said. "Sarah's not feeling well and is staying home. What's this about California?"

"Haven't put it together yet, so what's the problem?"

"Sarah's not coming out until Tuesday or Wednesday, as soon as she feels better. I thought you might call her this weekend."

"Does she know you're asking me?"

"No, it'll be our secret. I don't want her to think I don't trust her."

"I'll have someone check up on her, it won't be a problem. Are you in the Capitol?"

"In the middle of a ten-minute recess."

"Don't forget to call me tonight," said Stuart, feeling very much like an enamored schoolboy.

"I won't," she said and nearly giggled.

The moment that call was completed, Stuart dialed a number and heard "This is the Marlboro man."

"This is Captain Midnight," he replied. "Where is the congresswoman's daughter?"

After a few seconds' delay, the voice replied, "She's sitting on the steps of your daughter's house, chatting with your daughter and two other girls."

Stuart felt immediate relief. "Thanks, do you have her cell phone number?"

"Does a rhino have a thick skin?"

"Put me through." He waited less than ten seconds to hear Sarah Winston's voice.

"Sarah, this is Marilyn's father. Don't say anything out of the ordinary this conversation is being taped. I want you to walk away from the other girls and listen carefully." He heard movement and then Marilyn asking Sarah where she was going.

"Back in a minute," she told the girls. A moment later, she asked Stuart, "What's wrong?"

"You told your mother you weren't feeling well and that you were staying home this weekend. I have it on good authority that you were planning on going to San Francisco. I need you to change your plans." He heard her inhale and smiled. It was hard enough being a teenager without having someone from the telling you how to live your life."

"How did you know?"

"That doesn't matter," he said. "I've asked my mother to call Marilyn and invite her to California for a few days. In a few minutes, I'm going to call and invite Kenneth. It's important they all be there with you on Saturday. What you do on Monday or Tuesday is up to you, but for that weekend, you have to be in California."

"May I ask why?" she inquired, a touch of teenage petulance in her voice.

Stuart hesitated. The less she knew, the better. On the other hand, it was everyone's safety that was at stake. "I can tell you part of it, but you can't repeat it to anyone until next Tuesday, and then only to the people approved by me. Agreed?"

"Sure," she responded.

"If you've read the papers or watched television, you know that I've been assigned to the President's staff to look out for terrorists. All of a sudden, I'm on someone's watch list. This trip has to look like a family get-together, where your mom and I will be making an announcement."

"Are you?"

"No," he said quickly, and then felt a wave of disappointment. "On Monday, I'm slipping into Arizona, doing what I have to do, and then returning that night or on Tuesday."

"What are you going to do?" asked Sarah, clearly enjoying the role of co-conspirator.

"I can't tell you that part."

She went quiet for a moment, and then asked, "What do you want me to do?"

"I want you to go with your mother to California. My mother will fly with Marilyn, and Kenneth will meet them when they land. I want you to spend a day or two with us and then you can take off and do whatever you like."

"Mr. Taylor, do Marilyn or Kenneth know about this?"

"No, not yet," said Stuart. "But my mother is about to get in touch with Marilyn, and I'll be talking to Kenneth very soon. They'll both know all about these plans in the next two hours."

"Is anything bad going to happen?" Sarah asked, her voice barely above a whisper.

"Sarah, I'm going to make sure that everything will be fine. The problem is, I can't tell your mother because of her committees."

"Fine, I'll go, but only if you tell me how you knew about San Francisco."

"My organization looked into airline bookings for the next two days and your name popped up on the search."

"Anyone else's?"

"Your name only came up because they were tracking your mother's flight." Trying to keep his voice serious, he asked, "Is there someone else I should be tracking? If so, I can always do another search."

"Please don't," she responded at once. "I'll go with my mom."

"Who were you going with?"

Sarah didn't answer for a few seconds. "I wasn't going with anyone, but I was meeting Kenneth there."

"Kenneth . . . my son?" Stuart acted surprised.

"We were just going to goof around, maybe go dancing or something."

"I see," mused Stuart. "Well, this puts me in an awkward position, but I'll tell you what: I won't say anything to your mother and you don't say anything to Kenneth."

"You have a deal. I'll see you in California."

It was just after two in the morning when Stuart's phone rang. He let it ring twice before answering it.

"Did I wake you?"

He smiled when he heard Jessica's voice. "Of course you woke me, it's the middle of the night."

"I'm sorry. The meeting seemed to go on and on, and you did say to call."

"I'm only kidding," he told her. "I was working on some papers. Did you get anything accomplished?"

"I hope so. The leadership has some good ideas. Now it's up to us to bring the message to our constituents."

"You'll have to tell me about it this weekend."

"This weekend?"

Interjecting innocence into his voice, he said, "You haven't heard? I'm flying to California in the morning. My mother's going too, and she's bringing Marilyn. If I've worked it out right, Kenneth will be there to meet us."

"Kenneth and Marilyn? Too bad Sarah isn't going."

He smiled. "That's the other thing, Jess. Sarah is going. She and Kenneth may fly up to San Francisco later in the week, but she'll be there through Monday."

"How did you arrange all of this? And wait, what do you mean she's going to San Francisco?"

"Did you forget that I'm a secret agent who happens to be in love?"

"Oh really, with anyone I know?"

"My kids, of course!" he announced, and then laughed.

He's getting very good at laughing. "I'll see you sometime tomorrow, Mr. Taylor. Thank you."

"Before you hang up, there's one thing. Don't say anything to Sarah, okay? Let her tell you."

"I won't, now sleep tight."

Stuart was still smiling when he fell asleep.

Chapter Fifty-Nine

"Whoever this is, it'd better be good," Stuart said groggily, barely able to open his eyes. He looked at the clock and groaned. "It's four thirty."

"Stuart, it's me," said Michael. "The President wants to see us at six, which gives you an hour and fifteen minutes to get there. Don't be late."

Stuart pulled himself up and sat on the edge of the bed. Running a hand through his hair, it struck him that he was getting too old for this. "What's up?"

"Listen, when I get a call from the President at four in the morning, I just say 'Yes, sir' and show up. Which means when you get a call from me at four thirty, you say—"

"I'll be there, sir."

Stuart clicked on the television and then turned on the shower. "CNN has just learned that Israel has moved troops into Hebron. There have been more than sixty members of Hamas killed in retaliation over this week's bombing. A communiqué from Chairman Yasser Arafat's headquarters blames the United States for not taking stronger steps in controlling the Israeli government."

Stuart arrived at the White House at five thirty and found the building in darkness. There were some lights on across the street, at Blair House, but not enough to suggest that the government was awake and in emergency mode. The sky was beginning to show signs of morning, and there were government workers walking into the buildings. Stuart looked around and saw no sign of reporters. He didn't recognize either of the guards, but they were expecting him.

"Mr. Taylor, please park your car in the lot on the right. The golf cart will be here in a moment to take you to the meeting."

"Are the others already here?" he asked.

"What others, sir?"

Stuart was tempted to say something about the guard perfecting the noncommittal voice, but the arrival of the golf cart silenced him.

230

Stuart noted the four-passenger cart was blue, and that two others were riding in it. The driver looked straight ahead. In the back, a uniformed security guard stepped onto the pavement, her demeanor so serious that Stuart expected her to salute.

"You may keep your weapon," she stated, and Stuart nodded. "You won't be here long. I'll take your keys; you'll find your car outside one of the exit doors."

"Which is where?" Stuart asked.

"We're not sure yet, but it will be there."

They drove for less than two minutes, taking a shortcut across the lawn and behind the area designated for helicopter landings.

"Inside that door," she pointed, "you'll find someone who will take you to your meeting." She held out her hand. "I'll take your keys now."

Stuart removed his car key from the key ring and handed it to her.

"You didn't have to do that; I would've taken care of them."

"I'm sure you would, except that I'm seeing someone now, and it might have been embarrassing. I'm not allowed to give my keys to anyone but her."

He could see her blush even though the sun had not yet risen.

After being shown to a room that had hot coffee and muffins on a sideboard, Stuart was left alone. Five minutes later, the President entered with Michael right behind him.

"Stuart, thank you for coming," said the leader of the free world. The men shook hands, and the President took a seat. "You've heard the news from Israel," he began. "What you haven't heard is Israel killed over two hundred Palestinians. Arafat has decided to make a show of force, which has backfired, so now he's blaming us." The President stood and walked over to the sideboard. "I love the plain muffins. Have you had one yet?"

Stuart shook his head.

The President shoved one into his mouth and washed it down with a swig of coffee.

"What I want is for you to put together an organization that will formulate a policy on what we have to do if these crazies come after us. I have ninety days before Congress has to get involved. That gives me until October and gives you until the end of August. Get yourself a second in command, someone you can trust, really trust, and then start the ball rolling. This person must be able to pass a government inspection, so we're talking about someone already in, or just out of government work who can take full responsibility for dealing with the money and interfacing with Congress." He took another muffin. "Know anyone with those qualifications?"

"Yes, sir, I do. In fact, Michael knows him, although I don't think you do. His name is Peter Weber. He was my partner until he stopped a bullet. He's a money manager now, and I trust him with my life."

The President looked at Michael, who nodded.

"Then it's settled. Get your friend on board and keep me updated at our weekly meetings."

"Is there a salary cap?" Stuart asked as the President started for the door.

"It's less than what you're making. I don't know the numbers, but you do." Saying that, he left the room

Stuart looked at Michael. "What do you think?"

"I think it's a good choice, and I hope he takes the job. He always was a good man."

Stuart started out the door and then stopped, walked over to the muffins, and took two, along with a cup of coffee. "I like the ones with jelly," he said, smiled, and walked out.

The security guard was waiting outside the door. Stuart handed her a muffin, and she took a bite. "These are pretty good," she said. "But I like the plain ones the President gives me better."

So much for trying to be a smart-ass.

Chapter Sixty

"Peter, I have to talk to you."

"I'm not doing anything, talk."

"No, both you and Joan, and in person."

"Something wrong?"

"Not over the phone. I'm as close to my house as yours, so how about my place in thirty minutes?"

"We'll be there."

Peter hung up the phone and stood there, staring at the receiver. Turning to Joan, his face betrayed concern.

"Honey, what's wrong?" she asked.

"Stuart wants to see us in thirty minutes at his place. I said we'd be there."

"He didn't say why?"

Peter ran a hand through his hair. "What do you think he wants? That idiot Kinsella rented a car for a job somewhere in Arizona, and Stuart's people somehow found him."

"You always said he was sharp, I guess this proves it." Joan crossed to the window and gazed into her perfectly maintained garden. They had worked hard for this; she had no intention of losing it all now. "He still can't connect Kinsella to us. And don't forget, Kinsella only saw us in our disguises, so he doesn't know who or where we are."

Peter's concern was not reassured. "And how long do you think it'll take him to start checking on customers of that maintenance company? From there, it's a small jump to us."

Any semblance of calm slipped away from Joan's face. "My god, Peter, what are we going to do?" She sat down at the table and placed her face in her hands.

"If we leave now, we'll probably have a two-hour head start. We can take the money and transfer it somewhere, then go to the airport and take the next flight going south. Wherever we land, we'll rent a car and go to Mexico. From there, we could probably get to South America and live pretty well."

Joan jumped up from the chair. "Let's do it, I'll start packing. We'll take one bag each; we can buy whatever we need." She pushed the chair aside and started toward the bedroom when the front doorbell chimed. "You answer it," she said, her voice almost begging.

Peter walked slowly to the door, and the chime sounded again. Whoever was outside was impatient. Retracing his steps, he opened the top drawer of the buffet and picked up his pistol. Shoving it into his waistband at the small of his back, he pulled his shirt from his pants to cover it and opened the door.

Two men were standing on the porch. "Mr. Weber," said one of the strangers. "We're from the Cigar Store. Stuart asked us to bring you and your wife to his place. He thinks we'll make better time and he's in a hurry."

Peter turned away from them and called out, "Honey, Stuart sent some people to pick us up. Are you sure you're up to going?" Turning back, he said, "She hasn't been feeling well."

A minute later, Joan walked into the room. "I'm fine," she said. "I want to see what he's done with his house, let's go."

The four of them walked out to a large black limo, and one of them opened the door.

"We've got a refrigerator and some hot coffee in the back," said the younger of the two.

"Thanks," said Peter," but I get nervous in the back."

"That's fine. Rick's not such a good conversationalist anyway."

Peter smiled, thinking, *Shit, I must be slipping. I talked them into splitting us up.*

The ride started off smoothly and without incident, but Peter was uncomfortable with the darkly tinted glass partition that blocked his view of Joan. Halfway to Stuart's, the traffic started building up, and the driver, who had said nothing so far, turned off the beltway.

"You're going a different way," Peter stated.

"Just to get around the traffic."

Peter turned as he heard a knock on the glass. "They must want something."

"They probably do," said Rick, "but you just stay put and don't get nervous." He pushed a button that lowered the partition.

The first thing Peter saw was a pistol; the second was the smiling face of Joan.

"Tell the driver not to get nervous," she instructed, the weapon in her steady grip.

"What's going on?" Rick asked nervously.

"Just pull over," she commanded. "And then come back here and let my husband drive."

Rick pulled over and put the limo in park. "You people are making a big mistake."

"And if you think I won't shoot you, you're making one."

After both men were secured in the backseat, Joan settled next to Peter and explained, "When I heard them tell you who they were, I called Stuart. I was afraid if I didn't, he'd become suspicious. He did not send these men and told me that we should bring them to a place called Curious George's. He gave me the address." Peter glanced at the address and nodded. "You did the right thing. Now just keep that gun pointed at them, we'll be there in ten minutes."

When they arrived at the address, they found a closed restaurant, a panel truck parked in front, and Stuart walking back and forth on the sidewalk.

"I was getting a little worried. Did you have any problems?" Stuart asked.

"None, but it was Joan who did everything, I just drove."

Stuart kissed Joan on the cheek. "Thanks," he whispered, motioning for two agents to step out of the van. "Find out what these guys were after," he told them, "and then let me know. They must have our phones tapped. You know how to reach me."

One of them nodded as the other one ordered Rick and his partner to get out.

Stuart turned to Peter. "Let's go to my place, there's something we have to talk about, and I want Joan to hear it."

"Anything serious?" Joan asked.

"Very," Stuart replied.

Joan looked at Peter, who shrugged and followed Stuart to his car.

Chapter Sixty-One

Joan sat in the backseat of Stuart's car and listened to him talk about his trip to California, which he was planning for later that day. He was like a little boy in a candy store. His kids would be there along with his mother and new girlfriend. As he spoke excitement rose from his voice. She closed her eyes and sat back. All she could think about was Peter worrying about what Stuart wanted to discuss. *It couldn't be about the bank robberies, he could do that anywhere. I wonder if he wants to move his money to someone else and doesn't know how to tell us.* The more she thought about the situation, the more positive she was about what Stuart wanted.

They entered the house, and Stuart headed upstairs, calling for them to help themselves to whatever they wanted. Peter held a finger to his lips and pointed at his ear, signaling to Joan that the room might have a listening deVice.

"I think Peter wants to change his money manager," said Joan, pouring a cup of coffee.

"Why would he do that?"

"With ten million plus dollars, maybe he'd like a professional manager."

Peter's mouth turned into a scowl. "I've done a good job for him."

"We both know that the market has done a good job for him," she said.

"Well, wasn't I the one who suggested he switch most of his money from stocks to bonds? It's saved him more than two million over the past four months."

"Maybe he thinks you should've saved him more."

"Should've saved who more?" Stuart asked as he reentered the room.

Peter turned to face his friend. "We were second-guessing the reason for this talk. Joan thinks you want to take your account away from me."

"Aren't you taking good care of me?"

Peter turned to Joan and smiled. "So if you're not dumping me as your finance whiz, what's it about, and why here?"

"This place gets swept every day," said Stuart, pouring himself a glass of juice. "You've seen the papers, I'm the guy that's supposed to advise on terrorists. Until two weeks ago, I didn't know shit. Today, I'm supposed to be the expert. I met with the President early this morning. Israel's retaliated by killing over two hundred Palestinians, and Arafat is blaming us. The President gives me two months to put together a department that can stop terrorist activities."

"Can you do that?" Peter asked.

"I don't know if we can stop them, but with enough information, we might be able to slow them down. I've met with my counterparts from five countries, and information is starting to flow. We detained someone trying to enter through Canada with explosives, we've got the FBI investigating a couple arrested in Israel, and—"

"What did you do with the guy in Canada?" Peter interrupted.

"He claimed diplomatic immunity. The Canadians will put him on a plane for New York, and that plane will have engine trouble and land in Boston." Stuart looked at Joan before continuing, "In Boston, he's going to rent a car and drive to New York."

"How do you know this?" Joan asked.

Stuart looked at Peter. "Explain it to her later?"

Peter nodded and asked, "Why are both of us here?"

"The President wants me to staff the department with people I trust, someone with experience handling money and who can pass a security check. I gave him your name, and he wants you on board." He saw Peter and Joan exchanging glances and knew it was a done deal.

"You want me back in the government?"

"Peter, I want you to be the number two man in the department. You'll be responsible for funding, congressional interface, dealing with people, and all things I can't get to, including hunting down terrorists."

"How much does it pay?" Joan asked.

Peter looked at her and then turned to Stuart, a smile on his face. "Yeah, Stuart, how much?"

"I was told I could offer you less than I earn, which is seventy-seven, plus hazardous duty."

"I won't go to work for a dollar less than seventy-five," he said, looking quickly at Joan. She nodded. "Before you're official, there's something we have to discuss."

Apprehension appeared on Peter's face and he waited. "This is basically a desk job, but you could find yourself in the field. I'm asking Michael for the sixteen people who work for the Cigar Store. It's my belief that they're closing down, and these are good people. Until I get them, however, you could find yourself in difficult situations. I want both of you to be aware of what you're getting into. You're my best friend, but I can't let friendship get in the way of getting the job done."

"I wouldn't expect anything less," said Peter. He turned to Joan and added, "Neither would she."

Joan kissed Peter. There were tears in her eyes as she walked over to Stuart, put her arms around him, and gave him a squeeze. "Thank you," she whispered.

Stuart returned the hug and poured another glass of juice. "That's it then, you're hired; you'll start as soon as I return."

"When's that?" Peter asked.

"Probably next Friday. We'll all be there on Friday, Saturday, and Sunday. I'll be in Arizona on Monday, and hopefully, I'll spend the rest of the week with Jessica."

Peter smiled. "Something serious between you two?"

"Don't ask him that," Joan blurted out, and then turned to Stuart. "So are you serious?"

Stuart laughed. "I'll let you know, okay?"

Peter put his arm over Joan's shoulders, both of them visibly more relaxed than five minutes ago. "What're you doing in Arizona?"

"I thought I told you," said Stuart. "We ran a computer check on car rentals at all the major airports near those banks. I still think they were robbed by the same people. Anyway, the name, Kevin Kinsella, showed up a half dozen times, including a car rental next Monday in Phoenix. We haven't found out how he's getting to Phoenix, I'll be there when he picks up the car. I'll see what he looks like and maybe where he's headed. With any luck, he'll lead me to the man and woman who are his accomplices."

"You know it's a man and a woman?" Joan asked.

Stuart nodded. "We have pictures of all of them. I don't know which one is Kinsella, but I'll know him when I see him."

"What does he look like?" Peter asked.

"One of them is dark skinned, like he's been in the sun. Dark hair, maybe a little gray around the edges, and he walks like his knees hurt. I'm thinking maybe an ex-football player or a carpet layer."

"A carpet layer?" Joan laughed.

Stuart gave her a long look. "Maybe someone who works in his garden a lot." He saw the surprise on their faces.

"Need any help?" Peter asked. "This guy could be a terrorist in disguise."

Stuart smiled, "Thanks, but no thanks. This case has a low priority, and I think it's just my ego showing. I'll be fine. Now that we're agreed on your job and salary, tell me what we're going to do about my money."

Peter's answer arrived so quickly, it was clear he'd been thinking about this. "Tomorrow morning I'll convert all stocks to cash and buy government tax-free bonds. We can probably average about four-point-seven or eight. It'll mean having to exist on a half million a year. As long as you don't do anything crazy, I'm sure you can do it."

Stuart nodded, smiling. "You don't think I should keep some of the better stocks?"

"You probably should, but someone has to watch them. This way, the money takes care of itself. We'll instruct the brokerage firm to reinvest as they come due; you'll never have to worry."

"What about you and Joan?"

"Thanks to you, we're in pretty good shape. I'll do the same thing with my account."

"You'll be under scrutiny, so if you've got any mistresses or funny accounts for money laundering, now's the time to put them on the table." Stuart looked first at Joan and then at Peter.

"If he's got any mistresses," said Joan, "you're going to have to find another second in command."

Stuart instructed Peter to speak to Seth Roberts and Gary Williams. "Roberts is a company pilot," he explained, "and Williams is Secret Service assigned to White House detail. They both know a lot about the comings and goings in the capital, and I know we can trust them."

"Anything else?" That Green Tree Lawn and Garden Company you use for your place. Give them my address and ask them to come by and then show me some plans to make my place look good."

Stuart saw concern on Joan's face. "You don't like them?"

"They're okay, but awfully expensive."

They all turned as the phone rang, and Stuart answered at once. "This is Captain Midnight."

"Marlboro here. Those two guys you sent in are legitimate Secret Service. They said they got a call, were told what to do, and thought it came from Mr. Levitt's office."

"They didn't check?"

"They called back and were told he was unavailable, so they decided to go ahead."

"Where were they supposed to take them?"

"To a company van waiting ten minutes from where they were stopped by Mrs. Weber. We sent a team, but either we were too late or no one was ever going to be there."

"Hold them for forty-eight hours, or until I find Levitt."

After explaining to Peter and Joan, Stuart told them to take one of his cars and be careful. "Whoever the bad guys are, they have your name."

Chapter Sixty-Two

"Well, what do you think?" Joan asked as they headed home in Stuart's Porsche.

"I think it handles great."

"Peter," she said, frustration in her voice, "I'm positive he suspects something, I just don't know what. He's a black-and-white guy, no gray, no nuances. Everything's either good or bad."

"Would he offer you that job if he suspected us?" When he shook his head, she exhaled. "Then I guess there's nothing wrong."

Peter glanced over. "Don't worry," he whispered, reaching over for her hand. He kissed it and added, "We'll be fine."

Stuart got through to Michael minutes after the others left. "Peter accepted the job," he said. "He'll start a week from Monday. Before then, there are a couple of things I'd like."

"The President told you to get it done, so what do you need?"

"If and when you close the Cigar Store, I want those people." When Michael didn't respond, he continued, "I've given Peter two names of good men I want: a pilot attached to the FBI and a Secret Service guy at the White House."

"Why them?"

"They know people and things I don't know, and I trust them."

"You do know that the President hasn't said a word about my heading up the FBI. By giving you the Cigar Store team, I'm putting myself out to pasture."

"He'll do it, you're too valuable to lose. Weren't you the one who said you trusted him, which means I have to trust him too?"

"I'm having second thoughts."

"Michael, make it clear to him: if you don't get the job, I don't take the job." After a pause, Michael told him he would start the paperwork and give Peter a congratulatory call, adding, "By the way, how'd his wife take it?"

"Like I expected: relieved. I think he was getting antsy at home. Oh, and one more thing: our guys are holding two FBI people who said they took instructions from Jake Levitt to intercept and hold Peter and Joan. While I'm gone, can you look into it?"

"Anything else?" asked Michael, a hint of amusement in his voice.

"Since you asked, when you talk to your friend the President, ask him how long we're putting up with Chilicote. I have a funny feeling his finger's in this pot."

"I won't argue on that one. I don't know if I'll get an answer, but I'll ask."

"See you next week." Without waiting for a reply, Stuart hung up.

The company jet, an upgraded 727, ferried Stuart to the Van Nuys Airport, about fifteen miles north of LAX. There were two-dozen passengers, congressmen or their aides returning home for the holiday. The plane had sixty seats, all first class. Stuart was to sit in the back, away from the boisterous noise of people who started partying as soon as the wheels left the ground. His eyes were closing when someone touched his shoulder. Opening them, he recognized the young woman.

"Mr. Taylor, remember me?"

Stuart focused and smiled. "You're Marie, Seth's friend."

"I hate to bother you, but you have a call in the cockpit."

"Did they say who?"

She nodded. "It's the President."

Stuart stood and stretched. "Lead the way."

The revelers watched in silent surprise as Stuart was led past them and into the cockpit.

Taking the bulky instrument that passed for a phone, he said, "This is Taylor."

"Is this line secure?" the President barked.

"I'm not sure, Mr. President. We're at twenty-seven thousand feet, and I'm in the captain's seat, so I guess it's as secure as I can make it. Is there a problem?"

"Damn right, there's a problem. A Saudi diplomat was stopped crossing the border, and he was raising bloody hell. Said we had no right stopping him even though his car was full of explosives."

"I know the story, Mr. President."

"Then you know they put him on a plane to New York and made him leave the explosives behind."

"You've got the story a little backward, sir."

"I've got the . . . , okay then, let's have it."

"We didn't stop him, the Canadians did, because he was on their side of the border. I told them to hold him, and they informed me he was claiming diplomatic immunity. I suggested they put him on a plane and insist he leave his explosives behind."

"What's going to happen to the explosives?"

"If the Saudis wanted them, they can ask our State Department. I don't think they'll ask. Is this the problem?"

"No, they put him on a plane to New York, but it had some mechanical problem, and it landed in Boston. The passengers were held in a waiting area so they could clear customs in Boston, but this guy decides to rent a car and drive to New York."

"So?" Stuart asked, a smile on his lips.

"So he can't be found," barked the President. "No trace of him anywhere."

"He skipped?"

"I don't know what he did, but the Saudis are screaming bloody murder, and they're demanding to know where he is."

Stuart's voice turned cold. "Is that what you want me to find out, Mr. President?"

There was no answer, and Stuart remained there, waiting, the clock on the instrument panel ticking off nearly two minutes before the President spoke. "I don't care where he is. I know there's another question I should ask, but I don't want to know. You're an interesting person, Mr. Taylor. When you get back from your vacation, we must talk." With that, the phone went silent.

Stuart looked at the co-pilot to his right and the pilot standing at his shoulder. "Whatever you just heard or surmised, it's classified."

The men nodded, and Stuart rose, announcing, "Captain," he said with a sweeping gesture, "the plane is yours."

Chapter Sixty-Three

The woman at the Hertz counter thought the trip from the Van Nuys Airport to LAX would take about forty-five minutes. Friday traffic on the San Diego freeway doubled that estimate. Driving in gridlock, Stuart checked in with Sally and was told he received a call from Bill Cook in Canada and she was to give him the message verbatim. It was short, but not so sweet: *Duck, the shit's about to hit the fan.*

"Does that mean you've done something wrong again?" Sally asked sweetly.

"Anyone else called?"

"Oh yes, I forgot, the President called and asked where you were."

"He found me. Anything else?"

"Jose Vargas called from Mexico to say he was going to Tecate, could be reached by cell phone, and you have the number."

Stuart nearly hung up, and then remembered to tell Sally about Peter coming back to join the team. "We'll be moving to new offices, and he's to call you if he needs anything." When she didn't answer, he asked, "Did you hear me?"

"I heard you. It's just that the last few times I've seen him, he seemed a little strange, maybe too cavalier for the type of work we do."

"This new department is different. He'll be fine, and we'll watch him."

"You're the boss," she said, adding, "Have a great vacation. Oh, and if you decide to get married, don't forget to call!"

"It's not a vacation, and we're not getting married."

"I know, and you're not going to have good time." With that, she hung up.

Stuart dialed Kenneth's cell phone, which was answered on the first ring.

"Kenneth, it's Stuart. Have they arrived?"

"Dad, where are you? Grandmother and Marilyn are waiting for their luggage."

"I'm less than five minutes from the American Terminal, so give them a hand and I'll meet you at the curb. I'm in a white van."

"What time are the Winstons arriving?"

"They're flying directly to San Diego," Stuart explained. "That means they'll be there in three hours. We'll go straight down and pick them up. I'm entering the airport now, see you in a minute."

Stuart made the loop around the airport and noticed four police cars and two private security cars parked in front of the American Terminal. The police were directing traffic away from the building; Kenneth was facing the wall, his hands pressed against the building while he was being searched. Stuart saw his mother being escorted by a policewoman toward one of the security cars while Marilyn was being led to the other. He pulled up in front of the two cars and blocked them.

"You can't park there!" yelled one of the uniformed policemen.

Stuart got out of the rental, holding up his badge. "What seems to be the problem?" He heard his mother saying something to the policewoman, and they both stopped, the officer looking at Stuart. Marilyn yelled something he couldn't hear over the noise, but she was still being led away.

The officer looked at the badge. "The girl's father filed a complaint," he said. "It seems she stole over ten thousand dollars and then flew to California to meet her brother."

"What's private security doing here?" he demanded.

"The father's a big shot, and these guys work for him."

"And they're taking the two women where?"

"Can I see that badge again?"

Stuart pulled out the badge. "Who's in charge?" The officer began to fidget. Turning, he called out, "Hey, Sergeant!" over the din of impatient drivers and departing planes. When the man nearest Kenneth turned around, he added, "Some guy with a badge wants to see you."

The sergeant stared at Stuart, making no effort to move or respond.

Stuart stared back, walked to the man, and said, "While you're trying to decide if you'll speak to me, you better tell those rent-a-cops that if they touch either of those women they'll wish they hadn't."

"Is that a threat?" the sergeant asked.

Stuart stepped closer, holding out a card. "Here's the number of the White House, have someone verify it. Make sure they ask for the President of the United States and use my name. When he vouches for me, you will arrest those clowns on my authority."

The men looked at the phone number, and then back at Stuart. "Aren't you the guy that was just named head of the new antiterrorism department?"

"That's me."

The policeman's face changed perceptibly. He stood a little taller and dropped the bullying attitude. "What do you think is going on here?"

"Those are my kids and that's my mother, and I doubt if they have two thousand dollars between them."

"Mind if I check IDs?"

"Be my guest." Stuart looked at his watch.

"In a hurry?"

"We're supposed to meet Congresswoman Winston's plane in San Diego, but it looks like we're not going to make it."

"What time's it landing?"

"Around three."

The policeman looked at his watch. "You're right, you won't make it."

"Think you can get us out of here in the next twenty minutes?" Stuart asked, reaching for his cell phone.

"You gonna rent a plane?"

Stuart ignored the question and dialed. "Sally, a little problem. Call the LA office and tell them I need a helicopter at the American Terminal in thirty minutes. It has to be large enough to carry four. Have a van waiting in San Diego when it lands. Oh yeah, and I'll probably need cigarettes." He closed the cell phone and pocketed it.

"Just like that," mused the sergeant, his voice filled with respect. "I'm in the wrong part of law enforcement." He turned to his officers and instructed them to put the private security people under arrest. "Advise them of their rights," he added, "and let's get this traffic cleaned up."

"One more favor," Stuart, asked, watching Marilyn and his mother join Kenneth on the sidewalk. "Please call Hertz and have them pick up this van." Stuart glanced up just as a police helicopter approached the terminal. "Here comes my ride."

Across the street, on the second floor of the parking garage, a thin man dressed in shorts and a Hawaiian shirt watched the goings-on below. As Stuart Taylor led his mother and children into the terminal and the police arrested the others, he dialed a number on his cell phone.

"Mr. H., this is Andres. It didn't work. Taylor got here before they could take them away. The police arrested our people, and Taylor's headed into the terminal. My guess is they'll take the two forty-five to San Diego." He listened for a moment and then responded, "The boy was scared stiff, and the girl was crying. You better tell our people in San Diego to work fast. Taylor will land about fifteen minutes after the plane from Washington, so they'll have no more than that to get the congresswoman out of there."

Chapter Sixty-Four

Stuart's mother was the only one to ask questions as they were escorted through the terminal, down a flight of stairs and out to a waiting bus. "Do we have to go this fast? I need to use the ladies' room."

"There's one on the helicopter," Stuart replied, hoping he was right.

The blades turned slowly as they approached, Stuart and his family ducking reflexively even though the blades were four feet over their heads. He watched from the tarmac as their bags were loaded into the cargo area and then climbed the metal steps leading into the chopper. There were eighteen seats, and he saw Marilyn and Kenneth sitting halfway back, both of them next to windows. His mother was on the aisle in the first row, so Stuart took the seat across from her.

"I don't think I'm going to enjoy this," she said, stretching her neck to look out the window.

Stuart twisted around and yelled, "Are you kids alright?" his voice nearly lost over the din of the rotor blades.

The helicopter rolled forward like a car and suddenly ascended, tilted to the right, and was over the ocean. "Out the left window is Pacific Palisades," announced a voice coming out of overhead speakers. "Over there, on the right, that's Catalina Island." After a moment, the voice added, "This was a rush assignment, so I didn't have time to stock up, but there's a chest filled with Cokes, juice, and water, so please help yourselves. We should arrive in about thirty minutes. If there's anything I can do to make this trip more pleasant, just come on up and ask."

Stuart's mother tapped him on the arm. "Why did those people stop us?" she whispered, not wanting the children to hear. "I'm not sure," he replied. "But I'm guessing it has something to do with Jessica's arrival." Turning, he saw that Marilyn and Kenneth had moved up and were trying to listen to the conversation. "They, whoever they are, had to know that once I got there, they wouldn't be able to hold you. Your late arrival screwed them up. I'm sure they wanted you arrested and me to chase you down. That way, I wouldn't be at the gate when she arrived."

"Will we get to San Diego in time?" Kenneth asked.

"No problem," said Stuart. "I want to be there with you," added the boy.

Stuart looked at his son. "If I'm wrong and it's you and your sister they're after, I'm going to need you two to stick together where you can watch her."

"What about me?" Stuart's mother exclaimed.

"Kenneth is going to have to watch both of you."

"Dad, why did you have to invite us to California?" blurted Marilyn.

"Marilyn!" said Kenneth, his voice a reprimand. "It's not Dad who's doing this, it's Loring. He told the police you stole ten thousand dollars."

The girl looked confused. "But I didn't steal anything, Mom gave me some money in case I wanted to buy presents."

"How much did she give you?" Stuart asked.

Marilyn shrugged, reached into her bag and held out a sealed envelope.

Stuart unbuckled his seat belt and took a few steps. Accepting the envelope, he opened it and counted the money. "Ten thousand dollars," he said.

"Mom gave you ten thousand dollars?" sputtered Kenneth.

Marilyn shrugged, but her face mirrored confusion.

"Don't you get it?" urged her brother. "Mr. Loring had the police waiting to arrest you!"

Marilyn looked down at her knees and then up into her father's face. "Grandma told me not to say anything about you being on the trip, but I mentioned it to mom. A little later, Mr. Loring wished me a good trip and then Mom gave me the envelope." Tears formed in the corners of her eyes.

Stuart leaned down and draped his arm over her shoulder. "Don't worry about it," he soothed. "It's just a little inconvenience." Squeezing her arm, he added, "We'll get even someday."

Both of his children looked at him, doubt in their eyes.

"We'll become a really close family," he explained with a mischievous smile, "and it'll aggravate the heck out of him."

Kenneth and Marilyn started laughing, and it was their father's turn to be confused.

"Stuart," explained his mother, "I don't think your children take you for a *heck* kind of person. And to tell you the truth, I'm with them."

Before Stuart could respond, the pilot announced that they were approaching Lindbergh Field. Marilyn and Kenneth returned to their seats, and Stuart sat down. His mother reached across and squeezed his arm.

"Don't do anything stupid," she said quietly. "This is the start of a close knit family."

On the ground, Stuart put Kenneth in charge of the bags and told him to take the rental van and pull into the short-term parking across from the terminal.

"When you see us come out, drive the van to the curb. I'll take over, and you can sit in the back with—the girls."

Stuart moved quickly through the terminal, the arrival board showing Jessica's plane landing ten minutes early. That gave him fifteen minutes to survey the area. A man approached while he was still three gates away and asked for matches.

Stuart replied, "This is a nonsmoking facility."

The man nodded. "I have two cigarettes; just need something to light them with."

Stuart lowered his voice. "The congresswoman and her daughter are due to arrive in about ten minutes, but I have a feeling there are people in the crowd who would like to cause her some embarrassment. I want you and your friends to help me identify those people and make sure nothing happens."

The man looked around. "Any idea what they look like?"

"No, but I'm sure they know what I look like, so I'm going to stand by the arrival door and make myself visible. After that, I'm going to escort the congresswoman and her daughter to a van parked in front. If no one bothers us, you guys can get some coffee and go home. If they're here, you'll know what to do."

"Want us to follow the van?"

"I don't think so."

The man started to walk away and stopped. "By the way, one of the cigarettes is a Virginia Slim."

Stuart watched the man take a seat next to a woman in a nurse's uniform. After a brief conversation, the nurse walked two gates away and joined another man, this one with a baby stroller. When Stuart looked back at his original contact, the man was gone. *These guys are real pros,* he thought.

Outside, the plane from Washington was jockeying into position. Stuart strolled over to the arrival area just as the door opened, as one of the attendants passed through. He heard a commotion behind him and saw the nurse leading a man toward the exit. The man with the baby stroller was leaning against the wall, his eyes watching everyone in the area. He suddenly pushed himself away from the wall and maneuvered the stroller up to a man who was rushing toward a pay phone.

"Mr. Taylor, you made it!" Sarah was the first one out of the door. She looked around, disappointment on her face. "You're alone?"

"Someone has to watch the car," he replied, and a huge smile appeared on her face.

Jessica, who had been watching her daughter, approached Stuart and kissed his cheek. "It's so nice of you to meet us."

"Mom, that's no way to say hello to someone you haven't stopped talking about for the last four hours."

Jessica blushed prettily. "That's not really true; I caught up on some reading."

Stuart smiled, pulled Jessica close, and murmured in her ear, "We have a small problem, so let's stay together and head out to the van. It should be right out in front."

A look of suppressed alarm flashed across Jessica's face. She looked from side to side and took Sarah by the arm. "We have to hurry," she said, leading the girl toward the baggage area.

Stuart saw his original contact motioning to him. "I'll just be a second."

"There were only two of them," reported the man. "They both told the same story: they were supposed to escort her as far as Harper's home. He lives a few minutes from her, and he was concerned for her safety. One of them overheard part of a story where he's trying to make you look bad in the congresswoman's eyes."

Stuart shook the agent's hand and rejoined Jessica. "Nothing to worry about, it's a false alarm."

"What's a false alarm?" Sarah asked.

"I thought I had to go to work, but I don't. We can enjoy ourselves."

Outside the terminal, Kenneth stood talking to a traffic cop while waving his hands wildly. "Here they are!" he exclaimed, and waved his father to come over. "Dad, would you explain why I'm parked here?" The police officer turned with a humorless smile that instantly disappeared. "Congresswoman Winston! I'm sorry. I didn't know he was waiting for you. He kept saying something about the FBI and flying in on a police helicopter." He stopped and looked around. "Do you need any assistance?"

Jessica walked up to him, shook his hand, and read the name on his badge. "Officer Rogers, thank you for being so kind. Kenneth's dad is with the FBI, and I wouldn't put it past him to fly in on a police helicopter." She looked at Stuart, who nodded his confirmation. "We have everything we need, but thanks again for being so considerate."

Stuart got behind the wheel of the van. Jessica took the passenger seat, and the children squeezed into the back with their grandmother.

"The woman who hasn't said a word is my mother," explained Stuart. "She's usually not this quiet, but she's had a tough morning."

Jessica twisted around and shook Stuart's mom's hand. "I can't keep calling you Stuart's mother," she said with a smile. "What would you like me to call you?"

The older woman laughed nervously. "You could call me crazy, or maybe I'll call you crazy for ever getting involved with him. I should start a diary, but today alone would fill up fifty pages." Looking out the window, she added, "And the day's not even half over." Taking a deep breath, she smiled at Jessica and said, "I'm Barbara."

Jessica smiled warmly and turned back to Stuart. "So tell me, Mr. Taylor, what kind of day has it been?"

Stuart drove onto the freeway and suppressed a smile when his daughter piped up with, "Let's see, we were almost arrested, we had to get a police helicopter to get us here on time, and then the policeman came and I thought he was going to arrest us."

"It wasn't that bad," said her father, his voice placating.

"Sounds bad enough," replied Jessica.

"Your friend Harper arranged a ride for you, and the only way to pull it off was if I missed your plane. Harper's brother-in-law, who happens to be married to my ex-wife, nearly got my children arrested at LAX. Like I said," he added with a shrug, "no big deal."

No one spoke as Stuart negotiated heavy traffic. As the van broke clear, Jessica looked over her shoulder and said, "Barbara, you, Marilyn and I are going off by ourselves so we can talk about your son. He continues to amaze me everyday, and I figure I'd better find out all I can about him before we get more involved." She smiled and added, "Sarah, you'll have to take Kenneth somewhere while the other women chat." She reached across the seat and pinched Stuart on the thigh.

Chapter Sixty-Five

Jessica's home was nearly an hour northeast of San Diego, not far from Warner Springs. There was considerable chatter between the two girls. It was as if they hadn't seen each other in years. They ignored Kenneth, who sulked and stared out the window, watching traffic drift by. Jessica and Barbara swapped Stuart stories, which kept both of them in stitches, much to Stuart's dismay.

Stuart interrupted their conversation with "I made reservations at the Warner Springs Resort. How close is that to your home?"

"Ten or fifteen minutes," Jessica replied. "But there are five bedrooms, so you're welcome to stay with us."

"No, that's too much of an inconvenience," he told her. "However, I was hoping Marilyn could stay with Sarah. Sarah, could then show everyone around San Diego while I do some work?"

Jessica waved away his comment. "That's ridiculous, your mother will take the room with the private entrance, and Kenneth and Marilyn will have their own rooms. I won't take no for an answer." She glanced back at Barbara for support.

"Sounds like a good idea to me," said Barbara, in unison with her grandchildren.

"I have to visit some of my supporters and attend the requisite barbecues, so Barbara can spend some time with the kids or just relax. Or," she added, glancing back toward the woman, "you can join me. I heard your son mention he had to work."

"I do," said Stuart, his face turning serious.

Jessica looked closely at him and saw that same look he had during the run-in with those kids who harassed the girls. "I hope we can find some time to enjoy ourselves," she said. This time, she did not pinch his thigh, but squeezed it.

"I'd like to take in a ball game," said Stuart. "Maybe go to the zoo or cross over into Mexico. I have a friend in Tecate. What would you guys like to do?" He peered at them through the rearview mirror.

Barbara was the first to answer, "Count me in for the zoo and SeaWorld."

"Are the Padres in town?" Kenneth asked.

"How about Las Vegas?" suggested Marilyn, adding, "We're all old enough."

"I've got a friend," said Sarah. "His name is Martin Meridian, and I'm sure he'd love to go to Vegas."

A bell went off in Stuart's head, and he looked quickly into the rear view mirror. He'd been around too long not to recognize that inflection.

"Is he nice?" Marilyn asked.

"I've known him since high school," replied Sarah. "He used to be on the football team. He moved here with his mother about seven years ago. He's almost six feet tall, dark hair, very cute."

"Sounds nice, like we could have fun."

Jessica sensed Stuart's discomfort. "I didn't know you were still in touch with him, Sarah. In fact, I haven't heard his name for a long time."

"He called yesterday and said he was planning a trip to Washington and could I get him into places like the White House, Congress and—"

"If you want," Stuart interrupted, "I can probably get him a tour of the FBI building."

"I'm sure he'd love that. I'll ask him when we see him."

"Which is when?" Jessica inquired.

"I told him I'd call when we arrived."

"Hey, I got a great idea," Kenneth spoke up. "Let's take the ten thousand dollars and use it for Vegas. If we win, we return Mr. Loring's money to him; if we lose, it serves him right."

"Hold on, folks. Your stepfather's money is going back to him, untouched." Stuart's tone was hard, leaving no room for negotiation.

"Mom gave it to Marilyn to have a good time with," Kenneth replied petulantly.

Stuart ignored the irritability in his voice. "Like I said earlier, we're a family just starting to get to know each other, and we don't need his money. Let's give your mom the benefit of doubt and assume she didn't know how much was in the envelope."

"Your mom gave you ten thousand dollars and said have a good time?" Sarah asked, her voice a mix of awe and incredulity.

Marilyn grimaced. "It's a little more complicated than that."

Stuart spoke before Marilyn could explain. "The sign we just passed said five miles to Warner Springs. I'd like to go over some of the ground rules for the next three or four days."

The backseat filled with groans, which made Jessica smile. "It's tough being a dad even for a short period of time," she sympathized.

"Rule number 1: No one, and I mean no one, is to talk about any plans we have. Jessica's schedule will probably be in the papers, but the rest of us, including Sarah, will not discuss them with anyone." The van became very quiet.

"Rule number 2: If anyone is going to be away from Jessica or me for any length of time—for purposes of this conversation, make that thirty minutes—I must have the itinerary. Rule number 3: If anyone sees anything suspicious, they are to contact me quicker than I'm saying it."

"What about me?" asked Barbara.

"You're included in all of this." He paused a moment, mulling over how to deliver this information. "Over the past couple of months," he continued, "some strange things have been going on. Aside from the attack on the girls—and I needn't remind you some kids ended up dead—there was an incident in New York, and another at Jessica's house in Maryland, where more people died. The Secret Service is getting close to the answers, but we can't be too careful."

"Is my mother in any danger?" Sarah asked, leaning forward.

Jessica saw that look again in his eyes and knew that this would be yet another of those times when he didn't tell the truth, but also didn't lie.

"She's probably more in danger of getting hit by a car," he reassured the girl. "In fact, I'm more concerned about you. With me hanging around and the Secret Service on the job, if there's someone who wants something from your mother, it's going to be easier for them to grab you."

"What would they do with me?"

"Threaten your mother with your bodily harm unless she cooperates."

Sarah sat back hard against the seat. "You mean, I've been in danger?"

"No more than your mother," said Stuart. "But that's one of the reasons I wanted all of us to come to California. As long as you're with Kenneth, or the rest of the family, you'll be fine."

"What's the other reason?" asked Jessica.

"I've been on the trail of some bank robbers for over a year. We got our first break last week, and it looks like they're going to rob a bank in Arizona next Monday."

"And you're going to stop them?" asked Stuart's mother.

"I'm not that brave, Mom, but I think I may be able to identify one of them. If I do, he'll get picked up by the FBI."

"Dad," Marilyn asked, "what is it exactly that you do? Mom said you were going to end up in jail, but I'm getting a feeling she may have not been telling me the truth."

Jessica saw his fingers tighten on the steering wheel and answered the question for him. "I had your father investigated when you and Sarah had that run-in with those boys. Most of what he does is classified, but he reports directly to the President of the United States. Our first date was at the White House, where he told the President that if I wasn't invited, he was going home."

"It was a simple mix-up," Stuart interjected.

"Maybe so, but I was very proud of him that night." Jessica smiled and touched his shoulder. "He was my knight in shining armor. Ever since, I've been on everybody's list of people to be treated nicely."

"Are you like a secret agent?" Marilyn persisted.

"To make it easy, let's say yes. I'm an agent that has to keep secrets." Stuart laughed and announced, "I like that, an agent that has to keep secrets."

"Mr. Agent, make a right turn at the second light." Jessica pointed ahead.

Like in Maryland, Jessica and Sarah lived in a gate-guarded community. When the guard came out from the booth to say hello, she registered Stuart's car for easy access. They drove down several streets before coming to her home. It was a sprawling ranch model sitting on three acres of land. There was a three-car garage some twenty feet from the main house, attached to it by a covered portico leading to a side door. A white split-rail fence surrounded the entire manicured acreage.

Sarah yelled to Marilyn and Kenneth "Follow me!" and ran to the front door. When Stuart entered behind his children, he saw a formal dining room on the left and the kitchen beyond that. The kitchen opened to the backyard, the den, and a hallway led to the guest wing Jessica had mentioned. There was one more bedroom downstairs, to the right of the hallway, and a staircase leading to three more bedrooms, including the master bedroom suite, which had a small private deck and a stairway leading down to the pool.

"How big is this place?" Barbara asked in awe.

Sarah smiled and announced, "Seven thousand four hundred square feet, not including the garage."

Jessica came up to them and added, "We purchased the land and signed the papers seven weeks before my husband was killed. His insurance more than paid for the completion of the house. The sale of his business insured Sarah could go to the right schools. With a little care, I can live in the style to which I was accustomed. Being elected to Congress means I don't have to be quite so careful."

"It's lovely," said Barbara, admiring the furnishings.

While his mother gushed over the home, Stuart's trained eye looked for any signs of security deVices. There were smoke detectors in every room, but no alarm system. He heard the kids upstairs claiming rooms and watched Jessica lead Barbara to her room. From the window in the dining room, he could see two other homes with well-manicured lawns, one of them with a red Japanese maple tree. He also saw a panel truck and two men sitting in the front seat.

Chapter Sixty-Six

"Your mother is delightful," Jessica said, walking up behind Stuart. "I'm glad you decided to bring her and the kids; it's going to be a fun week." She looked over his shoulder at the panel truck. "That's one of Mark's."

"How do you know?"

"See the logo on the door? It's supposed to be a large oak tree with branches covering the entire southwest."

"He lives in this development?"

"Actually he doesn't, but his property backs up to it, and he has a gate that lets him use this street as a shortcut, if he's headed in this direction."

"The homeowners don't care?"

"There are only sixteen of us. Three of them work for his company; two of them are involved somehow with him, and he's an important patron of the arts. He doesn't abuse the privilege, so they just include him as one of the homeowners. He may even pay dues."

Stuart nodded. "I have to check in. What are we doing for dinner?"

"I planned a barbeque. I've invited the neighbors, including Mark and his wife." She looked at his face for any telltale signs of displeasure. Seeing none, she went on, "It's done by a Service, and they'll be here around five thirty to start setting up. I've told Sarah she can invite some of her friends, so the kids won't think it's a party for old people."

Stuart smiled. "It sounds like fun, and I'd like to meet Mark's wife." He looked at his watch. "It's four thirty, I'll be back in an hour or so. What do people wear to a California barbeque?"

"They start off wearing the same thing they wear in Maryland," she said. Leaning closer, she added, "And with any luck, they end up the same way they do in Maryland."

Stuart shouted goodbye, plugged the address he needed into the GPS system in the van, and started out the gate. He hadn't gone a half-mile before the panel truck was visible in his rearview mirror. He kept the speed a little over the limit, but not fast enough so they would lose sight of him. He had seen a motel on his way to Jessica's and headed back in that direction. Entering the driveway of the Dew Drop Inn, he felt satisfied it was just what he wanted.

"Any rooms available?" he asked the young man behind the desk.

"How long do you plan on staying?"

"Depends. Any bars around here with friendly women?"

The boy smiled. "Two or three, anything special you like?"

"Mostly friendly and willing."

"I can make a call for you, if you want."

"How much will it cost?"

"A hundred for the room, twenty for the call, and you'll have to negotiate the rest."

"How long will it take?"

"Half hour, maybe less."

Stuart took two bills out of his wallet. "Here's a hundred and twenty; I don't want to sign a register."

"Cost you another twenty."

Stuart handed over another twenty. "Give me the keys to the last room on the right."

The room was like he imagined. Faded yellow walls, two chairs, and a desk bolted to the wall. No phone, but a TV with a little sign instructing guests that access to the adult channels required a visit to the front desk and an extra fee. The one thing this room had that the others didn't was a side window. After putting the television sound on as high as it would go, Stuart climbed out the window. From his vantage point, he watched the two men enter the office and speak to the young man behind the counter. One of the men took some bills from his wallet and handed them over. After they finished registering, they parked their truck and walked to the room directly across from Stuart's.

Stuart circled the building and approached their truck unnoticed. Bending low, he let the air out of one of the rear tires and returned quickly to his room, climbing through the window and settling down in front of the TV. Fifteen minutes later, there was a knock on the door.

"Who's there?" he asked without opening the door.

"Room Service."

"Door's open, come on in."

The door opened and in walked a girl Stuart judged to be sixteen or seventeen. She wore jeans and a tee shirt that was a walking ad for Harley Davidson.

"You requested room Service?" Her voice sounded like she was two weeks out of Georgia.

"I did, but it was for my friends across the way."

She looked over her shoulder. "How many are there?"

"Just two, and I'm willing to pay extra. How old are you?"

"I'm twenty-four, and it's going to cost you four fifty."

Stuart knew he was expected to negotiate, but he was in a hurry. "Tell you what. I'll give you five hundred if you can keep them both occupied for an hour."

Her eyes lit up, and he could almost hear her thinking, *This is definitely going to be one of my better days.*

"They know I'm coming?" she asked.

"They're expecting you. And to show my trust, I'm going to give you three hundred now, and they'll give you the rest when the hour is up."

She held out her hand. "For an extra hundred, I'll include you."

Stuart shook his head and pointed to the door. He hadn't seen her arrive, and he was sure she had a friend or two waiting for her somewhere nearby. As she knocked on the door across the driveway, Stuart walked out of his room, got into his car, and drove away. From his rearview mirror he watched the men push past the girl as they fumbled for their keys. He was still laughing as he found his way to the Warner Springs resort.

Chapter Sixty-Seven

Jessica's barbeque was in full swing when Stuart returned. The caterers had supplied valet parking to go along with the cooks, waiters, waitresses, and bartenders. Stuart estimated over a hundred and fifty people standing around, watching children splash around in the pool or listening to a woman deejay telling jokes when the records weren't spinning. The women in the crowd were, for the most part, wearing western-style gingham sundresses, while the men were clad in jeans, plaid shirts, and cowboy hats. Stuart stood back and studied the crowd while thinking, *So much for "they dress the same way as in Maryland."*

A voice called him back with "Where have you been?" He turned to face his mother.

"Had to make some calls," he said, looking at the pool. "Are the kids swimming or dancing?"

"Girls are swimming and Kenneth is sulking."

"Because the girls are swimming?"

"Not bad for a new dad. You may want to talk to him."

"Where is he?"

"Last time I looked, he was by the steak table." She pointed toward a group of people standing around the barbeque, dinner plates at the ready.

"Ah think ah'll mosey on over thar and say howdy."

She compressed her lips.

"Don't be so provincial." Stuart said, "When in Rome and all that stuff,"

With a smile on her face she replied. "You do that, and I'll go check on the girls."

Stuart grabbed a beer off the tray of a passing waiter and approached his son. Stuart thought he was talking to another boy, but as he neared them, he realized that they were arguing. The boy was several inches taller than Kenneth, but Stuart focused on his eyes. They had the same mean look as his older brother, Augie.

258

"We do things differently out here," Martin Meridian was saying.

"What kind of things?" Stuart asked, and both boys looked at him.

"Dad, this is Martin, Sarah's friend. He was just telling me about the trip to Vegas."

Stuart held out his hand. "What trip?"

"I was just telling your son," said the boy, making *son* sound like something bad, "that we usually share rooms with the girls when we go to Vegas."

"What girls are going to Vegas?"

"Sarah and your daughter."

"When is that happening?"

"As soon as we figure out the room arrangements."

"How does Kenneth want them to be?"

"He wants four separate rooms."

This kid is spoiling for an argument. "Too bad the trip has been cancelled; it sounds like it could've been fun."

A look of uncertainty crossed the boy's face. "Who cancelled it?"

"I did," said Stuart. "I got a call from a friend in Mexico, and we've been invited to attend a fiesta."

Martin stared at the older man for a moment and then asked, "When're you going?"

"As soon as Mrs. Winston clears the date."

A man approached them from the crowd and declared, "Oh, there you are! I was looking all over for you." The three turned toward Mark Harper. "I heard you were in town," he informed Stuart. "I was going to invite you to my place, but no one could find you."

"I've been around. I seem to run into your people all over California."

"Really." The smile left his face. "If I would have known you were bringing Jessica home, I wouldn't have bothered to send one of my limos."

Stuart put a huge smile on his face. "Ever since someone killed those three boys who were hassling the congresswoman, the Secret Service has been keeping an extra watch on her."

Harper quickly glanced at Martin and then back to Stuart. "Yes, I heard about that. So I guess this protection is a good thing."

The two men locked eyes, no friendship offered on either side. "I arranged to have your men at LAX released after we departed," said Stuart. "The two at Lindbergh Field were supposed to be let go at five this evening. The other two, those men who thought Jessica was in the car I rented have probably left the motel by now. In the future, just ask where we're headed; the congresswoman's itinerary is an open book. The problem is, when we think she's being followed, we have to react. Luckily, no one was killed, but who knows what'll happen next time?"

Harper said nothing for a moment, as if unsure how to proceed. "I may have underestimated your ability to . . . protect Jessica. I won't do that again."

"Now, I'm glad it's settled, how about an introduction to your wife? I understand she's very nice."

Harper clenched his jaw, and his hands were nearly fists. He forced a smile that made him look almost ghoulish and said, "She's around here somewhere. As soon as I find her, I'll bring her over." He turned and moved into the crowd.

"Way to go, Dad," Kenneth said, and then watched Martin stalk away. "What say we keep this between us?" suggested Stuart. "I don't want to worry your grandmother." When the boy nodded, Stuart thought, *the kid's getting better every hour I'm with him.*

Kenneth ran off to look for the girls, and Stuart circled the crowd. He saw Jessica with a group of people having a good laugh. He also noticed the Virginia Slim agent from the airport; the woman's partners were somewhere nearby. Mark Harper was standing by the garage, the woman at his side making Stuart think of a top model. "Another beer, sir?" asked the waiter.

Stuart turned to reply and recognized his contact from the airport.

"Yes, thank you, and I'd also like the name of the blonde standing next to the man by the garage."

"That would be Mark Harper; the woman is his latest squeeze. I'll have a report at the front desk of the hotel in the morning."

Stuart tipped the beer in the direction of his contact and walked off toward the pool. Halfway there, in the shadow of some trees, he saw Sarah, dressed in a two-piece bathing suit arguing with Martin. The boy suddenly grabbed her arm, and she tried to pull away, but he tightened his grip. Stuart moved closer and heard the girl tell him to let her go.

"You said we could go to Vegas," Martin's mouth was a sneer.

Before Sarah could answer, Kenneth stepped in, "She asked you to let her go."

Stuart tensed but stayed where he was.

"Look, kid, this has nothing to do with you, so get lost."

Kenneth bristled and held out a hand for Sarah.

"I said to get lost," repeated Martin, except this time he swung and hit Kenneth on the side of the head. Kenneth half slipped to the ground, supporting himself with one arm. As he struggled to rise, Martin moved in.

"Don't hit him!" Sarah shouted.

Martin glanced back at Sarah and didn't see Kenneth coming at him. Kenneth threw a tackle sending them both to the ground, with Kenneth on top. Stuart let him hit Martin once before he rushed in and broke them up.

"Sarah, take Kenneth back to the pool to cool off." He leaned over to help Martin stand. "Let's call this one even."

Martin stood glaring at Stuart and then over his shoulder at Sarah and Kenneth, who were walking away. "This isn't over by a long shot."

"Oh, yes it is," Stuart, whispered. "I'm not as nice as my son. If I find you bothering either of them again"—he stopped and reconsidered—"just tell your boss if I find you bothering *anyone* I know, he'll hear from me personally."

"I don't have a boss," the boy stammered, but his eyes said something else.

Chapter Sixty-Eight

Stuart glanced at his watch for what seemed like the tenth time in the past half hour. The crowd started disappearing around ten, and now, at eleven, only a handful remained. Mark Harper never returned with his wife, and Martin Meridian was nowhere to be seen. Stuart lifted his third beer to his lips and thought about the night.

Barbara had gone to bed earlier after telling him about the nice couple who lived two houses away. The woman was a retired teacher and her husband had worked for a dot-com company until his retirement six months earlier. They had invited her over for tea, and she wanted to know if it was all right to visit.

Marilyn found him after hearing from Sarah and Kenneth about the fight with Martin Meridian.

"What are you going to do about it?" she asked indignantly, staring down at her father. "Martin is inches taller than Kenneth."

Her anger made him smile. "Your brother handled himself very well, and I think he's got Meridian wondering what he should do."

"Are we going to Mexico?" she asked, her voice changing moods as she spoke.

"We've been invited, I'll check with Jessica."

"Dad, you like her, don't you?"

Stuart nodded and realized it was the first time he had admitted his feelings.

"Why do you think Mom really divorced you?"

Stuart had taken another pull on his beer, stalling for time. His daughter had a way of changing gears that kept him on his toes. "I don't know if it makes a difference any longer. Why do you ask?"

"I heard Mom and Mr. Loring argue a long time ago. Mom was shouting if all he wanted was information on the Torres investigation, he could have bought it, he didn't have to marry her."

Stuart asked about Loring's reply, and Marilyn looked down at the ground.

"He slapped her and then told her that if she ever spoke that name again, he'd make sure she went to jail."

"Are you sure he said Torres?" Stuart had struggled to keep his voice under control.

"I'll never forget it. I searched all the papers, but there was nothing with the name Torres. Does it mean anything to you?"

Stuart shook his head. "How many years ago was that?"

Marilyn pursed her lips and spent a moment calculating. "Maybe a year or two after you got divorced. The only reason I remember was because the argument started over you. I remember you were being sent to some new job that no one knew anything about. The same thing happened last month, Dad. Mr. Loring got a call about your new job, and they argued again. The next day, when I asked Mom if the argument was about Torres, she said she didn't know what I was talking about. It's funny, but I had forgotten all about him until that day."

Stuart closed his eyes, wanting to make believe he didn't remember the Torres investigation. As if he could ever forget.

His was pulled from a stupor when someone kissed his cheek.

"Penny for your thoughts," said Jessica.

Stuart smiled, his eyes closed. "Lady, you throw one hell of a party." He opened his eyes and noticed she was seated across from him.

"My feet are killing me." She kicked off her shoes and rubbed her feet.

"Put them up here," he said, patting his knees. He adjusted the chair and then helped lift her feet onto his lap.

Jessica didn't say a word as he rubbed, but the sounds emanating from her indicated pleasure. "How are you on other areas, because I hurt all over."

"Pretty good."

She smiled. "I believe you. Sarah was telling me we're invited to Mexico."

"Jose Vargas, an agent assigned as liaison between Mexico and other Latino countries, is in Tecate, working with the Vice President of Mexico. If you have the time, he'd love to arrange a dinner between the two of you, families included."

Jessica sat up and let her feet drop to the floor. "The Vice President of Mexico? Of course I'll find the time. Thirty days ago he didn't have the time to say hello." She stopped and then added, "Did your friend say anything else?"

"He has something he wants to show me but wouldn't or couldn't talk about it over the phone. However, he did say Sunday afternoon around four would be great for a half-hour meeting, followed by dinner. The VP's wife and four children will be there."

"Sunday!" declared Jessica, standing quickly. "That only leaves me tomorrow, not much time to find out the names and ages of his wife and children, pick out an appropriate present, and figure out what to wear."

"What about the back rub you needed?" suggested Stuart, hoping to derail her for another few minutes.

"Who's got time for a back rub? Do you have any idea how important this meeting can be? I've got to get in touch with the Speaker. Who knows what deals we're working on?" She stopped and looked at Stuart. "You set this up, didn't you?"

"He wants to show me something, no big deal."

She leaned over and kissed him full on the lips. "Tomorrow, I'm having breakfast with some supporters and then lunch with a few big contributors. How about us planning on dinner somewhere without the family?" Jessica suggested the Warner Springs resort, and Stuart offered to make the arrangements.

He expected her to bolt and was surprised when she sat down and asked for his version of the altercation between Kenneth and Martin Meridien.

"Which version have you heard?"

"One from Mark, another from Sarah, and they're not even close. Mark said he was standing there as it took place and is very upset with you. He's going to complain to his friend, the President. He also suggested I no longer have anything to do with you."

"Suggested?"

"Well, his exact words were," and she lowered her voice to mimic Mark's, "I cannot continue to support someone who has anything to do with that person."

"What did you tell him?"

"That I wouldn't take support from anyone who didn't like that person. Now tell me what happened."

He explained what he saw, from Martin grabbing Sarah's arm to Kenneth stepping in to defend her, Kenneth being knocked to the ground and then getting in a few good licks of his own. "What's interesting," he added, "was Mark wasn't even there when this happened, so anything he told you is either hearsay or a lie."

"I guess you need to go." She looked up at him.

Leaning over, Stuart kissed her and whispered against her mouth, "Not that I want to, but I have some unfinished business."

Stuart started toward his car when the Virginia Slim walked up to him.

"There are four men, in two pickup trucks, waiting for you outside the gate. Nathan wants to know how you want it handled."

"How does he know they're waiting for me?"

"There the same guys from the motel."

Stuart led her back to the house where they found Jessica on the phone.

Chapter Sixty-Nine

"Mr. Speaker, I know it's one fifteen in the morning, but I consider this important." Jessica's voice had a pleading sound to it.

She listened for a minute and then explained, "The Vice President of Mexico has invited me to a family barbeque in Tecate on Sunday. My calendar is full tomorrow, and it's imperative I know what you want discussed." She caught sight of Stuart with the pretty waitress from the party, raised her eyebrows, and shrugged, as if asking what he wanted.

In a quiet voice, he too asked, "Hold the call for a minute."

Her eyes widened. Holding a hand over the mouthpiece, she whispered, "I'm speaking to Gary Brightwell, Speaker of the House."

Stuart held out his hand for the phone. Jessica handed it over with obvious uncertainty.

"Mr. Brightwell? This is Stuart Taylor. If you don't know who I am, I'll give you the President's private line to verify my credentials. I'm with six Secret Service agents, and I must ask you to please hold on for a minute. I'll personally call you tomorrow to explain the problem. Thank you, sir." He returned the phone to Jessica and told her, "I need your sweater and scarf now! There may be some strangers hanging around, and we want them to follow you."

Jessica removed the articles of clothing and handed them to the woman, who immediately slipped them on.

Stuart kissed Jessica on the cheek and promised to see her in the morning.

"You'll call me as soon as this matter is straightened out," she commanded. "I don't care what time it is."

Even with Jessica's clothing, Stuart wasn't sure he could pass the agent off as Jessica. This woman was taller and heavier. To cover this, he walked her out with his arm around her and had her look at the ground.

They got into the car, and Stuart turned to her. "Tell Nathan I'm heading toward the seventy-eight. There's a cutoff four miles before we get there, and I'm going to pull onto that road. A half-mile down, I'll stop. I want these guys incommunicado for at least seventy-two hours."

The agent nodded and clicked her cell phone twice. After repeating the instructions, she listened for a moment. "Nathan wants to know what to do if they're armed."

"Tell him to follow my lead; I don't want anyone getting hurt."

After the agent disconnected from the call, Stuart asked her name and she responded, "Susan."

"Okay, Susan, listen. When we stop, you stay down. Worst case, these guys are after the congresswoman. But if I had to guess, I'd say I'm the target. Let me and Nathan handle them."

She turned toward him, a scowl on her face. "You listen, Mr. Hotshot Washington guy. Working in the field is a lot different than some office job in the big city. So I'm telling you: when you pull over, *you* stay down! I can handle whatever has to be done, and what I don't need is someone from the home office getting hurt on my watch. We haven't had a casualty in over three years, and I don't plan having one tonight."

Stuart felt the verbal slap and was appropriately chagrined. He knew what it was to have a job to do. "Sorry, I was out of line." When he saw the tension in her face relax, he told her, "When I pull over, we'll both get down and out of sight. I want those jokers out of their trucks and on flat ground. If we do this right, no one has to get hurt."

Susan nodded and then smiled.

"Get Nate's location, we're coming up to the turnoff."

Susan made contact and reported that there was one car behind them, followed by Nathan's and two others.

"Tell him I'm slowing down so the car behind us can pass and precede us onto the road. A half mile up, have them stop and get out of the car. When we get there, we're going to wait for those bastards to get close. Tell your men to be ready."

After passing on the instructions, Susan asked, "Do you have as much clout as everyone seems to think?"

Stuart gave her an odd look. "Why are you asking?"

"Because Mark Harper has lots of friends inside the government. We've had congressmen, senators, even the White House chief of staff visiting him. Since you're playing with fire, I'm wondering if we're going to get burned."

Stuart made a quick turn onto the road. "Stay awake," he warned her. "And don't worry, you won't get burned."

Parking on the side of the road, he doused the headlights and pulled the agent close to him.

"Watch those hands!" she said as he simultaneously reached for the pistol in the small of his back. "Nate and I have something going, and I wouldn't want him to get the wrong idea." She laughed seductively, bringing a little smile to Stuart's face.

"Here they come," he suddenly hissed. "Stay down!"

The two pickups cut their lights the moment they turned onto the road. There was a sound of car doors and then footsteps quietly approaching. Stuart figured there were four of them.

"Tell Nate *now!*" he instructed, his voice an urgent whisper.

Susan conveyed the message, and in less than five seconds, the van positioned in front and facing them switched on its high beams. The four men, temporarily blinded, covered their eyes, giving Stuart and Susan time to jump out of the car.

"Don't anyone move!" boomed a voice through a loudspeaker.

One of the men tried to run toward the pickup. Stuart saw the flash before hearing the report of the gunshot.

The man stopped in his tracks and raised his arms.

His three cronies raised their arms at the same time, one of them shaking so hard he could barely stand.

Stuart separated them into two groups; the first comprised of the two men from the motel and the second, the two unknown men. After relieving all of them of their weapons, he asked the first two, "How was the girl I sent you?"

When neither man answered, he stepped over to the second pair. "Who did you think I was with?" When there was only silence, he prompted, "The congresswoman?"

One of them nodded.

Stuart turned to Nate. "You saw him nod, right?" When Nathan confirmed this, Stuart announced in his best FBI voice, "Under the federal law established for the protection of elected officials, you will all be charged with a crime that carries a sentence of twenty years to life."

"We didn't threaten any public officials!" shouted one of the men. "In fact, we didn't threaten anyone!"

"That'll be for the jury to decide," Stuart told him. "You do know the congresswoman has been threatened, and that the men were killed while they were attempting to do bodily harm."

The four men exchanged frantic glances. "We want to see a lawyer," demanded their spokesman.

Stuart made sure they saw his smiling face. "Under federal law, we can hold you for ninety-six hours before you see your lawyer. Give us his name, and we'll contact him for you . . . in four days."

The men appeared shaken. "We're also allowed one phone call each," insisted their leader, earlier signs of bravado no longer there.

"That doesn't apply under federal law," Stuart told him. "But I'll do you a favor, okay? Who do you want called? Come next Wednesday, I'll make those calls for you."

The men stared down at their shoes. Finally, one of the men asked, "How about my wife?"

Stuart sighed out loud. "You guys don't get it. You're each going to a different jail, in a different state. Four days from now, the process will begin. If we can still find you, we'll ask you who to call. If this takes more than four days, tough shit. Why will it take more than four days?" He asked rhetorically, clearly enjoying this interlude from guns and powerful insiders. "You'll be with the general population. In order to keep your identities secret, they'll be told you're child molesters. Gee," he added, trying to look sympathetic. "I hope you can stay awake until we find you."

"You can't do that!" insisted the leader.

"You're right, we can't," Stuart replied. "Remind me of that a week from now." Turning to the agents, he barked, "Take these assholes away."

As each man was led away, one of them turned back to Stuart. "I want to talk to Mr. Harper."

Chapter Seventy

It was almost two in the morning before Stuart entered his room at the Warner Springs resort. Perched on the edge of the bed, he thought about the last few hours. He had given instructions that the four men be taken to a facility where they would remain isolated until the sixth of July. Nathan had put in a call to Ray Bradley, the FBI's deputy director, and Bradley asked to speak to Stuart. After five minutes of animated conversation, Nathan had the approval needed to carry out Stuart's instructions.

Stuart pulled off his shoes and rubbed his tired feet. He smiled to himself, recalling the last conversation with Susan. "Big City Man," she started, "you certainly have the clout. Just want you to know, I'm putting your name in our little black book. If we ever need help, you're the man."

"I hope you never have to call," Stuart replied. "But if you do, I'll be there." Stretched out on the bed, he closed his eyes and continued to review the night. Harper would be looking for his men, come first light. Not finding them would probably generate calls to his brother-in-law, to Jessica, maybe even to the President. Bradley was right: once it was determined Stuart was the target and not the congresswoman, different laws and rules were in effect. He had asked Bradley how Jake was doing, and the answer was not good. The President would have to make a decision soon.

Stuart opened his eyes and looked at the clock on the nightstand. *Three o'clock, I must have dozed. Time to call Michael.*

The phone rang as he was pulling himself upright.

"You bastard!" It was Jessica and she was pissed.

"I was just getting ready to call you," he said, and the lie was even transparent to him.

"I hope I woke you. I've been sitting here worried stiff."

"I'm sorry, Jess, truly." When she didn't respond, he continued, "I got here a little after two. Something happened tonight that we'll have to talk about."

Again there was no response. "They weren't after you, they were after me. All of them worked for Harper, but they weren't part of his A-team."

"You keep referring to them in the past tense. Are they dead?"

"I told you I don't like killing people, remember? Too much paperwork." When the humor failed, he said, "We've taken them out of the game for a time."

"What's going to happen to Mark?"

"Probably nothing, for a while. That's why we put his men where he can't reach them. I'm hoping when they don't report back, he'll start making phone calls. So when you get yours, play dumb." He looked again at the clock. "I've got to get some sleep. I'll see you in a while."

Hanging up, he rose from the bed, went into the bathroom, and turned on the shower. When the temperature felt right, he stepped in and let the water run over his body as he turned the handle to cold. Fully awake, he picked up his cell phone and dialed.

"Good morning, Michael. And before you ask, yes, it is early. Or late, depending upon your point of view."

"Ray just called and said you've had a busy night."

Stuart nearly grinned. "I'd be lying if I said it wasn't fun. How are you feeling?"

"I'm feeling well. The weather's fine, and hopefully, I'll have a pleasant weekend." After a few seconds, he added, "You didn't call me to ask about my health or the weather. Something wrong?"

Stuart remained silent for a few seconds. "I don't know yet. Remember Torres?"

It was Michael's turn to be silent. "I remember the Torres case," he finally said.

"What do you remember?"

"Farm workers from Mexico were being beaten, their women raped, their living conditions below slave level, and Ferde Torres was going to organize them. Our office was working on catching the people responsible when Torres disappeared. We spent months tracking down leads but eventually had to give it up. You headed our team, so why are you asking?"

"I got a call from Jose Vargas. You remember him, from New York? He advised me they found Ferde's body in Tecate. They haven't released that fact and they won't until some things get checked out, but I remembered what you always said about coincidences."

"Something else happen?"

"Remember the guy I found dead, Augie Meridian? His brother's here, working for Mark Harper."

"There must be something else. You wouldn't call this early in the morning with next to nothing, and on a case we gave up on fifteen years ago."

"This one is, well, let's say some coincidences are hard to ignore." Stuart stopped talking and looked at the ceiling.

"It's six in the morning, talk!"

"My daughter mentioned a fight she overheard years ago between my ex and her husband. My ex said if all he wanted was information about Torres, he didn't have to marry her." In the long silence, Stuart knew Michael was processing this information.

"Maybe she got the name wrong?" he finally said.

"Maybe," Stuart replied. "Or maybe she got the name right."

"Let me go over those records and see if any of this makes sense. You'll be back in Washington when, Thursday or Friday?"

"Or earlier, if need be."

"We'll talk before then, get some sleep."

Stuart hung up, laid back on the bed, and stared at the ceiling.

Chapter Seventy-One

Stuart awoke, his body covered in sweat. Light was streaming in through curtains not fully closed. He glanced around, knowing something had awakened him, wanting to identify the source before jumping up and brandishing his gun. The digital clock moved from seven thirty-eight to seven thirty-nine; nothing else was moving. A loud knock on the door caused him to jump.

"Mr. Taylor, are you awake?"

"I'm awake, who's there?"

"Nathan, from last night."

"Hold on, I'll be right there." He got off the bed and moved quickly to the door. Looking through the security hole, he saw nothing. "Step back against the wall," he commanded. Peering through again, he saw Nathan holding two containers of coffee. "Door's open, come on in."

The man entered and handed one of the cups to Stuart. "Sorry to get you up this early, but I was told to give this to you in person." He offered him a folded piece of paper.

The President has received calls from Chilicote, Mark Harper, Harvey Loring, and Kenneth Hall. The senator said you threatened him, Loring says one of your kids took $10,000, and you had the police let her go. Harper is complaining about your threatening some eighteen-year-old boy who works for him, and Hall is their lawyer. He's threatening the President to pull campaign funds and support the opposition against the President and Winston. They're screaming for your scalp. I've spoken to Ray and Jake, and they're circling the wagons.

Michael

"Are there any copies of this?"

"No, and I was told to stand by for the transmission. When the President's chief of staff calls, I do exactly what I'm told."

Stuart walked over to the desk and picked up a book of matches. He lit one and put the flame to the paper, holding it over a trashcan. "Now the only copy is at the White House."

"Was that a smart thing to do?" Nathan asked.

"Probably not." Stuart shook the trashcan to be sure the entire note burned. "Thanks for bringing it over. And thanks for the help last night."

After Nathan left, Stuart took a hot shower, shaved, and dressed. He picked up another container of coffee in the lobby and left for Jessica's. "Dad!" Kenneth shouted as he entered the front door. "We decided to go to the zoo this morning, but Mrs. Winston says we need your approval."

"Who's *we*?" Stuart asked, looking around the empty room.

"Sarah, Marilyn, Grandmother, and me."

"Where is everyone?" Stuart asked, still evading the question.

"Sarah and Marilyn are getting dressed, I hope, and Mrs. Winston and Grandmother are in the kitchen."

"Let me talk to Jessica before I give my okay."

Kenneth left, going up the stairs two at a time.

"Good morning, everyone," he announced, entering the kitchen.

"You look like you didn't get any sleep at all," Jessica commented, rising to greet him. "Now can you tell me what went on?"

Stuart smiled. "You look lovely and yes, I can, but first let's get the kids on the road. There's a van with two Secret Service agents prepared to go everywhere they go. The only thing we have to tell the kids is, if anything happens, they'll have to listen to the agents."

The line between Jessica's brows deepened. "Is there any danger?"

"No!" Realizing he had answered too loudly, Stuart repeated, "No, there's not. This will be a learning experience for them. They get to act like adults with someone watching over them. I wouldn't let them go if I thought there was the slightest chance of anything happening."

Barbara leaned on her elbows, concern etched in her face as well. "Stuart, did anything happen last night I'm not aware of?" His mother glanced from Stuart to Jessica and back to her son.

Stuart poured himself a cup of coffee, picked up a muffin, and sat down at the table. "Okay, here it is. Last night, Mark Harper had four men waiting outside the gate. With the help of the Secret Service, and maybe some local FBI, we arrested them and told them we were charging them under a federal law that carries a twenty-year to life sentence."

"What law is that?" Jessica asked.

"Not quite sure, but it was for the protection of elected officials. Once they thought the woman with me was you, it was easy to make them believe." He took a bite of muffin. "These are great, did you bake them?" He looked at Jessica.

"I don't bake, now finish the story."

"Well, after twenty minutes or so, they told us Mark had sent them to do some damage to me and or maybe you. No one was sure if you'd be with me when I left, but they were told that if you were, it didn't make a difference. I had each of the men moved to a different prison for the next ninety-six hours, where they'll be kept without any communication with the outside."

"Isn't that illegal?" Barbara asked.

"Of course it is," Jessica, answered, her voice hard.

"According to my sources," said Stuart; "there's a law on the books which allows us to hold a prisoner incommunicado if having access to others could be detrimental to public officials."

Jessica's face looked like a question mark. "Is that true?"

"Close enough. I'm not sure of the exact wording, but it only works where public officials are concerned, and you are a public official."

"What are they going to do with Mark Harper?" Stuart's mother asked, changing the conversation.

"Nothing right now; he's part of an ongoing investigation. Harper, his lawyer, a congressman, and his brother-in-law have already called the President demanding my head. I'm expecting Jessica to get a call from the Speaker and Mr. Harper some time this morning. I'm hoping when they can't find the four men, they'll assume they've been killed."

Jessica looked skeptical. "You don't think the Speaker will be told the truth?"

"I trust the people in this room, and I haven't told you where the men are being kept. The President can honestly tell him, if he asks, he doesn't know either."

Before anything else could be said, they heard the children descending the stairs. Stuart turned to his mother. "Mom, you're in charge. Have a great time, don't forget to see the pandas, and make sure you're home in time to have tea with the neighbors. I had them checked out, and they're everything they claim to be."

It took another fifteen minutes for everyone to get ready and leave. Once they heard the rules, they decided to travel in the same car as the agents, their only guarantee of not getting separated.

Stuart and Jessica stood at the door and watched the agents van pull away.

"What do you mean, you had my neighbors checked out?" Jessica asked, closing the front door.

"Not a real checkout, just making sure they weren't somehow indebted to Harper."

Before Jessica could respond, the phone rang.

"Hello," she said in an exasperated tone.

She mouthed "Mark Harper" to Stuart, and he picked up the extension in the kitchen.

"Good morning, Mark. I hope you had a good time last night. I didn't see you leave."

"It was a great party, thanks. My leaving is one of the reasons I called. I went home through my secret entrance, and the four men who act as my bodyguards turned up missing."

"Where were they?"

"Parked in front of the gate. The guard said they left about a minute or two after Stuart, and I was wondering if they stopped at your place for anything?"

"I didn't see them, and Stuart is inside. I'll ask him."

"No, don't bother him, I'm sure he didn't see them. I'll just have to keep looking. Thanks again for the invite, we had a great time."

"I guess that means the next call will be from the Speaker," Stuart said, joining her in the living room.

"He's going to have to find me first. I have a meeting in twenty minutes, and I can't be late. I should be home by three thirty. Are you going to be here, or do you want to wait at the resort?"

"I'll pick you up here; it'll give me another ten minutes with you."

She gave him a quick kiss on the lips and headed out the door, calling over her shoulder, "I have a cleaning woman coming in about an hour, and don't get in her way." Waving, she was out the door, leaving Stuart standing there.

Using his cell phone, he dialed a number in Mexico. The call was answered on the first ring.

"Jose here."

"It's me. Have they verified it's Torres's body?"

"Not yet. Like I told you yesterday, we found his watch, his wallet, and his car keys. We also found a letter in a metal cigarette case. It's in bad shape, but we can make out your name on the bottom and some of the words."

Stuart closed his eyes. He knew very well about that letter: it was the one in which he had guaranteed the man's safety if he came forward. "Are you there?" asked Vargas.

"I'm here. We're arriving at three thirty. There's an airfield near Tecate that'll accommodate a small jet. There'll be six of us, maybe two Secret Service agents. We've had a little bit of excitement here."

"Anything we should be aware of?"

"No, I think it's personal, but better safe than sorry."

"Have you told the congresswoman the real reason for the visit?"

"All I've told her is as a favor to me, you've set up this barbeque and a meeting with the Vice President. She's very excited."

"It's a funny thing, but he's getting a little excited too. Who knows, maybe I can become a private secretary, if he becomes President." Jose chuckled. "See you tomorrow, amigo, vaya con Dios."

Stuart closed his cell phone and started out the door. He heard Jessica's phone ring and stopped to listen. After a long beat, the recording machine kicked in.

"Congresswoman Winston, this is Chuck Andres. We met three months ago when I did a story about you for the paper. Please call my office. We're trying to get verification of an altercation that took place at your home between Stuart Taylor and some young kid. After that last debacle, we want to make sure we've got it right."

Chapter Seventy-Two

"Do you think you can trust this American friend of yours?

Jose Vargas pursed his lips before answering the Vice President. "I met him around fifteen years ago, when he was trying to catch the people responsible for brutalizing our people who were crossing the border for work. He was honest, and he really seemed to feel for them. When Torres disappeared, he acted as if he had been betrayed." Vargas paused for a moment. "Some people believed Torres had been given a large sum of money and had fled with it, but Taylor never believed that. He was determined to catch the perpetrators. From what I heard, it cost him his wife and family."

The Vice President mulled over this information before speaking, "And now he's associated with this congresswoman."

Vargas nodded. "I've heard some stories about how they met. True or not, I do know at least six people are dead because they got in the way. Stuart Taylor is not someone you want to anger. And," he quickly added, "the answer is yes, I trust him as long as our goals are the same." Jose looked into the eyes of the man seated across the large mahogany desk. "At this particular time, our goals are the same."

"Michael, you've got to put a lid on Andres. He got the story from someone about the altercation at her party, and now he's trying to get confirmation from Jessica."

"The hell with him," shot back Michael. "Let me tell you what we've got. I've had people going through the archives, and one of the people questioned, mentioned they were transported by truck. The name on the truck was, and I'm reading from his notes, Okka-Tee Ranch. We couldn't find anything with that name, so the agent let it slide. After your call this morning, I checked and Harper's ranch is Oak Tree West."

"Close, but is it close enough?" Stuart replied glumly.

"Absolutely not, but I've got a funny feeling we're about to reopen the case. I'm meeting with the attorney general, and Ray Bradley first thing Monday morning. If you learn anything in Mexico, call me right away."

"What about Andres?"

"You handle him, but nicely. In the past, I've found him to be a friend." After saying their good-byes, Stuart placed a call to the journalist.

"Chuck Andres here. Is this Congresswoman Winston?"

"Caller ID will screw you up every time," said Stuart, identifying himself.

After a short delay, Andres said, "Mr. Taylor, I'm glad you called. I have a few questions about—"

"Before you ask me anything," Stuart interrupted, "whatever happened to getting back to me with a date for that meeting?"

"Couldn't get anyone else interested. My gut feeling is they're afraid."

"Are you taping this conversation?"

"Yes, yes, I am."

"Turn off the recorder; I have something to tell you."

"How do you know I'll really turn it off?"

"Until you prove otherwise, your word is good."

"Okay, it's off, so what've you got?"

"Get yourself booked on a flight to San Diego. Be at the civilian aviation terminal tomorrow afternoon, one thirty at the latest, and bring your passport."

"Where am I going?"

"You and I are going to have a conversation. If I like the way it goes, you'll be on a plane to Mexico. You'll return late tomorrow night and can schedule a flight home on Monday morning."

"Where in Mexico, and who else will be on that plane?"

"Chuck, listen to yourself. This could be the biggest story of the year, and all you've got are questions. Come on, this isn't the White House. I'm no one's press secretary. You coming or not?"

"Count me in," he quickly replied.

"Good, I'll see you tomorrow. Don't be late and don't eat on the plane."

Chapter Seventy-Three

Stuart wandered through Jessica's house before finding a comfortable sofa and television. Baltimore was playing the Yankees, and the game was getting started. Turning on the set, Stuart kicked off his shoes, stretched out, and pushed the mute button. *Watching baseball on television is like watching the grass grow* was the last thing he thought before the vacuum cleaner awakened him.

"Sorry, Señor," said the housekeeper. "I tried not to disturb you." She smiled sheepishly.

Stuart rubbed his hand through his hair. "I had to get up anyway," he told her. He looked at his watch and realized he'd been sleeping for almost three hours. "You've been very quiet, I didn't hear you come in."

"Señorita Winston told me that if you are sleeping, I should clean around you."

Stuart smiled and slipped into his shoes. As he stood, he saw that she was looking at him strangely. "Is something the matter?"

She smiled. "You don't recognize me?"

He studied her face but had no memory of having met her.

"I was only ten when we met. You were looking for my brother, and you came into our bedroom."

"Your brother?" he repeated. "I'm sorry, I don't remember. What is your name?"

"Ladena Rodriguez," she told him. "But when we met, I was Ladena Torres."

Stuart studied her face for a moment. "Ferde was your brother?"

"You remember him! Many people do not. They said he took some money and went to South America, but you never believed that. I always remembered you looked for him months after everyone else stopped."

Stuart searched her face, as if trying to remember. "They called you Dena," he said, his memory kicking in.

Her lips parted into a smile.

"Sit down, please," he said, holding out a hand. The woman shook her head. "I still have much work to do, and you've spent enough time with me." Having said this, she reluctantly took his hand and sat down.

"It's been fifteen years," he said. "What have you been doing? Do you have children?"

"My family never went back to Mexico. My parents were sure that someday, my brother would come back. Like you, they never believed that story. I graduated high school, became a citizen, and married Roberto, who was born in California. We have a little boy, he's four, and we named him Ferde." She used her sleeve to wipe away a tear. Stuart squeezed her hand. "Dena, what does your husband do?"

"He works for Oak Tree West," she said proudly. "He's the assistant manager of the vineyards. It's a good job and gives us medical benefits and a nice place to live. We're saving to send Ferde to college." The expression on her face changed to reflective. "This is why I work because my brother was the only one in our family to go to college. Little Ferde will be next."

"It sounds like you and Roberto are doing well. I may have a surprise for you. How can I get in touch with you both next week?"

"What kind of surprise?" she asked, her eyes alive with possibilities.

"I'm not sure, but I'll check on it Monday and get back to you."

Dena wrote down her telephone number and handed it to him. "I will now be on, as you say, pins and needles, until you call."

Stuart laughed. "One more thing: whatever happened to Ferde's girlfriend? I think her name was Doreen something."

Ladena's face turned to stone. "She married Mr. Harper. She's now a very fine lady, but I think very unhappy. He even made her change her name to Denise."

Stuart was surprised and unsure how to respond. He stood and announced, "I have to go, but I promise to call you very soon." Touching her shoulder, he left the room.

When Stuart arrived at the car, he had to brace himself, both hands pressed against the roof. *Son of a bitch.* He took a deep breath. *I'm not supposed to take pleasure in what I do.* He removed the cell phone from his pocket and scrolled down to Peter Weber's number. "Peter, it's me."

"You decided to get married?" Peter asked.

"That's not why I called. Remember Torres?"

"How could I forget?" *The Torres case cost him his family*, Peter thought to himself.

"They think they found his body." When Peter didn't reply, Stuart carried on a one-sided conversation. "They'll know for sure tomorrow or the next day, I'm calling because I just ran into his little sister. She's married and has a four-year-old son named Ferde."

"After her brother."

Stuart made an acknowledging sound and then repeated the conversation he just had, including the information about Roberto and Dena trying to save enough money to send their boy to college. "What I need," explained Stuart "is a dollar amount that I can put into a trust today and will earn enough compound interest to pay for little Ferde's education. Would you do that?" When Peter agreed, Stuart gave him the necessary information. "Set it up," he told his friend, "and I'll call on Monday for the particulars."

"Don't bother," said Peter. "Tomorrow, I'll be on the first plane to San Diego. And Stuart," he added, his voice taking on a gentler tone, "I remember the Torres case very well, and I want in. It sounds like a terrorist thing, and I'm part of your team. As for the financial stuff, I'll have it done today."

Stuart smiled to himself he could always count on Peter. "Okay, then you better bring Joan and your passports. There's a reporter, Chuck Andres, who's going to be on the eight thirty flight. Hook up with him, and I'll be there when you land."

Chapter Seventy-Four

Stuart spent the rest of the day in his hotel room, arranging for tomorrow's trip to Mexico. He called Peter again and briefed him on what he knew and what he suspected. He also instructed Sally to do deep background checks on Loring and Harper. Most of the information wouldn't be easy to find and, if found, would probably take three to four days. The Fourth of July celebrations were certain to slow everything down. Stuart contemplated getting agents in Phoenix to keep an eye on Kevin Kinsella but decided he had to do this one himself. At three fifty, his cell phone rang. When he heard his son's voice, he smiled.

"Dad, Marilyn went with Grandma to the neighbor's house for tea, and then they're headed to Old Town for dinner. Sarah and I are going to Sea World, and we wondered if you and Mrs. Winston wanted to join us."

"We'd love to, but I promised Jessica dinner here, at the resort. I understand they have a five-star restaurant."

"Oh, that's too bad. Well, have a nice time, we'll see you tomorrow." And he was gone.

"Too bad, indeed," muttered Stuart. They wouldn't even be missed! He arrived at the security gate of Jessica's development and was told by the guard he had missed his mother and daughter by minutes, and his son and Sarah by a half hour. Waving, he passed through and continued on to the house. There was a car in front. He pulled up and saw Susan, the Virginia Slim.

"The door's unlocked," she told him. "The congresswoman said you could go on in."

"Thanks," he replied. "We'll be at the resort for dinner, and I'll make sure she gets home okay. Take the night off."

"When I'm in the big city, you can tell me what to do," she said. "Until then, I take orders from Nathan."

Stuart shrugged and responded, "As you wish."

"Nathan said I could take off after you leave. Have a nice time." She winked at him and rolled up the window.

Stuart entered the house and heard Jessica singing upstairs.

"Jessica?" he shouted to be heard.

"I'm upstairs getting dressed!" she shouted back. "Make yourself a drink, I'll be right down."

Stuart climbed halfway up the staircase. "There's no hurry," he told her, no longer having to shout. "Our reservations are for six thirty, so you have time."

Jessica appeared at the top of the stairs wrapped in a white silk robe. "Then pour me a glass of red wine and bring it up, will you?"

Stuart walked into the den and opened a cabernet. He poured two glasses and headed up the stairs. "I'm on my way up," he announced. "Are you decent?"

"That depends what you mean by decent," she responded with a laugh.

Stuart entered her bedroom and stopped short. Jessica was in front of a full-length mirror, and he stared at her reflection. The black cocktail dress was molded to her body, ending several inches above her knees. She was wearing black stiletto heels that showed off her shapely and very appealing legs. Stuart worked his eyes up to her shoulders and saw they were nearly bare, the dress draping across the bodice. Her neck was long and graceful, adorned by a three-strand pearl necklace.

Jessica looked at him in the mirror. "See anything you like?"

"You're beautiful. No, I'm sorry I said that, because you are always beautiful. But dressed like this, you are spectacular."

She smiled and held out her hand for the wine glass. "You don't look so bad yourself," she commented, running a hand up his arm. "Maybe after dinner, if you're not too tired, we'll do a closer inspection."

Stuart felt himself turning red. He handed her the glass, and she reached for it, moving closer and brushing her lips across her mouth.

"Let me put these down," he murmured, holding up the wine glasses. "Don't bother, I have so much I want to talk about. We can go downstairs and talk."

"Can't we talk later?"

"I thought we had other things to do later," she teased, giving him her most alluring smile. "And don't be a baby! So many things happened today, I have to talk to someone."

Stuart pretended to frown and then followed her downstairs. When they reached the living room, they settled into the sofa and faced each other.

"Start talking," he told her. "But remember our reservations are for six thirty."

Jessica looked at her watch. "Good, that gives me an hour, plus ten minutes for you to bring me up to date on what havoc you've created." She blew him a kiss and smiled. "I must say you do look sexy, all dressed up." Before Stuart could respond, her voice shifted into its professional mode. "The Speaker of the House returned my call. There's a move afoot to give resident status to all Mexicans laborers who cross the border."

"Which means?"

"As it was explained to me, if they get sick they can go to a hospital and not worry about being deported. Their children can go to local schools, and they will get credit for the social security taxes taken out of their paychecks."

"Are we considering doing that?"

"The President would be in favor of some sort of modified plan, but there's a lot of opposition to its implementation, primarily because of the cost."

"Why would he be in favor?"

"We can't get enough field workers in California, Arizona, and Texas. Nevada is running almost zero unemployment and still building hotels."

"What do they want you to do?" asked Stuart.

"Probably more than I can. They think, and I let them, the Mexican government came looking for me. I didn't mention you set up the meeting as a favor."

Stuart finished his wine, looked at his watch, and announced it was almost time to leave. "We'll be a little early, but better early than late."

As they headed out the door, Jessica stopped and turned to Stuart. "How does one payback such a big favor?"

Stuart took two steps down and turned, a huge smile on his face. "Over dinner, I'll explain my problems about paying back. Afterwards you can show me how you pay back."

"Sounds like a plan, but I get the feeling my task will be a lot easier."

Over dinner they talked about everything but their children being out on a date. They discussed the party and what happened afterwards. They chatted about Stuart's mother and daughter visiting the neighbors, and Jessica brought up her meeting with her constituents and Mark Harper's boycott of those meetings. "Will his lack of support hurt your reelection plans?"

"Mark and his family usually donate in the ten to twenty thousand dollar range, which isn't enormous. However, his support had a big effect on voting day." She paused for a moment and thought further about the question. "The money is replaceable, but the support, I'm not so sure."

"The election's four months away," reminded Stuart. "If he pulls his support and finds himself arrested, that should help."

Jessica's eyes widened. "Arrested? Stuart, he may be a lot of things, but I don't think Mark's a thief." And then she stopped and stared expectantly at Stuart. "Is he?"

Stuart signaled for the check. "Let's talk in my suite. I'll have champagne and dessert sent up."

"Make it something fattening," she replied humorlessly. "I don't think I'm going to like the conversation."

Stuart tipped the man and closed the door. With champagne on ice and the aroma of chocolate soufflés wafting through his suite, they were ready to have that talk. He joined Jessica at the little table, poured champagne into the crystal flues, and took his seat.

"To us," he proposed, raising his glass. Jessica followed suit, but her expression remained borderline grim. Stuart saw no choice but to launch into the explanation.

"Fifteen years ago, I was the lead agent of a group assigned to shut down the smuggling of illegal aliens from Mexico. The pattern had gone on for decades: People were brought in, made to work in the fields for next to nothing, and that included their children. The living conditions were deplorable. The women were raped, as a regular course of events, and anyone who complained ended up back in Mexico, if we could find them. One day, a leader emerged. His name was Ferde Torres."

"I remember him. Didn't he take some money and leave the country or something?"

"That's what a lot of people thought." Stuart looked out the window at the setting sun. "I never believed the story. I met Ferde and believed he wanted better things for his people. During our few meetings, I learned to respect and trust him. He said he had proof of who was behind the smuggling but wanted assurances. He was willing to hand over that proof, but only if we agreed to prosecute and then protect the people who testified. I sent his request to Washington and was told to give him those assurances. I even wrote a letter and left it with his girlfriend, Doreen. After three days with no reply, I went looking for Doreen and was told she'd left town. Everyone I spoke to was convinced she'd left with Ferde for some South American country, carrying a bag filled with money. I searched for weeks, tracked down every lead, every sighting and mention of their names."

Stuart began pacing the room, clearly agitated.

Jessica wanted to comfort him, but she knew that he needed to tell this story.

"I was ordered home and found that my wife had a rich boyfriend and I was out. Strange," he added, as if speaking to himself. "I lost my wife and my kids and I didn't care. I was obsessed with the thought that someone sold me out. If it weren't for Michael, God knows where I'd be today."

"I guess this has something to do with Mark."

"I don't know yet, but I've learned never to ignore coincidences." He poured himself another glass of champagne and offered a refill to Jessica.

"When our kids got hassled on the street," he continued, "we all assumed that someone was after you. Since then, I've learned that the leader was a kid named Augie Meridian."

"Meridian? Isn't that the same last name as . . . ?" Her voice trailed off, and she unconsciously pushed away the soufflé.

"Brothers," he told her. "And there's more. When Marilyn was a little girl, she heard Loring and her mother having an argument. It seems that Linda yelled something like if all he wanted was information on Torres, he didn't have to marry her to get it. Marilyn was arguing with Loring a few months ago and threw this up at him." Stuart took a swig of champagne and carried his glass to the window. "Did you know that Loring and Harper are brothers-in-law?" Jessica's silence answered the question. "If that surprises you," he said, "listen to this. I just found out that Ferde's girlfriend, Doreen, married Harper and changed her name to Denise."

"My god," she gasped.

"Jessica, the dirty water runs even deeper. We have proof that Chilicote has been taking money from Harper. We also know that Chilicote was pushing Weaver into the number two spot at the FBI."

"Weaver?" she repeated, her brow furrowed. "I remember him because he called me after that trouble in New York. He's the agent who was killed in that attempted bank robbery."

"He's also the man who arrested a bunch of crooks who were later paroled by the President, at the request of Neil Chilicote."

Jessica pulled herself up. "I understand your frustration," she told him. "A lot has happened that seems to point at Mark and his brother-in-law, but we're a country of laws, Stuart. Before you act, you need solid proof of any wrongdoings." She stood and walked to the window. "You're trying to build a case that Mark paid off Torres, but you have no proof. And his wife can't be forced to testify against him."

Stuart turned, and there were tears in his eyes. "They found a body," he said. "They think its Ferde. They also found my letter tucked in a cigarette case alongside the remains. The only way he could've gotten it was from Harper's wife. We can make a case against her, and he'll take the fall."

Jessica touched Stuart's arm; her eyes cleared with comprehension. "They found him in Tecate." When he nodded, she said, "So this meeting is a smoke screen, intended to get you there without revealing anything."

Stuart nodded again. "We need to keep this very quiet until all the facts are in. No one wants old hatreds to surface. Coincidentally, the Vice President is intrigued by you and sees this as a golden opportunity to get close to an up-and-coming star in the political sky. He believes you know nothing about this, which will give him an edge."

"So why did you tell me?"

Stuart wrapped his arms around her. "Because, I care for you." Before she could respond, he lifted her off the ground and carried her into the bedroom.

Chapter Seventy-Five

"Your kids beat you home by fifteen minutes," the guard informed Jessica, pushing the button to raise the security gate.

Jessica glanced at her watch. "I know you and Kenneth haven't grown up together, but I hope it's not a case of 'like father like son.'"

Stuart smiled. "If Sarah is anything like her mother, I'm the one who should be worrying."

Jessica punched him lightly on the arm, just as their car pulled up behind Kenneth and Sarah. The two were locked in an embrace in the front seat. Stuart tapped the horn, and the children jumped, craning to see who was behind. Stuart thought of the "deer caught in the headlights" analogy and smiled.

The parents exited from one car and their children from the other. The expression on the adults' faces said they expected an explanation; their children's expressions were pure sheepishness.

"You're out a little late, aren't you?" Jessica asked.

Kenneth stepped forward. "Mrs. Winston, it's my fault. I've never been to Sea World, and I sorta lost track of time."

Jessica struggled to restrain any hint of a smile. "It's three o'clock in the morning, Kenneth. What times does Sea World close?"

Kenneth looked at Sarah, his eyes pleading.

"Mom, Kenneth had never seen the San Diego I know, and well, after we went on the rides and saw the shows, we started to sightsee."

Jessica looked at Stuart. "What do you think?"

Stuart felt for the children and sensed this was one of those moments when he could score some points with his son. "I think it's time to get to bed," he announced, his voice more casual than stern. "We've got a big day tomorrow."

"Good idea, Dad!" announced the boy. "Good night, Mrs. Winston," he added, and then started toward the house.

"Hold it," demanded Jessica. Kenneth turned around and rejoined them. "This conversation's not finished." She looked purposefully at both teenagers and then turned her gaze to Sarah. "Starting tomorrow, there's a curfew."

"Mom, I'm eighteen!" The girl's scowl made her look more like twelve. "A curfew is for kids."

Jessica glanced toward Stuart. "I'm sure Stuart is setting a curfew for Kenneth too. So if you're with him, you'll have no problems. Now let's go to bed, okay?"

With the children inside, Stuart laughed. "Good thing they didn't ask what we were doing out this late."

Jessica walked closer, placed both hands on his face, and kissed him long and hard.

Stuart still had a smile on his face as he approached the front gate of the resort and was waved down by Nathan. "You have a visitor," said the agent. His name is Michael Burnett, and he landed two hours ago with an Asian woman he called Sally. Their rooms are on the same floor as yours. Thought you might want to know."

Stuart sighed. "I owe you one. If you get anywhere near Washington, dinner's on me."

Nathan nodded and drove off, leaving Stuart to wonder what was so important that Michael and Sally would need to see him in the middle of the night.

Chapter Seventy-Six

Stuart checked with the front desk: there was no Burnett or Kim registered. He placed two twenty-dollar bills on the desk. "Anyone check in within the past three hours?"

"A Mr. Michaels and a Miss Sally, around midnight," the desk clerk replied, slipping the money into his pocket.

"Room numbers?"

"Sorry, sir," he smiled, "privileged information."

Two more twenties and the rooms were quickly revealed, along with information that coffee had just been sent up. Stuart took the stairs two at a time, not wanting the sound of the elevator door to give him away, and arrived in time to hear the phone ringing. *So much for the honor of the desk clerks of America.* He leaned against the wall, unable to be seen through the peephole. The door opened, and Michael came rushing out, looking down the hallway toward Stuart's room.

"You're getting sloppy," accused Stuart.

Michael jumped, as if hit with a cattle prod. "It takes you an awfully long time to say good night. You finished dinner over"—he looked at his watch—"six hours ago."

"I hope the coffee's still hot."

Michael grimaced and grumbled about desk clerks and big mouths. Stuart shrugged, recognizing his friend's poor attempt to discern how Stuart knew he was there. Entering the room, Stuart found Sally curled up on a chair and watching as Cary Grant walked around a sofa, Deborah Kerr stretched out with a blanket over her legs.

"This is my favorite part," said Sally, her eyes never leaving the screen. "I'd be crying now if I hadn't seen this picture at least twenty times."

Stuart poured himself some coffee. "You didn't come all this way to see a movie," he told her. "So what's happening?"

Sally clicked off the set, uncoiled from the couch, and lifted a briefcase that was resting on the floor. Opening it, she handed Michael a stack of papers. Michael fanned through them and then said, "They've identified the body in Tecate. It's Ferde Torres. Their President called ours to let him know the information will be held in strictest confidence. He also believes that it's only a matter of two or three days before word gets out. Your little trip, Stuart, has taken on major political significance. When your congresswoman friend arrived home tonight, she found a request from the White House to call at seven in the morning., Washington time." Michael looked at his watch. "That's twenty-five minutes from now."

Stuart picked up the phone and dialed the operator. "Any messages for Stuart Taylor, room 241?" After listening, he thanked the operator and hung up.

Michael appeared nonplussed by his friend's behavior. "She's taking her orders from the President of the United States, the same as you, so don't bother calling her now."

"What does the President want me to do?"

Before Michael could answer, there was a knock on the door. Sally crossed the room, peered through the peephole, and opened the door. In walked Jessica.

"What the hell is going on?" she demanded. "I have to call the President in fifteen minutes, so I called you and find out you're visiting friends!" She took a deep breath and turned toward Michael. "Good evening or morning, Mr. Burnett." Before Michael could respond, she looked directly at Sally, eyes instinctively sizing her up. She smiled, as if having decided this was neither competition nor a future threat, and extended her hand. "Jessica Winston," she said. "And you are?"

"Sally Kim," she replied, and then added, "Stuart's administrative assistant." If the congresswoman needed to be reassured, she was happy to comply. Jessica turned to Stuart and demanded, "Now tell me what's going on and what the President wants."

Michael bit his lower lip. "What you're about to hear comes under the heading of Official Secrets Act. If you're comfortable with that, we can get started."

Jessica stared at him and then at Stuart, who nodded.

"Let's do it," she said, taking the chair vacated by Sally.

"First, Sally will fill you in on what we know, and then what we're guessing." He motioned to Sally, who began to read from a document.

"Fact: Three years ago, the government of Mexico, as part of their land reform, turned over four hundred acres of land in Tecate to peasant farmers. Last week, when those farmers were starting to plant, they found the remains of a body. Nearby was a silver cigarette case containing a letter from Stuart. It was addressed to Ferde Torres, who has been missing for fifteen years. Fact: DNA results are in, and it was Torres. Fact: A few weeks ago, some kids accosted Stuart's daughter after having mentioned to her stepfather an argument she had heard years earlier, where the name of Torres was mentioned. The leader of these kids had been receiving paychecks from one of Harvey Loring's companies. The gang leader's brother works for Mark Harper's company. Harper and Loring are brother-in-laws, Harper's wife was Torres's girlfriend, and Loring's wife, who's Stuart's ex. She probably had information on the Torres case, since it was Stuart who led the lead investigation. After the case fell apart, Harper and Loring became millionaires. They're both connected to the ranch, the construction of houses, and a half dozen other projects. Now," she went on, "let me tell you what we think but can't prove. Harper and Loring had Torres killed when he got too close to organizing the people. Through the girlfriend, the two men had a pipeline into what Torres was doing. Tapping into Stuart's wife was the confirmation they needed."

"I never discussed the case with her," Stuart protested.

Sally looked at Michael, who continued the discussion.

"It wouldn't have taken much to figure out what we were doing. Knowing where you were, Stuart, where you had dinner and all, knowing those kinds of things would have put them on the right track. We also think, and maybe by Wednesday or Thursday we'll have the answers, that Chilicote has been getting rich working with these guys. He was pushing for Weaver to get moved up at the Bureau, and we know that the people Weaver arrested were on his list for Presidential clemency. All of them worked for one of the companies owned by Harper and Loring."

"What's the President going to ask me to do?" Jessica asked.

Michael shrugged and looked at his watch. "Make the call, you'll have the answer in less than five minutes."

Chapter Seventy-Seven

"This is Congresswoman Winston, the President asked I call at seven."

"What is your mother's maiden name?"

"Sarah Conway."

"Please hold, the President is expecting your call."

Jessica covered the mouthpiece. "They're putting me through."

A man's voice came on the line. "Congresswoman Winston, this is David Gastner. Please bear with us a second, the President is on another line."

"No problem, Mr. Gastner."

"Is Michael Burnett with you?" asked the chief of staff.

Jessica did her best to cover her surprise. "Yes he is, along with Ms. Kim." Jessica looked at Sally, shrugged, and added, "And Stuart Taylor."

"If your phone has a speaker, please activate it."

Jessica hit the Speaker button and asked, "Can you hear me?"

"Jessica, this is President Sherman. Sorry to make you wait." Without giving her time to reply, he rushed forward. "I understand that you're meeting with Mexico's Vice President in a few hours. I don't know how you arranged this meeting or why. However, you must convince him that we will do everything in our power to help them find the killer. Our position is simple: Ferde Torres was a Mexican national who was attempting to organize Mexican workers who crossed the border illegally. He was probably paid off by someone, we will try to find out who, and then killed by his associates for the money." The President paused, as if expecting an answer. When none came, he added, "This crime took place fifteen years ago. We'll do our best to help, but we can't promise anything."

Stuart stepped closer to the phone. "Mr. President, Stuart Taylor here. What do we do if we find out who's responsible?"

"Mr. Taylor," said the chief of staff, "maybe you weren't listening. We've offered to help. After fifteen years, it's beyond our capabilities of finding out who did it."

Stuart stared at Michael, who was shaking his head as a warning to be quiet and chose to ignore him.

"Mr. Gastner, sometime in the next seventy-two hours, I will know who was responsible for Ferde's death. One hour after that, the Mexican government will know. One hour after that, so will the media."

The silence in the room was complete, save the sound of audible breathing through the phone's speaker. "Mr. Taylor," said the President, his voice low and menacing, "you are an employee of the United States government." The President put the call on hold, leaving everyone anxious. After a long moment, he returned. "I'm issuing you an order," he announced. "You are to be on the next plane to Washington; I'll see you in my office today!"

"Mr. President!" Jessica intervened. "Stuart Taylor is the only reason the Vice President has agreed to see me. Without his presence, I'm not sure the meeting will be held."

"So be it!" stipulated the President. "Cancel the meeting. I will not be blackmailed by a civil servant who screwed up fifteen years ago."

Ignoring Jessica's warning looks, Stuart took a deep breath and announced, "Mr. President, I don't know who's advising you on this course of action, but they're a horse's ass. We know who was responsible. We just don't have the proof yet. That reporter, Chuck Andres, is on a plane this morning to accompany me to Mexico. He has the resources to get the information I need. The Mexicans are treating this as a terrorist act. After your speech on terrorism, you're going to find it tough to keep a lid on this." The phone again went silent, and it was nearly two minutes before David Gastner came back on the line. "I want to speak to Michael, and not on the speaker." When Michael picked up the phone, Gastner said, "The President has asked me to say that you're responsible for keeping a lid on this situation and making sure that his wishes are followed. He also wants you to understand any future promotion in this government hinges on your ability to contain this. Do you understand?"

Michael felt both anger and the humiliation of parental chastisement. "I understand."

"Good," responded Gastner tersely. "The President is available, put us back on the speaker."

"Michael, Jessica, I understand it's the middle of the night, so let's not argue. We all want to do what is right. I'm leaving the situation in your capable hands. Call me when you return from Mexico. And, Stuart, don't take any of this personally. This is your first venture into affairs of state, and we want you to succeed." With that, the phone went dead.

"He didn't even say good-bye to me," Sally quipped.

"That was fun." Jessica looked at Michael. "What did he say when you were off line?"

"It wasn't the President, it was the horse's ass." He smiled as he looked at Stuart. "Gastner can never remember I don't take orders from him, only the President. Everyone in this room heard the President tell me that we only want to do what's right and he was leaving it in our capable hands." He looked at all the faces for acknowledgment. "Good, so we'll do what's right and nail the sons of bitches. Any questions?"

Chapter Seventy-Eight

Stuart briefed Michael and Sally on what transpired over the past two days and left them with a plan of action to be taken while he was in Mexico. He grabbed a change of clothing and drove Jessica home, hoping to get some sleep on the sofa in her den.

Jessica unlocked the door and they entered.

"Good morning!" greeted Barbara, her voice making them jump. "This time difference is hard getting used to. Have you two been out all night?"

"It seems like it," Stuart replied. "We were actually here several hours ago but had to leave. Jessica needed to speak to the President, and it was more convenient from the hotel."

His mother smiled conspiratorially. "The President, of course, that explains it."

Stuart was about to reply but realized that she would be difficult to convince. "Mom, I've got to get some sleep." He turned to Jessica. "Set your alarm for ten, or thereabouts I'd like to get everyone moving by eleven. Peter, Joan, and Chuck Andres should be at the airport by noon."

Jessica nodded and then asked if he had rented a private plane. Stuart smiled. "Not quite, I do have some friends."

Four hours later, after hearing the sound of three teenagers tiptoe like a herd of elephants around the sofa, Stuart rose and began to orchestrate the day's events. He briefed everyone several times regarding the do's and don'ts of the day's festivities.

At eleven thirty, the van pulled into the parking area adjacent to the civilian aviation hangar at Lindbergh Field. Stuart waved at Peter, who was going over the plane with Seth Roberts. He walked over to Joan, who was in a heated conversation with Chuck Andres.

"Good morning, fellow travelers," said a jovial Stuart. "I see you've met each other."

Joan kissed him on the cheek, motioned toward the reporter, and said, "These liberals will be the death of me. I'm going to say hello to Jessica and the kids."

"How was your trip down?" Stuart asked Andres.

The reporter's expression shifted to grim. "Well, let's see, I spent the first three hours arguing with Peter and the second three arguing with her." He shook his head and then smiled. "Those were probably the best six hours I've had in months." Andres glanced at the others. "I know the congresswoman, and I'm assuming that one of those girls is her daughter. Who are the other three?"

"My son, my daughter, and my mother," Stuart responded.

A quizzical look spread across the reporter's face. "Can you explain what's going on in Mexico that involves your family?"

Before Stuart could answer, Seth Roberts and Peter approached.

"We're ready when you are," Seth said, sticking out his hand.

Stuart shook it and instructed the pilot to get everyone aboard. "Just give me a few minutes with Mr. Andres," he added.

Peter took charge and herded the group toward the steps of the plane while Seth climbed the steps, greeted the ever-present Marie, and entered the cockpit.

Stuart and Andres stood on the tarmac, the sound of the plane's engine drowning out their conversation. "It's a hastily called meeting between the Vice President and the congresswoman. They both see this as an opportunity to foster better relations between their countries."

The reporter nodded as he wrote on his pad. "Okay, that's the party line, now tell me what the hell's really going on."

Stuart studied the man's face and decided to proceed. "Fifteen years ago," he said, "I was the lead agent in an investigation. We were looking into what amounted to the enslavement of Mexican nationals who were crossing the border for work. I became friends with a Mexican who was trying to organize his people, and I was very close to closing the case when he disappeared."

The reporter nodded, his eyes practically dancing. "Ferde Torres! I was a rookie in Arizona when that story broke. Wasn't he purported to have run off with a sizable amount of money?"

"They found his body two days ago."

"Two, but how did they identify him so quickly?"

Stuart explained about the letter he had written and how it was hidden in a cigarette case found with the body.

"I wonder how they managed to keep it quiet," mused Andres, almost to himself. He stared at Stuart. "Of course, the meeting with the congresswoman. So when do you think the story will break?"

"It's yours in forty-eight hours, if you cooperate," said Stuart. "Right now, I need the meeting covered, with the families visible. We think we know who's responsible."

"*We?* But isn't this something for the FBI or the CIA?"

"The Mexicans are going to call this a terrorist plot or something like that, which will justify asking me to get involved."

Sweat was starting to appear on the reporter's upper lip. "Who, inside of our government, knows about this?"

Peter suddenly appeared on the steps of the plane. "Are you almost ready!" he shouted.

Stuart turned to Andres and smiled. "Are you coming?"

"Are you serious? This could be the biggest story of the year!"

"Good. Let's get settled, and I'll tell you about the altercation at the congresswoman's home. That's a story you can file tomorrow."

Chapter Seventy-Nine

"Next stop: Tecate," boomed Seth's voice throughout the cabin. "Marie has soft drinks for the kids and soft drinks for the adults. She also has snacks, if anyone's interested. The trip should take about an hour, so sit back and relax. Anything we can do to make your trip more enjoyable, all you have to do is ask."

"Anyone know how to play bridge?" asked Barbara.

All three teenagers raised a hand, and five minutes later, a game was underway.

Jessica and Joan cornered Marie, their conversation quickly turning to Seth. The women were planning a marriage, although no one had mentioned it to the pilot.

Peter was seated next to Stuart briefing him on the trust he had set up. "It's irrevocable," he explained. "Its only can be used for the boy's schooling or medical needs. Since there's no way to know how big the fund will become, any monies remaining after graduation will be given to him in three equal installments: age twenty-five, thirty, and the balance at thirty-five. I did a quick check, and I think a top university will run around two hundred thousand."

Stuart nodded and thanked Peter, confident in his friend's ability to handle this.

"I also put in a sell order on all your stocks," explained Peter. "I've left instructions to put all of the money into tax-free municipal bonds, except for seventy-five thousand, which we'll need to fund the trust. It should double in nine years, and then double again."

"You got the name right: Ferde Rodriguez."

"I got the name right. His parents have to sign the trust, which we'll have them do when we get back."

"You think selling all my stocks is the right thing to do?"

Peter nodded vigorously. "Especially in your new job, Stuart. You'll be dealing with lots of companies, and you don't want even a hint of impropriety.

On top of that, eight and a half million in tax-free bonds should net you over four thousand a week in spending money."

A voice from behind them suddenly said, "Pardon me?"

Peter and Stuart turned to the seat behind them and saw the reporter.

The man gave them what almost passed for an apologetic shrug. "I make a living listening in on other people's private conversations. Did I hear you say that Stuart has over eight and a half million dollars?"

"That's one of the things you can't report," said Stuart.

"How about the part about starting a trust fund for the Torres kid?"

"Another piece of privileged information."

Andres leaned his forearms on the top of Peter's seat and looked over the top of it. "Okay, then how about telling me what happened at the congresswoman's home the other night?"

"That I can do," said Stuart. "Get out your pencil and paper."

"Never take notes," he said, holding up a digital tape recorder that was no bigger than his thumb. "Just keep talking."

It took Stuart twenty minutes to fill in the reporter about what had happened.

Andres clicked off the recorder. "You know that Harper is a heavy-duty contributor to the President's reelection campaign, and that he's a regular guest at the White House. When I print this story, it's going to rock Washington."

"For tomorrow's edition only, you're going to leave out his name."

"Why?" asked Andres, his voice suddenly turning from friendly to challenging. "Sometime before July fourth, his name is going to be associated with the Torres case."

Chuck Andres's mouth opened, but no words came out.

"You're catching flies," Stuart said. Andres suddenly leaned back in his seat and declared, "Of course! It was Harper's workers that Torres started with and where he got most of his support."

Stuart nodded, without actually confirming the statement. "So can you live with what I've given you, not using names?"

A grimace appeared across the reporter's mouth. "I'm must be getting soft: I'm sitting on what could be the biggest story of the year while agreeing to wait a few days before reporting." He directed his gaze straight at Stuart. "No one else had better get wind of this."

Stuart nearly laughed. "You should be worrying about your paper not pulling your column rather than risking alienation from the White House."

Andres stared at Stuart. "You're serious!"

Stuart raised his eyebrows and said nothing.

"Then you don't know how the system works," protested Andres. "They pull my column, they pull me. The first call I make is to opposing papers or leading television stations; before you know it, I'm on the circuit making tons of money talking about the book I'm writing."

Marie's voice rang through the cabin. "Time to get back in your seats, folks." They were only thirty-five minutes into the one-hour trip.

"This is your captain," announced Seth. "The congresswoman's arrival has taken preference, and we've been given special clearance. We should be on the ground in five minutes."

True to his word, the door opened exactly five minutes later. Peter was first off the plane, acting as Jessica's security. Upon reaching the bottom step, he shook hands with Jose Vargas, took a long look at the honor guard, and then signaled for Jessica to join them.

Stuart watched from the window as Jessica was first introduced to the Vice President and then invited to walk with him past the row of the eight-soldier honor guard. As they reached the end of the line, a black limousine drove up, and the Vice President held the door for Jessica. She turned, shading her eyes from the sun, trying to see where the others were being led. When her eyes fell on Chuck Andres, she called him over and introduced him to the Vice President, who promptly asked him to join them in the first car.

Joan and Barbara accompanied the three teenagers into the second limousine. The two cars immediately left the airport, a jeep with four armed soldiers in front of them, another heavily armed jeep close behind. Local reporters were herded onto a bus, which quickly followed the procession. Stuart thanked Seth, Marie, and their copilot and descended to the tarmac. As expected, the heat was oppressive, and he felt sweat rolling down his back. Without a word, he shook Jose's hand and followed him to a waiting Lincoln Navigator.

"I have a message from Marc Frankel," Jose said, leaning his face closer to the air-conditioning vent. "That Saudi who disappeared on the flight deposited a hundred thousand into a Swiss bank account three days before he was stopped. It would help us if you could find the name of the person who gave him the money. Even better, if we knew the password for making withdrawals."

"I'll see what I can do," Stuart responded. "That is, if we ever find him. Now brief me on what's happening and how you think it should play out."

The men settled into the leather-upholstered seats, the frigid air providing welcome relief. "After Vice President Martinez spends an hour with the congresswoman in closed talks," explained Jose, "they'll meet with the media. In addition to the reporter you brought with you, there are four American and nine Mexican journalists. They'll be given fifteen minutes for questions, and then everyone will be invited to *la barbacoa*." He smiled and added, "Barbecue for you gringos. They'll have piñatas for the children to bang around, pictures will be taken, and everyone will have a good time. Oh," he added, a finger raised "Vice President Martinez would like fifteen or twenty minutes alone with you during the party. He'd like to discuss, what shall I say, our country's desires regarding the conclusion of this." And then he waved his hands and shrugged.

"I understand." Stuart shuffled his feet for a moment and then asked to see the remains of Ferde and the letter found near the body.

"Do you have any idea who did it?" Jose asked.

"I know who I gave the letter to," confided Stuart. "She's now married to Mark Harper in San Diego. I think we can build a case against her, and maybe through her, we can find out what really happened."

Jose exhaled. "Mark Harper is a name I have heard, even in Mexico. He's very rich, owns a lot of land, and has been instrumental in trying to get your government to open the borders wider for my countrymen to work. What you allude to will be very difficult."

"We may want your government to arrest the woman when she crosses the border to visit. Laws are a little different, no death penalty, for one thing, but you can hold her longer without charging her. I hear that being in a Mexican jail can be hazardous to one's health."

Jose smiled and shrugged again. "We can discuss this with Martinez later. For now, it's time to visit the gravesite."

"Four hundred acres doesn't sound like much, except when you're standing in the middle of it," Stuart said to no one in particular.

"Where is everyone?" Peter asked.

"It's Sunday and the story we've told is that the bones are over two hundred years old. The local peasants believe this is holy ground, and they avoid it when possible. Next week, when the story breaks, they'll be back."

Stuart approached the yellow strips that encircled the hole in the ground.

"What made them start farming in this place?" asked Peter, joining him at the pit.

Stuart explained how the four hundred acres had been divided among the area's hundred and fifty families, with each family getting two acres and the remaining hundred acres set aside for irrigation. He explained how a reservoir was to be dug on this spot, with fingers of water directed toward the fields soon to be covered with crops. The bones were found nearly four feet below the surface. "If it hadn't been for this reservoir," he added, "the bones never would have been uncovered."

Peter stood alongside Stuart and placed a hand on his friend's shoulder. "Don't worry," he said. "The worst thing that will happen is that you and I will make sure he's avenged."

The ride to the barbecue was made in silence, everyone lost in their own thoughts.

Chapter Eighty

"Try and blend in," Jose said, and then started laughing at his own joke. The van came to a stop at the front gate of a farm. There were two soldiers standing guard, the leader asking for identification. After inspecting each driver's license, he asked, "What is your business?"

"Our business is our business," stated Peter, his voice flat.

The soldier stared into the backseat, eyes locked with Peter's. "What is your business?" he repeated.

Stuart opened his door and stepped out. Both soldiers moved in almost imperceptibly. In fluent Spanish, he informed the soldiers that Peter was from Canada, on a secret mission to meet with the Vice President. He assured them Peter's name was on the guest list, but living so far from Mexico, he had no idea of what good manners were. Stuart asked for their names, promising to report their diligence to their commanding officer. The men smiled and then lifted the gate.

"What did you tell them?" Peter asked, the van rolling easily past the guards.

"I told them to get the hell out of the way or we'd kick their butts."

Peter nodded his approval, and Jose laughed.

They arrived just as Kenneth was swinging a broomstick and missing the piñata. Everyone was laughing, including the Vice President and Jessica. Stuart scanned the crowd and located everyone who was supposed to be present. His mother was seated next to a woman Jessica's age, who was staring at Marilyn and a boy with jet-black wavy hair. Stuart studied the boy, who was easily six feet tall and moved like an athlete.

"That's the Vice President's son," said Jose, standing at Stuart's shoulder. "He's home from Stanford on vacation. Nice looking, isn't he?"

"Very. What's his name?"

"Manuel. His friends call him Manny, a name his mother hates. That's his mother sitting next to your mother."

Kenneth took one wild swing and split open the piñata, an occasion for everyone to break into cheers. Sarah walked over, removed his blindfold, and kissed him on the lips, which started everyone cheering again. Stuart watched Jose pick up a piece of candy and walk over to the Vice President. He whispered in Martinez's ear, prompting the man to turn and look in Stuart's direction. The two men stared at one another across the courtyard and then Martinez nodded. He then turned and walked into house, followed closely by Jose who was motioning for Stuart and Peter to follow.

Once inside, Martinez held out his hand. "Mr. Taylor, welcome to Mexico."

"Mr. Vice President, I'm sorry we had to meet under these circumstances. My government and I wish to thank you for your efforts throughout this trying situation."

Martinez nodded diplomatically. "Would you or Mr. Weber like a drink?"

"Whatever you're having is fine."

"I'm having lemonade."

Stuart grinned. "Our favorite drink."

The Vice President sat behind a desk and began to speak, "I have spoken with the congresswoman. She is very intelligent and clearly understands some of the problems that exist between our countries. She explained your government's position about the Ferde Torres situation, but she could have saved the time. Your President's chief of staff already called to explain. Now, you are here. Will you also explain your country's position?"

"Mr. Vice President, there can only be one position for both countries."

"And that is?"

"To bring to justice not only the person who committed this senseless act, but also the person or persons behind him."

Martinez said nothing, looking first at Jose and then Stuart. "And how do you expect to do this without the backing of your President?"

"Sir, ever since Ferde disappeared, I've been working for an organization whose function is to bring criminals to justice. To me, justice doesn't always mean jail. You may have spoken to Gastner, but I take my orders directly from the President, and he has instructed me to do what is right. That is precisely what I will do."

The man looked pensive and then asked, "So what do you need from us?"

"Ninety-six hours, sir, and perhaps asking you to arrest someone and holding that person incommunicado."

"Who is this person?"

"I don't think you want to know, sir. But if you do, I'm prepared to tell you."

"Have you told Jose?"

Stuart nodded.

"Why ninety-six hours?"

"I know who's responsible, but I don't have the proof. However, I will in the next four days. The story will break in Washington on July sixth, which is why the White House reporter is with us."

Martinez leaned toward Stuart, his expression one of concern. "I have been told to trust you, Mr. Taylor. You have ninety-six hours to make us all happy."

"I didn't say you'd be happy," corrected Stuart. "I said I'd catch the bad guys."

"And you don't think that will make us happy?"

"I'm sure it won't. I could be wrong, but I doubt it. Your plans for housing, food, and payments into a Mexican bank for the people working across the border may be in jeopardy."

The Vice President shifted his attention to Jose, who shrugged. "Mr. Taylor, what if after further consultation with my President we decide on a different course of action?"

"You and your President can decide on anything you want, sir. The people responsible for Ferde's death are going to be punished."

"You're as stubborn as Jose said. Give me your cell phone number in case I need to contact you."

"If you need to reach me, ask Jose. I don't give out that number."

Martinez clenched both hands into fists, his body tensed, as if preparing to pounce. "Mr. Taylor, I fear I've made a deal with the devil." He stood and walked toward the door. "Shall we go back to the party? I'm sure I'll have to explain to my wife everything about you and your daughter."

"Maybe I should be asking the questions," smiled Stuart. "Your son is very good-looking, which my daughter seems to have discovered on her own."

Martinez broke into a friendly smile. "In that case, perhaps I should introduce you to my wife. Watching the two of you will be very interesting."

On the plane headed home, Marilyn sat across from her father. "Dad, did you know that, by car, Tecate's only sixty miles from San Diego?"

"Really?"

"Manny said he might drive over tomorrow."

"I think he'll find it's less than sixty miles," said Stuart. "But on those roads, it'll take him more than two hours."

"Do you think it'll be okay for him to stay with us? I mean, just so he doesn't have to take that long drive back home tomorrow night."

"You'll have to ask Jessica."

"If she says yes, is it okay with you?"

"Marilyn, why don't you clear it with her and let me get some sleep?"

"I already did, and she said it's fine with her if it's okay with you."

Stuart laughed to himself. Had it been that long ago when he'd done the same end run around his own parents? "He seems like a nice boy, and he certainly comes from a nice family. I guess it's all right."

Jessica and Barbara, seated in the row in front of Stuart, smiled at the same time.

Chapter Eighty-One

"Chuck, a minute before you go?" Stuart was jotting something on a writing pad.

"Sure, what do you need?"

He tore off the paper and handed it to the man. "Here's the name of Harper's brother-in-law and his attorney. Go back fifteen years and see what you turn up."

"Isn't easier for you to get this information?"

"Probably, but I want an independent person to do it."

"Am I allowed to know the reason?"

Stuart nodded. "Loring, Harper's brother-in-law, is married to my ex-wife. She may have been an unwitting conduit of information fifteen years ago; I don't want this investigation colored by my feelings."

"I doubt that could ever happen to you, but I'll get the information. May I ask you something?" When Stuart said nothing, he took a breath and forged ahead. "How did you ever amass over eight million dollars?"

"After this is over, I'll explain. Have a safe trip."

Stuart stood and walked over to Joan and Peter. "I have a little problem." They both looked at him. "I can't make Arizona tomorrow. How about the two of you going over and eyeballing this guy? I can give you the time he's expected to arrive. All I want is his picture and an idea of the next bank he's targeted. I'll have people waiting for him. After that, I can then close the case."

"What happens if he doesn't show?" Joan asked. "And why am I going?"

Stuart smiled rather mischievously. "For one thing, I don't trust your husband. He's liable to go off and shoot this poor guy or get himself shot. I can't afford to lose him right now." Glancing across the room in Jessica's direction, he said to Joan, "Three months ago, I would have let him get shot just so I could make a play for you. But now I want, . . . no, I need him to back me up. If the guy doesn't show, I'll have to go to plan B."

"You have the nicest way of saying things." She looked at Jessica who was about a hundred feet away. "She is very nice."

"I'm starting to feel the same way."

"I'm going to make our reservations," Peter said, picking up his overnight bag. "We'll call you from Arizona tomorrow."

Stuart leaned over and kissed Joan on the cheek. "Watch him for me," he whispered. "Don't let him do anything stupid."

Joan and Peter left the room, and Jessica appeared at his side. "Got some time for me?" she asked.

Stuart put a big smile on his face and held out his arms. Jessica walked into them and put her arms around him, her cheek pressed to his.

"It was a great day," she murmured. "Tomorrow's papers will have photos of all of us, except you, with the Vice President of Mexico. I don't think he was happy with what I had to say about the Torres situation, but unlike you, I do have to listen to the White House."

"I listen."

"And then you do exactly as you wish."

"Sometimes."

Jessica nuzzled closer. "The truth: when was the last time you did what they told you? That is, when you didn't intend to do it in the first place."

"When they told me to go meet some congresswoman."

She pushed away just far enough to see his face. "And how did that turn out?"

"I guess I should listen more often."

"Mom!" Sarah's voice bounced of the tarmac. "Stop fooling around, we have to go."

Stuart and Jessica smiled, walking hand in hand to the van.

Barbara was the last person out of the van when it reached Jessica's house. She was helped out by her son but held his hand tightly and refused to let go. Stuart looked at her questioningly.

"When you and Linda split up," she said, "I was so upset. Not so much at losing a daughter-in-law, but because of the children. Over the past fifteen years, I've wondered what you were doing and why you were doing it. I never saw a wife on the horizon, and I couldn't figure out how you were going to have an impact on your children. Over the past two months, Stuart, and especially the past two days, I've watched and listened. I am very proud of you and the way you are becoming a father." Before he could respond, she rushed ahead. "I just want to tell you this," she told him, looking directly into his eyes. "If you lose Jessica, I'm going to find a baseball bat and hit you over the head with it." Before he could answer, his mother released his hand and walked directly into the house. "What was that about?" Jessica asked. "She had tears in her eyes."

"She told me that if I didn't ask you to marry me, she'd hit me with a baseball bat."

"And what did you tell her?"

"Nothing."

"Nothing?"

"In ninety-six hours, this case should be finished. In ninety-seven hours, I will have a question to ask you. Right now, however, I need a favor." He paused and said, "I have to visit a Roberto and Ladena Rodriguez. He's an assistant manager of Harper's vineyards, and she's the woman who cleans up after your parties."

"You mean Dena?"

"Yes, and I'd like you to be with me."

"Of course, but I don't understand why do you have to visit them."

"She's Ferde Torres's little sister. They have a little boy, and I've set up a trust fund for him. I'd like you to be there when I tell them, in case there are any questions. If it's okay with you, I'm going to call them now."

"Give me thirty minutes to change," she said.

Stuart pulled out his cell phone and dialed the number of the resort. "Mr. Michaels, please."

"Mr. Michaels checked out two hours ago and asked that all messages and calls be forwarded to his secretary, Miss Sally."

"Please put me through."

The phone rang twice. "Miss Sally."

"Sally, it's me."

Before he could continue, she interrupted him with "Mr. Taylor, how nice of you to call. Mr. Michaels asked me to give you this message: Christine was correct in her assessment."

"That's it?"

"And he also heard from the White House. They were pleased with what the congresswoman said in Mexico. Oh, and he can be reached on his cell phone. His plane was scheduled to leave for Washington thirty minutes ago."

Stuart glanced at his watch.

"He was going to stop and buy some cigars, but I think it's too late. He'll try to reach you when he lands."

"How long will you be in town?"

"I'm leaving in the morning," she said. "I don't like red eyes."

"Thanks for the message. I should be taking off around nine, so maybe we'll make the same plane."

"That'll be nice, I'll look for you."

They hung up, and Stuart contemplated what he had just been told. *The last thing Christine had said was that she thought someone was looking over her shoulder. Michael just confirmed that. His plane was scheduled to leave, not him. I can reach him through the Cigar Store, if needed, and he wants to meet but not tonight. My choice of nine o'clock is acceptable, but I still don't know where we'll meet.*

"Dollar for your thoughts?"

Stuart blinked. He hadn't heard Jessica approach. "They used to be worth a penny."

"I'm an elected government official. When we're involved, everything always costs more. I'm ready to go, did you make the call?"

"I'll make it now." Stuart punched in the number he had been given.

"Hello!" said a man's voice.

"Mr. Rodriguez, good evening, this is Stuart Taylor. I don't know if your wife told you but—"

"I know who you are. Don't call us and don't talk to my wife again."

"I just wanted to—"

"I don't care what you want," he interrupted. "Don't ever call here again!" With that, the phone was slammed down.

Jessica shook her head. "You didn't need a phone for that conversation, just an open window."

Stuart leaned against the van. "I wonder what caused that."

"Give me the phone. I'll call Dena and see if I can find out."

Jessica dialed the number and waited six rings before it was answered.

"I told you not to call here!" Roberto screamed.

"Mr. Rodriguez, this is Mrs. Winston. Did I call at a bad time?"

"Mrs. Winston? I'm sorry, I thought it was someone else."

"Could I talk to your wife for a second? I have a house full of guests, and I'm going to need her tomorrow."

"I will put her on the phone. Is that Mr. Taylor still at your house?"

"No, he's staying at the resort. His mother and children are at my house, why?"

"No reason. I'll get my wife."

Jessica could hear voices in the background but couldn't make out the words. The only thing she was sure of was that there were more than two people talking.

"Mrs. Winston, good evening. How may I help you?"

"I'm going to need you tomorrow. There'll be no one home until around four, so if you could come around noon I'd appreciate it."

Jessica heard muffled voices before Dena came back on the line, "I have an appointment at three. If I can come at ten, I can finish by two."

"That'll be fine. The guard will have the key."

She hung up and looked at Stuart. "That was the best I could do." She smiled and added, "Now that we have all this time on our hands, do you have any suggestions?"

Chapter Eighty-Two

Stuart looked at the clock on the nightstand and saw that it was one thirty in the morning. He didn't move, afraid to wake Jessica, but he was sure he had heard a noise. He scanned the room. Aside from a sliver of light coming through the crack under the door, nothing seemed out of place.

Jessica stirred and was instantly awake. "Something wrong?" she asked, sitting up and looking around.

"I was just lying here thinking about you."

"I should hope so. If you were thinking of some other woman, I'd be really upset."

He turned toward her and said, "Jessica, will you marry me?" In the darkened of the room, he felt her surprise.

"Will I what!"

"Marry me."

"What happened to the four days and an hour?"

"I decided not to wait."

Jessica got out of bed and started to dress.

Stuart felt his heart racing. Had it been a mistake? He knew he was compulsive and didn't always think things through, but could he have misjudged this? "Where are you going?"

"Home," she stated.

"But—"

"Stuart, I don't think I ever really believed you'd ask me to marry you. Standing here half naked, I believe I would love to spend the rest of my life with you. But I need a reality check, and I can't get it here and now."

Stuart got out of bed and started toward her.

"Don't," she said. "You standing there naked might melt my resolve. I have a career, you have a very important job in the government, and we both have children to think about. This isn't something someone just says yes to." She put on the light and looked under the bed for her shoes.

Stuart noticed an envelope on the floor. *That's what must have awakened me.*

"If I said yes, when would we get married? And where?"

He shifted his focus back to Jessica. "Well, we could get married in Las Vegas. With our families all here . . ."

"What about our friends?" she interrupted, and then stopped. "You do have some friends."

"A few, yes. At least let me take you home," he said, more pleading in his voice than he liked. "We'll wake the kids and tell them the good news."

"No! I haven't accepted yet. Just give me the keys, and I'll drive myself home. We can talk about this when the sun is up."

"Jessica, it's almost two."

"I'm fifteen minutes from home, Stuart. Besides, this'll give me a few quiet minutes to think."

"Fine, but call me when you get home." He took the keys from his pants pocket and tossed them to her. "Don't want to get too close."

"Idiot!" she replied. Crossing the room, she kissed him and then waved good-bye.

As the door closed behind her, he picked up the envelope. He could tell it was from Sally because she always drew an X where the stamp would normally go. Before opening it, he dialed the number of the men assigned to watch Jessica. "She's driving my van home. Make sure she gets there."

Breakfast has been moved to eight at the IHOP, four miles from the resort. Pick you up at 7:45.

Stuart turned on the television, muted the sound and laid back down to await Jessica's call. At exactly two fifteen, the phone rang. He lifted the receiver and listened. "She's home, no incident."

"Thanks." Stuart hung up and waited. Less than a minute later the phone rang again. "It's me. I made it home without a problem."

"Who is this?" he asked, his voice laced with sleep.

"Who is, I'm sorry, what room is this?"

"I don't give out my room number to strange woman who call in the middle of the night. That is, unless they have important information for me."

"You know, I might just accept your proposal, just so I can aggravate you for the rest of your life."

Stuart grinned foolishly. "I'll take that as a good sign. Now, if I remember correctly, you have a breakfast meeting this morning with some of the party faithful. How about I meet you back at your house around eleven to talk to Mrs. Rodriguez?"

"I'll be there, and then I'd like to sit down and really talk about this marriage thing."

"See you at eleven." Stuart hung up and turned off the TV.

The knock on the door at seven thirty surprised him. If nothing else, Sally was prompt. Arriving early was out of character.

"Open up, I know you're in there."

Stuart recognized the voice of Martin Meridian. He sat down on the bed, trying to decide what to do. The knocking quickly increased to a banging.

"What the hell!" he said aloud and walked to the door. "Who's there?"

"It's me, Martin Meridian. Open this door."

"Why?" Stuart responded.

"Why? Because I want to talk to you."

Stuart looked through the peephole. Just as the boy was getting ready to knock again, he yanked open the door. Martin was thrown off balance and nearly fell into the room. Before that could happen, Stuart grabbed him and threw him into a chair.

"Let me up!" he shouted.

"After you tell me what's so important."

"Mr. Harper gave me a copy of today's Washington newspaper. It has a story about the fight I had with your son."

"So?"

"It also said you were involved with my brother's murder."

Stuart stopped leaning on the boy and sat down.

"Is that true?"

"I haven't read it yet, but I can tell you what happened."

"Mr. Harper said that you killed him. Did you?"

Stuart shook his head. "I found him, Martin, and two of his friends. They had been hassling my daughter and then the congresswoman, so I went to their apartment to ask them some questions. That's when I found him dead. Someone didn't want any of them answering any questions."

"Why would Augie hassle your daughter? Maybe he was just trying to pick her up."

"Maybe, but he had a strange way of doing it. He had a switchblade, and he threatened to cut off my ears."

"If Augie threatened to cut off your ears, he would've. He was real good with that knife."

"Not good enough." Stuart reached into his pocket and pulled out the knife he had taken from Augie almost two months earlier. He flipped it to Martin and said, "Here, it's yours."

The boy opened the knife, looked at Stuart, and then closed it. "Why would Mr. Harper tell me that you were responsible?"

"In a way, I was. If I hadn't been there to step in and stop whatever he intended, there wouldn't have been any reason to kill him. Why Harper sent you on a blood feud is beyond me, but I would suggest you leave San Diego and go somewhere else. People have a way of ending up dead when Harper's unhappy with them."

"I'm not afraid of him. He hates you, and you're still walking around."

"Martin, believe me, Harper doesn't know what real hate is, but he will soon. You can do what you want, but if I were you, I'd leave town." Stuart looked at his watch, *Seven forty five.*

Martin jumped at the sound of someone knocking on the door.

"Relax," said Stuart. "It's my administrative assistant."

"How do you know?"

"It's my job to know." He walked to the door. "For example, I know you work for Harper and your brother worked for Loring. Did you ever think of going to college and completing your education?"

"Stuart, you in there?" Sally called through the door.

"I'm here, hold on a second."

"I thought of it. It takes more money and time than I got."

"Here's a phone number. If you decide to further your education, maybe he can help."

Stuart opened the door for Sally. She stepped in just as Martin asked, "Who's this guy you want me to call?"

"Just a guy, but he may be able to help; it's up to you." He held the door open for Martin and Sally, and they walked out of the room. "Just remember what I said about leaving San Diego."

The three of them took the elevator to the lobby, no words passing between them. When they reached the parking lot, Martin turned to Stuart. "The only reason I believe what you said is that Augie always said that if you threaten to cut off their ears, they always pay attention. I still work for Mr. Harper, and I trust him. When I tell him what you said, I'm sure he'll change his mind."

"What was that all about?" Sally asked as they watched him walk away.

"It's a long story. Fill me in on what's happening."

Sally went through her short list, beginning with the Vice President of Mexico calling their President to say that he had enjoyed a very productive meeting with the congresswoman and an even better meeting with Stuart. "His exact words that he attributed to you were, 'He might not be happy with the results, but he had your word that we'd do the best we could.'" Sally glanced at him. "The President, according to Michael, is ecstatic."

"Okay, now for the important stuff," Stuart said as he climbed into the passenger seat of the bug-free car. He saw Sally's expression shift to serious.

"Michael found a bug in our phones. It only had a range of about a hundred yards, and our men were able to locate the listening post. They left it in place, but they took pictures and traced the background of the men inside that post. They work for a company headquartered in Washington. Michael asked Ray Bradley, at the Bureau and the name rang a bell. It seems that your dear, departed best friend, Weaver, hired this company as outside contractors. Bradley has the bill on his desk, and he's been trying to figure out what they were hired to do. Michael thinks it was to tap into our lines at the Cigar Store. Bradley thinks these bugs give us probable cause. As soon as they get the court order, which is expected early this morning, they're going to raid the place."

Sally pulled up in front of IHOP. "Michael's taken the back room for this meeting, so there's no way anyone could listen in."

There were two tables located closest to the back room. Seated at them were several men eating breakfast. Stuart recognized them and nodded slightly as he entered a larger room that had been set up with fifteen tables. Michael was seated at one of them and waved Stuart over as he continued to talk on the phone.

When he hung up, he said, "I hope you like Canadian bacon and eggs, cause that's what they're serving."

"It's fine, just bring me up to date on what's happening."

"I assume Sally told you about the bugs."

Stuart nodded.

"I just got off the phone with Ray. He said they raided the place and found out your ex's husband owns it, indirectly of course. The work order to bug your phones in San Diego was a verbal one given by Kenneth Hall, Loring's lawyer. Weaver hired them to put listening devices not on the premises, but on each of the secretary's phones. Christine was right when she said someone was looking over her shoulder."

"Do you think she found out something that caused her death?" Stuart asked, his voice a whisper.

"It was something she found out, or something they were afraid she was going to find out. Either way, they were responsible."

"By *they* we're talking about the same two people?"

"I'm counting three," said Michael. "I've added their lawyer to the list."

There was a knock on the door, and a waiter entered with three plates of steaming food and a pot of coffee. After he put them down and left, Stuart looked at Michael and then turned toward Sally. "Please take your breakfast outside," he told her. "You can pick up some coffee at one of the tables."

Sally stared at Stuart, as if preparing to object, and then picked up her plate and walked out.

As the door closed, Stuart spoke, his voice a monotone. "We don't have enough for a long-term conviction. Is my license still valid?"

Chapter Eighty-Three

"Of course your license is still good, but you can't go off half-cocked. We don't know who was responsible for her death."

"But I do know," said Stuart, "and so do you." He hesitated. "I asked Jessica to marry me. I also told her this would be over in ninety-six hours, which is the sixth of July. One way or the other, it will be."

Michael bit into a piece of toast, prompting Stuart to think, *He always puts something in his mouth when he's trying to formulate an answer.*

"I think we need a little more than three days," said Michael. "I've got the IRS checking back-tax statements. On the first pass, they found a few discrepancies that'll require a closer audit."

Stuart waved away the comment. "IRS trouble results in a penalty fee or short jail term. Neither is enough for the crime."

"You can't be judge and jury, Stuart. Give the system a chance."

Stuart's head bobbed up and down. "If anything else comes up, contact me. I'll be around at least until Thursday." With that, he got up, left the room, calling out, "Sally! I need a ride, are you ready?" When he saw his assistant was eating, he added, "Throw me the keys, I need to leave now."

Sally took one more gulp of coffee. "I'm ready, where to?"

"Drop me off at Jessica's, then get on the next flight home."

"I'm scheduled to leave with Michael."

Stuart glared at her for a moment and then took a deep breath. "Sorry, this job can be a royal pain in the butt."

Sally gave him a sardonic smile. "You should work for the people I work for."

Stuart scowled and then smiled. "This week is going to get worse before it gets better."

Peter and Joan sat in a Starbucks across the street from the car rental agency. "I don't know how this week can get any worse," he told her. "If this idiot shows up after I warned him to stay put in Maryland, I don't know what I'll do."

Joan touched his hand. "Let's see if he shows and then we can decide. Worst case, we turn it over to the FBI and they'll shoot him."

"With our luck, they'd miss."

"He's not on any flight coming into Arizona, so maybe he changed his mind."

Peter nodded, not at all convinced. "We have to do something about him. If not today, then eventually."

"My preference is it be eventually."

Three hours later, seated in the same window, Joan had reached her limit. "It's 108 degrees out there, let's go." "I guess he's not coming," agreed Peter. "Let's head back to San Diego."

Joan toyed with the coffee mug for a moment. "I've been looking at a map," she finally said. "It's one-third of the distance to Vegas. How about going there, seeing a show, and then leaving for San Diego in the morning?"

Peter looked at his wife. "You probably have the show picked out?" When she shrugged innocently, he smiled. "Fine, I'll call Stuart and tell him what we're doing."

Peter made the call and informed Stuart their perp was a no-show. "We've been here for over three hours," he explained, and then listened to the response.

"What happened?" Joan asked, hearing her husband's offer to grab a flight.

"An attempted robbery in Boulder City, Nevada. Two of the would-be robbers were shot and killed, a third is in custody." He fixed his eyes on hers. "One of the dead men had documents identifying him as Kevin Kinsella. Stuart wants us to fly there and see what we can get out of the survivor. We can fly into Vegas."

Joan looked relieved. "Well, I guess that week just got better. We're out of the woods, and I still get to see a show."

"Sally, tell Michael that Peter will be in Boulder City in the next hour or so."

Sally turned away from the keyboard and faced Stuart. "And Michael wants you to know the FBI agent reported there were four armed men waiting when the robbery started. They're the ones who shot Kinsella and his partner. He doesn't know what they were doing there. More news at eleven."

"I'm busy for the next three hours, so I'll check back when I'm finished."

Jessica was ten minutes late. From past experience, Stuart almost considered this punctual. He waited inside the guard shack, not wanting Rodriguez or his wife to see him before Jessica arrived home. When she arrived, he could see she was flustered.

"Sorry I'm late," she announced, having driven up to the shack. "Gastner called and wanted me to verify the story in today's paper. He's been getting calls from other journalists wanting information."

Stuart got into the car, and they headed to her house. "What did you tell him?"

"That I hadn't read the paper, and I'd received a dozen calls myself. I also told him I wasn't anywhere near that argument between the boys but I did hear it wasn't that big a deal, just two kids with differing opinions."

"I wonder if that'll hold him."

"Probably not, but I got the impression that wasn't the real reason he called. After I finished the story, he said the President was proceeding with the Mexican trade bill. After my great meeting with the Vice President, his evaluation, not mine, he felt my support would help the bill fly through Congress."

When Stuart asked if she supported it, she responded, "I haven't seen the final version, but I think so." Jessica peered at him, noted how his eyes seemed to turn color. He was not happy. "You don't think I should?"

"I'm paid to enforce the policies of our government, not decide if they're good or bad. But as long as you ask," he added, giving her an inquiring look.

"I asked."

"In that case, I fully support enforcing the minimum wage law. I also support the workers' right to have money deposited in a bank of their choosing for transfer back to their country. On the other hand, I don't support their right to cross the border at their whim, or that of their employer, nor do I believe that our government should house, feed, and transport them free of charge. There has to be a fee, or some kind of tax, paid by the employer. There should be a school where children under a certain age must attend, and the Mexican government should supply the teachers. There should also be some health care group that charges for medical expenses incurred only when that person is employed. Anyone not working must return home. I feel very strongly there should be no undocumented aliens running around the U.S."

"We're going to finish this conversation later," Jessica said, pulling into her driveway.

"Dena, I'm home!" she announced, stepping through the front door.

Dena called out, "In here, Mrs. Winston!"

Jessica, with Stuart on her heels, walked into the kitchen, where they found Dena standing, one finger pressed against her lips. "I should be finished in a half hour," she said, slipping a note to her employer. Jessica read the note and passed it to Stuart. It said, *I have a wire taped to me that allows Mr. Harper to hear what we say.*

Stuart saw Jessica's alarm. He pointed to himself and shook his head, indicating that he wasn't there. He then gestured for Jessica to continue talking. With a nod, Jessica asked, "Did you finish the upstairs?"

Dena nodded. "Yes, and all that's left is the kitchen and taking the clothes out of the dryer."

"The children are outside by the pool?"

"With Mr. Taylor's mother," said the young woman, concern in her eyes.

Jessica chewed on her lip for a moment and then said, "Dena. I know your husband doesn't want you to speak to Mr. Taylor, but he has something very important to tell you."

The young woman seemed startled but was comforted by Jessica's expression. "I admit to being curious, but Roberto says he's not a nice man."

Jessica turned to Stuart, who nodded and then shrugged.

Jessica sat down and gestured for the woman to follow suit. When they were comfortable, she said, "Ladena, Mr. Stuart knew your brother. When he found out you named your son after him, he was very touched. He put some money in a college fund for little Ferde. You and your husband are the caretakers of this fund, which can only be used for college or medical expenses." She paused, giving Dena a moment to absorb this information. The woman's eyes filled with tears. Before she could speak, Jessica added, "There's something you need to understand. By the time Ferde is ready for college, there will be more than a quarter of a million dollars in that fund."

Dena pressed a hand to her mouth to stifle the cry.

"You understand that's not what's in the fund now, don't you? It's what the fund will grow to over the years. Stuart needs your signatures, yours and Roberto's before he can transfer money into that special account."

Dena nodded, still overwhelmed by this unprecedented generosity.

The doorbell rang, and Stuart looked out the window and smiled. Walking to the door, he opened it and found Manuel, the son of Mexico's Vice-President. "Marilyn told me you might stop by," greeted Stuart, shaking his hand. "I hope you brought your bathing suit, everyone's out by the pool."

The young man held up a little duffel bag and laughed. "Mr. Taylor, it's so nice to see you again, and yes, I brought my suit."

Stuart led him toward the kitchen. "You can say hello to the congresswoman on your way outside," he said. "I'll be joining you in a minute."

Manuel greeted Jessica and was introduced to Dena. They spoke for a moment in Spanish, and he said something that made her blush. He smiled graciously and left to join the others by the pool.

"He said she is very beautiful," Jessica explained.

Stuart nodded and jotted something on a piece of paper. "Take off the wire?"

Jessica showed the note to Dena, whose eyes immediately widened.

"No!" she insisted.

Jessica understood the woman's fears and gestured for her to relax. "Stuart will give you the papers so that you and Roberto can look at them." Before anything else could be said, the front door was thrown open and in walked Harper, Roberto, and two other men. The latter two had their guns drawn. "Get out of my home," demanded Jessica. Turning to Harper, she said, "Mark, are you crazy?"

"I gather the weekend you spent in Mexico wasn't all fun and games," he told her. "If you think I'm going to let some small-time politician spoil everything I've got, you're crazy."

Jessica glanced toward Stuart, who gave an almost indiscernible shake of his head. We're outgunned, said that gesture. Let's not give them cause for alarm. "There are security guards outside," she went on. "So why don't you just leave?" Her eyes were beginning to show signs of panic.

Harper pointed toward the door. "There's a van outside, so get in without doing something stupid that'll bring harm to any of those children basking outside."

"You're making a very big mistake," said Stuart, uttering his first words since these men arrived.

"It wouldn't bother me one bit to leave you dead, right where you're standing, but my brother-in-law feels something for your brats." With that, he said, "Start walking."

At that moment, Manuel walked into the kitchen. "Mrs. Winston," he asked, "where can I change?" When he saw the scene, he began to back out of the room.

Harper blocked his route. "One less Mex in this world won't bother anyone. You're coming with us."

In a flash, Stuart dropped to the floor, pulled his gun out of its shoulder holster, and shouted, "Get down!"

With all eyes on Stuart, no one noticed Manuel pulling out a switchblade. In one swift motion, he pushed its button and threw it, hitting Harper directly in the throat.

Harper let out a garbled cry and reached up, grabbing the knife's handle. His goons stared openmouthed as their boss lay in a pool of blood and Stuart's gun was pointed at them. Defeated, they dropped their weapons.

"And one less gringo won't bother anyone either," said Manuel, hands on hips.

Stuart dialed the front gate. "Nathan, get some men up here in a hurry. I've got one dead and two who will be, if you don't show up fast." The next call was to Michael. "We've got a problem," he explained. "Manuel, the Vice President's boy, just killed Harper in self-defense. I've called our local people, but we'd better decide how this is going to play out . . . and we need to do it quickly." Hanging up, he turned to Jessica. "As soon as help arrives, I'm getting my family out of here." To Manny, he said, "You'll have to wait until we can figure out a believable story."

The young man nodded, eyes fixed on Harper. "Who is this man?"

"I think it's better if, for now, you don't know. Let me do my job, and I'll make sure you're filled in later." He instructed Jessica to have the children dressed and ready to move. "All hell's going to break loose any minute." When she didn't move, he shook her arm.

The blood which had formed a dark red pool on the floor, transfixed Jessica. She started to say something but turned and walked out the back door.

Nathan and two other agents entered the front door just as the back door closed. He motioned for one of them to take into custody the men standing there with their hands in the air. "What about those two?" he asked Stuart, nodding toward Ladena and Roberto.

"Keep them separated from these goons. Michael Burnett will be here in a couple of minutes, and we'll let him sort it out." Stuart walked into the dining room and dialed a number on his cell phone.

"Vargas."

"Jose, it's Taylor. We have a little problem. The Vice President's son just stuck a knife in Mark Harper's throat."

"Manny? Shit. Is Harper dead?"

"Yes, and I'm making up the story now. Tell the Vice President his son Manuel will be a hero on this afternoon's news."

"You're sure?"

I'm working on the story now. I have to go, I'll keep you advised." He ended the call just as Michael Burnett arrived.

Chapter Eighty-Four

"Just tell me you didn't plan this," said Michael, surveying the room.

"I wish I could say I did, but I'm not that smart."

Michael glanced out the back windows and saw Jessica. "What's she doing out there?"

"I told her to keep the kids away; she'll be back in a second."

Michael studied Stuart's face, his mouth grim. "Okay, give me the *Readers Digest* version of what happened, and then tell me what you think our next step should be."

"I put together a trust fund for Ferde's nephew," he explained. "The boy's mother and father have to sign the documents."

"Why?" Michael asked.

"Because I set them up as the executors."

Michael nodded and Stuart continued, "When I wanted to meet with them, they refused, so Jessica called her and asked her to come by and clean the house. She came, but she was wearing a wire." Stuart showed Michael the note. "During the conversation, Vice President Martinez's son, Manuel, entered." He saw Michael's attempt to get all the players straight and nearly smiled. "My daughter invited him here. Okay, so then he spoke to us briefly and went outside to join the others. Seconds later, the front door flew open, and Harper and these two idiots barged in."

When Michael asked how they managed to get past the guard, Stuart explained about the private entrance from Harper's property.

"Anyway," continued Stuart, "he was threatening to take Jessica and me somewhere when Manuel returned. That's when Harper informed the boy he was coming with us. I have to tell you, Michael, he was very menacing. I yelled for everyone to get down and pulled my gun. Before I could use it, Manuel's switchblade was in Harper's neck." He took a deep breath and said, "Now you know everything."

Michael pulled on his lip. "Everything except what we should do next."

"I've given it a little thought and—"

"I'd like to be included in your thought process," said Jessica, entering from the back door.

"You're always in my thoughts," said Stuart. He smiled at her, but she didn't smile back. "Have you taken care of the kids?"

"They're getting dressed. The FBI's assigned someone to watch them until we decide what to do. I've got to tell you up front," she added, looking first at Stuart and then at Michael. "I think we should call the police and let them handle it."

"The police have been called," Michael assured her. "But we have other fish to fry." He paused, looked at Jessica, and said, "You're going to have to trust us on this."

"Trust you, why? You live in a world of such great deceit that no one should ever trust you."

"I said *us*," corrected Michael.

Jessica was about to reply when Stuart entered the conversation.

"Jessica doesn't have to trust us," he insisted. "I consider her part of the decision making process. Whatever we decide, she'll have a say." He waited for a response from Michael and saw the man nod. "Now, we need to have someone pick up Harper's wife. We say that we think she's part of a conspiracy to—" He searched for the phrase.

"Kill the Vice President of Mexico's son?" suggested Jessica.

Michael nodded again. "That might work."

"It fits everything that's happened," said Stuart. "When the story breaks about finding Ferde's body, we can say it coincided with our visit to Mexico. The listening devices in our hotel rooms alerted Harper, causing him to attempt to get rid of us."

"What about your Loring?"

"We have him picked up on the same charge. Like Harper's wife, he'll probably make bail faster than we can fill out the paperwork, but at least it'll allow us to dig into his affairs."

"What are you going to tell the President?" Jessica asked.

"I'll be on a plane in an hour and will set up a face-to-face with him, Jake Levitt, and Ray Bradley the minute I land." Michael looked pointedly at Jessica. "I suggest you call the Speaker in six hours and inform him of what's happening."

Jessica's brow furrowed deeply. "Why Brightwell?"

"Because as soon as I leave the White House, I'm going to have Chilicote arrested. We have more than enough on him to start the process."

Stuart thought about this for a moment. "The only thing wrong with the plan," he said, "is being able to keep it quiet for six hours. But I guess that's my job," he added.

Police cars were starting to arrive as they entered the living room. Michael held up his badge and said, "FBI. This is a case involving the Vice President of Mexico, and we are claiming jurisdiction. We appreciate your taking possession of those two men and securing the scene from spectators. We also appreciate a total blackout for six hours until I can meet with the President of the United States. My assistant," he added, pointing at Stuart, "will be in charge until you hear differently." With that, Michael left the room.

Jessica stepped forward and faced the officers. "I'm Congresswoman Winston," she informed them. "This is my home and under the National Security Act, I'm asking you to comply with the FBI's requests. I will, of course, talk to your commanding officer, but I request you use landline phones when communicating with him. This will avoid having someone listening in on the police band." She turned to Stuart and winked.

He watched Jessica exit the room and thought, *She's starting to like this. I'd better be careful.*

Chapter Eighty-Five

Jessica looked at her watch. "Mr. Speaker, I know you're in the middle of dinner, but this is important."

"Mrs. Winston, Jessica, I'm having dinner with a friend of yours, Neil Chilicote, who sends his regards. Now tell me what's so important that you needed to bother me tonight."

His voice had a condescending tone that Jessica decided to ignore. "Mr. Speaker Gary, if Representative Chilicote is anywhere within listening distance, I suggest you take this call in another room."

"Don't be silly! I have no secrets from other members of our party, especially when it comes to what is going on in government."

You pompous ass, she thought. "As we speak, Jake Levitt, Michael Burnett, and the attorney general are meeting with the President. They are advising him that the son of the Vice President of Mexico's son killed Mark Harper this afternoon. They are also telling him warrants are being issued for the arrest of Harper's wife, his brother-in-law, Harvey Loring, and Representative Chilicote. I thought you'd appreciate being advised of these arrests prior to their happening." When the man screamed into the phone, Jessica nearly laughed. "Now will you take this call in another room?" The ensuing silence was so long Jessica thought she had been disconnected.

"Jessica," he finally replied, "hold on for a second, will you? I think I have a copy of that memo inside. Let me change phones."

The Speaker of the House was back on the line seconds later. "Okay now, explain to me what's happening."

"Mark Harper was killed when he attempted to kill Manuel Martinez, the son of the Mexican Vice President."

"Why in God's name would he do that?"

"They identified the body of Ferde Torres this weekend. He's the man who—"

"I know who he is, go on."

"They found proof Harper and his wife were involved in his death. Further checking has led them to believe Harvey Loring, Harper's brother-in-law, was also involved."

"What about Neil. Why are they after him?"

"I understand that's a different matter, yet somehow tied together. They have proof that he's been taking large sums of money. They think it's from Ken Hall, the lawyer for Harper and Loring."

"They *think*?"

"They know, but I don't, and they're playing it close to the vest until they tell the President. Chuck Andres is going to break the Torres story tomorrow and will be given the rest of the story the day after."

"What time were they meeting with the President?"

"The meeting should have started twenty minutes ago."

Before he could answer, there was a break on their line and a voice announced, "This line must be cleared for a call from the President of the United States."

Jessica turned to Stuart. "They interrupted us; a call from the President."

"I guess the President is going to brief the Speaker of the House."

Just then the phone connected to the front gate rang, and Stuart pushed the Respond button.

"We have a Peter and Joan Weber asking for admittance."

"Send them in," Stuart responded.

"I thought they were spending the night in Vegas," said Jessica, heading toward the front door.

Peter and Joan entered, faces grim. Stuart immediately recognized their exhaustion. "How was the trip?" he asked.

"Is anyone else here?" Peter asked, looking around.

"Just us, is there a problem?"

"Yeah, there is. The four men who killed the bank robber were Cigar Store people."

"So?" asked Stuart.

Simultaneously, Jessica asked, "What's a Cigar Store person?"

Stuart turned to her. "This is one of those items that comes under the secrecy act. If you're uncomfortable, we'll go outside and finish the conversation."

She sat down next to Joan, "In for a penny, in for a pound. Go ahead, I understand the rules."

Stuart nodded, took a swig from a bottle of water, and asked Peter, "How do you know?"

"How do I know? I know because I worked there for twelve years." Having tossed out this reprimand, he ticked off the reasons he knew. "They said they were private investigators working for someone they weren't allowed to discuss;

they had credentials and everything the police wanted, and all of their ID numbers were consecutive."

Stuart finished the bottle of water. "During the investigation of the robberies, I had Sally check all flights into airports serving the surrounding areas. She went back a few days prior to, and then a few days after, each robbery. The name Kinsella showed up, and we traced him to his workplace. Your names also showed up. Not as frequently as his, but enough to require some double-checking. When I found out you used the company he worked for to do your gardening, I decided to prove to myself that you weren't involved. I was having Kinsella followed. Once I knew where he was flying to and returning from, it was easy to get some of our guys to follow him to the bank." Stuart stared at the frightened faces of his two friends. "I'm not sure we got all of the crooks, but the report will read we did. The video we had from other banks shows this man was always ready to shoot. This time, he tried and he died, along with his companion. I proved to myself and anyone else that would be interested you two weren't involved, and that the case is officially closed." He looked unswervingly at both of them. "Am I right?"

Peter looked at Joan, who smiled, rose from the sofa, and kissed Stuart on the cheek. "Right," she whispered, and then returned to the sofa.

Peter took his wife's hand. "You've always been a black-and-white guy, Stuart. There never was an area of gray. Are you sure you don't want to pursue this further?"

"I don't think we have to. Besides," he added with a warm smile, "I can't have the best man at my wedding chasing all over the country, looking for someone who may not exist."

Joan turned to Jessica. "You're getting married?"

"I haven't said yes yet. Stuart still has three days of cleaning up this case; I told him he'll get his answer then."

Peter draped an arm over Stuart's shoulder. "Let's get it done, okay? I always wanted to be a best man."

Chapter Eighty-Six

Stuart, Peter, and four FBI agents, two of them women, went to Mark Harper's home. Jessica remained behind to deal with the Vice President of Mexico, who was flying to San Diego from Mexico City.

"Good evening, Doreen," Stuart said as a butler escorted them into a huge living room.

She looked at him for a few seconds before answering, "No one has called me that for years. Mark said you were in town, but I doubted if you'd remember me." She stood with both hands on her hips. "If you're looking for my husband, I think he said he was going to the congresswoman's home. You should check there."

"Doreen, your husband is dead," Stuart spoke the words as if he were asking for the evening paper.

The woman lost her balance and gripped the back of a chair for support. "What happened?" she whispered, eyes filling with tears.

"Before I go into that, I suggest you call your lawyer. These people are here to take you into custody as an accessory to murder."

"Accessory to murder? You're crazy, I never helped kill anyone."

One of the female agents stepped forward and read Denise her rights.

"Am I allowed to ask a question?"

"As long as you understand what I have told you, you've been Mirandized."

Denise Harper nodded at the agent and asked Stuart, "Who was murdered?"

"Ferde Torres," Stuart replied. "Fifteen years ago."

This time she did collapse, and two of the agents rushed to her side to support her. One of them ordered someone to get a glass of water.

"I don't believe that Ferde's dead," she told them, sipping the water. "They swore he went off to Argentina."

"Who swore that?" Peter asked.

"Mark and Ken Hall, Mark's lawyer."

"When did they tell you that?" Stuart asked quietly.

"The day after I brought them your letter. You remember the letter you wrote to Ferde promising him some things? I met you at the airport and asked you for Ferde's letter. I told you it was too dangerous for Ferde to be seen with you, and you gave it to me to deliver."

"How did you know I even had it?"

"My brother was seeing your wife. He called and told me to bring the letter to Mark. When I took it to Mark's house, he wasn't there, but his lawyer was. Ken told me he'd take care of it. The next day, Mark asked me to marry him. He told me Ken arranged for Ferde to leave the country and that it was for the best. That's when he said he had always loved me." Tears started down her face.

"And you accepted his proposal," said Peter, scorn in his voice.

"Not right away. I went to Ferde's, but he was already gone. I was left high and dry, I figured I could do worse. On top of that, my brother had become a partner with Mark in some businesses. It looked like a good deal, and it has been. He's treated me nicely even though I know he's fooled around a little." She looked around the room. "What makes you think I was an accessory?"

"We'll give that information to your lawyer," said Stuart.

"When can I call him?"

One of the FBI agents said, "As soon as you're booked, you'll be able to make a call."

Mrs. Harper looked at Stuart. "Is all of this necessary? Kenneth will have me released in minutes."

"Doreen—"

"My name is Denise!" she shouted before Stuart could finish.

"Denise. At this moment, Kenneth Hall is also being arrested as an accessory to murder. I would suggest you give some thought to whom you can call for help."

Her mouth opened, and the tears began anew. "This isn't fair, I didn't do anything."

"Neither did Ferde, except to try and help. I think you'll find being an accessory carries up to twenty years in jail." Peter regarded her sternly when he added, "When you find a lawyer, tell him you want to cut a deal and have him get in touch with me. I'll explain what I want, what I need, and what I'm prepared to give up for it."

"It's my brother you're after," she insisted, looking at Stuart. "He got your wife, and now you're trying to get even. I'm going to call him."

Stuart smiled and turned to Peter. "I told you she'd do that."

A look of doubt crossed Denise's face. "You don't think I should?"

"I think you should do anything you want." Stuart motioned for the agents to take her away.

"Mr. Vice President, welcome to my home. I'm sorry it has to be under these circumstances." Jessica extended her hand to the Vice President of Mexico.

"Where is my son?" he replied, acknowledging her greeting with a nod.

"He's by the pool with a security agent. Before you see him, I'd like to explain. Would you like something to drink?"

"As long as you assure me that he is fine."

"You have my assurances," she replied. "Earlier today—" She was interrupted by the phone and held up a hand. "I'm expecting a call from the President." She picked up the phone and was surprised to hear Michael's voice asking for Stuart. "He's not here," she told him, explaining that he was at Mark Harper's home.

"Congresswoman, please tell him that all is proceeding as planned. They've arrested Loring and are looking for Hall. Chillicothe has been detained, and I expect that to go as planned too. The President is taking a very big interest in this, so tell Stuart to proceed with caution."

"Vice President Martinez is here; may I tell him what's happening?"

"I'd rather Stuart did that, but you might as well."

"You don't think I'm capable?"

"Oh, I believe you're more than capable, but some things are best handled by Stuart."

"I understand, I think," she told him and promised to pass along the message.

"That's okay, I'll find him," said Michael and rang off.

Jessica went back to the Vice President and asked him to sit with her for a moment. "Pardon me for not being formal, but I'd like this to be one parent to another."

Chapter Eighty-Seven

The Vice President and the congresswoman spoke in hushed conversation for nearly twenty-five minutes. When they were finished, the Vice President said, "I certainly hope your President realizes what a gem he has in you. I thank you for your kind words, and now I'd like to see my son." He took Jessica's hand, raised it, and brushed it with his lips. Despite her worldliness, Jessica blushed.

Stuart and Peter returned five minutes later and found Jessica staring out the window at her guest, the Vice President and his son.

Stuart joined her and watched the father explaining something to his attentive son. "Michael reached me on my cell phone," said Stuart. "How did it go with him?" Stuart nodded toward the Vice President

"I explained what happened and told him what I thought he should do. I also told him you wanted to speak to him about how we—" Jessica stopped and took a deep breath. "How the government would like to handle the news."

"And what did he say?"

"He didn't say anything. I think he's receptive, but he didn't commit. He was anxious to speak to his son." She checked her watch. "They've been talking for ten minutes."

Stuart leaned closer to the window for a better view of the area. "I didn't see Jose Vargas."

Jessica gestured toward the pool. "He's there, somewhere."

Stuart walked over to the sliding glass doors and surveyed the yard. Jose was seated on a chaise on the far side of the expansive lawn. Wearing a gray suit with a white shirt and dark tie, he looked more like a businessman. The wraparound sunglasses added a stylish touch to his appearance. Stuart noticed how he didn't move. It was almost as if he were sleeping, except there was also a tension about him, a complete awareness that emanated from his body. Stuart slid open the door, and Jose immediately uncoiled snakelike from the chair and crossed to Stuart's side. "Amigo how goes the battle?" Jose asked.

"This one's almost finished," Stuart replied. "As soon as Rodriguez and I can come to terms on the wording and agree on what comes next, I'm ready to move on."

"Where will the next one be fought?"

"Come on inside, where we can discuss this in private." Stuart led Jose into the kitchen.

"I have to use the library for ten or fifteen minutes," he told Jessica. "If the Vice President comes in, please tell him where we are."

Stuart and Jose disappeared into the library, followed by Peter.

When the men were settled, Stuart asked, "Do you remember Mark Frankel's request?"

Jose frowned before speaking, "Something about finding the diplomat who disappeared off the plane in Boston?"

Stuart nodded. "And asking where he got his money. Our people just learned that the money came from a lawyer who helped this guy, his name is Asif something, open a Swiss account. The code name on the account is Oak Tree, and the lawyer's name is Kenneth Hall."

Jose leaned forward. "The same Kenneth Hall?"

"It'll take a couple of hours to verify, but we think so. He's also told them that there are at least eight more people like him heading into the U.S. from Canada and Mexico. Their plan is to blow up bridges, tunnels, and buildings. Asif supposedly wasn't one of the people doing the bombing; he was only delivering."

"This man has an awful lot of information. Has he volunteered the names and travel arrangements of these people?"

"Some of the names but no travel arrangements."

"And what is it you're going to need from us?"

"That's why I want to talk to the Vice President. We need a closer look at people crossing our borders. We anticipate the lines getting longer, and that it'll take perhaps an extra hour to get across."

"He is not going to be happy."

"None of us are, Jose. Hopefully, we'll have more information going forward."

There was a knock on the door, and the Vice President entered with Jessica.

"I understand there are some things you wish to discuss before we leave," said Martinez.

Stuart motioned for him to take a seat. "How's Manny?"

"My son is strong; he will get over his feelings of despair."

Stuart looked into the eyes of the man. He knew, and he was certain that this father also knew that Manuel felt no remorse. Both his movements and his words told Stuart that the boy would not lose any sleep over Harper's death.

Stuart smiled at the man. "That's good," he said, his voice suddenly shifting to a more serious tone. "The news will carry the story of Manuel being a hero and saving the life of my daughter." Stuart waited to see if the Vice President had any comments.

"He saved the life of your daughter, and not the congresswoman's or her daughter?" questioned the Vice President.

"The congresswoman and her daughter are protected by the Secret Service," Stuart explained. "For him to have saved them, there would have been a serious breakdown in security. No," he added, "Harper was after me because of my friendship with Ferde. He simply found my daughter first. Luckily, your son was there to save her life."

"What do you want from me in exchange for this favor?"

Stuart worked to suppress the smile. The rule was *quid pro quo* no matter what country. "As I just told Jose, we have information that terrorists are headed into the United States through Mexico. We'd like an increased presence at all borders. At the moment, we don't have their names or any knowledge of how they're traveling. What we do know is they're going to try and create a little havoc, but that's what we'd like. We're going to do the same thing on our side. Hopefully, we'll find them and stop them."

Martinez listened, but his expression was skeptical. "There's something else, am I correct?"

"Extradition," said Stuart. "Your country has a rule that unless we guarantee no death penalty, you won't hand them over. I want these people handed over with no paperwork and no guarantees."

The man smiled sardonically. "Neither the President nor our Congress will agree to that." When no one responded, he looked imploring at Jessica, who dropped her gaze to the floor and ignored his unspoken cry for help. He turned to Jose, whose eyes were hidden behind the sunglasses and whose face seemed frozen in time. "What you ask is impossible."

Stuart looked around the room. "It's also impossible to make your son a hero in the eyes of the world, but I will succeed in doing just that."

"When are you starting this inspection?"

"July sixth."

"I will talk to my President. I cannot promise, but I'll see what I can do."

"I understand," Stuart said and held out his hand.

This time, the man shook it. "Can my son leave the country?"

"Of course he can," said Stuart, "he's a hero! He may be asked to come back, if there's an inquiry, but there's no reason for him to stay." After a moment, he remembered Manuel had driven to Jessica's home. "What about his car?"

"My son tells me he has invited your son and daughter, and the congresswoman's daughter, to be our guests. Perhaps they can drive it home for him."

Stuart looked at Jessica, who shrugged and said, "I'm sure they'll have a better time at your home than he had here."

The Vice President smiled. "I doubt it. My son enjoys the limelight." His face quickly became somber. "Not that he enjoyed what he had to do, only the notoriety that goes with it."

Stuart looked at Jessica and knew just what she was thinking. The man's son was a major accident waiting to happen. He turned to the Vice President and said, "Before I let my children go, I need to talk with them. Their stepfather is being arrested as we speak, and the kids should have the option of going home to be with their mother."

A scowl crossed the face of the Vice President, which was rapidly replaced with a smile. "Of course you must. I can always have Jose drive it home, or he can drive the congresswoman's daughter, and your children can join them later on."

"I'm sorry, sir," Jose said. "I'm leaving from here and going directly to Canada, but I will have one of my men take care of it."

"Good, so that's settled," said Martinez. "Thank you for your hospitality. I'm sure we'll all meet again soon." He left the room and called out, "Manuel, we are leaving."

When everyone was gone, Jessica put her arm across Stuart's shoulder. "Thank you for interceding. I didn't know what to say to him."

"It's funny, but I could feel your concern. He's a nice boy, but he's headed for trouble, and his father's no help."

Jessica's eyes suddenly took on a sparkle. "Stuart, let's go back to Washington. I've had my name in the paper quite enough for any campaign, and I'm not comfortable here."

"Lady, you must have witches blood running through your veins, because I was just going to suggest the same thing."

She smiled and bared her teeth. "My great-great-grandparents may have come from Salem."

Stuart gave her a hug. "I'll request a plane for seven thirty in the morning, then call my mom and have her take the kids and check into a hotel by the airport."

"And where are you planning on spending the night?" Jessica asked.

"Use some of your witch's magic and guess," he replied.

After he arranged for the plane, he phoned his mother. "Mom, everything's fine," he told her. "Just be at the terminal with the kids in the morning." He hung up and shook his head at his mother's habit of worrying about everything.

The cell phone rang while he was watching CNN relate the specifics of Chillicothe's pending arrest.

"Stuart!" a voice announced.

"Yes" he responded, hearing the frustration in Michael's voice.

"The President wants to see you tomorrow. And before you tell me to go fly a kite, think it over. You've had three or four pretty good days, even if they weren't all vacation."

"I can be on a plane by seven thirty tomorrow morning. That'll get me into DC around three thirty. How about telling him I'll be there at five? He can have dinner ready."

"I'll tell him five but no dinner," responded Michael. After a short hesitation, he asked, "How come you're not giving me a hard time?"

"Because I think it's time I met with our leader and straightened out a few things. This seems like as good a time as any."

"Stuart, this is his meeting and his agenda, so don't be a smart-ass."

"It's his meeting and his agenda, and his every wish is my command."

Stuart closed the cell phone and started laughing.

"What's so funny?" Jessica asked.

Before Stuart could answer, Jessica's phone rang. Picking it up, he announced, "Winston Residence."

"The President of the United States wishes to speak to Congresswoman Winston."

Stuart handed over the phone. "Tell him it's a small problem, but you can make it."

With a puzzled look, she took the phone and listened to the President request her attendance at a meeting the next day at five. She looked at Stuart and mouthed, "What do they call a male witch?"

Chapter Eighty-Eight

Stuart and Jessica arrived at the airport at six thirty to find his mother and the three children waiting in the terminal. Peter and Joan walked in through another door at almost the same time.

Sarah walked up to her mother. "Mom, you look terrible. Didn't you get any sleep?"

Jessica ran her fingers through her hair. "I did, but the President called, and I'm expected at a meeting at five. It's a little stressful."

"Is something wrong?"

Stuart's mother and daughter turned and looked at Sarah. It was the first time they had heard concern in her voice.

Jessica reached over and tucked a strand of Sarah's hair behind her ear. "I'm getting the impression he's not happy with what happened between Mr. Harper and Manuel."

"You couldn't have done anything about it," insisted Sarah, glancing at Stuart. "Could she?"

"Absolutely not," he reassured the girl. "Your mother is in politics. The first rule is to be ready to blame someone else, especially if things don't work out. The President is the consummate politician, which means he might be willing to share the glory, but he wants someone standing in front of him if something goes wrong." Jessica smiled at Stuart's defense of her. "What Stuart hasn't mentioned," she explained to her daughter, "is the President also wants him back in Washington. I'm an elected official, and Stuart works for the President. If our leader is looking for a scapegoat, Stuart's an easy target."

Sarah chewed that over for a moment. "If he weren't here with us, would we still be in trouble with the President?"

Jessica nearly laughed. "First off, we are not in trouble with the President. If he has a problem, it's with me, not us. Secondly," she said, taking Stuart's

334

hand, "if he weren't here, I wouldn't be happy." She paused a moment and then added, "I might as well tell you now: Stuart asked me to marry him."

"No shit?" Kenneth blurted out. "What did you say?" Marilyn chimed in.

Jessica's eyes never left Sarah's. "I haven't answered him yet."

"Why?" Sarah whispered.

"I wanted to talk to you first."

"Time to get on board, folks," Seth Roberts yelled from the top of the plane's steps.

No one moved. Everyone's eyes were riveted on Jessica, who was gazing at Sarah.

"Mom, you've got to say yes. He's everything I could ever hope for in a stepfather, or you in a husband, unless,"

"Unless what?" Jessica asked

"That's okay, we can discuss it later."

"No, let's hear it now. I don't want to leave anything unsaid."

Sarah looked at the ground and kicked at a crack in the floor. She turned and walked through the door, heading out to the plane. Halfway there, she looked over her shoulder and called back, "Unless he's terrible in bed." With that, she took off running toward the plane.

Marilyn and Kenneth started laughing, and Jessica's face turned red. Barbara, Stuart's mother, walked up to her son and asked, "So is there a problem?" When he scowled, she began to laugh as well.

Chapter Eighty-Nine

After the bombshell Jessica dropped on the family, the flight back was uneventful. Sarah and Marilyn couldn't stop planning the wedding, while Barbara, Joan, and Peter debated honeymoon destinations.

Between drinks and sandwiches, Marie confided to Jessica that Seth had also proposed, certain that his new job with Stuart's organization would mean a raise in pay. They were keeping it quiet because he didn't want to aggravate his present boss but readily admitted that working with Stuart was going to be one of the great experiences of his life.

Four hours and twenty minutes after takeoff, Seth entered the main cabin with the news they were being given preferential treatment and would be on the ground almost forty-five minutes early. "There will be three limos waiting," he told Stuart. "One will take Barbara and Sarah home, the second will be for Marilyn and Kenneth. I don't know where they're headed, but the message is it's somewhere safe. You and the congresswoman will be taken directly to the White House for your meeting with the President."

Jessica nodded, but Stuart stared out the window and didn't reply.

"Something wrong?" Seth asked.

"Probably not," he replied. "May I use your phone up front?"

"They've cut off communications. The only thing we're getting are messages from the tower."

"Did they give a reason?"

"They said they're trying to keep reporters away. I have a suggestion, which didn't come from me, and I'll have to report you to the FAA if I catch you doing it." When Stuart said nothing, he explained, "I have a cell phone pilots carry in case of a high jacking. It's in my jacket that's hanging in the galley." With that, he walked toward the cockpit. "Time to fly the plane. We land in"—he looked at his wristwatch—"less than twenty minutes."

As soon as Seth closed the door to the cockpit, Stuart rose and walked to the galley. Taking the phone out of the pocket, he dialed Michael.

"Burnett!"

"Is there any reason I can't drive to the White House?" Stuart said without identifying himself.

"Why are you asking?"

"The pilot just got a message that there are three limos waiting for us. One for my kids, another for Jessica's daughter and my mom, and another for Jessica and me."

"I'm at the White House awaiting your arrival, but no one told me about you being picked up and delivered."

Stuart nodded, the wheels in his brain spinning faster. "We might be a little late. I want to make sure the kids get home okay."

"Stuart, give me ten minutes to find out what's going on."

"Don't have ten minutes," he said. "But don't worry, I've got everything under control."

"Every time you say that, someone dies. Be careful, help is on the way as we speak."

Stuart put the phone back in Seth's pocket and motioned for Peter and Joan to follow him to the back. He explained about the three cars. "The problem is that no one knows who sent them. Whoever did doesn't know that you two are on the plane. Michael is sending help, but it won't get here in time."

"What do you want us to do?" Peter asked.

"I want you two to leave first, pretending that you're Jessica and me. When you reach the bottom step, turn and tell the kids that you'll meet them for dinner around seven thirty. The car they ask you to get into will probably have their best men. I don't think they'll worry about the kids. I'll take care of the last two limos; you just make sure that the one you're in doesn't go too far. It shouldn't take more than three or four minutes."

"Stuart, don't tell me that you're going to take on people from two cars?" Peter's voice had shifted from helpful friend to concerned agent.

"I'll get Seth to help. Don't worry about me, just worry about yourself, and don't forget I'd like them alive."

"Spoil sport," Peter laughed as he headed back to his seat.

"Stuart!" resounded Seth's voice. "They've told us to taxi to the far end of the field where the limos will be waiting."

Stuart picked the microphone off the wall. "Don't, Seth. Pull up to the terminal and tell them that the congresswoman has instructed you to do this."

The plane took a slight turn and headed to one of the empty spaces in front of the terminal. Looking out the window, Stuart watched the three vehicles speed up to catch the plane.

"They're upset," said Seth.

When the plane came to a full stop, Marie opened the door and pushed the button to release the stairs. Peter and Joan were halfway to the ground when the first car arrived. As two men jumped out Peter turned and yelled, "We're on our way to the White House, we'll meet you for dinner around seven." and proceeded to the waiting limo. The driver climbed in behind the wheel, but the man-riding shotgun, remained on the tarmac, looking confused.

Peter called out to the driver, "We don't want to keep the President waiting." He helped Joan into the car and jumped in beside her.

The second man opened the back door and asked, "Are you Congresswoman Winston?" He found himself looking down the barrel of a gun.

"Get into the car or you'll never take another breath," Joan said, holding the weapon steadily with both hands. "What's going on?" asked the driver, lowering the window that separated the front seat from the rear. Turning, he too faced a gun.

"As soon as your friend steps into the car," instructed Peter, "start driving and I'll tell you where to go."

"You people are crazy."

The man facing Joan stepped into the car, leaving behind a pool of liquid. There was a large stain evident on his tan pants.

Joan shook her head. "Good help is so hard to find nowadays."

"Drive toward the exit, but don't leave the grounds," said Peter. He glanced out the back window, trying to see the chaos he knew had been planned.

The three teenagers descended the steps and jumped into one car. When the men tried to separate them, Barbara got into the second car with Seth.

"We have no instructions to take you anywhere," said a driver to Stuart, who was wearing Seth's jacket.

"You can drop us on the way to the congresswoman's home."

"We're not going that way, now get out."

Marie, at the top of the stairs yelled down, "Kenneth, Kenneth, please tell your dad that our equipment is working again. The seventh cavalry is less than one minute away from helping the Marlboro Man."

"What the hell is she talking about?" asked one of the four men.

"I think what she meant to say was—" Before Stuart could finish, everyone heard the door locks engage. The three kids, Jessica, and Stuart's mother were locked inside the car with the four men locked out. "There are security guards entering the tarmac," he continued. "If any of you wants to live to see tomorrow, you'll raise your hands and face the plane."

The four men simultaneously turned toward the doorway, which was closed, and then toward the cars, which were locked. That's when they saw Stuart, who stood half hidden and with a gun pointed at them. "Don't shoot!" one of them yelled. "It wasn't supposed to happen this way."

"How was it supposed to happen?" Stuart asked. The car in which Peter and Joan were riding made a wide swing and returned. Behind them were two other cars. The men inside appeared defeated. Stuart recognized the men in those cars from the Cigar Store.

Chapter Ninety

"You're going to get us killed driving like this." Jessica held onto the strap above the door. She was seated on the passenger side in the limo Stuart had taken for their trip to the White House.

"We don't want to be late, do we?" He took the corner on what felt like two wheels.

"I'd rather be late than not get there at all."

Stuart glanced up at the rearview mirror. "You would have thought at this speed, at least one cop would have stopped us!" He made a sharp left and then a sharp right, braking to a loud stop less than three feet from the side gate of the White House. Gary Williams, the security guard in charge, smiled when he recognized the limo's occupants.

"Welcome back, Mr. Taylor." Bending so he could look in through the window, he added, "And good afternoon, Congresswoman. The man stepped back and gave the limo the once-over. "If you'll pull this oversized town car into one of the parking places, I'll have someone come down and escort you."

Stuart waited for Jessica to get out before pulling the car into an empty spot. He stepped out and threw the keys to one of the guards. "I'd have this checked out," he suggested. "I borrowed it from some guys who are now under arrest."

The body language of all the guards changed quickly from easygoing, nice guys to alert and well-trained soldiers.

"Who's holding them and where?" Williams asked.

"We left them at the airport." Stuart jotted down a number and handed it to him. "Call and find out what's happening. Just tell your men to be careful."

A golf cart came down the path with two guards in the front seat. "Mr. Taylor, Congresswoman Winston, please come with us, we'll take you to the President."

Before the golf cart could pull away, Williams approached Stuart. "Mr. Taylor, I know it must be an oversight, but you forgot to give me your weapon."

Stuart smiled. "You're right, it was an oversight."

They stared at each other as Stuart handed over his gun.

"You don't have any other weapons on you, do you, sir?"

Stuart shook his head.

"Congresswoman Winston?" The guard said her name without taking his eyes off Stuart.

"Of course I don't."

"You can go," he said, motioning to the cart's driver.

Less than two minutes later, Stuart and Jessica were entering the White House through the lower level. Neither had said a word during the short ride, nor would they speak as the elevator carried them up to the third floor. When the door opened, the customary marine guard standing at attention greeted them. Several feet away, Michael Burnett was slouched against the wall.

Michael shook his head slowly, back and forth, and then motioned for them to follow. When they were out of earshot of the guard, he stopped. "I've heard from our men. The limos were sent by Gastner, with instructions to make sure you two arrived here, but late. The other limos were to take the occupants to a place in Virginia for debriefing."

"Debriefing of what?" Jessica asked, her ire rising quickly.

"Not quite sure. When you two arrived on time, Gastner announced he had to see someone and then left. The President is waiting in his office. I can tell you he's not happy."

"Not happy over what?" Stuart asked.

"Not happy that you put the arm on the Mexican Vice President, not happy with arrests being made all over town, not happy about losing Chillicothe's vote, and not happy at all with Gastner for leaving before your talk."

"Can I tell him what I'm not happy about?"

"No, you can't."

Before either of them could say anything else, the President's secretary stepped into the hall and motioned for them to follow her. The President was seated at his desk, the sleeves of his light blue shirt rolled almost to his elbows. He was taking a sip from a can of Diet Coke and was clearly avoiding eye contact with his visitors. Putting down the can, he stood and addressed them individually. "Jessica, it's always a pleasure. Mr. Taylor, it's always, how shall I say it, an experience." Without his chief of staff present, he was struggling to get to the reason for this meeting.

Michael stepped forward. "Mr. President, you wanted to talk to Stuart about Mexico."

"Yes, yes, I did." The President put on his glasses and studied some papers on his desk. "Your instructions were not to promise the Mexican government that we would find out who murdered Torres."

"I'm sorry, Mr. President, but your instructions to me were that I should, and I quote, 'do what is right.'"

The President was about to object, but Stuart didn't give him a chance.

"I did not go after Mark Harper even though I believed we had enough evidence. He surmised, after talking to someone here in Washington, I had proof and was coming after him. He broke into Congresswoman Winston's home with two other men and threatened bodily harm. Unfortunately for him, the Vice President's son was in the house visiting. When he was threatened, he threw a knife and killed Harper. The rest of the story you probably know."

"Assume I know nothing and tell me what you think I should know."

"Fifteen years ago, I was in charge of an investigation into beatings, rapes, and other violent acts against the people of Mexico here in the United States. I was authorized to guarantee the safety of Ferde Torres as well as guarantee our government would prosecute the people responsible. The condition was that he had to turn over to us the proof he said he had."

The President nodded but said nothing.

"As you may know, Torres disappeared. Everyone believed that he absconded with a large amount of money and left the country."

"And why do you think otherwise?" asked the President.

"When they found his body in a field near Tecate, they also found my letter of authorization. It was stuffed inside an empty cigarette case. The hitch is that I never gave it to him. Instead, I handed it to his girlfriend, who met me at the airport and told me he was afraid to be seen with me."

"How did she know you had a letter?"

Stuart pressed his lips together before speaking. "Mark Harper's future brother-in-law, Harvey Loring, was escorting my wife around town. At the same time, he was getting information from her about our investigation."

"Future brother-in-law?"

"I know it's confusing, but Doreen Harper, the girl Torres was seeing when he was killed, is Harvey Loring's sister."

"You're positive?"

Stuart looked at the President for a few seconds. "I'm positive."

Michael leaned forward in his chair. "Mr. President, this drama gets even worse. Ten years ago, Stuart's daughter overheard her mother and stepfather arguing about Ferde Torres. Around six weeks ago, the girl threw that name in Loring's face. From that moment on, the congresswoman was unknowingly involved. Her daughter Sarah and Stuart's daughter are friends. Some street kids started hassling them, and we assumed they were after the congresswoman. We tracked them through IRS and plane reservations only to find out they worked for Harper or Loring. In fact, they traveled with their lawyer, Hall, for whom we've also issued a warrant." Michael paused for a moment to give the President time to absorb this information. When no questions were forthcoming, he continued,

"For fifteen years, Harper, Loring, and their attorney, Hall, have built their farm and orchard into a multimillion-dollar empire. We have proof of their giving money to Chilicote. Proof, I might add, which would have remained quiet at the request of your chief of staff. When Chuck Andres, the reporter, got wind of the story, we had to move quickly."

The leader of the free world was visibly upset. "What's the next step?"

"Your chief of staff needs to be questioned, and I strongly suggest you start distancing yourself from him."

The President looked at Stuart. "Are you crazy?"

"Mr. President, I can't prove it right now, but three limousines pulled up at the airport today. After some persuasion, I learned that their instructions were to make sure that Jessica and I arrived late for this meeting. They were also told to take our kids to a place where we wouldn't be able to reach them. On top of that, there have been leaks to Loring, Harper, and Hall that could only have come from this office."

The President fell back into his chair. "I've known David for years; I can't believe that he's involved."

"Mr. President," Michael interjected, "we're not saying he's involved, just that we need to ask him some questions."

The President's face brightened. "Of course, I understand. Is there anything else?" Stuart looked incredulously at the President. They were being dismissed! "Mr. President, what about the Home Guard? We have information that terrorists are headed into the country, and we still don't have a definitive program from you."

"You're right," he replied. "As soon as this mess with David is cleaned up, we'll address that as our next order of business. Thank you all for coming and briefing me on the situation. Please keep me up to date." The President rose and walked out, leaving the three of them standing there shaking their heads in disbelief.

Chapter Ninety-One

"I've heard stories about this happening, but I never believed them," Jessica was talking as she followed Stuart and Michael as they walked down the elegant corridor.

As they approached the elevator, the marine pushed a button, and the doors opened. Michael entered first and turned to face Stuart and Jessica, his index finger pressed against his lips.

Jessica looked at him, nodded her head, and started speaking, "The President looks like he's working very hard. I certainly hope he takes care of himself. What we don't need is a sick President."

Stuart smiled and nodded. "He's got one of the toughest jobs in the world."

The same two guards that drove them to the meeting were waiting when the door opened.

"Your office sent a new car to take home," said one of them. "The limo you arrived in had a tracking device under the rear seat. They've asked you to call the Cigar Store for verification."

Gary Williams wasn't at the guard shack when they arrived, but one of the other guards handed Stuart the keys to a new Lincoln Continental.

"Where's the man who delivered the car?" Stuart asked.

"He left," the guard replied.

Stuart saw what a bad liar the man was: he didn't hold eye contact and drummed his fingers on his leg to hide his nervousness.

"Where's Williams?"

"I think he went to dinner."

"And left only two of you at the gate?"

Neither man answered, and Stuart dialed the Cigar Store.

"This is the Cigar Store, who's calling?"

"This is the Marlboro Man." Stuart intentionally used the wrong sign-in.

"What can we do for you?"

"Can you verify a car left for me at the White House?"

"A new Lincoln Continental."

"Color?"

"Dark Blue. Anything else?"

"I need a voice check, three, six, twenty."

The voice hesitated a second and then responded, "Twenty-nine."

"Thanks," Stuart said and broke the connection. Turning to the guards, he asked for his weapon.

Michael, who had been talking to Jessica, called over to Stuart, "Why don't you two come with me and we'll get something to eat. I know a great restaurant nearby."

"Sounds fine to me, I'll have someone come and pick up the car. You can drop me at my house, and I'll drive Jessica home."

One of the guards stepped forward. "You can't leave that car here."

"Someone will be by in fifteen minutes. I'll call the office and have it picked up. It'll save me two hours tomorrow."

The guards stood and watched Michael drive Stuart and Jessica out of the gate. "That Taylor is one big pain in the butt," said one. "We better call it in."

Stuart instructed Michael to drive to the Cigar Store. "I'm calling Jake and telling him to get some men over to the White House."

"We're on our way," said Michael. "I heard you break procedure and ask for a voice check. What did they answer?"

"Twenty-nine," replied Stuart, closing his eyes briefly.

"Idiots. Did they think it would be that simple?" Michael pressed down on the pedal and the car shot forward.

Stuart flipped open his cell phone and hit a code. "Jake, Stuart Taylor here. I have reason to believe our branch has been infiltrated and the guards at the White House have been replaced."

"Shit!" said Jake.

"I'm with Michael," Stuart told him. "We're headed to the Cigar Store now. Whoever took over didn't understand our security procedures." When the call ended, he told Michael that Jake was calling Ray Bradley and having all key members of Congress covered. "He'll take a dozen men over to the White House and check out the guards," he added, trying to push away an encroaching sensation of doom.

Stuart's next call was to Peter. "Where are you?" he asked before Peter could say a word. "Good, turn the car around and head to Curious George's, but don't go inside. Wait for Michael and me to arrive. We should be there about five minutes after you. I think the Cigar Store has been compromised."

He next turned his attention to Jessica. "I'm going to have Michael let you off at the shopping center six blocks from here. Call a taxi and go home. I'll call you later and let you know what happened."

"Michael, don't you dare stop this car," she commanded. To Stuart, she said, "It was only two days ago that you proposed." Her voice became suddenly louder. "If you were serious, you'd understand that, for better or for worse, I'm going with you." She sat back into the shadows. "If you're not serious, tell Michael to stop and let me out."

"That's not fair," he protested. "I was serious, I still am, but I can't let you get involved in something that might be dangerous."

"It sounds fair to me," Michael added. "Want me to stop?"

Stuart hesitated before speaking. Finally he said, "No, don't stop. But, Jessica, I need you to listen to me when we get there."

Peter and Joan arrived just as Stuart and Michael were getting out of the car.

"Joan!" Stuart called out. "You and Jessica make sure no one leaves through the alley."

Joan waved Jessica into her car and maneuvered it so that the alley alongside Curious George's was blocked.

Stuart, Michael, and Peter entered the closed restaurant.

"We're closed," said a man standing at the bar.

"We're not hungry," said Michael. "We just wanted a drink."

"I said, we're closed," the man repeated himself.

Michael pulled his revolver, motioning for the man to step out from behind the bar.

The man's eyes widened. "You're making a big mistake. I'm not a bartender, and this isn't really a restaurant."

"I know that," Michael replied. "How many more of you are in back?"

"In back? There's no one in back."

Stuart walked up to the man until they were practically touching. "You're good. On your tombstone they'll write, 'He lied in the line of duty.'"

"You don't understand," the man sputtered. "We're FBI agents, and we're following the orders of the President."

"So are we," said Peter, showing a mouthful of teeth. "And we have the guns."

Michael stepped forward. "My name is Michael Burnett, you may have heard of me." When the man's eyes became even wider, he demanded, "How many in back, and who's in charge?" The agent took a deep breath and exhaled slowly. "We were sent here by the President's chief of staff. He told us that this was a rogue operation that had to be shut down. There are four men inside; we're waiting for help from the Bureau."

Michael knocked on the door leading to the back room. "Listen carefully," he said through the door. "This is Michael Burnett. In about two minutes you're getting a phone call from Jake Levitt, the head of the FBI. He's going to tell you that your orders have been rescinded and to come out. Don't do anything foolish until you get his call."

"How will we know it's really Levitt?" came a muffled voice through the door.

"Anyone in there know Mr. Levitt, or his deputy, Ray Bradley?"

After a slight delay, the voice answered they did not. "Who do you know?" Michael asked.

"We know the chief of staff. And, of course, the President."

"Unbelievable," muttered Stuart. "Why not let me go in there and just shoot them?"

"Is there a problem?" Jessica asked as she entered the room.

"I thought I told you to wait outside," barked Stuart.

"We were relieved of our duties," Joan answered from behind Jessica. She entered with two men Stuart knew from prior encounters.

"Mr. Burnett," asked the first man, "what would you like us to do?"

"The men behind this door are holding three of our own. They work for the FBI and were told that we're a rogue unit. Unfortunately, they don't know Levitt or Bradley, except by sight, and they won't open the door."

Jessica walked over to the door. "This is Congresswoman Winston. Do any of you know me?"

"I've seen you on television," came back a voice.

"Then stop being moronic. Open the door and take a look. If it's not me." She struggled to contain her exasperation. "If it's not me, shoot me!"

The door opened, and one of the men stepped out. He glanced around the room, looking at each person present. "Congresswoman Winston, it's an honor to meet you." He shuffled his feet. "The chief of staff, David Gastner, gave us our instructions. We were told to shut this place down without hurting anyone. Our problem is that we have no way of contacting him for further instructions, and no one at the White House is taking our calls."

Jessica turned toward Stuart and shrugged.

Chapter Ninety-Two

"How many people know that we moved here?" Stuart asked Michael.

"Enough so that it's impossible to keep a secret."

Peter looked over the roomful of agents and grimaced. "What are we going to do with these guys? I've checked their IDs, and they work for the Bureau."

Before Michael could answer, his cell phone rang. "Burnett," he barked into the phone.

"Michael, it's Ray. These men at the White House all work for the Bureau. It's a story of the right hand not knowing what the left hand is doing. The chief of staff has a group of men assigned to him that work outside the normal process. They used to report to Weaver. Since his death, they've been reporting to Pettit. We haven't located Pettit yet, but it looks like Gastner gave the order, and these men just followed instructions. Security around the President was not compromised. I repeat: it was not compromised."

"We've got five more here. They're waiting for help from the main office, which doesn't seem to be acknowledging their calls."

"Jake had me contact Karen and put her in charge. He's going to put Pettit on leave, until we can straighten out this mess, once we find him. Have your men bring those five men over to headquarters, and we'll let Karen deal with it."

"What about Gastner?" Michael questioned.

"We've got an all-points out for him, and we've doubled the guards around key people from Congress, the Supreme Court, and the inner circle, just in case. Jake is in with the President now. The moment I hear anything, I'll give you a call."

Michael explained what was going on to Stuart and Jessica and told them to go home.

Twenty minutes later, as they crossed the bridge six miles from Jessica's home, Stuart said, "You've been very quiet. Is something bothering you?"

"It's just these past few days," she said. "There's been the meeting with Martinez, Mark's death, the arrest of a fellow representative, and now this business with the President's chief of staff and the President himself. It's all been terribly disconcerting."

Stuart reached over and took her hand. "Harper was a bad guy, Jess, and I'm sure we haven't heard the end of that story. As far as Chilicote, we're lucky that it's only one bad apple in an environment that could contaminate a bushel. What's disconcerting to me is Gastner. I'm not a fan of his, and I don't like all the things he's done, but I've always respected him. This is out of character."

"It's the President's fault: he's a spineless jellyfish." Her voice came out hard.

"Perhaps, but it's a tough job. Let's see what happens when Jake's finished with their meeting."

Jessica nodded. "I don't know much about Pettit or Karen Ortega. Are they good people?"

"I only met Jerry Pettit once. After Weaver was shot, he was at the funeral. Karen Ortega is a pretty good agent. I met her a few times when cases that we were working on crossed paths. She's fought her way up in the Service and will probably be a good number two or number three person."

"Is she attractive?"

"Average. Dark hair, about five foot four, weighs about one twenty. And if I remember correctly, she has three kids and a husband she adores. Why did you ask?"

"Just wondered about a woman in that position."

"She's a very good administrator, but I don't think she's tough enough to run the whole show."

"I think I'd like to meet her. Can you arrange it?"

Stuart stopped at the gate to Jessica's development. The guard looked inside the car and activated the gate. As Stuart drove through, his cell phone rang.

"Taylor!" he said, the gate closing behind him.

"We've found Gastner," said Sally. "He's dead." Her voice was matter-of-fact, as if mentioning an everyday occurrence.

"Where?" he asked. "How?" He felt Jessica's eyes on him and signaled for her to wait.

"They found him in his car, an apparent suicide, less than a block away from the Jefferson Memorial. Michael said to tell you that we'd check it out."

"Anything else?"

"Just that he still hasn't heard from Jake, and he'll call you as soon as he does."

Stuart repeated the news to Jessica, explaining the implications that went with it. "He was either involved above his head, or someone killed him to keep his mouth shut. By making it look like suicide, they, if there is a they have given us the opportunity to wash it away. We can say he was despondent over some illness or something not going his way."

"Why would someone say that?" Jessica was obviously very puzzled.

"If we don't, the conspiracy theorists have a field day. Once we release the suicide story, it will be almost impossible to prove that he was part of something bigger."

They sat in Jessica's driveway. Stuart turned off the headlights, knowing there was at least one more question on Jessica's lips.

"They can't let someone get away with this," she started. "But then, they have to protect the President and the government." She sat quietly for a few seconds and turned toward Stuart. "That's part of your job, isn't it? Aside from catching them, it's to make sure that criminals receive the full penalty for their actions."

Stuart winced. She was repeating his exact words he had told her when they were attacked at the Jefferson Memorial.

Jessica opened the door. "Thanks for bringing me home. Call me when you hear what's going on."

"You're upset?"

She stopped, her feet dangling out of the car. "I have no reason to be upset with you. You've been up-front with me since we met. It's just that," She fell silent and exhaled loudly. "Call me tomorrow." Pushing herself out of the car, she slammed the door and headed up the walkway.

Stuart watched until she entered the house. With her safely inside, he called Michael.

"I just had a thought. When Meridian tried to kill me, it was at the Jefferson Memorial. Maybe someone is sending us a message?"

"Which is?"

"We missed you before, but we didn't miss this time."

Michael didn't answer for a few seconds. "Why the Jefferson?"

"If I knew that, I'd have your job. I'm headed home; you can reach me there."

"I thought you'd be with the congresswoman."

"Her name is Jessica, and we're both tired." He closed the phone and immediately felt guilty about giving out a lame excuse.

Four days after the newspapers ran the story of Chief of Staff Gastner committing suicide, Stuart was seated at his desk at home, reading the newspapers and watching CNN. The note found near Gastner's body told of cancer spreading through him. He explained to his family that he had refused chemotherapy treatments because of the sensitivity of his position. The President had made a speech at the gravesite, praising his longtime friend and announcing how much he would be missed. No one took notice that there was no mention in the media of the doctors he was seeing. Stuart had spoken to Michael and was told both the doctors and the clinic he visited in secret would be named in a press release due to come out in two days. Denise Harper was released on bail and had disappeared along with Harvey Loring and their lawyer Kenneth Hall. Chilicote was screaming to anyone who would listen he had been framed because he refused to vote for certain legislation. He declined to tell reporters which legislation that was, insisting he wanted his day in court.

Stuart had called Jessica every day but had gotten nothing but voice mail and a promise from one of her staff that she would call back. August was quickly approaching, and the heat and humidity did nothing to calm his mood.

He adjusted the sound of the TV just as Jessica's picture flashed across the screen. She was with the Speaker of the House, Gary Brightwell. Even though everyone knew he was happily married, Stuart felt something unidentifiable turn in his stomach.

"Mr. Speaker"—the reporter held a microphone in front of Brightwell— "what do you think of Congressman Chilicote saying he was framed?"

"The congressman, like every American, is entitled to his day in court."

"Are the rumors of impeachment proceedings true?"

"Again, let me make sure that everyone understands: Until such time as the congressman is convicted of a crime, talk of any proceedings is inappropriate."

The reporter shoved the microphone in Jessica's direction. "Congresswoman Winston, the story circulating around Washington is that you were involved in the decision to have Congressman Chilicote served with papers. Is that true?"

"As I understand it, the decision was made by the attorney general."

Stuart turned off the volume. She was sounding too much like a politician. He shuffled through memos he had written to himself, and on top of the pile was the one he considered most urgent. He had received a call from Jose Vargas about the lines at the borders extending the wait for hours. The Mexican government was doing their part, but the Americans were not. If Mexico didn't get help soon, they'd have to revert to the old way. In the three days since the order had gone into effect, six hundred and forty people trying to enter the United States illegally were caught and sent back across the border. Eight of those six hundred and forty carried passports from Middle East countries. There were three from Palestine, three from Saudi Arabia, and two from Iraq. Five of the eight claimed diplomatic immunity and were released. They were still holding the other three men, but time was running out.

There had also been a call from Ray Bradley, wanting to talk about the house in Florida, which the people killed in Israel had been renting. His agents found receipts for flying lessons and were checking this out. Ray had decided to tell the airlines to step up their passenger screening. Unless an order came from the White House, he didn't hold out much hope of getting this done. It was just too expensive, and the airlines were already strapped.

The call that left him most perplexed was from Marc Frankel, in Israel. They had captured some Saudis and, after extensive interrogation, were given the name of bin Laden, the head of a network operating out of Afghanistan. Stuart had been in Afghanistan right after the Russians pulled out and couldn't figure out why anyone would choose to stay there.

He looked back at the television and wondered what Jessica would think about extensive interrogation.

The ringing phone snapped him back to reality. He knew very well what Jessica would think.

Caller ID told him it was his mother, and he considered letting his voice mail pick up the call. On the other hand, she would only keep calling.

"Hi, Mom, everything all right?"

"I missed the notice," she replied.

"Which notice?" *This was not starting off well.*

"The one where you and Jessica announced to the world that you were getting married."

Chapter Ninety-Three

Sally looked at her watch. The pilot just announced they were at forty thousand feet, and everyone could expect a turbulent-free ride into London. One of the great things about traveling with Stuart was that she got to sit in first class. She was glad Brett Daniels, the head of British Intelligence, had called to request a meeting on Monday at noon. Stuart had been storming through the office for more than two weeks, and she was hoping this trip would snap him out of whatever was bothering him. She believed it had something to do with the congresswoman, but the one time she broached the subject he had almost torn off her head.

"Would you care for some champagne or a glass of wine?"

Stuart glanced up and recognized the woman. It was the lovely Marie, Seth's intended. "Strange meeting you in a place like this," he remarked. "Is Seth at the controls?"

"You two know each other?" Sally asked, a quizzical look on her face.

"We're old friends," Stuart replied.

"I have a few magazines you might like to read," Marie said, bending closer. "There's a story in one of them about an agent who was traveling without his weapon. It seems that on the same plane, there were also two men who worked for a lawyer who was very angry at this agent for purchasing seats at the last minute."

Stuart took the magazines and surreptitiously slid the knife and gun between the seat cushions.

"Where?" he whispered, a smile on his face.

"Thirty-four A and B," she murmured, readjusting the little pillow. "Another agent's three rows back."

"Miss! Can I have a bottle of water?" asked the passenger seated behind them.

Marie smiled and made her way to the galley.

"You don't think they're crazy enough to try something here, do you?" Sally whispered. Stuart shook his head. "No, but it's interesting. Only a few people knew we were traveling today. They must have been following us."

"Unless someone on the other end told them we were coming."

Marie passed them and handed the passenger a glass of water. On her way back, she bent low and informed Stuart there was a call for him in the galley. Stuart waited until Marie was several yards ahead. He then got up, stretched, and headed for the toilets. As soon as he entered the galley area, Marie closed the curtain separating the preparation area from the passengers.

"Kenneth Hall is out of the country," said Michael. "Using global satellites, the Cigar Store was able to trace him to Ireland. Three days ago, after they met with Hall in Dublin, we followed the two men to Heathrow and then JFK. We didn't know what they were doing, or what they were supposed to do, until they suddenly purchased two tickets on your afternoon flight. We had their bags searched. They're not carrying, so they'll undoubtedly have access to weapons when they land. I've personally spoken to Daniels, and he's promised to have men standing by when you land. Find out what they're after, Stuart. And if possible, find out what Hall is up to."

"Anything going on in Washington I should know about?" When Michael responded in the negative, Stuart wasn't convinced. "Michael, let me reword that question: Is there something going on that I shouldn't know about?"

There was a slight hesitation and then, "You'll probably hear about this sooner or later anyway. It's about your girlfriend."

Stuart felt his stomach contract. "Has something happened to Jessica?"

"Nothing serious, relax. The party is going to fly a trial balloon hinting that she might make a run for the Senate."

"Good for her," said Stuart, drawing a circle on the partition with his finger. "Anything else?"

"It looks like we're making some headway on a replacement for Gastner."

"Anyone I know?"

"Probably. Meanwhile, let me know what's happening on the other side of the pond."

After he disconnected, Stuart stood in the galley and stared through the porthole. Marie broke into his thoughts with "Anything special for dinner?"

"How about starting with some scotch?" He turned away from the endless cloud formations and smiled. Stuart returned to his seat and turned toward Sally. "Do you know how old I am?"

She had heard this tone before and knew him well enough to recognize that something had made him unhappy. "If I remember correctly," she said diplomatically, "thirty-six. Or is it seven?"

Stuart stared at her. "Forty-four."

"So? My husband's forty-three, and you look much younger.

"Forty-four," he repeated philosophically. "And I have nothing to show for it."

Sally shot him an apologetic look. "Nothing except two kids, a great house, a good job, and the knowledge that you're doing an important job for your country."

"I don't have a wife."

"I thought you and the congresswoman were getting close?"

"I'm afraid that *were* is the operative word. I just heard she's considering a run for the Senate."

"Good for her. Our government needs more women in high places."

Marie arrived with two trays of food, which she placed before them. Stuart thanked her, adding, "Don't wake me for dessert; I have to get some sleep."

True to his word, he finished his meal and slept until the pilot announced they would be landing in fifteen minutes. Like a cat, Stuart opened his eyes, stood and stretched, all in one fluid motion. He entered the galley and asked the other flight attendant for some coffee. Cupping it in his hands, he edged over to Marie. "What are our friends doing?" he asked in a low voice.

"I'm not sure," she murmured, "but they seem very nervous."

He nodded, giving the information a moment to settle in. "Someone will probably meet the plane and pass guns to them. Let's make sure they're watched so that we keep an eye on whoever meets them, and they're all followed."

"I'll be the first one off the plane," Marie told him. "I'll be sure to pass that on. And remember that it's against the law for anyone to carry weapons in the UK."

Stuart offered a wry smile. "I'll try to remember that, thanks. When you deplane, can you take Sally with you?"

Two hours later, the BBC and CNN broke the news of two IRA hit men being killed at Heathrow Airport, purportedly in an attempted assassination of an American CIA agent. The American's name was not released for security reasons.

"Mr. President, I have Congresswoman Winston on the phone for Mr. Burnett. She says it's important."

The President looked at Michael Burnett. "You can take it at the phone on your left."

Michael picked up the phone. "How can I help you, Congresswoman?"

"Just tell me the son of a bitch is okay."

Chapter Ninety-Four

"The Home Secretary is very upset. He's threatening an investigation into how you managed to carry firearms aboard a plane, and a British one at that." Brett Daniels was speaking to Stuart and Marc Frankel at their scheduled meeting in a nondescript building overlooking the Thames. The three were seated around a magnificent mahogany conference table large enough for twenty people. Sally, along with two other men who had been introduced by first names only, sat on straight-backed chairs against the wall, all of them holding briefcases containing documents that might be needed during the meeting.

Stuart looked directly at Daniels. "Tell your Home Secretary the investigation indicated I took possession of those weapons after I landed. That should keep him happy."

"For future reference," interjected Marc, "I suggest you travel as an Air Marshall, which would justify the weapon."

"Won't work, Mark. Only El Al has Air Marshals."

The Israeli shook his head. "Ask your people to check. I think you'll find that quite a few airlines have them."

Stuart turned to Sally and nodded.

Mark shifted in his chair and announced, "Fine, now let's get started. I'd like to make the six ten flight back to Tel Aviv."

Brett Daniels signaled to the man introduced as Richard, who approached the table and handed each man a sheaf of papers. That accomplished, he walked over to a bank of switches and dimmed the lights.

"We've investigated the man that Marc's people gave us," said Daniels, "and we now know that his real name is Osama bin Laden. He's an exiled Saudi millionaire who's reputed to be the head of an extremist organization called Al-Qaeda. If you check with your FBI, you'll see he's been on their most wanted list since ninety-nine."

Stuart again turned to Sally, who was busy writing.

"He's the seventeenth of what we believe are fifty-two children born to a Saudi construction magnate. When our man's father died in sixty-eight, he took an active part in the family business, the bin Laden Group."

An image appeared on the wall; it was a headshot of a man with a beard and turban. "We first heard of him in seventy-nine," Daniels continued. "That's when he went to Afghanistan to fight against the Russians. He used his family's influence to raise money for the cause. In fact, your CIA poured over three billion into helping him and his friends. After the Russians pulled out of Afghanistan, he returned to Saudi Arabia and aligned himself with those groups opposed to the reigning Saudi monarchy. We next heard about him in ninety-one, when he turned up in the Sudan with an estimated quarter of a billion dollars. In ninety-seven, the Sudanese expelled him, so he went back to Afghanistan and joined up with the Taliban. Our sources tell us that he took over the group headed by Sheik Omar Abdul Rahman, when the sheik was thrown into prison."

A picture of the aged cleric appeared.

"Isn't that the guy serving a life sentence for trying to blow up the World Trade Center in New York?" Stuart asked.

"That's him. In fact, two of his sons have since joined with Osama, and they've forged alliances with fundamentalist groups in Egypt, Sudan, Somalia, Saudi Arabia, Iran, Iraq, and Yemen."

"Some of my country's closest friends," said Marc, the irony not lost on anyone in the room.

Brett acknowledged the Israeli's comment with a nod and then continued, "The attack on the U.S.S. *Cole* can be traced back to bin Laden, along with bombings in Kenya, Nairobi, and Dares Salaam. This is not a nice person."

"You could have sent us this information," said Stuart. "Why did you go to the trouble of bringing us here?" He looked at Marc for help.

Brett Daniels sighed and glanced at the three aides seated nearby. "If you three would like to take a break, this would be the moment."

Sally looked at the men on either side of her and then at Stuart. When he tipped his head toward the door, she rose and followed the other two out of the room.

When the door was closed, Daniels resumed his explanation. "I know how the world feels about the way prisoners are treated, which is why I asked only the two of you here. We know that this lawyer, Kenneth Hall, has been meeting with the people from the IRA. Our men picked one up last week and after some"—he stopped and pursed his lips—"persuasion, the man decided to tell us what was going on. It seems that bin Laden has been a supporter of several of Hall's clients and has been helping him get terrorists into the United States via Canada, Mexico, and several friendly countries. Hall is negotiating to have you and the congresswoman taken care of. That way, if he comes to trial, there will be no witnesses."

Stuart glanced at Marc and then turned his attention back to Daniels. "Fine, but why is Marc here if they're after me?"

"Hall left London last Wednesday for the Middle East. The IRA promised four men, two of whom we believe are now gone. He plans to ask Osama for a little help, just in case. Our informant has heard that Osama has a few other things going and doesn't think he's going to get help. With all the illegal people in the States, however, he's not sure. This has become a personal thing with him and has some terrible implications."

Stuart stood and walked to the window. The river was muddy, stirred up by another heavy rain. "You think this Osama is like the old Murder Incorporated?" When the Brit looked confused, he explained, "You want someone killed and someone takes care of it."

"We think that Osama is going to do damage to the United States. There's no doubt he's going to take revenge for Rahman's incarceration; the more people he kills, the sweeter that revenge will be. We also think that Marc's organization may have a chance of finding Hall. Through him, maybe we can stop what Osama is planning, without the whole world getting involved."

"Let me get this straight," said Marc. "If we can find Hall, you want us to exert pressure and find Osama, and then?"

"What we want is for you to find Hall, get the names of his contacts, and learn what Osama is planning. Most important, make sure he doesn't bother us again."

"May I add something to that?" Stuart asked.

Marc and Brett stared at the American.

"Find out where Harvey Loring is hiding."

Marc walked over to the window and stood near Stuart. "If we find Hall, and if we get the information; and if we stop these terrorists from operating inside of the United States, what do we get in return?"

"What do you want?" Brett asked.

"We want visible pressure put on the Palestinians to sit down and figure out how we stop the bombings and the senseless killings of civilians."

"What do you mean by visible?" Stuart asked.

"We want your President to publicly denounce Arafat for the useless piece of shit that he is. We also want your President to demand that the Arab countries work with us to figure out how to stabilize the area."

Brett Daniels studied the Israeli's face for a long moment. "Any particular countries in mind?"

Marc responded to that question with a dry smile. "Jordan, Saudi Arabia, and," He stopped. "It doesn't matter which as long as some of them participate."

"In other words," said Stuart, his voice hard, "there's always going to be a quid pro quo for everything." Marc looked down at the river, the muscles in his jaw twitching. "In the last three weeks, thirty-one civilians have been killed and another two hundred and forty injured. We don't have enough people in our country for this to continue. It must come to an end."

"Perhaps your government should change its policies with regard to Palestine," suggested Brett icily.

"And perhaps your government should change some of its policies about Northern Ireland," Marc fired back.

Stuart looked at the two men. "While we're at it, how about my government changing its policy with regard to Cuba?"

All three men looked at each other and then Stuart smiled. "That's right, we don't make policy, we just see that it's carried out. Listen, I can't speak for the President, but I will carry the message. Marc, unless you find Hall, you have nothing to negotiate with. Who knows? Maybe you'll find out something you can use."

Marc looked at his watch, his movements clearly indicating this meeting was about to end. "You have the name he's traveling under?"

Daniels began to pull together the documents spread out before him. "R. Sherman, the same name as the President. In this case, however, the R stands for Robert."

"We'll find him," promised the Israeli. "Give me a day or two."

"One more thing before you go," said Stuart, holding up his hand. "I don't think we're going to change our policy toward Cuba. There are still too many people out there who are convinced that Castro had Kennedy shot." He laughed out loud, adding, "Have a safe flight."

"You can be sure I will," smiled Marc. "I'm allowed to carry a weapon." He shook hands with Daniels and Stuart and left the room.

When the door was firmly closed, Stuart turned to his British counterpart. "And now, if you'll get me to a secure phone, I know a congresswoman who needs some help."

Chapter Ninety-Five

After talking to Michael, Stuart arranged for passage on an air force jet that was leaving for Atlanta within the hour. The plan was for Michael to arrange for engine trouble, forcing the jet to land in Washington where Stuart, Sally, and Marie would deplane. This would insure that there was no record of them taking a flight.

"The two other hit men must be after Jessica," Stuart explained to Michael. "There's a good chance they're already in place. Call her, tell her to stay indoors, and make sure we have plenty of men covering her."

"I'm taking care of it," Michael replied. "This isn't amateur night."

"I'll be there in about five hours," said Stuart. "And by the way, you don't have to tell her I'm involved."

Michael hung up without responding. *These two are going to drive me crazy.*

The air force jet suffered engine problems as it approached the United States and was forced to land at Dulles. Three of its passengers disembarked. Seth was waiting for Marie and was standing with Donald, Sally's husband. The concern about the recent events was etched on their faces.

Stuart watched as they embraced and felt his face grow warm. *Better go and check on the congresswoman.*

It took him almost two hours to reach her development, because of the late afternoon traffic. There were three guards at the gate, two he knew. There was also a car parked inside the gate, with two Secret Service agents in front. Stuart spoke to each one, ascertaining the congresswoman knew of a threat and had been given a set of procedures to follow. She wouldn't leave the house for any reason, without telling the guards on duty.

Stuart stood in the guard shack watching Jessica's street. After thirty minutes, aware that he was making the men on duty very nervous, he decided to go home. As he walked toward his car, he saw Jessica's coming toward him.

Not having heard a phone ring in the guard's shack, he was surprised she would leave the house without calling. As the car approached the gate, he realized it was Sarah driving. He watched as the car slowed, the girl waved to the guard, and then picked up speed as the guard waved back. Stuart ran to his car and drove in the same direction, making sure he kept a safe distance. There were four cars between them until she turned into a shopping center. The first car kept going, but a van and a Buick following the van turned into the parking lot. Stuart passed the entrance, opting to enter at the next entrance, several hundred yards ahead. He entered a parking aisle, a Safeway looming ahead. As he neared the end of the aisle, Sarah's car entered from the top of the aisle. There were three empty parking spots, and Stuart pulled into the closest. Sarah pulled into a spot across from him, and the van took the spot four spaces away. The Buick was nowhere to be seen. Through the rearview mirror, Stuart watched Sarah get out of her car and walked towards the supermarket. The man in the van waited until she passed him and then exited his car. Stealthily, he moved to Sarah's car and crouched down. It was only seconds before he stood and returned to the van. Stuart saw the man signal to someone and then drive away. Stuart quickly got out of his car and approached Sarah's. The left back tire was flat, and there were nails lying all over the ground.

"Damn," he mumbled, walking toward the market. He had no doubt that these people were planning to do something to Sarah. Taking out his cell phone, he started to punch in the number of the Cigar Store. When he noticed he had no cells, he said "shit" so loudly a woman walking by gave him a nasty look.

"Mr. Taylor! What are you doing here?"

Stuart recognized Sarah's voice and turned. "Don't talk to me," he instructed, the expression on his face conveying the seriousness of the situation. "Just turn around and go back into the store, I'll be right behind you."

"What's the matter?" she asked, fear crossing her face.

"Now, Sarah! No talking, just move!"

The girl rushed back into the store. Stuart grabbed a shopping cart and followed. Once inside, he passed her while taking boxes off the shelves and filling the cart. When he was sure she wasn't being followed, he asked for her cell phone.

The girl removed it from her backpack and handed it to him. "Is something going on?"

"Nothing we can't handle," he told her, smiling as he punched in a number.

After explaining the situation to the guards covering Jessica's home and then arranging for backup, Stuart enlightened Sarah as to his plan. "You'll have to trust me this will work, and you might even enjoy it."

"Maybe I should tell my mother," Sarah suggested quietly.

"Haven't time; we don't want these guys to get away."

Sarah began to chew the skin on the back of her hand. Taking a deep breath, she said, "Let's go."

Stuart was first out of the busy supermarket, with Sarah ten feet behind. As he walked past her car, he paused to look at the flat tire, and she nearly collided with him.

The man driving the van was able to hear the conversation between Stuart and Sarah. Confused, he dialed his partner and brought him up to date.

"It's definitely not the woman," he said, "so it must be her daughter. Some guy was looking at the tire when she came out and has offered to drive her home. She's agreed, saying someone will come and change it. They've just entered his car, a new Lexus, and are driving away from where you're parked. I'm right behind them. If you step on it, you should be able to catch up."

Stuart drove out of the parking lot at a leisurely pace and headed toward Sarah's home. When he was sure he was being followed, he pressed a little harder on the gas pedal and turned off onto a road a good mile from the development.

"Something's wrong," reported the man in the van. "He's pulled into what looks like a deserted road. I'll wait for you to catch up. Hurry."

Less than a minute later, the Buick pulled alongside the van. "Where are they?"

"His lights went off about a hundred yards ahead. It looks like he promised to help her, and now he's going to try to have sex with her."

"Bloody Americans," the man said, removing his leather jacket and throwing it on the hood of the car. "Let's teach him some manners." He pulled a pistol from the holster strapped across his chest.

"Actually, he's done us a favor," said the driver of the van, following his friend down the road. "He's made it easy for us to grab the daughter."

The two men approached Stuart's car, bending over so they couldn't be seen from the inside. "I'll take the right side, you take the left," instructed one of them as they knelt behind the car.

"On the count of three, we open a door." Silently they mouthed the count and yanked open the doors. The car was empty.

"He's dragged her off somewhere!" shouted the taller man. "We have to find them."

After five fruitless minutes, the one giving all the directions called off the search. "We can't spend any more time looking. We'll try again tomorrow."

"What about the girl?" the other man asked.

"The hell with her, I hope she enjoys it."

When they got back to their vehicles, they discovered both had flat tires.

"Bloody hell," the leader cursed. "Let's just change yours. The rental company can change the other one when they find it." Using a jack, they pulled off the tire. "That's strange," mumbled the shorter man. "This tire has been slashed."

"What?" said the leader, letting go of the jack. Before he could turn around, the beams of a half dozen flashlights were blinding them. In seconds, they were on the ground, hands cuffed behind their back.

Stuart and Sarah stood over the two men. "Sarah, let me introduce you to the pride of the Irish, Murder Incorporated. Gentlemen, let me introduce you to Sarah. You can thank her for your survival tonight. Right now I have to take her home, but you and I will be seeing each other again, very soon."

"You can't do anything to us," the leader challenged. "It's against the law."

Stuart nodded and grinned. "You're right, and if you were in this country legally, you'd be allowed what they call *due process*. Since you're not, however, you're entitled to nothing . . . except what I'm willing to grant you. Think about that until we meet again."

Stuart led Sarah to a waiting car. "Now comes the hard part." She looked at him questioningly. "I don't want your mother to know I was involved."

"Why, she's your girlfriend, isn't she? Aren't you two getting married?"

Stuart was touched by the hopefulness in her face. "I'm not sure, Sarah. She's been very busy the past couple of weeks and we haven't had much time to talk."

Sarah nodded but didn't reply.

"So I'd appreciate it if she didn't know my part in this. We can't hide what happened, but we don't have to spell it all out either."

Sarah sighed dramatically. "Alright, I won't say anything."

Ten minutes later, Stuart let the girl out of his car at the security gate. Her car was waiting for her, its tire changed. "Don't forget," he said as she went through the gate.

Sarah entered the house, put down the packages, and yelled, "Mom!"

"I'm up here, why are you yelling?"

"I have something to ask you." Sarah climbed the stairs and entered her mother's room. "Why didn't you tell me that you and Mr. Taylor were having a problem?"

"Why do you think we're having a problem?" There was more than a little concern in her voice.

"Because he told me so, just a few minutes ago."

"You saw Stuart?"

Sarah shrugged. "No big deal, he was just saving my life." Jessica stared open-mouthed and pulled her daughter onto the bed. "Suppose you start from the beginning."

Chapter Ninety-Six

It had been three days since Stuart had finished questioning the two men, with last night's session lasting until almost midnight. He glanced at the clock on the wall and then at his watch.

"Maybe I'll call my mother," he said just as his private line rang. He shook his head. "Probably her," he mumbled. At six thirty on a Friday morning, who else would call?

"I'm glad I found you at home." It was Jessica. "I understand you've been very busy, and I need to ask a favor."

"You do know that I've tried calling every day for two weeks, but I've never been able to connect." The minute the reprimand was out of his mouth, Stuart wished he could take it back.

"I had some things to sort through."

There was a lengthy silence, broken when Stuart asked, "What's the favor?"

"I've been invited to a White House dinner, and I need an escort. I was hoping you could see your way clear to go with me."

Stuart looked at the ceiling. "Of course I'll go with you. When is it?"

"Saturday night."

"That's tomorrow!"

"Are you busy?" she asked quietly.

Stuart felt his heart leap. "Jessica, I'm never so busy that I can't go dinner with you."

"Good, then I'll pick you up at six thirty. I have a limo at my disposal." When he didn't speak, she added, "It's black tie."

"What's the occasion?"

"I'm not sure. The President's secretary called and just told me to be there."

He waited for her to continue. When she did not, he said, "I'll see you tomorrow."

Twenty minutes later, he was on his way to work. He had alerted the Parks Department to the possibility of a terrorist attack against the Lincoln, Washington, or Jefferson memorials. The two IRA soldiers had independently verified each other's story. Neither of them knew exactly what was planned, but both had overheard conversations about terrorists blowing up America's shrines. Both men denied ever having met Hall. When they were shown his photograph, they both identified him, each man using a different name. Stuart had sent the names to Marc and had tried calling him in Israel. There was no answer on his private phone, and the person answering the office phone refused to give any information. Stuart decided Marc was probably out of the country on assignment.

He drove past the Tidal Basin to take another look at the Jefferson Memorial. When he arrived at his office, the first thing he did was to have Sally call the Parks Department and have them increase coverage at the Jefferson.

The Parks Department earlier asked if he had any reason to pick one location over another and he said no. Now, as he looked at the map on his wall, he decided it had to be either the Jefferson or the Lincoln. Both sites offered easier escape routes than the Washington Memorial. Aside from the psychological motives, he could see no reason to blow up the shrines. Wouldn't it make more sense to go after the White House, the congressional building, or CIA headquarters in Virginia?

Stuart had spoken to his counterpart in London before going to bed and revealed what he had learned so far. He also told Daniels, arrangements would be made for him to be present when he turned the two men over to Marc for further interrogation. It was against British policy to turn I.R.A. members over to another government without legal representation. Twelve hours later, Stuart reflected on his conversation with Brett and the information the Americans were able to force out of the detainees.

Daniels had asked, "How much were they being paid to kill you and the congresswoman?"

Stuart understood the amount of money indicated the importance attached to the job.

"One hundred thousand for the congresswoman, two hundred and fifty for me," Stuart had revealed. He still felt strange about the amounts, with his worth valued more than twice that of Jessica.

"One hundred is the right amount for her," said Brett Daniels. "But it's you they consider the heavy hitter. I would be very careful, Stuart. These people will most likely try again. In the past, they got 25 percent up front and the balance upon completion."

Stuart thanked him for the information but did not put that statement into his report.

"How about a cup of coffee?"

Stuart looked up and saw Peter enter his office holding two cups.

He accepted a cup and took a quick sip. "Anything happen after I left last night?"

"Nothing important," said Peter with a little shrug. "We put them on a plane headed to Russia, making one stop in Jerusalem. They should be there about now." Peter glanced at his watch. "I spoke to Brett and confirmed the time of arrival with him." The man lowered himself into the chair facing Stuart. "He's concerned, and so am I, about the amount of money they're willing to pay to have you killed."

"When we get Loring, they'll forget all about me."

"Fine," responded Peter, "but what about Jessica? The word around the office is that you two are having problems."

Stuart tensed and told himself to pause before speaking. "Tell you what," he finally said. "The next time we have a plane headed to Russia, remind me to put Sally on it. Maybe you too. As it happens, we're having dinner tomorrow night. We've both been very busy."

Peter stood and picked up the coffee mug. "Call me on Sunday and let me know if you want Jessica's detail doubled." Without waiting for an answer, he left the office.

Stuart spent the balance of Friday reading reports. On Saturday morning, he drove to the firing range and practiced shooting.

When six thirty rolled around, Stuart felt ready. He rehearsed what he wanted to say a dozen times, and anticipated every answer Jessica could possibly give. His greatest hope was that she would be willing to listen. He already decided if it made a difference, he would give up his government job and try something in the private sector. If she would say yes, and if she would agree to marry him, untold changes and adjustments could be made.

Seated in his living room, he watched the security camera as the limo driver ran to the rear door and held it open for Jessica. She was beautiful. She wore a long black dress, a string of lustrous pearls draped around her neck. He watched her walk to his door and ring the bell.

"I'll be right there," he said into the intercom, watching her reaction to his voice. A smile crossed her face, and he pushed a button that would take her picture. *Just in case this doesn't work out,* he thought. He rushed to the door, took a deep breath, and flung it open. Jessica leaned into him and kissed his cheek. "You look very nice. Let's hurry, I don't want to be late."

Look very nice, indeed! "And you look lovely. You're going to make every man at the party envious of me."

The ride to the White House took only fifteen minutes, during which time she never stopped talking about the goings-on in Congress. With her explanation long and the drive short, Stuart never got the chance to say the things he had rehearsed.

The driver pulled up to the front gate, and Jessica lowered her window. "Congresswoman Winston and guest," she called out.

Gary Williams stepped closer and smiled. "Good evening, Congresswoman. I don't have the name of your guest on my list."

"I think you know him. His name is Stuart Taylor."

Williams looked in the window and smiled. "Mr. Taylor, I was told the congresswoman would be alone." The smile left his face. "You're not on my list."

"Please call the President," said Jessica sweetly. "I'm sure there's been a misunderstanding."

"I'm sorry, there's no misunderstanding. My instructions are in writing from the President."

Jessica looked at Stuart and shrugged. "I guess I misunderstood the invitation."

"I'm sure we can have someone take Mr. Taylor home. He, of all people, must understand how the system works." The man's smile was forced.

"That's not necessary," said Stuart. "The driver can take me home and come back for the congresswoman."

"Don't be ridiculous," argued Jessica, and then turned to the guard. "Please tell the President that I'm sorry, but I can't make his dinner. I've promised Stuart, Mr. Taylor, that is, we were dining together. For three weeks I've been putting off giving him an answer to a very important question. Tonight, he gets his answer."

Stuart, fuming over the course of events, sat straight up.

"You're going to answer now?" Stuart asked, his adrenaline rushing. "And the answer is . . . ?"

Jessica nearly laughed. "I really wanted to wait until after dinner, but I guess this place is as good as any other." She turned back to the guard. "Tell the President that the next time he wants me to join him for dinner, he'll have to include my future husband. That is, if he'll have me as his wife."

"Jessica, I don't understand. I thought you were mad at me." Stuart realized that the window was still open and felt his face turn hot."

She placed her hand on his. "Stuart, I've never been mad at you, but I have had to come to grips with your job. After Sarah told me what happened, everything made sense." She put her arms around him.

Stuart embraced Jessica, calling out to the driver, "Take us home."

After the limo left the guard station, Gary Williams picked up the phone and dialed. "Mr. President, I did as you instructed. He offered to go home, but she wouldn't hear of it and left with him."

"Was anything else said?" asked the President.

"Yes, sir. She said I should tell you that if you invited her to dinner again, you would have to invite her future husband."

"Thank you, Williams."

When the call was completed, the guard returned to his post. At the same time, the President turned to Michael and said, "The things you have to do for people just to get their vote in Congress is unbelievable."

Michael smiled broadly, "It sounds like her plan worked, but don't be too sure of her vote: she's tough. Now what's really for dinner?"

The shrillness of the phone awoke Stuart and Jessica. Simultaneously, they looked at the clock. It was six thirty on Sunday morning.

"One of your old girlfriends?" she asked, sitting up and letting the sheet fall to her lap.

"There's only one really old girlfriend with this number, and that's my mother."

"Let me answer it," Jessica said, leaning across Stuart. "Who's calling?" she asked, a distinctive lilt to her voice.

There was no answer.

"Is someone on this phone?" she asked.

"I'm not sure I dialed the right number," said a woman's voice. "Is Stuart there?" Jessica recognized Barbara Taylor's concerned voice immediately.

"This is Stuart Taylor's fiancée," she responded, elbowing Stuart. "May I tell him who is calling?"

"This is his mother. Jessica, is it you?"

Jessica laughed and gave Barbara the good news. "Your son accepted my proposal of marriage last night," she said. "When the phone rang, he told me it would be you. Barbara, I'd like you to help me plan the wedding. Don't you think September is a great month for weddings and honeymoons?"

"Jessica, you've made me the happiest woman in the world. Tell him, no, don't tell him anything, I'll tell him when I see him." With a girlish laugh, she hung up the phone. Jessica stretched out across Stuart and cooed as he rubbed her back from her neck to her ankles. "Your mother said to call when you're finished, maybe sometime late this afternoon."

Stuart acknowledged the message with his lips lightly brushing her shoulder.

Chapter Ninety-Seven

Monday morning came too soon for both of them. They spent the better part of Sunday dressed only in robes, if anything at all. Occasionally, they would remember to eat; but mostly they reveled in being together, lying in bed, watching television, and making love. Sometime during the day, Stuart called his mother, and Jessica brought Sarah up to date. He also left messages for his children, advising them of his upcoming marriage.

They left for Jessica's just as the morning sun was rising. Jessica needed time to change and meet with her staff prior to her meeting with the congressional leaders.

"We didn't decide when we should announce our engagement," she declared as they approached her home.

"You could call a press conference, or we could hop over to Vegas and just do it." "Be serious!" she exclaimed. "I'm a representative from the state of California. We may not like it, but whatever I do is news."

"You may not believe this," Stuart said, "but I have actually given it some thought. I heard you tell my mother September was a good month for weddings. How about September the ninth, in California?"

"Why the ninth," she asked, her brow creased. "And why California?"

"The ninth will allow us to take a honeymoon after Labor Day, when it's not so crowded, and aside from your home being in California, it's a good jumping off spot to Hawaii, Australia, Bali, Singapore, and points east."

"I've never been to Australia. Is it nice there in September?"

"It's the start of their summer—" he told her but was interrupted by his cell phone's ring before he could continue.

"Your mother again?" Jessica smiled.

Stuart read the little screen. "My office."

Pulling over to the side of the road, Stuart answered as always, "Taylor."

"Stuart, it's Peter. We just received an alert from Israel: Marc was found dead."

"Shit." He pressed his forehead against the steering wheel.

"What is it?" Jessica put her hand on his arm.

"Someone I liked died," he replied through clenched teeth.

Jessica sat back. She knew this was a part of his life to which she would never adapt.

"How?" asked Stuart.

"We'll go over that when you get here. Where are you now?"

Stuart felt awkward telling his friend that he was with Jessica at ten to six in the morning. "I'm on my way in. I should be there within a half hour."

"Was he a close friend?" asked Jessica, the car nearing her house.

"I wouldn't say close, but he was someone I trusted. He was helping us find Loring and Hall."

"Is that why he was killed?" Stuart took a deep breath and released it slowly. "Unlike my job, his put him in contact with some of the worst terrorists in the world. He was a line person as opposed to a planner."

"He wasn't an American?"

"No, he was Israeli."

"Did you know his family?"

The question left Stuart numb. Did Marc even have a family? He had no idea. "I've never met his family," he admitted. "I think I'd like to."

Stuart sat at his desk, his focus shifting from the clock on the wall to his watch. Two hours earlier, when he arrived at the office, Peter had given him the specifics. Marc had been found in a car in Milan. The car had been illegally parked for three days before the authorities decided to tow it away. While lifting it onto the truck's bed, they noticed blood dripping from the trunk. Marc's identification, watch, and money were all there. Whoever did it wanted them to know that it wasn't robbery. What the murderer didn't know, Peter told him, was that Marc wore a digital recorder attached to his collar and a ten-minute tape embedded in the heel of his shoe.

"The Israelis aren't telling us what was on the entire tape, but they did mention that one of the questions was about you."

"What did the bastards want to know?"

"They wouldn't tell me," said Peter. "But if you call them at nine our time and ask for Gabrielle Weiss, she'll fill you in."

Stuart still had fifteen minutes to before it was time to make that call. He had spoken to Brett Daniels, who already heard about Marc's death, and then to Bill Cook, who hadn't. He again looked at his watch: ten more minutes. He'd never heard of Gabrielle Weiss, but his instinct was she'd have plenty to tell him. Sally interrupted his musings. "Stuart, Michael on line 1."

"Ask if I can call him back, will you?"

"He said it's urgent, and he's at the White House."

Stuart hit the blinking button. "Yeah, Michael," he said.

"Stuart, this is the President." First name basis! He wondered what was up.

"Sorry, Mr. President, my secretary said it was Michael Burnett."

"I'm here too," chimed in Michael.

"Let me get right to the point," the President started. "I've just heard from the Vice President of Mexico. Your friend, Jose Vargas, was gunned down outside of his home near Mexico City last night. A witness reported that he approached a car, had a short conversation, and was shot. The street was crowded, and several people came to his aid. The only thing he said was to call Taylor." The President stopped talking and waited. When Stuart didn't respond he asked, "Did you hear me?"

"I heard you, Mr. President. That makes two of the top antiterrorists in the world."

"Two?"

"Marc Frankel was found dead this morning."

Michael's voice came on at once. "Stuart, can you be here at two? We have to talk."

"I'll be there."

"Come prepared. There may be others present."

"Sally! Peter!" Stuart yelled through the open door. "I have to see you now."

At ten minutes before two, Stuart drove through the gate at the White House. Twice he had received messages to call Jessica; twice he had called and received no response. He knew the rule for members of Congress: cell phones had to be turned off when Congress was in session or when the individual was meeting with congressional leaders.

The guard stepped forward at the security gate. "I was told to wave you through, sir, and get you to the rear door immediately." The man signaled for the golf cart. "Please leave any weapons you might have with them." He nodded toward the two men who were seated on the cart.

When the cart arrived, a uniformed Marine walked him to the waiting elevator, explained, "This will take you to the situation room." When the elevator stopped, Michael was waiting for him.

"There'll be three or four people from Congress, the head of the Joint Chiefs, the secretaries of State and Defense, along with Karen Ortega and Ray Bradley."

"Jake's not attending any meetings?"

"Some, not all. Now listen," instructed Michael. "Warning flags are flying all over the globe. The FBI, during a routine investigation, found out that Hall's father was a Saudi. He was attending college in the States when he met his wife, who was part of the radical fringe at Berkeley. After they met and married, they ceased their political activities. He became a citizen, and they raised little Kenneth. During his formative years, Kenneth visited Cuba, Yemen, Saudi Arabia, Egypt, you get the picture. His law firm only has a few clients. Loring and Harper are the big ones, but not necessarily the ones that pay the largest fees. We haven't checked out all the leads, but a good part of that money was coming from offshore clients whose names are impossible to find. What you're going to hear today may piss you off. Don't lose your temper and don't show surprise." Michael held the door open for Stuart.

The first person Stuart saw was Jessica, and he did a poor job of hiding his surprise.

Chapter Ninety-Eight

"Stuart," the President called out above the conversation that was buzzing around the thirty-foot table. "I think you know everyone here," he said, motioning with both hands. "There's an open seat next to Jessica. Take it and we can start the meeting."

Stuart nodded to the people seated around the table. He walked over and handed a disc to the naval officer who was sitting in front of the computer running a PowerPoint presentation. When Stuart sat down, he glanced at Jessica. She had a notebook opened in front of her and was busy writing. When she felt his gaze, she took the top piece of paper and slid it toward him. On it was "I've been trying to call you!"

When he nodded, she stuffed the note into her attaché.

The President leaned back in his chair and nodded for someone to lower the lights. "Stuart, bring us up to date on the recent killings in Italy and Mexico."

Stuart looked around the table, occupied by some of the most powerful people on earth. "This news is breaking as we speak. Here's what we know."

The presentation took almost thirty minutes, and everyone in the room, including the President, was mesmerized by what they saw on the screen. Stuart began with the meeting in New York. He discussed the information they received from the Saudi arrested in Canada and the IRA members, plus what they had gleaned from sources all over the globe. He included what he knew and what he surmised about Loring, Hall, and Chilicote. He left out any mention of Gastner, deciding that prudence was the better part of valor. When he finished, he asked that the lights be turned on.

The first question came from the secretary of Defense. "These men you've received the information from, when can our people talk to them?"

Stuart had anticipated this question and knew his response would not be well received. "Mr. Secretary, we work for the same government, and it was our own people who asked the questions. If you're asking if a different agency can talk to them, that's not possible. These men are either dead or have been turned over to another government."

"You mentioned Congressman Chilicote," said Speaker of the House Brightwell. "And then you tell us that some of the men who spoke out against him are dead. Is this fair treatment of an esteemed member of Congress?" He looked around, making certain that everyone at that table understood his message. "Mr. Speaker," explained Stuart, "I've heard Senator Chilicote say repeatedly that what he wants is his day in court. I've listened to Congresswoman Winston tell everyone he's innocent until proven guilty in a court of law. If you start proceedings tomorrow to get him arrested and thrown out of Congress, I'm prepared to show you proof today."

"So what you're saying is that we shouldn't give him his day in court?"

"There's a bounty of a hundred thousand dollars on Congresswoman Winston's head and a quarter of a million on mine. I assumed the reason for this meeting was to discuss that . . . and the deaths of seven antiterrorists."

"Seven?" The President's voice was low, incredulous. "My god, I thought there were only two!"

Stuart waited for the buzz around the table to die down. "I'm sorry, sir. After your call today we did further research and found there have been five other deaths in the past six days. These others were not as high on the exposure level as Frankel and Torres, but every bit as active."

"Who are the other five?" the President asked.

"One Israeli, an Egyptian, two Englishmen, and a Russian."

Jessica turned slightly so she could face Stuart. "What do you think it all means?"

"A call has gone out worldwide to find Osama bin Laden. He's believed to be the head of a terrorist organization operating out of Afghanistan. From what we can learn, it has ties to a very wealthy Saudi family. The thinking is that Harper, Loring, and Hall had been working with bin Laden to perpetrate some act of terrorism here in the States."

"But why?" came the question from someone near the far end of the table.

"Money, most probably," answered Michael, seated on the President's left.

"Too bad we don't have Harper to question," said another man snidely.

"What's too bad," shot back Stuart, "is that he tried to kill the son of the Vice President of Mexico. Had he not, he might still be alive. Stuart did not like where this meeting was going.

The same voice came back with, "I've heard that anyone who disagrees with the way you think seem to end up dead."

"Just a moment, hold it!" announced Karen Ortega, practically jumping to her feet. The way she confronted the man making these accusations, Stuart expected her to go mano a mano with him. "If you have something to say about the way Stuart Taylor conducts business and let me add that it's always in the name of the U.S. government, then stand up and say it. Otherwise, keep your snide remarks to yourself. I'm tired of you sniping at someone I've worked with in the past, and expect to work even closer in the future. And, I might add, for whom I have a great deal of respect."

The man was left openmouthed, searching frantically around the table for any sign of support. His eyes came to a stop when he reached Jessica. "I hear you know a lot about the way he works," said the man. "So how about letting us in on what you've seen and heard?"

Jessica slowly pushed back the chair and stood. "Many times over the past few years," she said, "I've listened to you and thought you were a bright person. As of this moment, however, I'm of the opinion that you're an ass. I've seen Stuart have to kill, and I've seen the pain on his face because of it. Do you want to know what I've learned? I've learned that he will do anything within his power to preserve the peace and protect the innocent. I've also learned that if everything goes according to plan, he and I will be married on September ninth." Jessica took a moment to compose herself, an overwhelming anger threatening to burst free. "I will also tell you he is a fighter. If you think you can insult him, or take cheap shots at him, you are mistaken. He has a long memory and so do his friends. They will defend him, as will I. If I were you, I'd shut up and listen to what he has to say. It very well could save your life."

The man chewed on his lip, two red splotches appearing on his cheeks. With a sheepish expression, he finally made eye contact with Jessica. "I'm sorry," he told her. "But I think I'm out of my depth here. I've never listened to a more bizarre story in my life. We're being told some religious fanatic is having people killed all over the world and intends to attack the United States. If Mr. Taylor had said the North Koreans or the Iraqis were instigating this, I might find it believable. But some outcast Saudi, living in the caves of Afghanistan? Sorry, that stretches believability way too far for me."

The President directed a question at Stuart. "What do you think we should do?"

Stuart rose and turned to face his commander in chief. "Mr. President, I think we must create another department for handling this terrorist threat. The FBI is chartered to work inside the United States; the CIA is designed to work outside. I propose an organization capable of working in conjunction with both of them, but also able to move from domestic to international. If you so specify, this department would report directly to the attorney general, as should every law enforcement agency in this country."

The President said nothing for a very long moment. When he finally spoke, he asked, "Any other thoughts?"

"Would you need any of our special forces?" asked the head of the U.S. Navy.

"If you mean Delta Force or the Seals, I doubt it. Right now, I envision a group of dedicated people who will ferret out terrorists and their organizations, and then use all available means to put them out of existence."

"Stuart." Jessica raised her hand. "Terrorists don't have to be from another country. Would this group also go after groups inside the United States?"

"Once identified, I think the FBI. or the ATF could handle domestic terrorists."

The chairman of the Joint Chiefs cleared his throat loudly, and the room fell silent. "How would you differentiate between those people wanting a change in the government and terrorists?"

"I wouldn't," answered Stuart. "Anyone advocating the violent overthrow of the government would go on the list and be handled by the appropriate agency. By handled, I think we should go after their money supply, their leaders, and any outside governments supporting them. People wanting a change are entitled to all the protection we can give them."

Stuart sat back down, and all eyes turned toward the President.

"I want to thank all of you for coming. I hope to make a decision before the end of this month, and I will get back to you as soon as that decision is made." The President turned to leave the room. When Stuart called out "Mr. President!" the leader stopped and turned.

Stuart took several steps closer and said, "Excuse me, but I don't think we can wait until the end of the month. At least seven are dead, and this bin Laden is looking to add more names to his list."

Michael stepped between Stuart and the President. "The President can't authorize a new department without more thought, but I'm sure he wants our people protected." He gave Stuart a meaningful look. "I've seen you work, Stuart, and I'm confident that you'll do the right thing. Until this decision can be made, I suggest you continue acting as liaison between our present agencies and foreign governments."

Stuart looked at Michael. The man had just given him the green light to act while the President was making up his mind.

"I can do that," he replied. "As long as I can report back to you."

Michael looked at the President, who nodded and left the room.

Everyone stood and followed the President. Everyone, that is, except Jessica.

"You did very well," she whispered, unable to suppress the smile.

"Why are you whispering?" he mouthed without making a sound.

Jessica leaned over and wrote, "Listening devices?"

Stuart nodded, took her by the arm, and led her toward the door. Before they stepped through it, he turned and said, "I love you, Jessica," and then walked out.

Chapter Ninety-Nine

It was late afternoon before Sally was able to establish contact with Gabrielle Weiss. When she finally put the call through, there was no doubt their conversation had not gone well.

"The bitch from Israel's on line 1" was all she said.

Stuart nearly laughed but knew better than to encourage his assistant. He picked up the receiver. "Stuart Taylor here." When the woman inquired about the purpose of the call, he explained he was seeking the details of Marc Frankel's death and had been referred to her.

"What is it you want to know?" she asked, her tone abrupt, cursory.

"Everything," he responded. "I called earlier, but you were unavailable."

"I was busy."

"Ms. Weiss, I'm also busy, so how about getting off your tank and giving me some information."

There was silence, and for a moment, Stuart thought she had hung up. "Ms. Weiss?"

"I'm here," she said and then launched into the details. "Marc was found by the Italian police in the trunk of a car perhaps two miles from the Villa D'Este, where he was registered. His money, his watch, everything he owned was still on his body. He was shot three times; any one of those bullets would have killed him. They did not know he had a hidden tape recorder in the collar of his shirt and a ten-minute tape in his shoe."

Stuart listened to the recounting of information already supplied. He let her go on uninterrupted, hoping to glean some new piece of information. "I understand my name was mentioned on that tape."

"Among others," she told him.

"Which others?" he probed, feeling as if he were being forced to drag every answer from this woman.

"Congresswoman Winston, Jose Vargas, and Brett Daniels."

"Have you notified Mr. Daniels?"

"He is en route to Israel to have a talk with the two IRA men you sent us. I'll tell him when he arrives."

"What did they ask about the congresswoman and me?"

"They asked about a meeting you had in New York and wanted to know if the congresswoman had been there."

"What was Marc's response?"

"His exact words were 'Mr. Hall, you can't run fast enough or far enough, and I'll bet you a thousand shekels Taylor catches you before my people do.'"

"Did Hall respond?"

"He said there were five men at that meeting, and he'd bet a thousand dollars that his people would get them all before they realized what was going on. He laughed and then we heard the three shots."

Stuart felt something twist in his gut. "When were you going to advise the five men present that they were in danger?" His voice was hard, angry.

"That meeting was supposed to be secret, and we're still trying to determine who leaked the information. We know that it wasn't Marc or was it Jose Vargas. We're assuming it wasn't you, and some time today we'll be sure about Brett Daniels. That leaves Bill Cook from Canada and two more Americans."

"If I remember correctly, there were a dozen others hanging around. Did you get the names of the two women agents from Canada, a few uniforms from Great Britain, and a family from Israel?" That edge in his voice was turning sharper. "Certainly you checked on all of them."

"We're working on it."

"And why haven't you asked for help?"

"Who would we ask?" she said, the disdain unmistakable.

"Me."

Weiss was silent for a few seconds before answering, "I'll see what my superiors want me to do. I assume that's all?"

Stuart had one final question that had been under his skin for days. "Ms. Weiss, before you hang up, did Marc have any family?"

This time, her silence was prolonged. "Yes, Mr. Taylor, he did."

"Would it be against policy for you to put me in contact with them? I'd like to tell them how sorry I am."

"I will pass it on."

"I'd like to tell them myself."

"Mr. Taylor, I will tell my son that you are sorry. It may take a few years for him to understand, but he will know you asked. If you are finished, I have things that must be taken care of."

"Your son? Marc was your husband?"

"Marc was my husband."

Stuart was stunned and felt slightly ashamed. "I'm sorry, I didn't know." He took a deep breath. "When is the funeral?" he asked, not knowing what more he could say.

"Friday morning."

"I'll try to be there."

The call ended, and Stuart picked up a pencil and circled Friday on his desk calendar. This was one funeral he needed to attend. "Sally, get me on a plane to Israel on Wednesday, and then find Bill Cook in Canada. I want to speak to him."

Stuart glanced at the full moon as he entered Jessica's house.

"Come on in," Jessica said, holding her arms open. "Have you had anything to eat?"

He yawned and rubbed his eyes. "I'm not hungry, thanks. It's been a tough day. I just wanted to tell you I'm going to Israel on Wednesday. I need another crack at those two IRA guys"

"Would you like me to go with you?"

"No, you have things to do here. But I have assigned two more agents to watch over you and Sarah."

"That makes how many, ten, twelve, more? Stuart, you can't take that many people out of the system because I'm your fiancée."

"Of course I can . . . and I am. Say anything you want, Jess, but they'll be watching you until I return."

Jessica knew better than to think she could win this argument. "I don't like it," she told him. "Please, just tell them to stay out of my way!"

Stuart heard the phone ringing in the kitchen. It stopped after the second ring. A few seconds later, Sarah yelled down from upstairs. "Mom, is Mr. Taylor here?"

"Yes, he is, why?"

"Sally's on the phone, she says it's important."

"I left word I would be stopping here on my way home," he explained, walking into the kitchen. "Yeah, Sally."

"We just received a call from a Martin Meridian. He said to tell you he was instructed by Kenneth Hall to bring something to Paris. He's supposed to pick up tickets tomorrow morning, at the John Wayne Airport in Orange County, for a flight to Dulles. He'll be met there, given a package to deliver, and will get another ticket to Paris. He doesn't know what flights he'll be on, but he thinks there won't be much of a layover. He also said to tell you you're now even."

"Did he say who would be in Paris to receive the package?"

"I didn't ask. He was trying to be secretive but not doing a good job."

"Sally, give me Karen Ortega's home number and stick around. I'm on my way back into the office." He turned to Jessica and gave her a perfunctory kiss. "I'll call you from, actually, I don't know where, but I'll call you."

She nodded and pressed the palm of her hand against his cheek. "Be careful, please."

He kissed her again and left. On the way to his office, he reached Karen Ortega.

"I need at least a dozen agents at the John Wayne Airport tomorrow morning," he told her. "Give them pictures of Meridian and have four of them board the same flight. Have the rest follow anyone who takes an interest in him."

"For me to have four men on that plane," she told him, "I'm going to have to get tickets on every plane leaving for Dulles."

"Karen, I have a feeling he might be connecting somewhere like New York or Atlanta. Whatever plane he's on, I need it met and the same procedure followed again.

"Where will you be?"

"I'll be in Paris. I know what he looks like, and I know what Loring looks like. If he goes anywhere else, call my cell phone or Sally. It's payback time."

"Stuart, be careful."

"I will, thanks."

Arriving at his office, he found Sally waiting at the door.

"Peter already left for the airport. Seth Roberts has a flight to Egypt that we're diverting to Paris. Is there anything else you need done?"

"Have the Villa D'Este brings up the names of anyone who has checked out in the last three or four days. I want to know where they came from and where they were going. I know Marc Frankel and he wasn't staying at one of the most expensive resorts in Italy because he liked the food. Call Michael after the plane takes off and tell him I'll try and work through the Cigar Store, but I can't promise anything. You can also tell him if we're lucky, my ex becomes a widow by Friday."

"Stuart, be careful," she said as he turned and raced back to his car. He had little time to get to the private plane.

Stuart and Peter slept through most of the flight to Paris. Before taking off, he contacted Marc's wife to fill her in. She listened attentively before stating the obvious. "This could be an elaborate trap."

"I know. I also know it could get me close enough to Hall or Loring to make it worthwhile."

"Stuart, Marc had a lot of faith in you, be careful."

"What did she say?" Peter asked without opening his eyes.

"She said be careful."

He nodded and went back to sleep.

Seth was announcing their approach to the Charles De Gaulle airport when the copilot handed Stuart a phone. "It's from your boss."

"Michael, what's up?"

"Stuart, what the hell are you doing?"

"I was sleeping."

"You know what I mean. You're not a field agent anymore. I need you back here at a desk. We've got other men that can do what you're doing."

"I'll ride that desk when the President makes up his mind," he said. "Until then, I've got a job to do."

"I expected you to say something like that. Karen has done what you asked, and Ray has alerted Paris and Rome to expect your call. The President received a call from Israel, and they have people available for you, if you need them. Stuart, I know I don't have to remind you but please, be careful."

Peter glanced up as Stuart handed the phone back to the copilot. "What did he say?"

"He told me to be careful."

"There's an awful lot of that going around."

Walking on the tarmac at Charles de Gaulle, they were met by four men and a woman. The first man asked Stuart if he had any Cuban cigars to claim; Stuart replied he only smoked cigarettes. The man shook his hand, introduced himself, and then proceeded to introduce two of the other men as French police. Stuart looked at the woman and saw something familiar in her face. When he wasn't introduced to her, he said nothing. As the six of them passed one of the doors, the memory came back. Turning, he held out his hand. "Mrs. Weiss, I'm sorry we had to meet under these circumstances."

"How did you know it was me?" she asked.

"I saw you at the airport in New York, when Marc and I met. I just didn't put it together until now."

"Marc said you were intuitive."

"Let's hope he was right. Otherwise, our trip to France could be a terrible waste."

They were escorted to a VIP conference room in the main terminal where Stuart and Peter were introduced to the fourth man, whose name was given as David. Aside from his name, no other facts were forthcoming. The man was stocky yet well built, and his eyes never stopped moving. He was alert to the point of vigilant, and his back always seemed to be against a wall. David had retribution written all over him. Stuart hoped he could wait until they got all the information they needed.

They settled into leather chairs and waited. The first call they received was from the FBI, and it proved Stuart half right. Meridian was given a ticket to New York, but from there the connection was London. The next call he received was from Sally. According to the records of the Villa D'Este, no one named Loring was registered. However, when shown photographs, the desk clerk positively identified Stuart's ex-wife. The man she was with called himself Boris Rashti, and the clerk did not believe they were married. The forwarding address they left was a Marriott in London.

"We should make arrangements to meet the plane," announced Gabrielle Weiss.

"I still believe they're coming here," replied Stuart. He saw Gabrielle glance at David, who shook his head. Before the conversation could go any further, Stuart's phone rang.

"They've lost him," Sally shouted. "Someone wearing the same jacket got on the plane but didn't take the assigned seat. We have four men on that plane, and no one at the airport knows where Meridian is."

"Are there any flights to Paris that left at the same time?"

"No, I already checked."

"Anywhere near Paris?"

After a slight delay, she said, "A flight to Nice left twenty minutes earlier, but he's not on the manifest."

"That's got to be it. Keep checking, Sally. If you find him, let me know."

From behind Stuart came a question: "Your people lost him?"

Stuart and Peter both turned. These were the first words David had spoken, and neither man liked his tone.

"No one asked you to this party," said Peter. "If you don't like what's happening, you can leave." The words came out of Peter's mouth, but it was obvious he spoke for both of them.

"You Americans never understand," said the man. "You think you can outsmart everyone. These people, they must be taught a lesson. The Bible tells us, an eye for an eye."

"David, be quiet!" barked Gabrielle. "Marc had faith in this man, and we will honor his memory."

"You honor him your way, and I will honor him mine." David turned and left the area.

"Where's he headed?" Stuart asked.

"He's probably going to London. David is Marc's brother, and he won't rest until Marc's death has been avenged."

Chapter One Hundred

Stuart left Peter and Gabrielle at the commuter flight to Nice and then headed toward a restaurant on the second level. There was still no word on Meridian's whereabouts or anything about his ex-wife and her traveling companion. Peter would arrive in Nice a comfortable forty minutes before the flight from New York. If Meridian were on it, Peter and Gabrielle would follow him to his next destination. Stuart could only hope it was Paris.

While he looked over the menu posted on the window, a familiar voice caused him to turn. Standing there was Miriam, Weaver's former secretary and girlfriend.

"What am I doing here?" he reiterated. "The question is, what are you doing here?"

She appeared confused and didn't reply. Stuart quickly scanned the crowd. "I'm just seeing the world," she stammered.

Stuart took her by the arm and led her down the escalator and back to the room in which he had been waiting. "Are you by yourself?" he asked, holding the door open.

"I'm meeting a friend."

"What's his name," Stuart demanded. "And what time is he arriving?" As he spoke, he led her to a group of chairs and a sofa.

Miriam smiled coquettishly. "What makes you think I'm meeting a man?"

"Miriam, this is no time to be playing games. Just answer my questions."

Her expression changed to that of a petulant child. "I'm meeting someone you wouldn't know. His name is Boris Rashti, and he's an older gentleman from Russia. I was introduced to him in New Jersey about a year ago, and he recently got in touch. He sent me first-class tickets from Washington to Switzerland. It's strange because when I arrived, there was a letter explaining he had to go back to Russia. He enclosed first-class tickets to Paris and said I could expect him tomorrow."

Stuart's head was spinning with names, information, and possibilities. He leaned forward in his chair, trying to control his impatience. "Miriam, who introduced you?"

"Weaver did, why?"

"Are you out of your mind!" declared Stuart, throwing his hands in the air. "Weaver was no good, and anyone he was involved with is probably no good."

A flicker of panic raced through the woman's eyes. "You're just saying that to scare me."

"How did you get out of the States? I thought you were being held for your own protection?"

"When Weaver was killed and Chilicote got himself in trouble, they weren't worried about me anymore, so they let me go."

"And how'd this Rashti get in touch with you?"

Now she faltered, uncertainty clouding her face. "I don't know."

"You must have some idea, think! Did you get a phone call or a letter?"

Her face brightened a bit. "Yes, he phoned me."

"How did he know how to get in touch with you?"

"Maybe my lawyer told him."

"Your lawyer? What's his name?"

"Kenneth Hall. Eric introduced me to him a few years ago, and he set up the foreign bank accounts for me. I called him when I was released so I could get money transferred to a Swiss account." Her eyes took on a faraway look. "Do you think he told Rashti how to contact me?"

Stuart pulled on his lower lip, trying to reason this through. "Probably," he finally said.

"Do you think he's coming to meet me?"

He looked Miriam straight in the eye. "For your sake, you'd better hope not. Rashti is wanted for murder."

Her eyes widened with fear. "My god, murder? Who did he kill?"

"It doesn't matter," responded Stuart, waving away the question. "What matters is when he's supposed to arrive."

"Tonight at six."

"Where's he coming from?"

"I don't know. We're supposed to meet at . . ." She rummaged through her purse and pulled out a folded sheet of paper. "Here it is, the Bristol."

Stuart walked over to the courtesy phone and recalled Gabrielle's remark. *This could be an elaborate trap.* He dialed the local number he had been given. After connecting with his contact, he barked out the instructions.

"Have someone check all reservations at the Bristol Hotel for arrival tonight. Get me the city they're coming from and length of stay." Looking at his watch, he did a quick calculation. "It's four o'clock, and I must have the information by five." He listened as the man on the other end gave a lengthy explanation of why it couldn't be done. "It's now five after four, so you have fifty-five minutes."

Miriam approached Stuart and asked where she could find the ladies' room.

"Last door against the back wall," he told her, pointing across the room.

Miriam clutched her purse to her side and then put it down. Hesitating, she picked it up again and started to walk. The movement struck Stuart as strangely clumsy for a woman who always seemed in control of herself.

"Miriam," he said, "where's your luggage?"

"Oh, it's downstairs, I'll go get it." She turned and headed toward the front door.

"Leave your purse."

"It's not heavy, and I might need coins for the ladies' room."

"Miriam," he repeated, leaving no doubt as to the urgency, "leave your purse!"

"I have to take it with me," she insisted, her voice anxious.

"Don't leave," he told her. "It's not safe."

She looked at her watch. "I have to go." Turning, she rushed toward the rear of the room. Before she could exit, the phone rang. "Don't answer it!" she yelled, running toward Stuart. She put her arms around him, holding him tightly. "I've always had a thing about you," she said. "I know you have feelings for me." Her hands ran down his body. "I understand you not wanting to have sex with me back in the States, but no one cares here."

Stuart held her at arms length and looked into her eyes. She was more than scared. She was terrified. He pulled her toward the ringing phone on the table.

"Don't answer it," she cried.

Stuart picked up the receiver and heard the voice of the agent he had called ten minutes earlier.

"That was easy. There's no one scheduled to arrive at the hotel tonight or tomorrow."

"Are you sure?" Stuart asked, turning to face Miriam.

"Of course I'm sure. Is there anything else?"

"Get some men over here in a hurry. I have a feeling I'm going to need some help."

"We don't have any men left. Three got on the plane to London with the Israeli, another two are with your associate and the woman."

"We only have five men?"

"We have sixteen, but some are at the Villa D'Este and some are at the airport in Milan. You and the boss have us stretched thin."

"My boss?" Stuart looked puzzled. "How about you?"

"I'd love to, but I'm in a wheelchair thirty miles from the airport."

Stuart looked at Miriam, whom he was holding at arm's length. "Send me anyone you can get in touch with. Tell them when I ask who they are, they should say they're Camels bringing water to put out the fire."

"That's very American. I don't know who I can call, but I'll try."

The man hung up, and Stuart hoped he could find someone. He pushed Miriam toward one of the sofas. "When?" he asked.

She looked at her watch. "Any minute."

"How do they know where you are? You haven't left the room."

"They gave me this." She reached into her purse and pulled out a calculator. "They said it would find me wherever you took me."

Stuart opened the back and saw the chip. If he weren't looking for it, he never would have noticed it. "How many of them are there?"

"Five. Three Arabs, an Irishman, and Mr. Hall."

There was a knock on the door. Stuart tensed as Miriam squirmed and tried to bury herself in the cushions of the sofa.

"Stuart, it's me, open up."

Jessica! What's she doing here? Stuart went to the door and asked, "Are you alone?"

"Right now I am. Michael is downstairs making a call."

Stuart opened the door, pulled Jessica inside, and looked up and down the hall. "What the hell are you doing here?" he asked, locking the door and shaking it to make sure it was secure.

"I called Michael after you left, and he made arrangements for me to fly over on the next plane. I was so concerned he came with me."

"Michael's with you?"

"He thought you might need help with the locals."

"Michael came with you!" Stuart repeated.

Jessica's face showed surprise. "That's what I said. He's downstairs talking to some people. He'll be right up. I thought he called you."

Stuart picked up the phone; there was no dial tone. He took out his cell phone and found the same thing, no tone. "Jessica, did you bring your phone?"

She nodded, her face reflecting concern as she rummaged through her traveling case. "What's wrong?" she asked, noticing Miriam for the first time. "I can't find it." She turned the case upside down. "I know it was here, I used it on the plane." She threw the case on the floor. "Who's she?"

"Miriam was originally Chilicote's secretary, and then secretary and girlfriend to Weaver. Her last known place of residence was under protection of the government."

"What's she doing here?"

Stuart leaned closer to Jessica. "I think she was sent here to die. It looks like Hall and his friends are trying to put everyone who can harm them in one place."

Miriam threw her shoulders back and announced, "That's not true! They promised me a million dollars and safe passage to South America, just to make sure you stayed here."

"Miriam, a million dollars? My god, won't you ever learn?" Stuart crossed to the door and shoved one of the chairs in front of it. He turned over a table and broke off one of its legs. He handed it to Jessica and said, "Hit anyone but me, and hit them hard."

"Why don't we just leave?" Miriam asked.

"We open the door and we're dead." He stared at Miriam. "Do you have a cell phone?"

She nodded and pulled it out of her purse.

Stuart smiled as he dialed a number.

The knock on the door made both women jump.

"Who's there?" Stuart yelled.

"It's Michael. I hope you've finished your reunion, let me in."

"Hold on a second." Stuart pointed to the far corner of the room. He leaned over, kissed Jessica on the cheek, and whispered, "Watch her."

"Door's open," called out Stuart as he moved the furniture.

The door opened, and Michael entered. Stuart kicked the door closed behind him and pointed his gun at Michael's head.

"Are you crazy?" demanded Michael.

Stuart held his gun in one hand and the table leg in the other. He swung the leg, hitting Michael across his shoulder. The man collapsed onto the carpet. "Don't say a word," he told him. "If they come through that door, you go first and then Loring or Hall. If they don't come, you have a chance of living."

"Stuart, what's the matter with you? I came here to help."

"I know that. It's who you're helping that bothers me. I've been doing some thinking, Michael. Christine told you about her suspicion that someone was listening to what was going on, so you had to get rid of her. You told me too many people knew the address of the Cigar Store, which is why we couldn't find out who was responsible. You were one of the outsiders at the meeting in New York, which was why the terrorists knew their names. You were the one person I never suspected, but the one person besides myself who had access to everything taking place. You kept throwing more curve balls than Sandy Koufax. What is it you're after?"

"Stuart, listen to me. The reason I'm up here alone is to talk to you. These people have more money than the mint. All they want is to be left alone. They don't want the U.S. government bothering them. They've told me to offer you five million as a down payment and two million a year, every year, going forward. Loring has to be exonerated, and he goes back to running his business. Hall is never indicted, and you become the number one man in the Homeland Defense.

Three years from now, you retire and go live anywhere you want. The money will continue to find you."

"What about Jessica?"

Without looking at her, Michael said flatly, "They don't want her alive, but I think it's negotiable."

"And the terrorists?"

"Every year, you'll catch eight or ten of them. As far as Israel and her neighbors, the United States will break with the present Israeli government. There will be a small skirmish, and the boundary lines will again be redrawn. Our friends can live with the new lines."

"Will any of our or should I say my friends be killed?"

"They don't have to be. We can cut deals with almost all of them. Frankel's wife is a problem, but you just met her, it shouldn't be too big of a problem."

"How many people have they already cut deals with?"

"Loring, Hall, me, that's all that's left. Weaver, Gastner, and Harper are all dead."

"That's it?"

Michael nodded.

"What about Chilicote?"

"He's going to be tried and found not guilty, but he'll resign from Congress anyway."

"And if I say no?"

"Then they're going to kill you and the congresswoman." Michael looked at Jessica. "Maybe you should ask her what she thinks. If you turn them down, she's going to die and so will her daughter."

"Jess?"

"I don't want to die; I don't want Sarah to die." She stood tall against and took a deep breath. "I love you. If you said yes to them, you wouldn't be the man I fell in love with. I would rather take my chances getting through this with you then have to live the rest of my life in shame."

Michael shook his head. "Stuart, don't be stupid. If you say no, you're going to die." Michael stood up, rubbing the soreness in his shoulder. "Let me at least tell them you're thinking about it. I can buy you another two hours. That's when the plane from Nice lands."

"He did go to Nice, I was right."

"I always said you were smart." Michael started toward the door. "You've got two hours." Michael took one step and then screamed as a bullet from Stuart's gun blew out his kneecap.

Stuart was on him like a cat, shoving a napkin into his mouth. "Listen carefully. I may not get out of this alive, but you can bet the farm if I don't, you don't."

Jessica ran over with a tablecloth. "We'll have to wrap that leg and try to stop the bleeding, otherwise he'll die."

Tears streamed down Michael's cheeks. He was starting to gag on the napkin, and the smell of urine permeated the room. He yanked the napkin out of his mouth. "You're making a mistake, both of you. I'm your only way out of this room."

His face was turning pale, and his eyes were starting to close. Jessica cried out, "Do something! He's going into shock! He'll die."

Stuart took out Miriam's cell phone and hit the redial button.

"How's everything going out there?"

Peter replied, "Not so good. We've got an Arab and an Irishman. Two of the Arabs died trying to defend themselves, and Marc's wife slit Hall's throat. I tried to get her to stop, but she was too quick for me."

"Any sign of Loring or my ex?"

"None."

"Better get a doctor in here. Michael may be the only one we'll get any information out of."

Three hours later, Stuart, Peter, and Jessica were seated in the first-class section of a jet crossing the Atlantic. The plane had been requisitioned by Presidential order to fly them back to the United States. There were twenty-one others in the tourist section guarding Michael and the two other prisoners. Miriam was on another plane, along with Martin Meridian, who kept yelling he only wanted to help Stuart. The President had personally called the prime minister of Israel to protest the way Marc's wife and brother behaved, but the prime minister told him he didn't have the slightest idea who those people were. The President told Stuart he was expected at a debriefing at noon the following day.

"All in all," mused Stuart, "it wasn't a bad day. It'll take some time, but I'm sure Michael will tell us where Loring and bin Laden are hiding."

"I don't imagine any of us will be up for a barbeque on Labor Day," Peter said with a heavy sigh.

"All I want to do is sleep," Stuart replied. Looking at Jessica, they said simultaneously, "And make plans for our wedding."

Chapter One Hundred-One

The meeting at the White House went as well as could be expected. Michael's involvement with Harper, Hall, and Loring threw everyone into a *cover-your-ass* mode. Jake Levitt was appointed chief of staff, and Ray Bradley was put in charge of the FBI. After some heated discussions, Karen Ortega was appointed deputy director. Jerry Pettit was nowhere to be found, and the feeling was he never would be. There was a lot of finger pointing at everyone but Stuart, who turned out to be the shining knight in the whole affair. Until further information could be obtained from Michael, no one quite knew what to do or say. After four and half hours, the President thanked everyone for attending and told them there would be a follow-up meeting on the fifth of September. He asked Stuart and Jake Levitt to stay for a few minutes after everyone had left.

"Stuart," he began, "I want to personally thank you for your efforts. I must admit I had my doubts about your ability, but I'm beginning to think it was clouded by what Gastner and Burnett were saying. Jake has a plan for presenting this to the press and the rest of the world; he's going to need your help."

"Anything I can do, just ask."

"Good. You're going to have to talk to some of our allies. Their story will have to be close to ours."

"Which is, Mr. President?"

"We don't know yet. You'll have to find out from Michael if we have more skeletons in our closets."

Stuart nodded, his mouth set into a grim line. No matter how much time elapsed, he knew he might never recover from that betrayal.

"I understand you've made friends with Chuck Andres." The President looked at Stuart for confirmation. When Stuart nodded, the President added the White House wanted Andres to run the lead story.

"All you have to do is feed it to him," said Stuart. "I'm sure he'd love to do it." Stuart was puzzled by something in the President's tone. It was only a moment before his suspicions were confirmed.

"In the past, whenever Andres was given a story, he was always diligent about double-checking his information. We don't want the story we give him double-checked."

Stuart, who had been sitting on the edge of the chair, leaned back and studied the President's expression. So the story would be false, and they expected him to swear to the lie. Something unsaid bothered Stuart. He tried to bring it forward from the depths of his mind but he couldn't find the words. He rose to leave when it came into focus. "What about the Home Guard?" he asked. "When do you envision that department being set up?"

"Well, that depends on what Michael has to say. However, the feeling is that we've pretty well taken care of whatever they had planned."

Stuart turned to Jake. "You can't possibly believe this."

Jake bristled at the accusation. "I was in the minority, Stuart. I've instructed the attorney general not to let our guard down, but it does cost money to keep everyone on high alert."

"Fine," said Stuart, resignation in his voice. "What do you want me to do?"

"Talk to Andres, keep questioning Michael, and let's get back together next Friday, the seventh." Jake wrote in his book. "Nine thirty looks good."

"What about the meeting on the fifth?" asked Stuart.

Jake looked uncomfortable. "The President thought it best if you didn't attend. It seems your presence intimidates some of the people. On top of that, you have to get ready for your wedding. If I'm not mistaken, it's two days later."

"Which *some of the people* do you mean, Jake?"

"That really doesn't matter!" interrupted the President. "What's important is, I want a free exchange of ideas, and some of the people have said you make them nervous."

Stuart rose and stared first at the President and then at Jake. "I think you're making a mistake, but I'm just a hired hand." He walked to the door, turned and said, "I'll talk to you on the seventh."

Throughout the weekend Stuart received phone calls from Jessica, his mother, and his daughter. What should they serve for dinner? Who should they invite? Where were they going on their honeymoon? After the first wave of calls, Stuart realized his primary function was to say "that's good" or "that's nice," and he was starting to enjoy it. Jessica, being a sitting member of Congress, was almost obligated to invite many members of both the House and the Senate. Stuart, on the other hand, found himself inviting *members of the working class*, as he called them.

During that week, Stuart arranged for lunch with Chuck Andres and gave him the party line. He then told him the truth but asked he not print it until after the wedding, to which he was invited. He also made sure his list of invitees included the top antiterrorist agents from a half dozen different countries. He laughed when he told Jessica there would be enough firepower present to invade Iraq.

It was on the sixth of September when Michael finally started providing information that meant something.

The people in Florida were taking flying lessons for something that was supposed to happen on Labor Day. When Stuart was able to acquire their address, it foiled their plans. Nevertheless, they were regrouping in New Hampshire although Michael didn't know where.

Hall, Loring, and Harper had been responsible for hiding the men who sneaked in from Canada or Mexico as well as for paying off government officials who could be bought or bribed. Michael provided eleven of those names. In addition, he told Stuart where to find copies of records listing donations made to public officials and from groups that didn't know they were being used. Michael believed they were going to ask for the release of the cleric being held for the attempted bombing of the New York Trade Towers. He wasn't sure, but he believed Loring and his wife, Linda, were in Pakistan.

By the morning of the seventh, Stuart had checked and rechecked everything he had learned from Michael. Now he was ready for his meeting with the President.

As usual, the head of the free world was running late. Jake had come into the waiting room at nine thirty to inform Stuart it shouldn't be more than another twenty minutes. Five minutes later, Stuart's cell phone rang. It was Sally.

"I'm going to patch through a call from a woman named Gabrielle. Caller ID says she's in Berlin, but I wouldn't swear to it."

"It's Marc's wife. Put her through."

"Mr. Taylor," her voice sounded tired. "I thought you'd want to know that Harvey Loring was found today in India. His head and hands were severed, and the only way he was identified was through a woman claiming to be his wife. This woman has been charged with his murder and is presently in jail. There will be a trial, and the chances of her being found not guilty are highly unlikely."

Stuart saw Jake Levitt wave to him from the Oval Office. "Thank you for the information. If you ever need anything, please don't hesitate to call. I'm sorry I couldn't be with you today."

"Your conversation with your President must come first. Good luck."

I wonder how she knew that. Stuart disconnected the call and went to his meeting.

Thirty minutes later, Stuart was walking down the steps of the White House. He had found an ally in Jake Levitt, but the President, after hearing what Michael had said before he died, decided the threat was over. He fervently believed whatever the terrorists had planned for Labor Day was foiled. With Hall and his friends gone, life would return to normal. Stuart was again thanked and told to enjoy himself on his honeymoon. Jake promised to talk to the President later in the day but couldn't guarantee he'd change his mind.

An hour before the wedding, Stuart asked Marilyn and Kenneth to join him and Jessica in a room at the hotel. It was there he told them about their mother and her husband. He promised he was doing all he could to get her released and back to the States. When asked why he told them at his wedding, he responded they were old enough to handle the news, and he didn't feel comfortable holding out on them. He was right.

The wedding was a resounding success. Every major player was there even some from the other side of the aisle. The newspaper coverage seemed endless. Had Jessica been up for reelection, her opponents would have been buried.

When Stuart and Jessica had a rare moment alone, he told her he had tendered his resignation, effective immediately. When they returned from their honeymoon, he was opening a private practice.

"I'll believe that when I see it," she laughed as they boarded the plane.

The phone in the bridal suite jarred them awake at three thirty in the morning. Jessica picked up the receiver and noted the time on the nightstand clock.

"May I please speak to Stuart Taylor?"

"He's sleeping, is it important?"

Stuart was already sitting up, rubbing his eyes.

"Yes, Mrs. Taylor, this is very important."

"Who is this?" she demanded.

"Jake Levitt," came the terse reply.

She handed the phone to Stuart and shrugged.

"This is Taylor."

"Turn on your TV."

"What station and why?" He motioned for Jessica to hand him the remote.

"It's on all of them, Stuart. Terrorists have hijacked at least four planes and crashed two of them into the Twin Towers of the World Trade Center. Another plane was flown into CIA headquarters in Virginia and a fourth has crashed in a field somewhere in Pennsylvania. The President says he's sorry, but you're needed in Washington as soon as it's humanly possible."

"Hold on," said Stuart, quickly explaining the situation to Jessica. By this time, she was watching with horror as the scene unfolded. "Listen carefully," Stuart told Jake Levitt. "Tell the President not to allow any planes to take off from any airport in the United States. Furthermore, he's to have all planes that are in the air land at the closest airfield. All inbound foreign are to land in Canada or Mexico. If they won't listen, send them back. Have fighter planes sent up to enforce his policy. I also suggest we close the borders until we can get more people to the checkpoints. Tell him to be decisive."

"Will do. Meanwhile, there's a plane waiting for you at the Honolulu airport. Please hurry."

"Remind the President I'm now an independent contractor, and my hourly rates are outrageous."

"You can tell him yourself when he appoints you to head the task force."

Hanging up the phone, Stuart found Jessica's hand and held it tightly. "It looks like I'm back on the payroll."

Jessica leaned over and wrapped her arms around him. "Darling, they couldn't have found a better man for the job." She kissed the tip of his nose. "How much time do we have before you start earning that big paycheck?"